Praise for *A Stolen Heart*

"Readers will enjoy the surprising ending as well as the romance always found in Cabot's books."

—Publishers Weekly

"Moments of humor provide a nice balance to the heartwarming scenes and the mild suspense thread."

—RT Book Reviews

"Cabot's nonpreachy inspirational romance features characters who genuinely try to live honorable lives, and their story has broad appeal for readers of gentle fiction and historical romance as well as for readers of Christian fiction."

—Booklist

"*A Stolen Heart* would be a good book to put on your 'to read' list! I can't wait for the next one in this series."

—Interviews & Reviews

"From the opening lines, Amanda Cabot's *A Stolen Heart* made me want to curl up under a quilt with a hot cup of tea and just read."

—Jane Kirkpatrick, award-winning author,
This Road We Traveled

A Borrowed Dream

Books by Amanda Cabot

Historical Romance

TEXAS DREAMS SERIES

Paper Roses

Scattered Petals

Tomorrow's Garden

WESTWARD WINDS SERIES

Summer of Promise

Waiting for Spring

With Autumn's Return

CIMARRON CREEK TRILOGY

A Stolen Heart

A Borrowed Dream

Christmas Roses

One Little Word: A Sincerely Yours Novella

Contemporary Romance

TEXAS CROSSROADS SERIES

At Bluebonnet Lake

In Firefly Valley

On Lone Star Trail

CIMARRON CREEK
TRILOGY · 2

A BORROWED DREAM

AMANDA CABOT

Revell

a division of Baker Publishing Group
Grand Rapids, Michigan

© 2018 by Amanda Cabot

Published by Revell
a division of Baker Publishing Group
PO Box 6287, Grand Rapids, MI 49516-6287
www.revellbooks.com

Printed in the United States of America

ISBN: 9780800727574

Library of Congress Cataloging-in-Publication Control Number: 2017059739

This book is a work of fiction. Names, characters, places, and incidents are the product of the author's imagination or are used fictitiously.

18   19   20   21   22   23   24   7   6   5   4   3   2   1

For the members of
Front Range Christian Fiction Writers.
It's a privilege to share learning, laughter,
and an occasional lunch with you.
Can you believe it's been ten years?

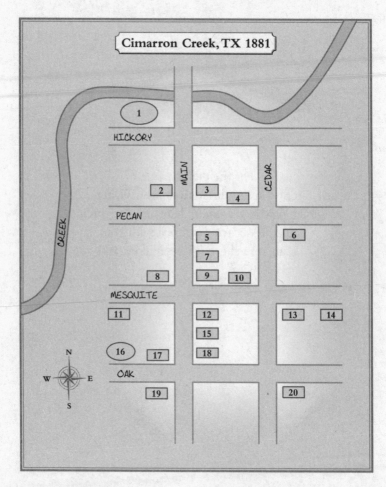

Cimarron Creek, TX 1881

1 – Town park
2 – Silver Spur Saloon
3 – Livery stable
4 – Vacant house
5 – Mercantile
6 – Lydia and Travis's home (a Founder's house)
7 – Apothecary
8 – Doc Harrington's home and office
9 – Dressmaker's shop
10 – Opal and Edgar's home
11 – Catherine's home

12 – Sheriff's office and jail
13 – Jacob Whitfield's home (a Founder's house)
14 – Charles, Mary, and Warner Gray's home
15 – Mayor's office/post office
16 – Cemetery
17 – Church
18 – Cimarron Sweets
19 – School
20 – Matthew Henderson's home (a Founder's house

Descendants of Emil Henderson

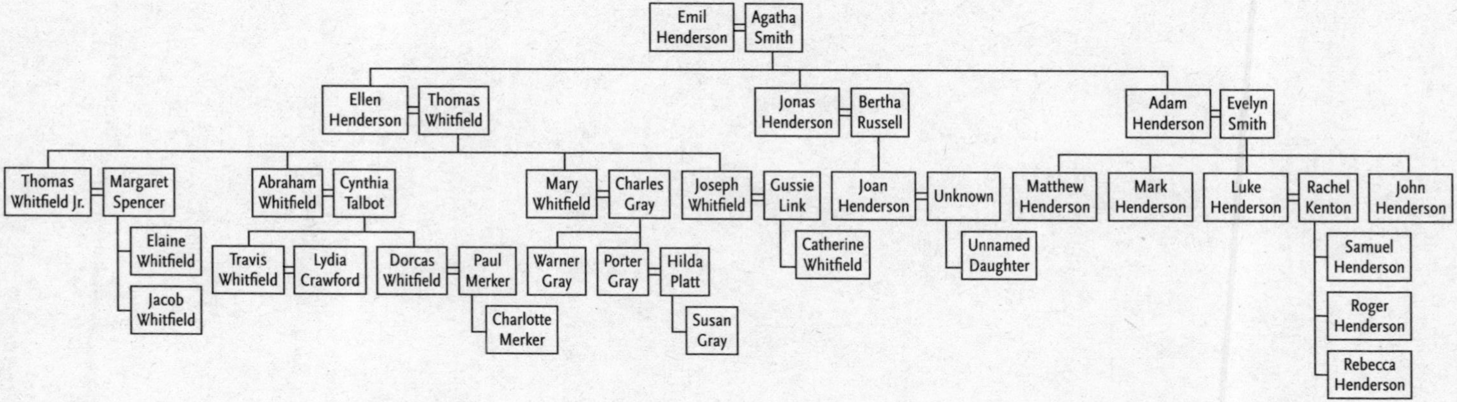

1

January 3, 1881

It was only a dream.

Catherine Whitfield fumbled with the lamp on her bedside table, taking a deep breath as light filled the room. There was no reason to be upset.

She swung her legs over the side of the bed and took another deep breath. This was far from the first time she'd dreamed that she was in Paris, walking along the left bank of the Seine toward Notre Dame. She'd had that dream many times over the years, but never before had it ended this way. In the past, she had awakened with a smile on her face. Tonight . . .

Catherine took another breath, trying to calm the trembling of her hands as she opened her watch and stared at it. Though she had thought it no later than midnight, it was already five in the morning, only an hour earlier than she would normally rise. While school did not begin until 8:00, pupils started straggling in by 7:30, and she needed to have the building open and warm before the first one arrived.

It was foolish to go back to bed. With the memory of the dream reverberating through her brain, she'd never fall asleep. She might as well get dressed. Reaching for the skirt and shirtwaist she'd laid out the night before, she paused. Was that the reason her dream had turned into a nightmare? Was she distressed over the thought of putting away her mourning clothes so soon?

Catherine shook her head as she fastened the last button. Mama wouldn't have expected her to wear black for a full year. She knew that Catherine had loved her and that in her heart she would mourn her for far more than a year. It was only the fact that others in Cimarron Creek might not be so progressive that had kept Catherine in unrelieved black for four months. Her pupils would appreciate the white shirtwaist and the navy skirt.

No, her clothing choice wasn't the reason the dream had ended the way it did. More likely it was the result of the stomach ailment that had plagued her all weekend. She had thought she was fully recovered last night, but perhaps some of the illness had lingered.

Catherine twisted her hair into a low chignon, forcing a smile to her lips. She wouldn't think about the dream. Instead, she'd make breakfast, then spend the extra time at the schoolhouse, preparing for the week ahead.

She had just removed the grounds from the coffeepot when the kitchen door swung open.

"Are you all right, Catherine?"

She turned at the familiar voice, and for the first time since she'd wakened, she felt peace settle over her. "I am now that you're here," she said as she hugged her early-morning visitor.

Though Lydia Crawford Whitfield had been gone less than two weeks, Catherine had missed her more than she'd expected. From the day she'd arrived in Cimarron Creek, the pretty blonde who was now the sheriff's wife had been Catherine's bulwark, her confidante, the sister she had always wanted, and with her away visiting her husband's family, Christmas had been dismal for Catherine. The new year was supposed to have been better, but getting sick had not been an auspicious beginning, and then there was the dream.

Though Lydia settled into a chair while Catherine filled two cups with coffee, she kept her gaze fixed on Catherine.

"Tell me about your trip," Catherine urged. Lydia's stories would help banish the memories that refused to be dislodged from Catherine's brain.

Her friend shook her head. "Not until I know you're all right. I woke this morning feeling that you needed me, and then Opal mentioned that you missed church yesterday," Lydia said, referring to the woman who helped her run the town's confectionary.

Catherine wasn't surprised that Lydia's partner had noticed her absence or that she'd reported it to Lydia. Even when the candy store wasn't open, the Cimarron Creek grapevine was active.

"I was sick all weekend," she admitted. "I don't know what it was, but I couldn't keep anything in my stomach. Fortunately, I'm fine now. I even managed to eat a bit of toast while the coffee was brewing."

"You don't look fine. Are you sure you should go to school today? You might still be contagious."

"It's not that." Catherine took a sip of the coffee, debating how much to tell her friend. "I had a dream—more like a nightmare—and I can't forget it."

Lydia stretched out her hand and clasped Catherine's, the warmth of her palm reassuring Catherine as much as the concern she saw in her friend's eyes did.

"Tell me about it," Lydia said.

Though she was reluctant to put the dream into words, perhaps sharing it with Lydia would lessen its power over her. "I was in Paris, walking along the Seine," she said slowly.

"That's a good dream, isn't it? You've told me that's been your dream for years."

"It was different this time. As I got closer to Notre Dame, I saw a woman staring at me. She looked a bit like me—the same dark hair and eyes—but she was taller and older, and her face . . ." Catherine shuddered, remembering how helpless she'd felt. "I've never seen such despair. When she turned away, I started to run toward her, but no matter how fast I ran, I never got any closer. I kept trying and trying. When she looked at me again and saw that I was coming, she . . ."

Catherine closed her eyes, not wanting to continue, but knowing she must. She forced her eyelids open and faced her friend. "Oh, Lydia, it was horrible. She jumped into the Seine."

"And you woke up." Though Lydia's words were matter-of-fact, Catherine saw the concern in her expression.

"Yes."

"So you don't know if someone rescued her."

Lydia was trying to lessen the horror of the dream, but she couldn't. No one could.

"No one rescued her. I'm sure of that. What I don't know is why my dream ended that way and why I couldn't help her. There must be a reason."

Lydia shook her head as she stirred sugar into her coffee. "Not all dreams are messages."

"But some are. Think about how many there are in the Bible."

Though she'd told herself she was going to put the dream out of her mind, Catherine had been unable to do that. While she'd ground the coffee and boiled water, the memory of the desperate woman had haunted her. She'd never before had a dream like this, one that lingered in her mind once she wakened. Memories of happy dreams would flit in and out, making her smile, but this one hovered, filling her with a sense of dread.

"Maybe this is God's way of telling me I should give up my dream of visiting Europe."

"And maybe it's not. Maybe it's just a dream." Lydia was

14

silent for a moment, sipping her coffee with a contemplative expression. "I know you're upset, but I think you need to focus on happier things. Promise me you'll try."

When Catherine nodded, Lydia said, "It seems we missed a big event at church yesterday."

"You mean Reverend Dunn didn't give his normal a-new-year-means-new-beginnings sermon?"

"Oh, he did, but I'm not sure how many people listened." Lydia's lips curved in a smile. "Opal was bursting with the news that we have a new family in the area. She didn't get to meet them, but Mrs. Moore stopped her after the service to say she was hired to keep house for them. It seems the man bought the Saylor ranch. The way Mrs. Moore tells the story, he's from Oklahoma and wanted a ranch of his own. Apparently, he's a widower."

Catherine couldn't help smiling at her friend's eager recounting of the news. "You're starting to sound like Aunt Bertha with her long stories." The woman who'd been Catherine's great-aunt had been famous for her monologues. "Is there a special reason I need to know about this rancher?"

Lydia nodded. "According to Opal, he's a good-looking young man. She's sure every mother with a single daughter will be inviting him to supper."

But Catherine no longer had a mother, and even if Mama were alive, she wouldn't have engaged in such blatant match-making. "At least he won't go hungry."

"Catherine." Lydia gave her a reproving look. "Don't dismiss the man sight unseen. He might be almost as wonderful as Travis." A sweet smile crossed Lydia's face as she pronounced her husband's name.

Travis Whitfield, the town's sheriff and Catherine's cousin, was a fine man and the perfect husband for Lydia. The new rancher was another story. Even if he were as wonderful as

Travis, he was a widower. That meant that whoever he married—assuming, of course, that he was interested in marrying again—would be his second wife.

Catherine took another sip of coffee, hoping the strong brew would clear her head. There was no point in arguing with Lydia. As a happy newlywed, Lydia believed every woman should be married. She wouldn't understand that Catherine had no intention of becoming the rancher's or any man's second anything. She'd learned that lesson last summer when Nate, the man she had expected to marry, had fallen in love with Lydia. Even though Lydia had done her best to discourage him, the damage had been done. Catherine would rather remain a spinster than be some man's second choice.

"Unless the widower comes to church, I doubt I'll ever meet him."

Lydia shook her head. "Oh, but you will. He has a school-age daughter."

Austin Goddard tried to ignore the anxiety that had been his constant companion from the moment he'd opened his eyes. There was no reason to worry, he told himself. Hannah would be safe. Of course, she would. That was why they'd come to Texas.

Forcing a smile, he looked at his daughter as she slid into the chair across the breakfast table from him. "You look nice this morning." Mrs. Moore had taken special pains with Hannah's hair, securing the ends of the braids with bright red bows that matched one of the colors in her plaid dress.

Though Hannah glanced at him, she remained silent, her expression more eloquent than words. Whatever Austin thought about school, his daughter did not agree.

When the three of them were seated, he closed his eyes and thanked the Lord for the food, adding a silent prayer for his daughter. Mrs. Moore was right. School would be good for Hannah. He didn't need the housekeeper to tell him his daughter needed to leave the ranch and be around other children, that she needed to laugh and play. Austin knew it wasn't normal for a child to be so quiet, but then again, it wasn't normal for a child to be forced to leave everything familiar not once but twice.

Hannah didn't remember her birthplace any more than she remembered her mother, for she'd been less than a year old when the two of them had left Paris, but there was no doubt that she remembered their last home, even though she'd obeyed Austin's command and never spoke of it. Perhaps that was part of the problem. Perhaps he should have allowed her to talk about their former life, but he couldn't take that risk.

Though Austin tried to smile at his too silent, too thin daughter, his heart yearned for the girl who'd once giggled as she tried to convince him to let her have at least a spoonful of coffee in her milk. Now she accepted the glass of plain milk without comment, deepening Austin's distress. He could run the ranch. He was confident of that. He only wished he were confident that he could restore his daughter's happiness.

Almost as if she'd read Austin's thoughts, Mrs. Moore addressed Hannah. "You'll like school," she said as she poured syrup over her pancakes. The woman who'd become Austin's housekeeper as well as Hannah's nanny liked her sweets, a fact reflected in her plump hands and the extra rolls of flesh around her neck. Though she was in her early fifties, her light brown hair held only a few threads of silver, and her eyes had not lost their sharpness. Most importantly, she seemed genuinely fond of Hannah.

"Miss Whitfield is a good teacher," Mrs. Moore continued. "Firm but fair, or so I've heard. My boys were out of school long before she took over."

Hannah looked up from the piece of pancake she'd been chasing around her plate. "I don't want to go."

Though his heart ached at the pain he heard in his daughter's voice, Austin kept his own voice firm. "You'll like it once you get there. You'll find new friends."

A vigorous shake of the head was Hannah's only response.

Austin looked at her still-full plate. "You need to eat more than that." As far as he could tell, she'd consumed no more than two bites of pancake and one strip of bacon. His daughter had always been slender, but she'd lost weight since they'd come to Texas.

Hannah kept her gaze fixed on her plate. "I'm not hungry," she announced.

With a sympathetic look for Austin, Mrs. Moore turned to Hannah. "I packed you a good lunch. There are some extra cookies to share with the other girls."

Hannah made no response, simply continued to push the piece of pancake in circles around her plate.

Realizing there was nothing he could do short of force-feeding her, Austin rose. "Get your coat on, Hannah. It's time for us to leave."

Though she complied, she moved as if her feet were encased in cement, her displeasure evident in the scowl that marred her normally pretty face. This wasn't going to be easy.

When they emerged from the farmhouse that was now their home, Austin found the horse and wagon waiting by the side door. Mrs. Moore had not exaggerated when she'd said her son Kevin would make a good ranch hand. The man had more than earned his wages in the week since Austin and Hannah had arrived, seeming to know what Austin needed even before he asked for it. Today Kevin had somehow realized that Austin planned to buy supplies while he was in town and had harnessed the wagon.

"It'll be all right, Hannah. You'll see," Austin said as he guided the horse toward Cimarron Creek. If only Hannah would adjust, it would be all right. They'd begin a new life here, a life where Hannah would be safe.

When they reached the main road, Austin's mood lightened. This part of Texas was more beautiful than he'd expected, with rolling hills that were still green, unlike the brown grass he would have seen at this time of the year back East. Even better, the sky was a vivid blue, promising a clear day, not one of the gray, rainy mornings so common in Paris in January.

Austin nodded, his determination ratcheting up a notch. This might not be the life he had planned for himself and Hannah, but he would do everything he could to ensure that it was the best life possible. The first step was to get Hannah to school.

Fifteen minutes later as they reached the edge of Cimarron Creek, Austin turned to his still-silent daughter. "It's a pretty town, isn't it, Hannah?" Predictably, there was no response. Austin refused to let discouragement stop him. "Look at the way the trees shade the street. They're like a canopy."

He'd heard that the Texas Hill Country was beautiful, and it was. When he'd gathered his daughter into his arms that last night in Philadelphia, he'd had no idea where they would go, but each time they'd reached a fork in the road, Austin had felt an inner urging telling him which way to turn, where to spend the night, where to head the next morning.

They'd spent weeks traveling, meandering across the country as Austin tried desperately to ensure that no one was following them. When Hannah had asked where they were going, he'd attempted to reassure her but had refused to lie. The truth was, he didn't know where or when they'd finally stop until the day he'd heard about a ranch for sale on the outskirts of Cimarron Creek. That day Austin's doubts had disappeared and he'd been filled with the belief that they were meant to live on that particular ranch. Surely it had been God's hand that had led them here.

The buildings lining Main Street were considerably smaller than the ones in Paris and Philadelphia, but that was to be expected. Cimarron Creek was a small town, not a big city, its population less than two hundred. Still, the stores and offices were attractive and well cared for, bearing witness to the residents' pride. That was one of the things Austin had noticed when he'd first driven through the town, yet another indication that this was the right place for him and Hannah to make their home.

He tugged the reins, stopping the horse in front of the stone building, its bell and the swing in the side yard announcing as clearly as a sign that this was the school. "We're here."

Hannah's eyes filled with tears, and when he lifted her from the wagon and placed her on the ground, she clung to his hand.

"There's no reason to be afraid," Austin said, his heart thudding at the realization that while his fears had diminished, his daughter's had not. "There'll be other girls your age." Some were already here. Though Austin had hoped to give Hannah a chance to meet the schoolmarm and settle in before anyone else arrived, he'd failed. Half a dozen children played outside the school.

Hannah glanced at them, her grip on his hand tightening as he led the way up the steps to the schoolhouse. "It'll be all right." Austin opened the door and ushered his daughter inside. If only Hannah would believe him.

The school was similar to the one he'd attended as a boy, the hooks on the wall of the first room identifying it as a cloakroom. He led his daughter through it into the main room. Like the one Austin recalled from his childhood, this classroom had a center aisle separating two rows of desks. Maps of Texas and the United States hung on one side wall, with portraits of President

Hayes and Governor Roberts on the other. As he'd expected, the teacher's desk was located between the pupils' desks and the blackboard that covered most of the front wall, and while there was no dunce stool in the corner, an adult-sized chair sat at one side of the teacher's desk. Perhaps that was the modern substitute for the stool.

Austin's gaze moved around the room again, noting the cleanliness and order, then returned to the woman who stood at the blackboard, writing today's Bible verse and assignments.

As if alerted by the sound of his footsteps, she turned, and he felt the blood drain from his face. The teacher had the same glossy dark brown hair, the same chocolate brown eyes as his wife, but Geraldine had been several inches taller than this woman, and Austin could not remember Geraldine ever wearing such a welcoming smile when she greeted a stranger. She had been reserved when she first met people, only warming to them after she'd come to know them. Hannah had apparently inherited that reticence from her mother.

Wrenching his thoughts from his late wife and her legacy to their daughter, Austin cleared his throat. "Good morning," he said, grateful that his vocal cords still functioned properly. "You must be Miss Whitfield. I'm Austin Goddard, and this is my daughter Hannah."

The teacher's smile broadened as she closed the distance between them. "Welcome to Cimarron Creek, Mr. Goddard. As you surmised, I'm Catherine Whitfield." She looked down at Hannah, her eyes radiating genuine warmth as she said, "I'm so glad you're here, Hannah. How old are you?"

Her hand still clutching Austin's, Hannah stared at the floor and said nothing.

"She's six."

Apparently unconcerned by Hannah's silence, Miss Whitfield nodded. "That's perfect. Rebecca needs a partner."

Up close, Austin saw that Catherine Whitfield bore little resemblance to his wife beyond the color of her hair and eyes. Her features were finer, her face heart shaped rather than oval, her skin slightly darker, perhaps because of the warmth of the Texas sun.

"I pair older children with the younger ones," she explained. "That works well for both of them. The older ones learn responsibility, while the younger children have role models." She bent down until she was at eye level with Hannah. "Rebecca will be so happy that you've come. She was the only girl without a partner."

As if on cue, the door opened and several girls entered the schoolroom, giggling as they made their way toward their desks.

Miss Whitfield straightened. "Rebecca," she said with obvious pleasure, "your prayer has been answered. Come meet Hannah Goddard."

Austin gave the girl who would be working closely with his daughter an appraising look. He guessed her to be eleven or twelve, with blonde hair, blue eyes, and a warm smile. Though he'd thought Hannah would make friends with girls closer to her own age, perhaps Rebecca would be able to break through the silence more easily than a younger child.

When Miss Whitfield had made the introductions, she nodded at Rebecca. "Please show Hannah her desk. I need to talk to her father."

As the two girls headed to a desk on the right side of the room, Austin followed the teacher toward the front. "Hannah's always been shy," he told her, "but moving here has been difficult for her."

Miss Whitfield nodded, her expression warm and sympathetic. "That's only natural. And losing her mother . . ."

Before she could complete the sentence, the door opened and a gangly boy entered the room, his appearance silencing the teacher. Austin could see that she registered the same things he did: the pallor, glassy eyes, and unsteady gait.

"Good morning, Seth." To Austin's surprise, the teacher's voice did not reflect the alarm he'd seen in her eyes. This sounded like a normal greeting. Turning her desk's side chair so that it faced the blackboard rather than the classroom and would give the boy a modicum of privacy, she gestured toward it. "Come here, please."

Though Seth looked as if he were on the verge of collapsing, somehow he made it to the chair before he practically fell onto it. Slumping forward, he gripped his head with both hands.

"He needs a doctor." Austin had no doubt that the boy, who appeared to be around thirteen, needed medical care. In addition to the symptoms he was exhibiting today, the dullness of Seth's light brown hair and his extreme thinness told Austin he was not only underfed but also malnourished. That combined with the spasms that were now wracking his body could be dangerous. And then there were the bruises that marred his face. Although not caused by any illness, they were alarming.

Austin turned to the teacher. "If you tell me where to find him, I'll fetch the doctor."

Though he had expected her to agree with him, Miss Whitfield stared at him with what could only be called horror. Unlike the momentary alarm she'd shown when Seth entered the classroom, this was a deep-seated emotion, one she appeared unable to control.

"We need to do this," Austin said, hoping his deliberately calm tone would allay her fears. "Seth needs a doctor."

Catherine Whitfield's reaction was instantaneous. "Never!"

2

Y ou're fools, all of you." Sherman Enright looked at the four men standing in front of him. These were his most trusted minions, the men he could depend on to obey his commands as if their lives were on the line, which, of course, they were. Never before had they failed him, but never before had the stakes been this high.

This morning their faces were pale, befitting the gravity of the situation. They kept their eyes fixed on the floor, as if staring at the Persian rug rather than him sitting behind the oversized mahogany desk would somehow lessen his anger. Nothing short of success would do that, and they'd failed to deliver it.

Shorty was shaking, and though Tucker tried to hide it, the beads of sweat forming on his forehead told Sherman just how much he feared what was to come. The other two stood like stone statues in the vain hope that he would not notice them.

"A man and a child can't simply disappear," Sherman said, his voice as cold and firm as steel. Anger, he had long since learned, was best delivered without fanfare. "They can hide," he told the men, pointing out what should have been obvious, "but they cannot disappear. Finding them ought to have been easy. A man who's carting his whelp with him can't move as quickly as one who's unencumbered."

As he looked from one man to the next, Sherman realized

that only Tucker understood his final word. True, he'd hired these men for their brute strength and their intense loyalty, not their brains, but perhaps that had been a mistake. His quarry wasn't dumb; he knew what was at stake. The man his minions had failed to locate claimed his scruples wouldn't let him do what Sherman needed. Scruples! Though Sherman kept his face impassive, inside he scoffed at the idea. The man would see just how much protection those highfalutin scruples provided. Once he'd done his job, he'd be as dead as the others who'd dared cross him. But first they had to find him.

"We looked everywhere, sir," Shorty said. Though Tucker seemed to agree, he said nothing when Shorty offered the flimsy defense. "Obviously, you did not look everywhere, or you wouldn't be standing here without the man." If there was anything Sherman hated, it was feeble excuses. "Now, get out, all of you, and start looking again. I expect a better report next time."

As the men filed out of the room, he saw the fear they'd tried to disguise. He didn't have to spell it out for them. They all knew the consequences of failing Sherman Enright.

Austin Goddard was looking at her as if she were crazy. Catherine could see it in the skeptical expression he didn't bother to mask. She wasn't crazy; she was simply cautious. "Seth does not need a doctor," she said firmly. "Not Doc Harrington or any other physician."

The reason she kept a box well stocked with medical supplies here in the schoolhouse was to ensure that none of her students had any reason to consult the town's sole physician. Catherine could not prevent their parents from taking them to Doc Harrington, but while they were under her care, they would not be subjected to his barbaric treatments.

"The boy is ill." The expression in Mr. Goddard's blue eyes said that his resolution was as strong as hers.

Opal had not exaggerated when she'd told Lydia the new rancher was good-looking. He was more than that. He was handsome. Though he was blond, blue-eyed, and approximately the same height as Nate, that was the extent of their similarity. Mr. Goddard's hair was more golden than Nate's, his eyes a darker blue. While his shoulders were broad, he lacked Nate's heavy muscles, and his hands bore none of the calluses that Nate's did. If she hadn't known otherwise, Catherine would not have imagined him to be a rancher.

The man was handsome, but he was also wrong. Seth had no need of Doc Harrington's ministrations. Turning her attention away from Austin Goddard, Catherine laid her hand on Seth's shoulder in an attempt to reassure her pupil. "I can see that he's ill."

She looked at the boy who was the center of the discussion. "Have you been vomiting?" He nodded. "Are you dizzy?" Another nod. "I know how you feel," she said softly, not wanting her words to carry to the other students. Though they appeared to be engrossed in their own conversations, she knew some were curious about Seth's presence in the side chair as well as the appearance of a strange man in the classroom.

"I felt the same way over the weekend," she told Seth. "When did you start feeling ill?"

"Saturday."

She nodded as she did the mental calculations. "Then you should be much better by tomorrow." Though the ailment was unpleasant, at least it did not linger.

Catherine looked up at the man who'd questioned her diagnosis. "What Seth needs is a bit of ginger root, some chicken soup, and lots of rest. He can get that at my house."

When Mr. Goddard raised an eyebrow, Catherine continued.

"It won't be the first time a pupil spent a day or two in my spare room." Admittedly, it would be the first time Mama wasn't there to care for the child while Catherine was teaching, but she would find a way to make it work.

Seth shook his head. "I can't do that, Miss Whitfield." His voice was weak, betraying both his illness and his fears. "Pa'll be mad. I gotta milk the cows." His left hand covered his cheek, as if to prevent another blow from landing on the already bruised skin.

Before Catherine could respond, Mr. Goddard did. "You're in no condition to milk cows. Miss Whitfield is correct. You need rest."

Though Catherine appreciated his support, she did not like the slightly officious tone of his voice. In that moment, he sounded like Doc Harrington making a pronouncement.

"I can take care of Seth," she told him. Removing her hand from Seth's shoulder, she nodded toward the rear of the schoolroom. "I want you to lie down in the cloakroom until recess. Then we'll go to my house."

Though she hadn't thought it possible, the boy's face lost even more color. "But Pa . . ."

"I can take his horse with me and explain the situation to Seth's parents."

Catherine gave Mr. Goddard a grateful smile. Though Boone Dalton wasn't much of a father, he needed to know why his son wasn't coming home today. "Seth walks to school, so you don't have to worry about a horse, but I'd appreciate your talking to his father. He's a widower like you." Though she would say nothing in front of the boy, she knew that Boone Dalton made Seth's life difficult and that he was quick to inflict physical punishment when Seth did something to displease him.

Mr. Goddard merely nodded, but the way his eyes narrowed at the sight of Seth's bruises told Catherine he'd suspected their cause.

"Thank you, Mr. Goddard. The Dalton farm is next to your ranch, so you won't have to go out of your way." She gave him directions. "Now, Seth, let's get you to the cloakroom."

As the boy rose, Catherine addressed her students. "Please take your seats, boys and girls. Seth is ill today, but it's nothing for you to worry about. He's not contagious."

Though Catherine hoped that was true and that he'd passed the communicable stage, she was not completely certain. The medical book she'd consulted for her own symptoms had been of little help. Still, she did not want to alarm the other children.

Once she'd situated Seth on a pallet of blankets in the cloakroom, Catherine walked to the door with Mr. Goddard. His expression told her he wanted to talk, and so she followed him outside, standing on the top step while he descended to the ground.

"The boy could benefit from a doctor," he said bluntly. "He looks malnourished to me."

Catherine wouldn't dispute that, nor would she tell this man that she often brought extra food from home to share with pupils like Seth who came without lunches. Instead she focused on Mr. Goddard's first statement. "How would bleeding or purging help with malnutrition?"

He seemed taken aback by her question. "It wouldn't."

"That's all Doc Harrington knows. When my mother was ill, he kept bleeding her, even though it made her so weak she couldn't get out of bed. Then he administered purges. That made her even weaker." Catherine tried not to shudder at the memories of her mother's final months on Earth. "And then he put those horrible patches on her, saying blistering was the only way to help her."

She looked at Mr. Goddard, whose eyes were now a few inches below hers, willing him to understand. "If it hadn't been for that doctor, my mother would still be alive. There was a lesson in that, and believe me, I learned it well. No pupil of mine will ever go near a doctor if I can help it. Doctors kill people just as surely as men with guns."

She was wrong, Austin reflected as he headed out of town. He'd finished his shopping, and with his wagon loaded with supplies, he was on his way to the Dalton farm and then home. All the while he'd been in the mercantile, buying everything from nails to ribbons for Hannah's hair, he'd replayed the pretty schoolmarm's comments.

She was wrong. Oh, she was right about how to treat Seth's most pressing symptoms. Austin had overheard several women at church say their husbands were suffering from a stomach malady. The only thing Austin might have added to Miss Whitfield's plan was willow bark tea to help lower the boy's fever. She was right about the ginger root to settle his stomach, and chicken soup had cured more patients than bleeding ever did.

She was right about Seth's immediate needs, but the boy still needed a doctor to address his malnutrition. A doctor—a good doctor—would sort through the quack medicines that had become so popular and choose the one that would help build up Seth's strength. A good doctor would counsel the parents—in this case, the parent, singular—about the foods a growing boy needed: eggs, milk, meat. Unfortunately, if Catherine Whitfield was correct, Cimarron Creek did not have a good doctor.

Austin tightened his grip on the reins as he thought of what she'd said about the local physician. It sounded as if he was stuck back in what Austin thought of as the Dark Ages, practicing what some called heroic medicine: bleeding, purging, and blistering. No modern physician would employ those techniques. Austin never had and never would. Catherine was right. Heroic medicine had resulted in many unnecessary deaths. Surely this Doctor Harrington knew that.

If he could have, Austin would have visited the town's doctor and done his best to educate him. But he could not. Though he wished it were otherwise, his days of practicing medicine were over. That part of his life had ended.

No one, especially the schoolmarm who so obviously distrusted the entire medical profession, could know that he had graduated from one of the foremost medical schools in the East and had studied with renowned surgeons in Europe.

Dr. Goddard was his past, a past that could never be revealed. For as long as Sherman Enright lived, he was simply Austin Goddard, Texas rancher.

3

Catherine kept her arm wrapped firmly around Seth's waist, knowing that even though he hated the visible reminder of his infirmity, he was too ill to walk without assistance.

"We're almost there," she said. Though it was only two blocks from the school to her home, bearing most of Seth's weight had left Catherine breathless. She guided them onto Mesquite, giving thanks that her home was now in sight.

"Need some help, Catherine?"

She froze for an instant, her brain recoiling from the very thought. Why oh why did the town's doctor have to be standing on his front porch at this particular time? It was bad enough that he lived on the same block and that she had to pass his house every time she left home, but at least he was rarely outside.

The easiest thing would be to pretend she hadn't heard him. That was what she did whenever she could. But Seth was with her today. After all the times she had chided her pupils for not being polite to one another, she could not ignore the doctor. She was an adult, and she needed to set a positive example.

"No, sir," she said as sweetly as she could. "I have everything Seth needs."

"Suit yourself, but I've got a couple hungry leeches here."

Both Catherine and Seth shuddered.

The Dalton farm was suffering from neglect. Austin saw that the moment he turned off the main road. As the wagon lurched from hitting yet another pothole on the narrow lane leading to the farm buildings, he frowned, his opinion of Seth's father sinking another notch. Though he tried not to form judgments about people without meeting them, the picture of Mr. Dalton that was emerging was not a pleasant one.

A day or two of work was all it would have taken to fill in the potholes and cut back the cactus that encroached on the edges of the road. Though the fields were plowed, the rows were crooked, and weeds had begun to overtake whatever crop was supposed to be growing. Neglect, plain and simple.

When he reached the farmhouse, Austin wasn't surprised to see that it had suffered equally, its paint peeling and the windows so encrusted with dirt that he suspected they hadn't been washed in years.

Had Mr. Dalton fallen on hard times or did he simply not care? Perhaps the burden of being a widower and trying to raise a child alone had taken its toll on him, leaving him either overwhelmed or apathetic. Parenting without a wife was not an easy life. Austin knew that firsthand.

As the wagon rattled its way onto the yard, a heavyset man an inch or two shorter than Austin emerged from the barn. His pants were frayed at the cuffs, his shirt missing a button, the brown hair visible beneath his hat in sore need of a cut. The man appeared as neglected as his farm.

"Are you Mr. Dalton?" Austin asked, trying not to frown at the hostility he saw on the other man's face. Though Texans were noted for their friendliness, there were always exceptions, and this man appeared to be one.

"Yeah, I'm Boone Dalton. Who wants to know?" As Boone Dalton approached the wagon, Austin climbed out, hoping the man would be more welcoming if they were on equal footing.

"I'm Austin Goddard, your neighbor."

It was an innocuous statement, or so Austin thought, but his neighbor's reaction said otherwise. The man's face flushed, and he balled his hands into fists. "So you're the one what stole the ranch from me." There was no mistaking the venom in his voice or the anger flashing from those brown eyes so like his son's. As far as Austin could see, the shape and color of his eyes were the only traits Seth had inherited from his father. That was probably good.

Austin kept his expression as neutral as he could while he considered the implications of Boone Dalton's words. The man who'd arranged the sale of the ranch had told him there had been another person interested, but that he hadn't been able to meet the price. Austin hadn't expected to encounter the other potential buyer, especially under these circumstances, and he couldn't help wondering why a man who obviously neglected the land he already owned would want to acquire more.

Deciding to ignore Boone's comment and the questions it had raised, Austin said, "Miss Whitfield asked me to stop by. Seth was ill at school." And had obviously been ill before then, although Boone gave no sign that he was aware of it. Austin had trouble imagining how the boy had managed to walk into town in his condition. It must have been sheer desperation that propelled his feet that far.

"She's going to keep him at her house until he's well enough to come home," Austin continued, watching the other man as carefully as he would a coiled snake. Instinct told him Boone Dalton was as dangerous as a riled rattler.

"She dang well better not expect me to pay for no doctor." The man practically spat the words.

Austin might have laughed at the thought of Catherine Whitfield consulting a doctor if the situation hadn't been so serious. "I can assure you, there will be no doctor's fees."

"Dang right there won't be. I ain't paying nothin' for that useless boy. He's always gettin' sick and sloughin' off his chores. Them cows gotta be milked regular like."

He pounded his right fist into his left palm in what seemed to be an attempt to vent his anger. Instead of being concerned that his son was ill, Seth's father only cared that he might have to milk a cow. It wasn't the first time Austin had seen men who apparently lacked paternal instincts, but Boone might be the worst example he'd encountered.

"You wouldn't want your livestock to catch whatever's ailing your son, would you?" he asked, trying to deflect some of the man's anger from Seth. He hoped Boone was as ignorant of the probability of interspecies infections as he was of paternal love.

Austin's comment hit its mark, for the man shook his head. "Dang right, I don't. Them cows are worth more than the boy."

Though the boy had a name, his father didn't seem to use it. Boone's bulbous red nose told Austin the man drank to excess; his reaction to Seth's illness told Austin he hadn't been mistaken in thinking the yellow patches he'd seen on Seth's face were bruises and that his father had been the one to inflict them. Boone Dalton was a brute, just like those thugs Sherman Enright had hired.

Austin tried not to sigh at the sadness of the situation. So far, he had been able to keep Hannah away from Enright's henchmen. Unfortunately, there was little he could do to protect Seth. Even if Austin told the sheriff that Seth was being mistreated, the law would side with Boone. A man had a right to raise his child the way he saw fit, or so the law books claimed.

"I missed you at church yesterday."

Catherine turned at the sound of the familiar voice, clutching her cloak more closely around her shoulders as she leaned forward on the porch swing. Despite the evening's chill, once she'd been satisfied that Seth was asleep, she'd ventured outside for a bit of fresh air, not expecting anyone to come calling.

"I was ill," she told her visitor, "but I'm better now."

Nate Kenton climbed the three steps to the front porch and leaned against the railing, the sliver of a moon illuminating his face. There had been a time when Catherine had considered that face handsome, but tonight it seemed like a pale and poor imitation of Austin Goddard's. Why hadn't she noticed the way Nate looked at a spot beside her rather than meeting her gaze? Why hadn't she noticed that his voice was harsh rather than firm? Why hadn't she . . .

Her thoughts were interrupted when Nate shook his head. "You may be well, but Seth Dalton isn't. I hear you've got him staying with you."

Catherine suppressed a sigh at the evidence that the Cimarron Creek rumor mill was as active as ever. "I hope he'll recover as quickly as I did."

Though she knew it was futile, she wished concern over her health was the reason Nate had come to town. The man whose peaches and goats were famous throughout the county lived a few miles outside of town and came in only for church and an occasional trip for provisions now that his weekly dominoes games with the sheriff had been discontinued. He'd never visited her on a Monday evening, but it was also true that she rarely missed church services.

"I worry about you," Nate said, dipping his head ever so slightly. "You should be caring for your own children, not someone else's." Though the words were slightly different from the previous time, Catherine had no doubt where this conversation was headed. She said nothing, letting him continue. The sooner he said his piece, the sooner he would leave.

"You're good with children. You're a good teacher and a good nurse. You'd be a good mother."

Catherine hadn't minded when Mama had said the same thing, but Nate was not Mama. "I'm not certain God intends me to be a mother," she told him. A year ago that had been one of her dreams, but the year had brought so many changes that she'd begun to believe that being a wife and mother was one of the dreams that would never come true.

"Of course he intends you to be a mother," Nate insisted, "just as he intends me to be a father." He took a step forward, reaching for Catherine's hands. When she kept them firmly fixed on her cloak, he simply shrugged at the rejection. "I want to marry you, Catherine. You know that. And now that you put off your mourning clothes, I know you're ready."

"I'm not." Catherine shook her head. "Just because I'm not wearing black doesn't mean that I've stopped mourning my mother. Even if I wanted to marry you, I wouldn't consider doing that until the full year is over. Waiting that long is my way of honoring my mother."

"Oh." Her declaration appeared to have left Nate speechless.

The silence stretched between them, broken only by an owl's hoot and the soft soughing of the live oak leaves. It would have been a night to savor, if only Nate hadn't come.

He squared his shoulders, as if preparing for something unpleasant, then announced, "I'll even take you to Europe if you agree to be my wife."

Catherine blinked in surprise. Was this really Nate Kenton, the man who had always scoffed at the idea of traveling more than fifty miles from Cimarron Creek? When she'd spoken of

France and Switzerland, he'd told her he had no desire to go to a place where everyone spoke a foreign language. But tonight he was acting as if he'd changed his mind.

"I know you had your heart set on going abroad last summer. If you marry me, that can be our honeymoon trip."

The dream of Europe with its fabled cathedrals and castles had sustained Catherine through difficult times, but like so many other dreams, it had been buried along with her mother. Now Nate was offering a second chance. A year ago, she would have been overjoyed at the thought of seeing the famous sites of Europe with him, but that was a year ago.

"I'm sorry, Nate." And indeed she was. She was sorry he hadn't turned out to be the man she had thought he was. She was sorry that he might be hurt by her refusal, but she wasn't sorry enough to risk a life of unhappiness. "You're a good man, but I can't marry you."

He straightened his back and looked down at her, his expression mirroring his disbelief, though this was not the first time she'd refused his proposal. It was, however, the first time the proposal had included a honeymoon abroad. Nate must have thought that would change her answer.

"Why not? You know that I care about you."

"The way you cared about Lydia?" Catherine couldn't resist shooting the barb. At the time, she'd been hurt by his infatuation with the town's newest resident, but the pain had turned to relief that she'd been saved from making a huge mistake. Nate's attempts to court Lydia had shown Catherine that he'd never loved her. Oh, he cared for her, but that wasn't the same thing. Even tonight he hadn't claimed that he loved her.

"Lydia was only a passing fancy," Nate insisted. "You're the woman I want to marry. Say yes, Catherine. We can have a good life together. We'll get married, we'll go to Europe, and when we come back, I'll take care of you. You won't have to teach another year." His eyes darkened as he added, "I know you never really enjoyed teaching."

"That's changed. I've changed." But one thing that hadn't changed was Catherine's determination to never be a man's second choice. Nate might not be a teacher, but that was one lesson he'd taught very well.

She was smiling. Just before the rooster's crowing had wakened her, she had been dreaming of Paris, and this time there had been no disturbing end to the dream. It was her familiar dream of walking along the banks of the Seine, admiring the spires and flying buttresses of Notre Dame, with one variation. Instead of being alone, she had been strolling arm in arm with a man. He was tall, with blond hair like Nate, but though she hadn't seen his face, Catherine knew her companion was not Nate. The way he walked reminded her of Austin Goddard.

It was foolish to be dreaming of Austin. Admittedly, he was handsome, but there were other handsome men. What distinguished Austin was the way he treated others. Though she'd spent less than an hour in his company, she'd been impressed by his kindness and concern. He didn't dismiss children as inferior beings, simply because they were not fully grown. Instead, he'd seemed genuinely concerned for Seth.

They'd discussed the boy's plight when Austin had returned to pick up Hannah at the end of the day. Though their conversation had begun on a formal note, they'd soon agreed to use each other's first names. Austin had reported on his visit with Boone Dalton and had asked Catherine whether she'd considered giving Seth willow bark tea, seeming pleased when she told him she'd already given the boy some of the fever-reducing concoction.

Though the subjects had been serious, Catherine had felt

oddly energized by the way Austin seemed to regard her as an equal. There had been none of the slightly condescending attitude so many men in Cimarron Creek had toward her, even Nate. Especially Nate.

When Nate had declared that he would take care of her, Catherine had wanted to tell him she was perfectly capable of caring for herself. What she wanted—what she needed—was to be loved. She wanted the kind of love Mama said she and Papa had shared, a love so strong that even twenty years after Papa's death, the memories still warmed his widow.

Perhaps it was foolish, perhaps she was making a mistake, but Catherine wanted to be a man's first and only love. That meant that no matter how handsome and kind he was, Austin could never be more than a friend. Still, friendship was good.

Fifteen minutes later, dressed and coiffed for the day, Catherine knocked on the door to the spare room. Even though she would never have wished illness on Seth, she hadn't realized how empty the house had been or how much she'd missed having company until she'd settled him into the small room across the hall from her.

"Good morning, Seth," she said as she entered the room. "It looks like you're feeling better." Her patient was sitting in a chair by the window, a pencil in his hand, when only twelve hours earlier, he'd been flat on his back, almost too weak to move.

"It must be your chicken soup," the boy said, his face lighting with a smile. Surely the smile was not caused by the fact that she had fed him, carefully spooning the warm liquid into his mouth. Boys Seth's age didn't appreciate being invalids.

"My head doesn't hurt anymore," he told her. "I even read one of the stories you told me I could. I liked that headless horseman."

Catherine smiled as she laid a hand on his forehead, confirming that the fever had broken. Whether it was due to the chicken soup or the willow bark tea did not matter. What was important was that Seth was healing. And if Washington Irving's tales could help, she didn't regret giving him permission to touch the three books he'd noticed when she'd been feeding him.

Seth had seemed fascinated by the worn bindings, confirming Catherine's belief that his home contained few of the things she thought a growing boy should have. Knowing he would be careful with them, she'd explained that the books had been her father's and were the only things she had of his but that Seth was welcome to read them.

"I want you to spend another day recuperating," Catherine told her patient. "If you keep improving, you can return to school tomorrow." She might have allowed another pupil back in the classroom sooner, but knowing that a return to the school-house also meant a return to the farm where there would be no opportunity to rest and where he might be subjected to Boone's fists, Catherine decided to keep Seth here for at least one more day.

His smile faded. "My pa won't be happy."

Catherine did not doubt that. "Mr. Goddard spoke to him. He understands that you're not ready to milk the cows." Though Catherine had laughed at the story Austin had told Boone, she would not repeat it to Seth. The boy didn't need to know that his father was so easy to fool.

She glanced at the pad that he'd turned over in his lap. "You don't need to worry about your lessons." Seth was one of her brightest pupils. He'd have no trouble catching up with the others even if he missed a full week of school.

His face flushed with what appeared to be embarrassment as he looked at the pad. "It's not lessons."

"Then what are you doing?"

"Drawing." Seth turned the pad face up and handed it to her. Catherine stared at the sketch, amazed by the talent it revealed. Seth had captured the view from the window: the small garden Mama used to enjoy, the picket fence separating the yard from the cemetery, the headstones and monuments in the graveyard. They were ordinary things, and yet Seth had imbued them with such realism that Catherine felt as if she were standing in the middle of her yard.

"This is excellent work." She rested her hand on Seth's shoulder, watching as his face lit with pleasure over the compliment. "I didn't know you could draw." While other students often doodled on their slates, she'd never seen Seth doing that, yet the boy had more natural talent than any pupil she'd had.

The spark of enthusiasm that had lit Seth's face faded. "Pa won't let me draw. He says that's for girls."

And anyone who defied Boone Dalton paid the price. Catherine's heart ached at the realization that the boy who had so few pleasures was denied this one. Surely there was a way for Seth to use his talent.

4

It had been a good service, Austin reflected as he rose and turned toward the end of the pew. Even though it had made him uncomfortable, the pastor's sermon about neighborly love had struck a chord within him. The discomfort had come with the realization that he'd been remiss. He hadn't prayed for Boone, but that would change. Inspired by the sermon, Austin had already offered a prayer for the man and his son, neither of whom had come to church. Those prayers would continue. While Austin might not be able to open Boone's heart, there was One who could.

"Can we leave now?" Hannah tugged on Austin's hand, her eyes darting from one side of the church to the other in what Austin recognized as a nervous gesture. She had sat quietly during the service, but now that the congregation had risen and was making its way out of the sanctuary, Hannah was clearly anxious to be away from the crowd. Since they'd arrived in Texas, Austin's once-gregarious daughter had become as timid as the proverbial mouse.

He shook his head. "We need to wait until it's our turn to greet Pastor Dunn." Unlike the large church they'd attended in Philadelphia, this one had no side door. Everyone filed out the front, murmuring a few words to the minister before they departed.

Though Austin looked forward to telling the pastor that his words had touched at least one man's heart, he was not looking forward to what came after that. If today was anything like last Sunday, he'd feel as if he'd run a gauntlet before he and Hannah reached their wagon. They had no sooner emerged from the church last week than three women had cornered him, introducing him to their daughters, each of whom was of marriageable age, and issuing invitations to dinner. Though Austin had explained that he and Hannah were still getting settled as he refused the invitations as gently as he could, he wasn't sure how long that excuse would hold.

"We're almost there," he told Hannah. Just two more pews. Austin glanced to his left, surprised that one family remained in their pew. Normally those in the back of the church exited first, but this trio had not. A man, a woman, and the inevitable daughter stood at the center aisle side of the pew.

"Good morning, Mr. Goddard." The woman stepped into the aisle, effectively blocking Austin's path, then nodded for her husband and daughter to follow her. Of medium height with dark brown hair and eyes, she was a moderately attractive woman, or she would have been if she hadn't been regarding Austin with what appeared to be triumph. He tried not to sigh at the thought that the gauntlet had moved indoors.

"I didn't have a chance to meet you and your charming daughter last week," the woman continued, "but I told Mr. Brooks that we mustn't let another week go by without making your acquaintance."

So she'd positioned herself at the rear of the church to ambush him. Austin nodded, accepting the inevitability of listening to whatever she had to say. His experience last week had told him that the encounter would be shortened if he refrained from responding until the woman had completed her speech, for he had no doubt that she intended to sing her daughter's praises and then invite Austin and Hannah to dine with them.

"I'm Henrietta Brooks, and this is my husband Henry." The man, who was only an inch or two taller than his wife, gave Austin a look that seemed to convey his sympathy as the woman tittered. "Henry and Henrietta. Folks said we belonged together because of our names. They must have been right, because we've been happily married for over twenty years."

Mrs. Brooks put a hand on her daughter's arm, drawing her further into the aisle so that she was directly in front of Austin. The girl, whom Austin guessed to be no more than sixteen or seventeen, looked as embarrassed as her father, but the mother had no such shame. "The good Lord blessed us with the best daughter anyone could want. Anna, say hello to Mr. Goddard and Hannah."

As the girl complied, Mrs. Brooks fixed her gaze on Hannah. "Two beautiful daughters with such similar names. Anna and Hannah sound nice when you say them one after the other, just like Henry and Henrietta, don't they?"

Rather than respond, Hannah kept her eyes on the floor, but she grabbed Austin's hand as Mrs. Brooks continued her monologue.

"When I heard your name, I told Mr. Brooks it was a sign and that you and Anna were meant to be together the way he and I were."

She looked back at Austin. "We can't ignore signs, can we? That's why I plucked my largest chicken for today's dinner. I hope you and Hannah will join us."

When Hannah tightened her grip on his hand, this time looking up with beseeching eyes, Austin smiled at his daughter, hoping to reassure her. He extended his other hand to Mr. Brooks. "I'm glad to meet you, sir," he said as he shook the man's hand, then nodded at Anna and her mother. "I appreciate the invitation, but Mrs. Moore has prepared a meal for us. I wouldn't want to disappoint her."

"What about next week?" It appeared that Mrs. Brooks was not easily discouraged.

Austin gave her what he hoped was a regretful smile. "I'm afraid I can't make any plans right now, but thank you."

Her lips pursed in obvious displeasure, Mrs. Brooks shepherded her husband and daughter toward the minister. A backward look at him told Austin he might have won the skirmish, but the war wasn't over. The mothers of Cimarron Creek were nothing if not persistent.

As he waited his turn to praise Pastor Dunn's sermon, Austin took one final glance around the church. Though he tried to tell himself he wasn't looking for anyone in particular, the jolt of excitement that raced through him when he spotted Catherine said he'd been lying to himself. Even though he'd stared at her back several times during the service, this was the first time he'd seen that beautiful face today.

Catherine had been seated in the second pew from the front when Austin and Hannah had arrived, and unlike some other parishioners who turned to see who was behind them, she had kept her attention focused on the altar. Others' attention had been focused on Catherine and her navy dress.

"She's out of mourning clothes," the woman seated at the other end of Austin's pew had announced to the man at her side.

"Who?" The question sounded perfunctory rather than triggered by curiosity, making Austin think the man was accustomed to his wife's tendency to gossip.

"Catherine Whitfield," the woman hissed. "It's only been four months since her mother was laid to rest. She should still be in black, especially since Gussie was her last parent."

If the man replied, Austin did not hear him. Instead, his

thoughts had centered on the schoolteacher and her loss. Austin's heart had clenched at the realization that Catherine was now alone in the world. Was she as vulnerable as Geraldine had been after her parents' deaths? Austin hoped that was not the case. He also wondered why, though she had given him the history of what felt like a hundred of Cimarron Creek's residents, Mrs. Moore had neglected to mention that Catherine Whitfield was recently bereaved.

Thoughts of Catherine had occupied Austin until the service began, making him want to offer his condolences, even though they were belated. Now she stood in the aisle, speaking with the woman who ran the candy store and her husband, the sheriff. Unfortunately, they were too far away for him to join the conversation.

As if she sensed his gaze, Catherine looked directly at Austin and gave him a conspiratorial smile, making him suspect she was aware of his encounter with the Brooks family.

How typical of her! Though he'd spent only a few minutes with her at the end of each school day, Austin had discovered that Catherine was a fundamentally optimistic person, one who tried to find something good in every situation, no matter how dismal it might seem. Her unfailing cheerfulness, so different from Geraldine's volatile moods, must be an asset in the classroom. And when she married . . . Austin shook himself mentally. There was nothing to be gained by speculating about the schoolmarm's future mate.

"Papa, I don't like that lady." Hannah whispered the words, and for a second Austin thought she was speaking of Catherine. She had said little about school, barely responding to his and Mrs. Moore's questions about classes, other pupils, and the teacher. While he knew Hannah did not like living on the ranch, she had given no sign of disliking Catherine, and yet it was clear that she disliked someone. Austin was about to ask her why when he saw that Hannah's attention was focused on Mrs. Brooks.

He took a quick breath as relief flowed through him. Though he shared his daughter's opinion, he wouldn't admit it. Instead, he smiled at Hannah. "At least she didn't pinch your cheek." Two of the hopeful mamas had done that last Sunday, much to Hannah's displeasure.

She shook her head. "I still don't like her. I don't want a new mama." And, knowing Hannah, there would be no changing her mind. It was a good thing Austin wasn't searching for a second wife. At least not now.

⁂

"I saw Henrietta Brooks talking to you," Mrs. Moore told Austin as she slid a sheet of biscuits into the oven. When he'd entered the kitchen, she had poured him a cup of coffee and gestured toward a chair, somehow realizing that he wanted to talk.

Austin nodded. "She invited us for dinner."

"And you refused."

"Of course. Hannah and I wouldn't miss your pot roast for anything." He took another sip of coffee, then sniffed appreciatively. Mrs. Moore might not have been able to coax Hannah out of her sulks, but she was a superb cook. If anyone could help his daughter gain some much-needed weight, it would be Mrs. Moore.

The housekeeper narrowed her eyes as she looked at Austin. "You won't get off that easily. I've known Henrietta since she was a girl, and she's not likely to give up. The way she sees it, you need a mother for Hannah, and her daughter needs a husband."

Grateful that his daughter was still playing with a doll in her room and didn't have to hear this discussion, he said, "Hannah and I've been managing by ourselves for a long time."

They had done more than manage. Hannah had seemed

happy or at least content in Philadelphia. Unfortunately, that was something Austin couldn't say now. He wanted to believe that Hannah's melancholy was the result of the changes she had endured and that she would recover quickly, but if she did not, he would have to seek other remedies.

Would giving Hannah a new mother solve the problem or would it merely create new ones? His marriage to Geraldine had certainly been fraught with difficulties, but despite the way it had ended and the grief he had endured, Austin could not regret it. If he hadn't married Geraldine, he would not have Hannah, and that was unthinkable. Even now, when she was clearly unhappy, Hannah brought joy to his life.

The question was how to restore her happiness. Would a stepmother be able to succeed if Austin continued to fail? It was a question that had flitted through Austin's brain more than once this week.

"Henrietta's wrong about a lot of things, but she's right about this. Hannah needs a mother," Mrs. Moore announced.

Austin glared at his housekeeper. "I'm not going to marry just because some busybody matchmaking mother decides I should."

What Austin didn't say was that if there were a guarantee that a stepmother would make Hannah happy, if he found a woman he could love, and if he knew that Enright was no longer a threat, he might consider remarrying. The problem was, those were all major "ifs." Judging from Hannah's reaction to the women who'd been presented to them, introducing another woman into the household would worsen her moods. Austin had yet to find a woman he wanted to share the rest of his life with, and Enright, like Henrietta Brooks, was not one to give up easily.

"Anna Brooks isn't the only girl in town." Mrs. Moore was becoming as persistent as the matchmaking mamas.

"That's good, because she's not the right one for me." Austin tried not to frown, but it was ridiculous to have to defend himself like this.

He drained his cup as he reflected that Hannah wasn't the only one who hadn't been impressed with the matrimonial candidates paraded in front of them. Not one had ignited even the smallest spark of interest inside Austin. Unlike Catherine, not one had seemed to have a mind of her own. Unlike Catherine, not one seemed to have any interest in Hannah. Unlike Catherine, who appeared mature beyond her years, they appeared to be young girls with their heads in the clouds. If he remarried—and Austin doubted he would—he would choose a woman like Catherine.

"You're not the first man Henrietta's run after," Mrs. Moore continued. "She had her sights set on Nate Kenton as a son-in-law, but now that he's courting the schoolmarm, you're her best bet."

Someone was courting Catherine? The coffee that had seemed delicious a moment ago now churned in Austin's stomach. "I don't think I've met Nate Kenton," he said, pleased that his voice betrayed none of the turmoil that knotted his stomach at the thought of the schoolteacher as a bride.

"He raises goats and peaches. Has a farm on the other side of town." Mrs. Moore lifted the lid on the pot roast that had been simmering all morning, then speared a piece of meat with a fork to test its tenderness. "Nate's a mighty fine man. I always thought he'd be a good match for Catherine." She punctuated her sentence with a nod. "They'll probably wait until fall when her year of mourning is over, but mark my words: they'll be married before the year ends."

It was ridiculous that the idea bothered him. It wasn't as if he were planning to marry again, but if he were, Austin wouldn't choose a recently bereaved woman. He'd made that mistake once, and he had no intention of repeating it.

It wasn't as if he harbored tender feelings for Catherine. He hardly knew her. While it was true that he liked what he knew of her, that he was grateful she was Hannah's teacher, that she had the characteristics he sought in a friend, that was all Austin wanted from Catherine: a teacher for Hannah and a possible friend for himself. That was all.

5

"What do you know about the new rancher? I heard he's got a daughter, but that's about all anyone knows."

Catherine tried not to sigh. Sunday dinner with Aunt Mary and Uncle Charles was often difficult. The combination of poorly prepared food and constant criticism of others made her dread the weekly event. If it weren't for Warner, she would never have agreed to come, but she couldn't desert him. He and Travis were her favorite cousins, but while Travis had found his true love in Lydia, Warner was still single and living with his parents. Though she would have refused the invitation, when Warner had added his plea to his mother's almost imperious decree that Catherine join them, she had agreed. Warner deserved an ally at least once a week, and so here she was, enduring the Sunday ordeal. The only positive aspect was that Lydia and Travis had agreed to join her.

"Hannah is six and seems very bright," Catherine told her uncle by marriage. Though it was normally Aunt Mary who began the inquisition, today it was Uncle Charles who'd asked the question as soon as he'd blessed the food. Catherine wondered whether he would notice that she hadn't said anything about Austin but had instead spoken of Hannah. That had been a deliberate move on her part, an attempt to deflect her sometimes cantankerous uncle's attention.

According to Mama, when he'd first come to Cimarron Creek, Charles Gray had been a young man with an eye for the ladies. The owner of the town's prospering livery, he'd apparently been as sought after as Austin Goddard was now. Perhaps that was why he was curious about the newly arrived rancher.

Catherine had heard various opinions about the Grays' marriage. Though Aunt Mary claimed it was a love match, others were less charitable and maintained the reason Uncle Charles had married her was that she was a Whitfield and a woman whose position in one of Cimarron Creek's two leading families overcame her lack of beauty. What no one disputed was that their marriage had produced two sons, one of whom was now deceased.

"Someone mentioned that Mr. Goddard grew up in Oklahoma," Aunt Mary said as she passed the bowl of green beans to her surviving son.

The seating arrangement was the same each week. Aunt Mary and Uncle Charles had their customary seats at the ends of the table, with Lydia and Travis on one side, Catherine and Warner on the other.

"Is it true?" Uncle Charles kept his gaze fixed on Catherine, waiting for her response. At least he hadn't patted her thigh today. Catherine gave silent thanks for that. Her skin had crawled the day he'd done that, and she'd shifted uneasily in her chair, wanting more than anything to leave the room. If it weren't for Warner, she would have made excuses not to return, but she couldn't abandon Warner.

"I'm afraid I can't help you," Catherine said. "I see him and his daughter every day when he brings her to school, but I didn't know Austin was from Oklahoma."

"Austin?" Aunt Mary's voice rose with disapproval. "You're on such familiar terms with him?"

"Yes." Though Lydia shot her a commiserating glance, Catherine refused to defend herself, knowing from experience that there was no reasoning with Aunt Mary when she became fixed on an idea. She had already told Catherine it was too soon for her to have put aside her mourning clothes. Now she was concerned about another aspect of social protocol.

"I'm worried about you, Catherine," Aunt Mary said. "Your mother, rest her soul, claimed you had good judgment, but I'm not so sure. You're a woman alone. That means men might try to take advantage of you. You oughta do what I do and keep a gun in your house. You need to be prepared to defend yourself. Why, I had to shoot a snake just the other day."

Uncle Charles nodded and wagged a finger at Catherine. "Mary is right. You got to be careful about newcomers. They can be more dangerous than snakes." His gaze landed on Lydia, who was seated at his other side.

"Newcomers like my wife?" It was the first time Travis had spoken since they'd gathered around the table. Though he was normally quiet during these meals, Catherine knew he would not allow anyone to insult Lydia. His question was brief, but his steely tone left no doubt that he was displeased.

Lydia had faced resentment and outright hostility when she had first arrived in Cimarron Creek, and though she was now accepted by most of the townspeople, Travis was determined to protect her.

While Uncle Charles seemed oblivious to the unspoken threat, Aunt Mary recognized it and shook her head vigorously. "Charles didn't mean anything bad, did you, Charles?"

"Of course not." Uncle Charles laid his hand on Lydia's. "I don't think of you as a newcomer anymore. You're part of the family."

And family was important, at least to the Whitfields. That was why Uncle Charles and Aunt Mary had accepted Lydia: she'd married a Whitfield. Family was why after their younger son's tragic death and their daughter-in-law's move to Austin, they'd begged Catherine to live with them.

"You're all alone," Aunt Mary had said. "I'm lonely too. We could help each other."

Catherine had refused the plea to join the Grays' household, preferring occasional loneliness to her aunt's obsessive mothering and Uncle Charles's bold stares and unwelcome touches. Even Warner's presence would not have made living here pleasant. Her sole concession had been agreeing to join her aunt and uncle and Warner for Sunday dinner once she'd convinced Lydia and Travis to come too.

"Misery loves company," she had told Lydia, not certain whether she or Warner was the more miserable at the meals. Fortunately, Travis and Lydia's company had seemed to mute Aunt Mary's complaints a bit.

"I saw Henrietta Brooks corner the new man today," Aunt Mary announced as she buttered a hot roll. "She probably figured he's so desperate for a wife that he'll overlook Anna's buck teeth."

Lydia raised one brow as she said, "Anna has a lovely disposition. I've never heard her say an unkind word about anyone."

Aunt Mary ignored Lydia's veiled barb and continued to dissect the Brooks family and Anna's chances of snaring a suitable husband, not seeming to remember that she herself had been married for her money and position, not her beauty.

An hour and a half later, Catherine took a deep breath of air as she and Lydia left the Grays' home and headed toward Catherine's. As often happened on a Sunday, Travis had remained to play horseshoes with his cousin.

"Was it only me, or did Aunt Mary seem more critical than

normal?" Catherine asked as she and Lydia headed east on Mesquite. It was less than three blocks from the Grays' home to hers, but there were times when Catherine felt as if she were entering a different world when she emerged from her aunt and uncle's ornate house. The one she'd shared with her mother was only a fraction of the size of the Grays', but Catherine would not have traded the serenity she found there for all the marble and polished wood in the other house.

"It wasn't your imagination," Lydia assured her. "I noticed it too. Mary's started coming to Cimarron Sweets almost every day. I think she's lonely."

"That's understandable." Though Catherine wasn't a daily visitor, she stopped in Lydia's candy store at least three afternoons a week, more for her friend's company than the delicious confections Lydia sold. It was likely that Aunt Mary felt the same need for companionship during the day when Uncle Charles was at the livery and Warner at his apothecary.

"I'm not surprised that she's lonely. Aunt Mary doted on that granddaughter of hers, and now she's gone. What I find strange is that she never speaks of either Hilda or Susan. It's as if they never existed."

Lydia looked in all directions before she responded, as if she wanted to be certain she would not be overheard. "You'd know better than I, but that seems to be a Whitfield tradition. Look at how Aunt Bertha never spoke of Joan."

Though the January sun was weak, there was no reason Catherine should have shivered. Still, although she'd lived in Cimarron Creek her entire life, she felt a chill run down her spine at the mention of a name she had never heard. "Who's Joan?"

Lydia's face mirrored her astonishment. "Oh, Catherine, I'm so sorry. I thought you knew." She looked around again before giving a brisk nod. "Let's wait until we're inside. Then I'll tell you what I know."

When they reached her home, Catherine brewed a pot of tea before leading the way into the parlor where she'd spent so many happy hours with her mother. After Mama had taken ill, Aunt Bertha had been a frequent visitor, sitting in this room, sipping tea or coffee, delivering some of her famous monologues, but to the best of Catherine's knowledge, she had never mentioned anyone named Joan.

"Who's Joan?" Catherine repeated her question when she and Lydia were seated in the room's most comfortable chairs, a low table with the teapot and cups in front of them.

Her blue eyes solemn, Lydia said, "Joan was Aunt Bertha's daughter."

For a second, Catherine was speechless, trying to digest the revelation. "Aunt Bertha had a daughter?" As far as Catherine knew, Aunt Bertha and Uncle Jonas had been childless.

Lydia nodded. "She left Cimarron Creek when she was fourteen. That was back in '59."

"I was only a year old." While she would have had no memory of Joan, surely someone in Cimarron Creek would have mentioned a girl who'd lived here for fourteen years, especially one who was also the daughter of a founding family. "It doesn't make sense. Why has no one spoken of Joan in all those years, and how did you learn things that I never heard about my family?"

Lydia reached over to clasp Catherine's hand. "Please don't be upset. I'm sure Aunt Bertha wouldn't have wanted you to feel hurt or excluded."

But Catherine did. She felt as if she'd been the victim of a conspiracy of silence. Mama had been here while Joan was alive. She must have known her, and yet she'd never said a word.

Lydia's eyes radiated sympathy. "You weren't the only one who didn't know. Travis didn't, either. I doubt Aunt Bertha would have said anything to me, but I came home from the store unexpectedly one afternoon and found her crying over

Joan's daguerreotype." Lydia took a sip of tea, then shook her head slowly as she said, "Perhaps I shouldn't have pressured her, but I insisted that she tell me what was wrong. That's how I learned what had happened."

"Will you tell me?" Catherine was still reeling over the thought that she had an unknown cousin.

Nodding, Lydia said, "As much as I know. Aunt Bertha said the Whitfields and Hendersons have always been concerned about their image in town. I think it's connected to what you and I called the sense of *noblesse oblige*, where everyone in the founding families is expected to serve the town in some manner."

That was the reason Catherine had become a schoolteacher, even though she hadn't found it a rewarding profession until Lydia had given her some wise counsel.

"Saying the town's founders were concerned about their image is an understatement. Look at those three Founders' houses. They're the epitome of opulence."

Lydia chuckled. "I have to admit that Travis and I are enjoying ours. I never thought I'd live anywhere so beautiful." Though many in Cimarron Creek had been shocked when Aunt Bertha had left her mansion to Lydia, Catherine understood the reasons.

"It's always seemed to me that the first generation of Whitfields and Hendersons were obsessed with serving as an example for everyone else." Though she was a Whitfield, Catherine and her cousins were less concerned with the family image than their grandparents had been. "Quite honestly, I don't understand why, but the first generation—and that included Aunt Bertha—seemed to believe that since they founded Cimarron Creek, they needed to be above reproach."

Lydia took another sip of tea. "That was the problem. Joan's father didn't believe that she was above reproach. When Joan discovered she was going to have a baby, Uncle Jonas wouldn't believe she had been attacked and had no idea who the father was, so he and Aunt Bertha sent her to live with Aunt Bertha's cousins."

A child born out of wedlock. The very thought sent a shiver down Catherine's spine. She had no trouble imagining the scandal that situation would have caused, particularly if the mother was a Whitfield or a Henderson. No wonder Aunt Bertha and Uncle Jonas had tried to cover it up. There were no unwed mothers in Cimarron Creek, although a few girls had left town to visit relatives for six or seven months, leading some of the matrons to speculate that a not-so-blessed event had occurred while they were gone.

"Is Joan still with the cousins?" Perhaps Aunt Bertha's daughter had found a welcoming home there.

"No." Lydia dispelled that possibility. "Joan ran away as soon as the baby was born, and no one knows where she went. When they heard the news, Uncle Jonas insisted that Joan was dead and decreed that no one mention her name."

"And because he was a Henderson, everyone listened to him." The Whitfields' and Hendersons' grip on the town had lessened a bit in the intervening twenty years, but Catherine knew that an edict from Jonas Henderson would have had the force of law at that time, in part because he was a lawyer and a man no one dared cross.

Her throat suddenly dry, Catherine raised her cup and sipped the hot beverage before she asked whether Joan had indeed died.

Lydia's eyes clouded. "I don't know. Aunt Bertha believed she was alive and tried her best to find her, but even the Pinkertons couldn't trace Joan. Aunt Bertha couldn't do much while Uncle Jonas was alive, because he was adamant that Joan be forgotten, but she never gave up hope of being reunited with her daughter. That's why we went to Ladreville last fall. She was hoping to find a clue."

"Did she?" Catherine feared she knew the answer, but she had to ask the question.

As expected, Lydia shook her head. "No one there had any idea where Joan had gone. Some thought she might have searched for her baby at some point, but the couple who adopted her baby was from another town, and no one kept in touch with them. It's as if they all disappeared from the face of the earth."

What a sad, sad story.

6

"I don't know what to do, Miss Whitfield." Rebecca Henderson twisted one of her blonde braids between her fingers in a rarely used gesture of frustration. The girl had come back into the schoolhouse before the end of lunch and had perched on the chair next to Catherine's desk, clearly agitated. "She won't play with us at recess."

Catherine nodded slowly. It had been four weeks since Hannah had started school, and she was still silent and distant. Fortunately, she wasn't a sullen child, but her behavior was definitely not that of a normal six-year-old.

"It's not your fault, Rebecca. I know you've tried."

Her eyes shining with unshed tears, Rebecca bit her lower lip. "I gave her a doll today. Mama and I ordered it specially for Hannah, but it didn't make her smile."

And that had hurt Rebecca. She was as generous as her mother, but like Rachel, she was easily frustrated. Catherine had seen that frustration last summer when she had refused Nate's offer to escort her to the Founders' Day dance, a refusal Rachel had considered insulting to Nate, even though Catherine had used her mother's illness as the reason for not accepting Nate's invitation. Rachel, it seemed, was almost as protective of her younger brother as she was of her three children.

A glance at the clock told Catherine it was nearly time to summon the pupils, but before she did that, she needed to find a way to console the girl who'd made such an effort to welcome Hannah to Cimarron Creek and its school. Even though Catherine had seen her frustration when Hannah did not respond to her friendly overtures, today was the first day Rebecca had complained.

Catherine touched Rebecca's shoulder, hoping the gesture would provide as much comfort as her words. "Sometimes people smile on the inside."

And sometimes they smiled on the outside when they were crying on the inside. Catherine wouldn't tell Rebecca that, but ever since she had heard the story of Joan Henderson, she had been haunted by the realization that although Aunt Bertha had appeared to be happy, she had borne a great sorrow. It made Catherine wonder what other secrets Cimarron Creek's residents harbored and whether she truly knew any of her fellow townspeople.

"Smiling on the inside." Rebecca pursed her lips and stared at her stomach, as if searching for a hidden smile. "Do you think that's what Hannah's doing?"

"Maybe." Though Catherine doubted that was the case, she didn't want to discourage Rebecca. "Some people are naturally shy. It takes them a long time to make friends."

Catherine had been one of those. As an only child, she had not had any ready-made playmates. Fortunately, her cousins Travis and Warner had allowed her to tag along on some of their adventures, even when Warner's brother Porter had protested. The boys' natural exuberance had broken through Catherine's barriers and opened her to friendship with girls her age.

Rebecca seemed dubious. "Mama says I'm supposed to be friends with everyone."

"And you are. You've been a good friend to Hannah, and by

doing that, you're helping me. Thank you, Rebecca." Catherine patted her shoulder again. "When I see your mother, I'll tell her what a good job you're doing."

Rebecca flushed with what appeared to be embarrassment. Surely Catherine's praise hadn't flustered her. When the girl bit her lower lip, Catherine knew something else was at work.

"Oh, I almost forgot," Rebecca said. "Mama wants you to come for dinner next Sunday. Uncle Nate's going to be there too."

Catherine bit back a sigh. It seemed Rachel was back in matchmaker mode. Catherine knew she should have expected that, especially since Rachel had mentioned that one of her cousins in San Antonio was looking for a teaching position. If Catherine married Nate, the cousin would have a chance to become Cimarron Creek's next schoolteacher. But Catherine was not going to marry Nate, no matter how happy that would make Rachel or her cousin.

"Please thank your mother, but tell her I won't be able to come. I always have Sunday dinner with the Grays." And though dinner with her aunt and uncle was far from the highlight of Catherine's weeks, it was preferable to a meal with Nate and his matchmaking sister.

Rebecca grinned as if she'd anticipated Catherine's refusal. "Mama knows that. She talked to Cousin Mary, and it's all right."

Which meant that Catherine couldn't refuse without being rude. "Then I'd be happy to join you." She'd be happier—far happier—if she could break through Hannah's shell.

Three hours later Austin entered the schoolhouse, his eyes scanning the desks looking for his daughter. Many afternoons Hannah remained inside, sitting quietly at her desk while she waited for her father, but today was different.

"She's outside, playing on the swing." Catherine was surprised Austin hadn't noticed that when he'd arrived. Though she refused to join in the other children's games during recess, for the past few days Hannah seemed to like to swing, perhaps because that was an activity she could do alone. The fact that the school had only one swing meant that she would have no companions there.

"I'm sorry I'm late." Austin sounded almost sheepish. "Something broke into the chicken coop last night, and it took more time than I'd expected to repair it." He raised his left hand, displaying the bandaged thumb. "There were some unplanned delays."

Catherine rose from her desk and made a show of inspecting his hand, just as she would have had he been an injured pupil. Boys—big or little—liked to flaunt their battle wounds. As she studied his thumb, Catherine realized the last month had wrought changes in Austin's hands. They were now more tanned and more callused than when she'd first met him, more what she would have expected of a rancher.

"It seems you were wounded in the line of duty." Catherine couldn't tell what had happened to the thumb, but whoever had wrapped it had done an excellent job.

"I'm afraid the hammer got the best of that round, but Kevin and I made sure the critter—he thinks it's a javelina—won't find our chickens such easy pickings again."

"I'm glad to hear that."

It was an ordinary conversation. On an ordinary day, Catherine would have enjoyed it, but today her thoughts were focused on Hannah and the discussion she and Rebecca had had. Though Hannah had kept the doll at her desk, not once had she looked at it. Even during recess, when the other girls had asked to see it, she had said nothing, merely held the doll up for them to admire.

Austin lowered his hand, and when Catherine resumed her

seat, he perched on the corner of the desk rather than using the chair next to it. "You look as if something's bothering you." He was close enough that she could smell the soap he'd used to wash off the grime of the day.

Catherine nodded. Once again, Austin had proven to be more perceptive than most of her students' parents. "I'm concerned about Hannah," she admitted. "I know it's difficult for a child to be uprooted, particularly after just losing her mother, but I thought she would have settled in by now. Instead, she's like a turtle, hiding inside her shell."

When Austin made no response other than a short nod, Catherine continued. "Hannah's very bright. Whenever I call on her, she knows the answer, but she never volunteers to speak, and she won't play with the other children at recess or lunch. I'm concerned."

His eyes dark with emotion, Austin rolled his shoulders, as if to release the tension that had gripped him while Catherine had been speaking. "So am I. Hannah wasn't always like this. It started when we moved here."

Though Austin might not have realized it, that was good news. It meant that this was probably a temporary condition. If Catherine could find the key, perhaps she could accelerate Hannah's return to normalcy.

"Did she have special friends in Oklahoma? She probably misses them."

Catherine had expected a straightforward answer. Instead, Austin seemed uncomfortable with what she thought was a simple question and seemed to hesitate for an instant before he spoke. "There was no one she was close to in Oklahoma." Perhaps she had only imagined his discomfort, for his reply was smooth.

Catherine didn't know a great deal about ranches in Oklahoma, but if they were as large as some in Texas, it was possible

Hannah had made few trips into the nearest town. Until this year, she had not been school age, which eliminated another source of social contact. Even church might not have provided opportunities to mingle with other children, since many ranching families worshipped at home when churches were hours away.

"I keep hoping she'll come out of her melancholy," Austin continued. "To be honest, I thought school would be the answer."

He crossed one knee over the other and stared at the far wall, the set of his jaw telling Catherine how deeply he felt about his daughter's problem. She understood. For many children, being part of a group was therapeutic, but that hadn't been the case with Hannah. Not yet.

"I'm not giving up on her," Catherine said firmly, "but I wanted you to know what I've observed. I plan to talk to Lydia about her."

When Austin looked surprised, Catherine realized he might not have known that Lydia had not always been a candy maker. "She taught at a girls' school back East and knows more than I ever will about young girls."

It had been Lydia's advice to remember what she had liked—and disliked—about school that had changed Catherine's perspective on teaching. Thanks to Lydia, it was no longer drudgery but a calling that brought her great satisfaction.

Austin looked dubious. "I doubt that's true, but thank you. I hope she can help. I'm not ashamed to admit that I'm at my wits' end." He slid down from the desk and strode to the window where he could watch Hannah on the swing. "I don't know what to do, but somehow there has to be a way to break through her shell. Hannah's all the family I have left, and I'm failing her." The last words came out as little more than a whisper.

Austin looked so sad and discouraged that Catherine's heart

ached. She would have tried to help any parent in Austin's situation, but from the day she had met him and Hannah, they had become special to her. They had both touched her heart in unexpected ways, making her want to do everything in her power to restore Hannah's cheerfulness and relieve Austin's anguish.

Catherine couldn't promise that Lydia would have any ideas or, even if she did, that they would have an effect on Hannah, but she longed to comfort Austin. She wanted to give him something positive to counterbalance the discouragement he felt about Hannah. If he drove his daughter back to the ranch in this mood, Austin would only depress her further. Instead, he needed to know that his efforts had helped someone.

Catherine thought about the changes she'd seen in another pupil and the reasons for those changes. "You're not a failure, Austin. Some problems take longer than others to resolve, but you're a good parent. I know you are. I see it in Hannah and in Seth. He may not be your son, but you're helping him. He told me you drive him most of the way to and from school."

Austin shrugged as if that were of little importance, when in reality it kept the boy from being so tired that he dozed during classes. The chores that Boone assigned him meant that Seth got little sleep, and having to walk an hour each way, particularly when he had had no breakfast, drained the boy's strength.

"I hated to see him walking when I drive the same road." Austin returned to lean against Catherine's desk, crossing his arms, his bandaged thumb a startling contrast against his blue chambray shirt. "Did Seth tell you he insists on getting in and out of the wagon far enough away from the farm that his father doesn't know he's riding? I can't say that I approve of the deception, but I know Boone Dalton is a difficult man."

"That he is." Difficult was an understatement. Though Catherine had seen no new bruises, she knew it was only a matter of time until Boone used his fists again. Still, Austin's driving the boy to and from school had helped him in more than one way.

"Seth may not have told you, but the fact that you're giving him a ride lets him do something he loves—sketching. That extra time has made a big difference in his life."

Austin's raised eyebrows told Catherine he was unaware of Seth's artistic bent. "Is he any good?"

"I think so."

"Then I'm glad I can help. I like Seth. He's got a good head on his shoulders. I wish I could do more for him."

"You're already doing a lot. I'm sure it's no coincidence that Hannah always has more food than she can eat and that she leaves her basket where Seth can find it." The hollows in the boy's cheeks had begun to disappear, and his skin was a healthier hue, thanks to an improved diet.

Catherine smiled at Austin. "That's another example of how you're a good father. You're raising Hannah to be kind and generous."

"If only she were happy."

7

I wish I had more ideas," Lydia said as she swished a saucer through the soapy water before rinsing it and handing it to Catherine.

Though the two women normally sat in the main room of Cimarron Sweets when Catherine visited, by the time she'd arrived, the shop was about to close. Lydia had taken one look at Catherine's face and had insisted she come inside. "We can talk while I clean up," she had said. "I do my best thinking when I'm washing dishes."

But even with the stimulation of hot, soapy water, Lydia had had no suggestions. "You're doing everything I would have," she declared when Catherine recounted her efforts to coax Hannah out of her shell.

Though she had feared that would be Lydia's response, Catherine was still disappointed. "Days like this make me miss my mother even more than usual," she told Lydia as she placed the saucer on the shelf. "Mama never taught school, but she used to have good ideas about how to manage the children."

"And even if she didn't, she'd give you a hug, and everything would seem better."

"Exactly, but how did you know?"

Lydia's smile said the answer should be apparent. "Because that's what my mother did. I imagine it's what all mothers do."

And that brought Catherine back to the reason she'd sought Lydia's advice. "I wonder if Hannah is so withdrawn because she doesn't have a mother. I know Austin is doing his best, but it's not the same." Catherine bit her lower lip as she mentally chastised herself. "Who am I to say that? I don't remember my father, so I don't know if he would have been as demonstrative with his love as Mama was."

Lydia dumped baking soda inside her Blue Willow teapot and began to scrub the stains, her expression thoughtful. "I think his love would have been different from your mother's. My father left us when I was eight, so he wasn't a typical parent, but my mother assured me that he loved me in his own way." She rinsed the teapot, then inspected it for other stains. "I remember him telling me stories when I was afraid of the dark, but I don't remember any hugs or being held on his lap. I do remember that I always felt safe when he was around."

Safety wasn't the problem. Catherine had no doubt that Austin would keep Hannah safe. Love wasn't the issue, either. Not really. She knew that Austin loved his daughter. The question was whether Hannah realized that, whether he lavished enough physical proof of his love on her that she felt secure. Though Catherine was comfortable discussing almost anything with Austin, that was one question she was reluctant to raise.

"Children need both parents," Catherine said as she dried the now spotless teapot.

"Yes, they do."

Surely it was only Catherine's imagination that Lydia's smile hinted at a secret.

"Has there been any change?"

Catherine looked up from the papers she'd been correcting to smile at Austin. It had been a week since they'd discussed their concerns about Hannah, a week in which Catherine had endured Sunday dinner with Nate. The meal hadn't been as bad as she'd feared, in part because she had made a point of treating Nate the same way she did his brother-in-law Luke: as a friend, nothing more.

When Rachel made pointed comments about how much happier she was since she'd married Luke, Catherine had nodded noncommittally. It was evident that Rachel and Luke were happy together. Furthermore, she was confident that marriage to the right man would bring her the same kind of happiness, but she also knew beyond the shadow of a doubt that Nate was not the right man. Watching him now, it was hard to believe she'd ever hoped to be his wife. Nate was a good man, he was a kind man, but he was not the man God had chosen for her.

Eventually, the meal had ended, and Catherine had returned to her quiet home and the thoughts that continued to whirl through her brain. She had spent more hours than she could count thinking about Hannah . . . and Hannah's father. Though she hadn't admitted it to anyone, Catherine looked forward to the time she and Austin spent together every afternoon. It was usually only a few minutes, but those minutes had quickly become the highlight of her days. And today for the first time she had something positive to report to Austin.

"There has been a little change," she told him. It might be nothing, but it felt like something. "Today when I came inside after lunch, I found Hannah studying the globe. She asked me where France was. I tried not to show how excited I was, but this is the first time she's initiated a conversation. It seemed like a step forward."

Austin did not look excited. Though it made no sense, he looked worried. "Did she say anything more?"

"Not at first. I pointed to France on the globe, then told her how I'd always dreamed of traveling to Europe." Catherine swallowed, trying to dissolve the lump that had formed in her throat at the memory of the dream that was unlikely to become reality.

"My mother and I had planned to go there last summer," she explained. "We intended to visit England, France, Germany, and Switzerland, but then Mama was too ill. Thanks to Doc Harrington . . ." Catherine stopped. Austin had already heard how the doctor had killed her mother. She would gain nothing by repeating the story.

Forcing a smile onto her face, Catherine looked up at Austin. "As I traced the itinerary we'd planned, Hannah listened the way she always does. Then she surprised me. She said she was born in France."

Catherine continued to watch Austin, trying to gauge his reaction to his daughter's statement. "I didn't contradict her, even though I doubt it's true."

He looked solemn, almost sad. "Hannah didn't lie," he said flatly. "She was born in Paris. My wife and I were living there at the time, but when Geraldine died soon after Hannah's birth, I knew it was time to return to America. I swore then I'd never return. There was nothing left for me in France."

The sorrow on Austin's face was more poignant than words. Though she had dozens of questions, including the reason a rancher would have moved to Paris, Catherine would not ask them. Austin might be a friend, but there were some subjects that were too delicate to discuss, even with friends. Austin's grief was one of them.

Catherine took a deep breath, trying to calm her turbulent thoughts. "I'm sorry I doubted Hannah. Somehow I thought you'd always lived in Oklahoma and that your wife's death was recent."

"No." Austin's eyes darkened with emotion. "I'm the only parent Hannah has ever known."

Though she knew there was more to the story, Catherine would not pry. It was obvious that Austin was still grieving for his wife. No wonder the town's matchmakers had been unsuccessful in pairing him with one of the eligible young women. His heart had been broken and might never mend. What kind of woman had Geraldine been to have inspired such a love?

He had stayed later than normal that day. His assistant was gone; the outer office was empty, but Austin still had two more files to update. The day had been so busy that he'd done little more than jot notes about each patient he'd treated. Knowing from experience that he'd forget critical details if he waited until tomorrow to record them, not to mention that tomorrow might be as busy as today, he'd decided to remain at the office until everything was complete.

His head was bent over the sheets of paper when he heard the opening of the door and footsteps on the wooden floor.

Austin looked up, startled by the sight of a well-dressed man in his mid-forties. The impeccably tailored suit, the crisp white shirt, and the ornate gold cuff links left no doubt of the man's prosperity. If it weren't for the steely glint Austin saw in the visitor's gray eyes, he might have been just another of his affluent patients.

"I'm sorry, sir, but office hours ended a long time ago."

The man raised his head ever so slightly and stared down his prominent nose at Austin. "That is precisely why I waited until now to come. I've been told you're the only person in Philadelphia—perhaps in the whole country—who can do what I need done."

"And what would that be, Mr. . . ." Austin let his voice trail off.

"Enright. Sherman Enright."

Thank goodness for the years of training that allowed him to

72

mask his emotions. That training had proven invaluable when dealing with patients, and it did not fail him now. Austin looked steadily at the man, knowing his face did not betray the thoughts that tumbled through his brain.

The name alone was enough to make grown men shake in their boots. Sherman Enright was the head of an organization that extorted money from at least half of the small businesses in the city. Shopkeepers were forced to pay a substantial percentage of their profits to Enright's men or risk having their shops destroyed and their families hurt. The rumor was that Enright took pleasure in torturing the victims himself. And now the man who personified evil to many of Philadelphia's residents stood in Austin's office.

"What is it you'd like me to do?"

Whatever the man had in mind, Austin doubted he would agree. Though his patients included both the city's wealthiest and its poorest, he had no room in his life for people like Sherman Enright.

Enright's lips curled into a sneer, as if he noticed and dismissed the way Austin had phrased his question. "What you're going to do," he said, emphasizing the words, "is change my face." He pointed to the hawk-like nose, the high cheekbones, and the square chin that distinguished him from thousands of other men.

"Every policeman within a hundred miles knows what I look like. They've got a warrant out for my arrest, but they can't arrest me if they can't find me." Enright's laugh sent a shiver down Austin's back. "I'm leaving Philadelphia. It's been good for me, but there's more potential in New York City than here. It's time for big changes—a new face, a new town."

There was no question about it: Sherman Enright was evil. "You want me to make it possible for you to continue your business in a different place."

"Precisely."

"What happens when people start recognizing your new face?"

The man who had wreaked such havoc with Philadelphia's honest shopkeepers shrugged. "They won't. You're going to make me so ordinary that I'll blend in everywhere, just the way Tucker does." Enright turned toward the still open door. "Come in here, Tucker."

The man who entered Austin's office was as ordinary as anyone he'd met. As Enright had said, Tucker could blend in anywhere. His hair and eyes were medium brown, his features so ordinary that they would draw no one's attention.

Tucker, Austin surmised, was one of Enright's henchmen.

"I see." What Austin saw was that Sherman Enright believed Austin would use his talent to ensure that he could continue robbing and hurting innocent people.

"I thought you would." Enright nodded as if he'd received Austin's agreement. "I know you need a day to prepare. I'll be back tomorrow at the same time." He turned toward the door, then pivoted and fixed his gaze on Austin. "And, Dr. Goddard, in case you have any thoughts of telling the police where I'll be, I want to remind you that you have a pretty little girl. I would hate to have something bad happen to Hannah."

Enright's laugh was echoing in Austin's ears when he woke, drenched with sweat, his heart pounding at twice its normal rate. If only he could dismiss the nightmare, but he couldn't, because it wasn't simply a nightmare—it was a memory. Sherman Enright had threatened him. More importantly, he had threatened Hannah.

Austin lit the lamp and walked quietly to his daughter's room, hoping he had not cried out in his distress and disturbed her sleep. He cracked the door open, then peered inside, his heartbeat slowing when he saw his beloved daughter curled in a ball, deep in slumber.

74

Hannah was safe. There was no reason to fear. He'd covered his tracks well. No one knew he was in Texas. Besides, Enright was looking for a doctor, not a rancher. Hannah would be safe here.

Austin closed his eyes and whispered a prayer. "Please, God, keep her safe."

8

The children loved having Cimarron Sweets, Lydia's candy shop, catty-cornered from the school. Although they were not allowed to visit it during recess, those whose parents gave them a few pennies would venture inside at lunchtime, bringing back peppermint sticks, licorice, or lemon drops.

Catherine saved her own visits for late afternoon when she knew none of her pupils would be there, stopping in a couple times a week for a piece of Lydia's justly famous fudge, a cup of coffee, and a few minutes of conversation with the woman who'd become as dear to her as a sister. Like the time she spent with Austin, these visits brightened Catherine's day.

"I was hoping you'd come in today," Lydia said, greeting Catherine with a warm smile and a hug. "I made penuche this morning and want your opinion." She gestured toward the window seat where customers were encouraged to rest for a while and sample pieces of candy.

When she'd turned the previously empty building into a confectionary, Lydia had realized that the sun would melt anything she placed in the front window and had converted that part of the shop into a tasting area, creating the window seat and pairing it with a small table and two chairs. The location had become a popular spot for the ladies of Cimarron Creek to gather and was one of the reasons the shop was so successful.

A minute later, Lydia emerged from the back room bearing a tray with two coffee cups and a plate of candy. She pointed toward the cream-colored piece. "Taste this first. Then you can tell me about Hannah."

Catherine paused, her hand halfway to her mouth. "I didn't realize it was that obvious."

"Only to someone who knows you as well as I do. You get a distant look when you're trying to find a solution to some problem. I doubt anyone else would see that."

Reassured that she wasn't telegraphing her distress to the entire town, Catherine took a bite of the penuche, letting the flavors swirl along her tongue before she swallowed it. "It's very good," she told Lydia a few seconds later, "but . . ."

"But what?" Her friend leaned her arms on the table, concern etching furrows between her eyes. "I knew something must be wrong, because only one customer bought any, even though half a dozen sampled it. The problem was, no one said anything."

Catherine took another small bite, wanting to confirm her initial impression. "This will probably sound strange coming from me when you know how I like sweets, but this seems too sweet. I didn't think that was possible with candy."

Lydia's worries vanished, replaced by a wide grin. "I knew I could count on you. I'll put a pinch more salt in the next batch and increase the vanilla by a tablespoon or two." She took a sip of coffee, then laid the cup back on its saucer. "It tasted fine to me, but . . ." With a quick shake of her head, she said, "Never mind about that. Now that you've helped me, tell me about Hannah."

"It's not just Hannah. There's Seth too. They both need help, but I don't know what to do."

Lydia's expression sobered. "Is Boone Dalton hitting Seth again?"

The sweetness of the penuche disappeared, replaced by the sour taste that thoughts of Seth's father always aroused. "Seth won't say anything, but I saw the way he was holding his ribs today. I'm afraid one is cracked. I asked Austin, but he hadn't noticed anything different when he drove him to school this morning."

Lydia closed her eyes for a second, and Catherine suspected she was praying for the boy. "I've talked to Travis about Seth, but there's nothing he can do as sheriff. Boone has the right to discipline his son any way he sees fit."

Though Lydia's words did not surprise Catherine, they saddened her. "That may be what the law says, but that doesn't make it right. From everything I can see, Boone treats Seth like a slave, beating him for the slightest infraction or maybe for no reason at all. Hasn't he heard that Mr. Lincoln freed the slaves almost twenty years ago?"

Lydia shook her head. "Be careful, Catherine. You're starting to sound like a Yankee, and I can tell you from personal experience that Yankees aren't particularly welcome here."

"I know." Catherine remembered the prejudice Lydia had had to overcome when she'd first arrived in Cimarron Creek, her Northern accent leaving no doubt that she was what one resident referred to as the Cursed Enemy. "It's just that I wish there were some way to get Seth away from Boone. I know it's wrong to listen to gossip, but I can't help remembering that when Martha Dalton died, there was speculation that Boone had killed her."

"Was Martha Boone's wife?"

Catherine took a deep breath as she nodded. The delicious aromas that filled the confectionary normally soothed her worries, but they were having little effect today. "Martha was a gentle woman. I think she tried to stand up to Boone, but she was no match for him, just as Seth isn't.

A moment of silence followed Catherine's words. Then Lydia gave a quick nod. "I'll ask Travis again, even though I doubt he'll have any ideas. He says Boone's tighter with money than anyone in town. No one thinks he loves his son, but having Seth work on the farm keeps Boone from having to hire someone. From what I've heard, you aren't far off with your assessment that Seth's little more than a slave."

Lydia pushed the plate toward Catherine and pointed toward a piece of candy. "Try this. I won't claim that fudge can resolve anything, but chocolate always makes me feel better."

Catherine popped a piece in her mouth, recognizing that although she wished the situation were different, there was probably nothing she could do for Seth. "This is wonderful." She tipped her head to one side as she considered the mélange of flavors coating her tongue. "Did you put coffee in this?"

Lydia nodded. "I knew not everyone would like it, but women who enjoy coffee as much as you do seem to think it's a good flavor."

"It is. It's perfect!" Catherine reached for another piece, then stopped herself.

"Go ahead," Lydia encouraged her. When Catherine shook her head, Lydia's expression turned somber again. "All right. Let's talk about Hannah. What's changed?"

"Nothing, and that's the problem. I've tried everything I know and everything you've suggested. I talked to Austin, but nothing is helping. I thought there had been a breakthrough one day when she spent some time with the globe, but the next day she was back to silence." Catherine took a sip of coffee. "It's the strangest thing. I feel as if she's afraid to talk, as if she's hiding a secret and doesn't want to risk letting it out."

"What kind of secret could a six-year-old have?"

79

"I don't know, but I do know that she was born in Paris."

Lydia's eyes widened. "Paris, France?"

"That's the place. Home of the Seine, the Louvre, and Notre Dame." The city that figured in so many of Catherine's dreams. "I don't know why, but Austin and his wife were living there when Hannah was born."

Laying down her cup, Lydia stared at Catherine. "I'm surprised you didn't ask. I've told Travis more than once that you're a born interrogator. You're subtle about it, but you get people to tell you things they'd never say to Travis or me."

Though it was a compliment, it brought Catherine no pleasure. Her heart clenched as it always did when she remembered the day Austin had spoken of Paris. "I couldn't do it. I couldn't ask him." Catherine kept her gaze fixed on Lydia, willing her to understand. "You didn't see his face, Lydia. It was filled with pain. I'd almost say agony. There was no way I would do anything that might increase that pain."

She took another deep breath, although she doubted it would soothe her. "I feel so helpless. Hannah's the unhappiest child I've ever seen. I want to help her and Austin, but all I can do is pray that I'll find a way to reach her."

Lydia's expression turned stern. "Never underestimate the power of prayer."

It was a good reminder. "I don't. It's simply that I have trouble waiting for an answer." Catherine forced her lips to curve in a smile. Even though nothing had changed, she felt a bit better simply because she had shared her worries with Lydia.

"Let's talk about something more pleasant. You looked especially happy when I came in today, and I know it's not the customers' reaction to the penuche."

Lydia shook her head, her blue eyes once again reflecting happiness. "No, it's something much better. I'm going to have a baby."

A baby! That was indeed good news. Catherine reached across the table and hugged her friend. It hadn't been her imagination that Lydia had worn a secretive smile the day they'd talked about children needing both parents.

Catherine smiled, and this time her smile was genuine. "How wonderful! I'm so happy for you." Catherine had seen the longing in Lydia's eyes every time she held someone else's baby and knew that she was praying for children of her own. Her prayers were being answered.

"When is the blessed event going to happen?" As she pronounced the words, Catherine's mind shifted to the memory of a Cimarron Creek resident for whom the birth of a child had not been a blessed event. Poor Joan. Catherine's heart ached for the young girl who'd been ostracized by her own parents. Fortunately, Lydia's story would have a happier ending than Joan's had.

Oblivious to the direction Catherine's thoughts had taken, Lydia smiled again. "Mrs. Steele says it'll be late September. I was relieved when she said she doesn't know of any other babies due at that time and that she'll be able to attend me."

Catherine nodded, remembering what had happened when the town's midwife had been called to deliver a rancher's wife's baby. While she was on the ranch, a woman in town had gone into labor, and her panicky husband had called Doc Harrington. Neither the baby nor the mother had survived. But Mrs. Steele would be here for Lydia, and if she was somehow called away, Catherine would do everything she could, including delivering the baby herself, to ensure that the doctor did not come near Lydia. The man waved at her every time he saw her and—compelled by common courtesy—she responded with a wave, but that did not mean Catherine would trust him with anyone's life.

As the church bell chimed the hour, she blinked at the

realization that she had been here longer than usual. Normally her visits lasted only a few minutes, and, more often than not, they were interrupted by customers entering the store. Today Catherine was the only person at Cimarron Sweets besides Lydia. The timing couldn't have been better for the discussion they'd had.

Her face glowing with happiness, Lydia helped herself to a piece of fudge. "Travis and I are so excited that it's practically all we can talk about when we're alone. We haven't chosen names, but one thing is definite: we want you to be the baby's godmother. Will you do that for us?"

"I'd be honored." Catherine had no trouble picturing an infant with Lydia's blonde hair and Travis's square chin. Would it be a boy or a girl? Only God knew that. What Catherine knew was that this child would have two loving parents. This baby would not suffer the way Hannah and Seth did. "Thank you, Lydia. I can't wait to hold your baby."

Her friend's smile widened. "Before you know it, it'll be your turn to choose godparents."

The conversation that had been so positive had taken a wrong turn. Catherine sipped her coffee as she tried to compose her thoughts. Though she would have liked to ignore Lydia's comment, she knew her friend would not let her off that easily.

"A year ago, I would have agreed with you. Now I wonder if I'll ever marry." And that thought brought more pain than Catherine had expected, especially when she witnessed Lydia's happiness.

"Nate hasn't given up."

Neither had Rachel, but the problem wasn't Rachel. It was Nate himself. "I always knew that man was stubborn. Now I think he must also be deaf, because he refuses to listen when I tell him I'm not interested in marrying him."

Lydia raised an inquisitive eyebrow. "Are you certain?"

"I am. I told you that last summer, and I haven't changed my mind."

This time silence followed Catherine's declaration. When Lydia spoke, her question surprised Catherine. "What about Austin? From everything I've heard, he's a fine man. Marrying him could be good for everyone. You'd have a husband, and Austin would be able to go to church without Henrietta Brooks and the other mamas parading their daughters in front of him. Besides, maybe a stepmother would solve Hannah's problems. We both know it's better for a child to be raised by both a mother and a father."

That was true, but marriage ought to be more than a convenient arrangement. "I care for Hannah—there's no doubt about that—and Austin has become a friend, but those are not good enough reasons to marry."

Lydia's eyes narrowed, and she looked at Catherine as if trying to read her thoughts. "Are you sure Austin is just a friend? You get a gleam in your eye when you speak of him."

Once again, her friend was seeing more than Catherine had realized. She chose her words carefully. "Austin is the most intriguing man I've ever met. I can talk to him about anything." Except his wife and their life in the city of Catherine's dreams.

"Last week he asked me what I thought about President-Elect Garfield and whether he was really involved in the Crédit Mobilier scandal. We argued about whether that should have disqualified him from becoming president and whether the country would be better served by General Hancock." Though the Southern states, including Texas, had voted in favor of the general, he'd lost the election. What concerned many in the South was that the defeat had been by only a few thousand votes.

"Austin listens to me," Catherine continued. "Really listens. I know you said Travis does that for you, but my experience has been that males over the age of sixteen rarely admit that a woman has a brain."

Lydia chuckled, as if she had had the same experience, then turned serious again. "So, tell me, if you're attracted to Austin—and you seem to be—and if he treats you like an equal, why wouldn't you consider him as a potential suitor?"

They'd reached the heart of the matter. "Because he'd never love me the way he did Geraldine. I saw the way Austin looked when he spoke of her. It's been close to six years, but his grief is still raw. If he even considered marrying me, it would only be for Hannah's sake. I'd be his second choice." Just as she would have been Nate's second choice once he met Lydia. That had hurt Catherine's pride, but this would be worse, much worse.

Catherine swallowed, trying to dislodge the lump that had settled in her throat at the realization that Austin could never love her the way he had Geraldine. A love like that came only once in a lifetime, or so Mama claimed. "It may sound foolish, Lydia, but I want to be my husband's first and only love. That's why I refused to let Nate court me last summer."

Her friend looked dubious. "I won't argue with you about Nate. He probably isn't the right man for you, but Austin is different. Yes, he's been married before, and that means you would be his second love, but it seems to me that being his last love is more important than being the first." Lydia's gaze shifted to the window, her expression leading Catherine to believe she was recalling a memory.

"There are many kinds of love," she said softly. "Sometimes what we call first love is nothing more than infatuation. That was certainly true for me. Last love is what endures. That's what everyone deserves."

Catherine considered her statement. "You make a good argument, Lydia. It's almost as good as your fudge, but . . ."

"There are no buts. I'm right."

"So you say."

He'd put it off long enough. As much as he hated revealing his past to anyone, Austin had no alternative. The only way he'd know if he and Hannah were safe was to enlist Travis's aid, and so he headed toward the sheriff's office after taking Hannah to school.

He pushed open the door and paused to let his eyes adjust to the relative darkness. As he'd expected, this building bore little resemblance to the Philadelphia police department's head-quarters. There was no bustle of activity, no uniformed officer to greet him, just one man sitting behind a desk.

Austin felt his tension begin to subside at the realization that Travis was alone. Though he had no reason to mistrust the deputy sheriff, he'd lived with the need for secrecy long enough to be reluctant to involve anyone else in his problems.

Travis rose and extended a hand. "What can I do for you, Austin?"

One of the things Austin had noticed about the sheriff when he'd met him at church was that he didn't waste time on social niceties. That was fine with Austin. He had no need for those.

"I'm hoping you can help me, but before I say anything more, I need to be sure that you won't repeat what I'm going to tell you to anyone. That includes your deputy and your wife."

Though Travis's gray eyes narrowed, he simply nodded and pointed to the chairs in front of his desk. When Austin was seated in one, he said, "You've probably heard that I'm the town's attorney as well as the sheriff. I practice client confidentiality, but if there's a crime involved, that's a different story. I can't ignore my duties as a peace officer."

If the situation hadn't been so serious, Austin might have

laughed. "Oh, there were crimes involved, but I wasn't the perpetrator."

"I didn't think you were," Travis assured him. "In my profession, you get to be a fairly good judge of people. I figured you for a law-abiding citizen who was hiding something."

Austin blinked, surprised by the man's perceptiveness. Travis was indeed a good judge of people. "You're right. I am hiding some things."

"Including your name?"

"Not that." Austin had considered changing his name but dismissed the idea, fearing that would be too difficult for Hannah. "I had a different life in Philadelphia." There was no point in dissembling. If the sheriff was going to help him, he needed the full story. "I was a doctor there, but when one of the city's worst criminals threatened Hannah, I had no choice. I fled."

He clenched his fists, remembering the fear that had accompanied him. "Before I left the city, I told the police where he'd be the next day so that they'd have a chance to apprehend him, but Sherman Enright—that's his name—is wily. Although I alerted the police, I'm not sure Enright's behind bars, and even if he is, I'm afraid he's got people looking for me and my daughter."

There was a moment of silence as Travis absorbed Austin's story. "You want me to find out what happened." He made it a statement.

Austin nodded. "Yes. I won't feel safe until I know that Enright's either been executed for his crimes or has left Philadelphia. His plan was to dissolve the Philadelphia operation and start over in New York City." Austin took a deep breath, inhaling the aromas of overcooked coffee and chocolate. It appeared that Travis and his deputy were as fond of Lydia's candies as the rest of the town.

Silently, Travis pulled out a sheet of paper and made a few notes. When he looked up and saw Austin's skeptical expression, he shook his head. "Don't worry. I'll burn this once I'm done. I just want to be sure that I have the details correct." He fixed his gaze on Austin. "When exactly did you leave Philadelphia?"

Five minutes later, the page was covered with writing. "That should be enough to get them started. I'll send a telegram to Philadelphia to see what they can tell me. If this Enright is still running his operation there, I'll check back every month." Travis laid down his pencil. "Why don't you stop in tomorrow morning? I should have an answer then."

Austin spent the rest of the day trying not to think about Sherman Enright but failing miserably. Even Mrs. Moore commented on his mood, asking if he wanted some of her dandelion tonic. "It's good for whatever ails you," she assured him.

But no tonic, no matter how potent, would stop his worries, and when he saw Travis's expression the next morning, Austin knew without asking that his fears had been confirmed.

"They didn't catch him." Travis held out the telegram he'd received from the Philadelphia police chief. "You were right in saying that he's wily. Enright must have seen something that alerted him, because he didn't return to your office the next night, and he hasn't been seen since. It appears that his operation is continuing, which makes the police believe he's holed up somewhere in the Philadelphia area."

That meant that Sherman Enright was still looking for Austin. And Hannah.

9

I s something wrong, Seth?" Catherine kept her voice low as she stood next to his desk. The boy, who was normally one of her best students, had made several errors on what should have been simple arithmetic problems. Now he appeared almost listless as he looked at the day's reading assignment. Though she saw no signs of physical abuse, Catherine couldn't help wondering what had happened at home to cause such a difference.

He shrugged, then closed his McGuffey's Reader. "It's these stories, Miss Whitfield. They're not as exciting as the ones in your books."

"My books?" For a moment, Catherine wasn't certain what he meant. Then she remembered how Seth had entertained himself when he'd been recuperating at her house. "You mean my father's books?"

Seth nodded. "Those were good stories." He scowled at the slim volume that was the designated text for pupils his age. "Can't we read them instead? That Mohican story sounded like a good one."

Catherine couldn't disagree. James Fenimore Cooper's book was far more exciting than the ones on the approved reading list. So were her father's other cherished books, Washington Irving's *Sketch Book* and Daniel Defoe's *Robinson Crusoe*.

She looked at Seth, wishing she could satisfy his request. It ought to be simple. She wouldn't be breaking any rules if she brought the books to school and let the students read them, so long as they completed their normal work, and yet the thought of sometimes-careless children handling the only keepsakes she had from her father made her cringe.

"We'll see."

Seth's lips flattened. "That means no, doesn't it?"

"No, Seth, it doesn't necessarily mean no. It means we'll see."

Austin looked at the sky and smiled. There were only three days left in February. It might be the shortest month of the year, but it had also been the busiest one of his life. Calving season had begun, and Austin had been riding the range for the last week. His lips curved into a grin. A year ago if anyone had told him he'd enjoy being on a horse all day and sleeping on the ground at night, he would have scoffed, but that was exactly what he'd been doing. And, while he had to admit that the hard ground lacked the appeal of a real bed, despite his ongoing worries about Sherman Enright, the experience had been satisfying.

As he'd ridden under the blue sky and felt the sun beating down on his head, Austin had felt closer to God than when he was inside a church. This land was God's creation. He was only the steward, but thanks to God's help, he was proving to be an adequate one. His fears that he would hate ranching as much as he had as a boy were unfounded.

His father had always said that if Austin gave ranching a chance, he would discover that it was good, honest work that a man could be proud of. As a third-generation rancher, Pa scoffed at the idea of Austin becoming a doctor, declaring that if ranching was good enough for his grandfather, his father, and himself, it was good enough for Austin. Austin had not agreed. Far from it. He'd hated the physical labor and the need to be outdoors regardless of the weather. Most of all, he'd hated the fact that he was being given no choice.

Though he'd appealed to his mother, Ma had sided with her husband, saying they'd spent their lives making the ranch prosper so they'd have a legacy for him. He was their only son, and as such, it was his duty to remain on the ranch.

Austin's grin faltered as he recalled the bitter arguments. Neither of his parents could understand that he didn't want the ranch. For as long as he could remember, Austin had wanted to be a healer. And so, though his parents had disapproved, he'd left home when he was sixteen and made his way to Philadelphia, determined to do whatever he had to to become a physician. He'd succeeded, but now he was once again on a ranch.

The smile returned, a bittersweet one this time. If Pa were still alive, he would surely be laughing at the fact that a dozen years later, Austin was a rancher and that he didn't hate what he was doing. To the contrary, using his medical training to help a cow through a difficult delivery today had been the culmination of a good week.

Austin knew that if he hadn't been there to turn the calf and ease it out, both the cow and her offspring would have died. As it was, when he watched the wobbly-legged calf begin to suckle, a feeling of deep satisfaction had welled up inside him. It might not be the same as saving some of Philadelphia's neediest residents from a life of shame and ostracism, but there was no denying the exultation that had flowed through him at the sight of the calf. He couldn't have chosen a better way to end the week.

And now he was on his way home. A hot bath to wash off the week's grime, one of Mrs. Moore's delicious suppers, and the reunion with his daughter—what more could a man want?

"I'm glad to see you're back." Mrs. Moore swiveled at the sound of his footsteps and nodded her head, then lowered the flame on the stove as he entered the kitchen an hour later.

"Right on time too." Austin had promised to return no later than 5:00. According to his watch, he had another fifteen minutes before he'd be late. The grin that accompanied his statement faded as he looked at his housekeeper. Instead of the welcoming smile he'd expected, he saw distress. "Is something wrong?"

She nodded and wiped her hands on a towel. "It's Hannah. She hasn't spoken a word since you left, and as far as I can tell, she hasn't eaten a bit. When she's not at school, she just sits in the corner of her room."

Austin tried to keep his expression neutral. Though he'd been concerned about Hannah's possible reaction to his being gone, he had thought she'd understood when he'd explained what he was doing and when he'd return. It appeared that even if she had understood, something had changed. Something serious. Something dangerous.

Mrs. Moore took a step toward Austin. "I'm worried, Mr. Goddard."

"So am I."

March had arrived. Catherine tried to slow the pounding of her heart as she gathered the books she'd used for today's lessons and arranged them carefully on the shelf. While her pupils were celebrating the end of the shortest month, she found no cause for celebration. Not only had February seemed longer than normal, but the past week had been particularly difficult.

When Mrs. Moore had brought Hannah to school last Monday, she had explained that Austin was riding the range. Though Catherine had expected Hannah to miss her father, she had not been prepared for the changes in her most difficult pupil. The girl had looked like the last vestiges of life were being drained from her, making her as pale as Mama had been after one of those dreadful bloodlettings. For the first time since she'd started school, Hannah had refused to respond when Catherine asked her a question. She merely sat at her desk, making not a sound. She had remained silent all week, fading a bit more each day.

Catherine had seen troubled children before, but she had never seen a case so extreme. Though she knew she had to tell Austin what she'd observed and what she feared, he hadn't attended church on Sunday, and Hannah had not come to school yesterday, only adding to Catherine's worries. Fortunately, the girl had returned today, but though Seth had mentioned Austin giving him a ride this morning, Catherine had not seen him.

She glanced out the window. Nothing had changed in the five minutes since she'd last checked on the children. Hannah was still on the swing, simply sitting there rather than swinging, and Seth was seated a few yards away, busily sketching something. Where was Austin? He was normally here by this time.

As if on cue, the door opened. Catherine turned, her heart leaping at the sight of the handsome rancher. "I'm so glad to see you!"

He removed his hat as he approached her desk. "You might not be when you hear what I have to say." His eyes were dark with worry, and the rings beneath them told Catherine he'd been sleeping poorly.

"If it's about Hannah, believe me, I've noticed the difference. I'd have to be blind not to. She seemed to fade away while you were gone." Catherine looked directly at Austin as she asked, "Did that happen in Oklahoma?"

Surely it was her imagination that he seemed uncomfortable with the question. Austin shook his head. "No. This is the first time anything like this has happened." When Catherine settled into the chair behind her desk, he took the one next to it.

"Perhaps I should have expected it, but I didn't. I'm worried." Austin shook his head. "Worried doesn't begin to describe what I'm feeling. I'm terrified."

Catherine stared at him, confused by the fervor she heard in his voice. Surely terror was an extreme reaction. She could understand concern—deep concern—but not bone-deep fear, and yet that was what he was exhibiting.

"Do you want to talk to me about whatever it is that's terrifying you?"

Austin shook his head again. "I don't want to, but I need to. You spend more time with Hannah than I do. I need you to be on the lookout for signs." Catherine hadn't thought it possible, but his expression darkened. "I also need you to promise that you will not share what I'm going to tell you with anyone, especially Hannah."

Though she was grateful Austin trusted her enough to confide in her, Catherine couldn't suppress her concern about what he might reveal. "Of course," she said, infusing her voice with certainty.

"Thank you." He leaned forward, placing his hands on the desk. "No one else knows what happened. I didn't want anyone to know, but I can't risk Hannah's safety."

Each word he pronounced made the situation sound worse. "You're scaring me, Austin."

"That wasn't my intent. There's no easy way to tell this story, so I won't even try to dress it up with pretty words." He took a deep breath, exhaling slowly as he stared at the wall behind Catherine. When his gaze once again met hers, he began his tale.

"My wife was a woman of volatile moods. I didn't notice it when we were courting, but then her parents died of influenza, leaving Geraldine alone and bereft. We'd planned to marry when I returned from Europe, but I couldn't leave her behind when she was so terribly distraught, so we married only weeks after she buried her parents."

Austin ran his hand through his hair, leaving it as disturbed as his thoughts appeared to be. "At first, I thought it was grief. Then I blamed it on the fact that she'd been taken from everything familiar and was now living in a country where she could barely communicate. Finally, I gave up trying to understand why she was acting the way she did and simply tried to cope with her moods."

Though Catherine wished there were something she could do or say to comfort Austin, she knew that what he needed most was someone to listen to his story. Only when it was complete would she respond.

Austin stared at the floor for a second before continuing. "Some days Geraldine would be the happiest person I'd ever known, laughing and singing and acting as if she didn't have a care in the world. Other days she'd be in the depths of despair. I never knew which Geraldine would get out of bed in the morning or if she'd even make the effort to leave the bed."

Catherine's heart ached at the pain both Austin and Geraldine had endured. Though she had never experienced anything like what he was describing, she recognized the symptoms. "I read about something like that in one of my medical books."

For a second, Austin appeared surprised. Then he shrugged. "That's right. You're an amateur doctor."

"I don't claim that distinction," Catherine told him. "I simply want to keep my pupils from being hurt by Doc Harrington." Catherine turned the conversation back to Austin's daughter. "I haven't noticed any mood swings in Hannah. For as long as I've known her, she's been melancholy, but having you gone seems to have deepened that. I would call her melancholia extreme now."

"So would I. I'm afraid she inherited that tendency from her mother. That's what terrifies me." Austin paused, and Catherine suspected he was choosing his words carefully. "Geraldine changed after Hannah was born. There were no more happy days. Instead, she seemed to sink further into melancholy. I don't know what made that last day any worse than the others, but when I came home, Hannah was alone, screaming because she hadn't been fed or her diaper changed. There was no sign of Geraldine. No note, nothing."

Austin stared into the distance for a long moment before he said, "They pulled my wife's body out of the Seine the next day."

10

A shiver made its way down Catherine's spine as she remembered the dream—no, the nightmare—she had had just hours before she met Austin for the first time. Perhaps it was only a coincidence, but she did not believe that. Somehow, someway she had dreamt about a woman who'd done the same thing Austin's wife had.

Though she tried, Catherine could not control her trembling. For her, the Seine had always represented beauty and peace, the culmination of one of her dreams. For Austin, it was the site of a tragedy, the loss of his beloved wife. "What did she look like?"

"Geraldine?" Austin appeared confused by the question, as well he should be. That was not the typical question someone asked upon learning that a man's wife had killed herself.

Catherine closed her eyes for a second, praying for a way to help this man who had suffered so greatly. "I'm sorry, Austin." She hoped he knew her words were sincere.

"I'm sorry your wife was so unhappy. I've heard that sometimes happens to women after a child is born, but your wife's condition sounds extreme." The violent mood swings even before Hannah's birth hinted at an underlying condition that would have made what Cimarron Creek's midwife called the baby blues even worse.

Geraldine's suffering was tragic, but so was its effect on Austin. "I'm sorry for what your wife endured, but I'm even sorrier for you. I can't imagine what your life must have been like." Catherine reached out to put her hand on Austin's. It might be forward and unladylike, but she had to do something to show him how deeply his loss touched her.

Austin laid his other hand on top of hers, as if he were giving rather than receiving comfort. "I kept thinking I should have been able to stop her, that there was something I could have done."

"There wasn't. She had made up her mind, and no one could stop her."

Austin's eyes widened. "What makes you say that? You never met Geraldine. You know hardly anything about her."

Catherine had wondered why a dream that usually made her happy had turned into an unforgettable nightmare. Now she knew the reason. The nightmare had given her new insights, insights she could use to comfort Austin, to help assuage his pain and lessen his feeling of guilt.

"Did Geraldine have hair and eyes the same color as mine?"

He nodded.

"Was she a couple inches taller and a few years older?"

He nodded again. "How did you know?"

"The night before I met you, I had a dream. It was a dream I've had many times before. In it, I was walking along the Seine, approaching Notre Dame. This time was different, though. I saw a woman at the edge of the river, the woman I just described to you. She looked so unhappy that I wanted to help her, but as I ran toward her, she shook her head, rejecting my help. Then she jumped."

The blood drained from Austin's face, leaving his eyes in sharp contrast to his pallid cheeks. "What was she wearing?" he asked, his voice hoarse with emotion.

Catherine closed her eyes, trying to recall what she had seen that night. "A red dress," she said as the memory resurfaced. "It had a black collar and cuffs." She opened her eyes and stared at Austin. Though she hadn't thought it possible, his pallor had increased.

"I don't understand how you know all that, but that's the dress Geraldine was wearing when they pulled her out of the river. It was her favorite gown, the one she wore when I took her to a nice restaurant to celebrate our anniversary. She only wore it that one time. When I asked her why she didn't wear it again, she said she was saving it for a special occasion."

Austin pulled his hands loose and covered his eyes, his shoulders shaking with silent sobs. "I should have stopped her."

"You couldn't have. Everything you told me and what I saw in my dream says she had made up her mind. No matter how much you loved her, you couldn't stop her from doing what she planned."

Lowering his hands, Austin looked at Catherine, his blue eyes bearing an expression she had never seen in them. There was pain, almost agony, but also a glimmer of hope. "I want to believe you're right."

"Believe it," she said as firmly as if she were admonishing one of her pupils. "I didn't understand the dream at first. I thought God might be telling me to abandon my plan to go to Europe, but now I believe I was meant to assure you that you couldn't have stopped Geraldine. Believe me, Austin. There was nothing you could have done."

As the words registered, his expression changed from skepticism to acceptance. "I feel as if you've knocked a burden off my shoulders. Thank you, Catherine."

She nodded and managed a small smile. "I feel better too." For the first time, her memory of the nightmare did not fill her with dread.

Austin hoisted himself to his feet and stared out the window. "I may not have been able to save Geraldine, but that doesn't mean that I can't help Hannah. Somehow, I have to break through her shell. I just need to find a way."

Catherine walked to his side. She wouldn't touch him again, but she wanted to be close when she gave him the only advice she knew would work. "You could ask for God's help."

Catherine had never seen the weather change so quickly. She had prayed and prayed, asking God to show Austin or her a way to reach Hannah. She had not prayed for this. Though the sky had been cloudy when she'd released the children for lunch, the air had been warm. Now, less than an hour later, freezing rain was pelting the schoolhouse, and ice had begun to form on the windows. If this continued, within minutes everything would be covered with ice.

Catherine tapped her pointer on the floor, her signal that she wanted her pupils' attention. "Children, you need to listen carefully." She gestured toward one of the windows. "That's a blue norther out there, and it's dangerous. I'm going to dismiss you early today. Those of you who live in town are to go directly home. No stops at Cimarron Sweets."

Though the children's faces had brightened at the idea of an early closing, a few groans accompanied Catherine's admonition to not visit the candy shop. She doubted Lydia would have opened it today, anyway, but she wasn't taking any chances with her charges' safety.

"Be very careful walking. The roads will be slippery. The rest of you will stay here until your parents arrive." Catherine prayed that the parents would recognize the changing weather and come before the roads became impassable.

Rebecca raised her hand. "Mama had lunch with Aunt Mary,

so she's in town already. We can take everyone home who lives on our side of town."

"Thank you, Rebecca. That's a good idea." Catherine addressed the four youngsters who lived south of Cimarron Creek. "When we leave, go with Rebecca. Mrs. Henderson will drive you home." That left only two pupils stranded.

Rebecca raised her hand again. "Will we have school tomorrow?" Though the girl was one of her best students, Catherine could see that she was looking forward to a long weekend. Today was Thursday, meaning that if Catherine agreed to cancel school tomorrow, the students would have three days off.

Looking at the sky, she made her decision. "No school tomorrow. We'll have extra lessons next week." As she had expected, cheers greeted her announcement. "Get your coats and remember to be careful." Catherine looked at the girl seated next to Rebecca and the boy in the back row. "Hannah and Seth, I need to see you both."

Once the other students had crowded into the cloakroom, Catherine addressed the two remaining children. "I doubt Mr. Goddard will be able to get into town today."

When she'd seen him this morning, Austin had mentioned being concerned about some of the cattle on the far side of the ranch. Even if he'd reached the cattle before the storm began, riding back to the house through the sleet would be much slower than normal, and driving a wagon into town would be decidedly dangerous. Only one thing made sense. "You can stay with me tonight."

Though Hannah said nothing, she appeared wary. It was Seth who shook his head, his eyes darkening with fear as they had the day he'd been so ill. "I gotta get home. Pa needs those cows milked." He wrapped his arms around his ribs in a protective gesture that told Catherine more clearly than words what

100

would happen if Seth didn't perform his chores to his father's satisfaction.

"You'll never make it on foot. Look at the sky." What had been rain was now sleet, and the ground was shiny with ice. "You could easily fall and break an arm or leg. If that happened, it could be weeks before you were able to help your father."

Though Seth nodded, he was still apprehensive. "He'll be mad."

"He'd be angrier if you needed Doc Harrington to set a broken bone." Not that Catherine would have allowed that. If Seth had fractured a limb, she would have set it herself, following the illustrations she'd found in one of the medical books she'd bought last year. But when she spoke to Boone Dalton, she wouldn't say that. She'd let him think that she'd done him a favor by saving him a hefty doctor's fee.

"When the roads are clear, I'll rent a buggy and take you home. That way I can explain the situation to your father." She wouldn't ask Austin to be her messenger this time. He had enough worries of his own without dealing with a fractious neighbor.

Seth was unconvinced. "I gotta go now, Miss Whitfield."

"I can't let you do that. As your teacher, I'm responsible for you. It's called *in loco parentis*."

Though Hannah remained silent, her eyes sparkled with interest at the unfamiliar words, but she left it to Seth to ask what they meant.

"That's a Latin phrase," Catherine explained. "The translation is 'in place of parents.' What that means is that when you're at school, I have the responsibility of keeping you safe just as if I were your parent." She could see that Seth wasn't impressed, probably because *safety* wasn't a word he associated with his father. One way or another, she had to convince him to remain with her. She pulled out the big guns.

"You wouldn't want me to lose my job, would you?"

Seth's response was immediate. "No."

"Then it's settled. You'll both come home with me."

As they left the schoolhouse, she tacked a note to the door, explaining where Hannah and Seth were, then locked the door behind them, shaking her head slightly at the necessity. The lock had been installed last year when the town had experienced a string of thefts. Though the person responsible had been caught, the residents were still wary, and Cousin Jacob's mercantile had sold more locks in a single week than in the whole previous year. Travis himself had insisted on Catherine securing the schoolhouse, pointing out the value of the desks.

"Come, Hannah, take my hand."

Hannah ignored Catherine until she slid on the ice. Then she gripped the extended hand so tightly Catherine almost winced.

"What are we going to do at your house?" Seth asked as they walked north on Main Street. As Catherine had expected, Lydia's shop was closed, and there were no lights on in the mayor's office. Cimarron Creek's residents were taking no chances with the weather but were staying indoors.

"I thought we might make popcorn and read a story," she told both children.

The furrows that formed between Seth's eyes had nothing to do with the ice he was so carefully traversing. "I've never had popcorn."

Catherine knew she shouldn't be surprised. From everything she'd heard about Boone Dalton, he wasn't a man to provide anything more than basic sustenance to his son, and judging from what she'd seen, he'd provided very little of that.

"Popcorn is one of my favorite treats," she said. Turning her attention to the girl who gripped her hand like a lifeline, she asked, "What about you, Hannah? Have you eaten popcorn?" Surely Austin had introduced his daughter to that simple pleasure. But Hannah shook her head.

"Then we definitely need to make some." As they turned west on Mesquite, Catherine gave a silent prayer of thanksgiving that they were no longer walking into the wind. Though the sleet continued to pelt them, at least it was not hitting their faces.

"Seth, you're going to be the man of the house, so I'll show you how to make popcorn. Hannah and I will be ladies of leisure while you work." She'd no sooner spoken the words than Catherine regretted them. Her comment, which she'd meant to be innocent, probably reminded Seth of life at home where work was the one constant. She looked at the boy, hoping he wasn't distressed, and was surprised to see a broad grin creasing his face.

"That means I get the first taste."

"It does indeed."

When they reached the house, Catherine unlocked the side door and led them into the kitchen. After hanging their wet clothes on hooks near the door, she gestured toward the woodpile that she'd brought indoors yesterday. "Seth, would you put more wood in the stove?"

As they'd walked, she had decided that they'd spend the rest of the afternoon in the kitchen. Seth could read or sketch at the table, and Hannah could . . . Catherine's thoughts had reached a dead end. She wasn't certain what Hannah would do. In all likelihood, the girl would simply sit silently in a corner.

"Will I sleep in the same room as before?" Seth asked as he struggled to carry more logs than Catherine would ever have considered lifting.

"Yes. That's my spare room."

"What about her?" Seth raised his chin in Hannah's direction.

Catherine hesitated. Hannah could share her room. The bed

was certainly large enough, but since neither of them was accustomed to sharing a bed, it might be uncomfortable. There was an alternative; it was simply one Catherine hadn't considered until Seth raised the question.

Taking a quick breath, she smiled at Hannah. "I have another room specially for you." No one had used Mama's room since she'd died, but Catherine knew her mother would have been the first to offer it to Hannah. "Let me show you where you'll be sleeping. Seth, I'll be back in a minute to teach you how to make popcorn."

Hannah followed her down the hall into the room that had been unused for six months. It was an ordinary room, a bit crowded with the mahogany bed, bureau, armoire, and nightstands. Mama had claimed that made it cozy and had painted the walls a pale green and placed light-colored rag rugs on most of the exposed floor to counteract the heaviness of the furniture.

Catherine turned to Hannah, trying to see the room through her eyes. It was an older woman's room with nothing to interest a young girl. "This is where you'll sleep tonight. Do you want to put your schoolbag there?" She gestured toward the bureau. Hannah nodded.

"I'm ready!"

Hearing the excitement in Seth's voice, Catherine returned to the kitchen, leaving Hannah to get settled in her room. She pulled a saucepan from one of the cabinets and retrieved a bag of popcorn from the pantry.

"First we melt a little butter." She drew the butter plate from the icebox and handed it and a knife to Seth. "About this much," she said, pointing to the tip of her pinky.

Seth eyed the butter as if the fate of the world depended on his measuring the correct amount. Catherine started to tell him that precision didn't matter when she noticed that he was holding the knife in his right hand.

"I thought you were left-handed." When he wrote his lessons or sketched, he used his left hand.

Color flooded Seth's face. "I am, but I eat with my right hand. Pa didn't like it when I used the other one. He said something's wrong with lefties, so I learned to do everything except write with my right hand."

And that had been enough to pacify Boone.

When the butter was melted, Catherine handed Seth the corn. "You need to keep shaking the pan so the kernels heat evenly and don't burn."

Seth nodded, as if this were an everyday occurrence for him. "I can do that. You don't have to watch."

But Catherine did, for she wasn't sure how much experience he had with stoves. Rather than quench his enthusiasm, she nodded. "I'll get our milk ready." It wasn't what she would have drunk with popcorn—water would have been her choice—but both children needed extra nourishment. She placed glasses, bowls, and napkins on the table as the corn started to pop, darting glances at Seth whenever she thought he'd be unaware of her oversight.

A delighted chuckle told Catherine Seth was enjoying the transformation of ordinary kernels of corn into a puffy treat. "Look, Miss Whitfield. They're turning big and white."

"That's what happens when they pop."

He grinned. "This is fun."

Catherine relished the sight of simple pleasure lighting Seth's face and wondered if the ice storm had been a gift from God. Perhaps God had known Seth had had far too few experiences that could be considered fun and had given Catherine this opportunity to introduce the boy to one.

"Eating it is even more fun," she told Seth. As the pan filled with the fluffy white pieces of corn, Catherine turned and called out for Hannah. There was no response.

"Hannah, the popcorn is almost ready." When there was still no response, she turned off the stove and asked Seth to pour the popped corn into their bowls while she brought Hannah back to the kitchen.

Catherine moved quickly down the short hall, stopping when she discovered that the door to Mama's room, which she was certain she had left open, was closed. Turning the knob, Catherine walked inside and discovered Hannah sitting on the floor, oblivious to her arrival. This was the girl she'd taught for two months, and yet she looked so different that Catherine blinked in astonishment. An expression of pure joy transformed Hannah's face, making the girl almost radiantly beautiful. The reason wasn't difficult to find. Mama's music box sat on the floor in front of her, its familiar tune filling the room with music and memories.

Catherine bit her lip, trying to control her emotions. She'd hidden the music box in the top drawer of the bureau the day Mama had died, not wanting additional memories of her mother's final months. During the worst of her illness, Mama had wound the music box with ever more frail fingers, claiming that the sweet melody would cheer her after one of Doc Harrington's treatments. At the end, when Mama had been too weak to turn the knob and wind it, Catherine had done it, placing the music box on the nightstand closest to her mother.

She wanted no reminders of those days and the fact that thanks to Doc Harrington, her mother no longer walked the earth. That was why Catherine had put the music box away, never intending to play it again.

The music wound down, ending as it always seemed to in the middle of a bar. For the first time since Catherine had entered the room, Hannah looked up, suddenly aware that she was not alone. Her hands reached out to clasp the music box, then dropped to her side.

"I'm sorry, Miss Whitfield. I know I shouldn't snoop. Papa

told me ladies don't do that." Her face turned red with embarrassment, and Catherine feared tears would soon fall. "I couldn't help it. When I looked at the bureau, I just had to see what was inside. I was only going to peek, but when I saw the music box, I had to play it."

Hannah picked up the music box, her expression almost reverent. "Isn't it beautiful?"

It was indeed. The intricately carved mahogany box had been Mama's most treasured possession, a gift from Papa their first Christmas as husband and wife.

Hannah's brown eyes radiated joy. "It looks like the one I had before, but the song is different." When Catherine said nothing, her smile faded. "Please don't be mad, Miss Whitfield. I didn't hurt it."

Catherine couldn't be angry, not at this girl who bore so little resemblance to the previously sad and silent child who'd caused both Catherine and Austin so much worry. Her prayers had been answered, at least for the moment. Now, instead of sitting without saying a word, Hannah was acting as if an internal dam had broken, letting words tumble out.

"I can see that you didn't hurt it." Catherine seized on one part of Hannah's explanation. "You said there was another music box. What happened to it?"

Tears filled Hannah's eyes. "I had to leave it. Don't tell my papa. He doesn't know I found it. I wasn't supposed to go into the attic, but I did. I had nothing to do one day, so I snuck up there. That's when I found a big trunk there with pretty dresses," she said, her expression beseeching Catherine to understand. "I think they were my mama's. I found the music box in the middle, wrapped in a long piece of white cloth. There were dresses and shoes, but I didn't care about them. I only wanted the music box. Nobody knew, but I used to go to the attic and play it when I was lonely."

Catherine's heart ached, for she suspected that Hannah's loneliness and her trips to the attic had been frequent. Despite the girl's pleas for secrecy, Catherine knew she would have to talk to Austin. He needed to know about Geraldine's music box and how much Hannah missed it, but right now, Catherine would do nothing to diminish the child's pleasure.

She gestured toward the music box that Hannah still cradled in her hands.

"That was my mother's. Like you, she played it when she was sad, and it made her feel better. I know she'd be glad you're enjoying it."

"Then you're not mad at me?"

"No, Hannah, I'm not."

11

At least he didn't have to worry about whether his daughter was safe. The animals were a different story. Austin stared at the thick coating of ice on the chickens' water. They didn't have enough strength to break through it, which was why he was out here with a mallet as well as some extra grain for the poultry. Hopefully, the cattle would know how to reach the life-giving water. Kevin claimed that they'd done that before, using their hooves to break the ice. Austin could only pray that today would be no different.

Weather. It was one of the things he had disliked most about ranching. You couldn't predict it; you couldn't control it; all you could do was endure. That was part of the reason he had not wanted to continue the family tradition of ranching, but here he was with a ranch of his own.

"You shouldn't go out without eating," Mrs. Moore announced when he returned to the house for a warmer coat. "Nothing's gonna change in the next fifteen minutes except that your stomach will get emptier."

She was right. Austin knew that, and so he took his usual seat at the table and helped himself to a generous serving of scrambled eggs and bacon while he wondered what Hannah was eating.

"I miss the little one," Mrs. Moore said as she spread strawberry jam on a biscuit.

"Me too." Even though Hannah rarely spoke, the house seemed emptier without her. "I'd have gone into town if I could have, but that seemed foolhardy with all the ice."

"Catherine Whitfield's a good woman. She'll take care of Hannah and Seth."

Austin nodded. When he'd realized that the roads were impassible, he'd known that Catherine would take any stranded children home with her. Her house might not be the largest in Cimarron Creek, but it would be warm and welcoming to anyone who needed shelter.

As he took a slug of coffee, Austin nodded again. Warm and welcoming. That described Catherine as well as her home. She was a naturally nurturing woman. Look at what she'd done for him. It wasn't an exaggeration to say that she'd changed, if not his life, at least his perspective on it.

He still didn't understand how it had happened that she had dreamed of Geraldine—the only explanation was that God had given Catherine that dream at that particular time—but hearing her recount what she had seen had released the burden of guilt Austin had been carrying. There was still uncertainty in his life, like whether or not Enright was still searching for him and whether he would ever be able to return to medicine, but the anguish of believing he could have stopped Geraldine from taking her life was gone.

Now if only they could find a way to heal Hannah.

Catherine woke to a winter wonderland. She smiled as she drew the curtains aside and stared at her yard, marveling at the transformation the storm had wrought. A day ago, everything had been brown and green. Now a thick coating of ice encased the tree branches, and with the sun shining on them, they shimmered like diamonds. It was a scene that deserved to be in a picture book—beautiful to behold but dangerous for anyone who needed to be outside.

A glance through the side window told Catherine the street in front of her house glistened with ice, making her grateful she'd canceled school. While the children would enjoy sliding on the ice, perhaps pretending they were Hans Brinker, she didn't want them to risk falling and injuring themselves.

It was the perfect day to stay at home. If she had been alone, Catherine would have spent most of the day reading, but she was not alone. She had two children staying with her, and when the roads cleared, she had to talk to two very different fathers. She had offered extra prayers for both children last night, praying that finding the music box marked a genuine turning point for Hannah and that Boone Dalton would not be angered by his son's absence. Only time would tell if those prayers had been answered.

Catherine dressed quickly, then hurried to the kitchen to make breakfast. As she'd dressed, she decided to serve pancakes with the syrup she'd made with some of Nate's peaches. It would be a treat for both her and the children. They might not be as excited by the split pea soup she planned for their midday meal, but at least that combined with pieces of cornbread would ensure that they did not go hungry.

As she measured flour and baking powder into the bowl, Catherine wondered whether Hannah would prove to be as moody as her mother and would have reverted to her silent self this morning. But when the girl emerged from her room, the music box cradled in her hands, she was smiling and chattering about the ice.

Thank you, God. One prayer had been answered. Unlike Hannah's interest in the globe, which had faded quickly, her pleasure with the music box seemed to be more lasting. Boone's reaction to Seth's failure to do his chores yesterday and this morning was still unknown.

"Good morning, children." Catherine enlisted their help in setting the table, then smiled as both of them devoured the pancakes and the strips of crisp bacon she'd decided would be a good accompaniment.

The morning passed quickly. Though she had feared that they might be bored, Seth seemed content to spend the time sketching, while Hannah chattered about everything from the ice storm to the wallpaper in the parlor as she played the music box so often that even Catherine, who loved the melody, grew tired of it. It was with a feeling of relief that she announced lunch was ready.

As she had hoped, Hannah and Seth ate the soup without complaint, although she noted that neither one asked for a second helping. Catherine bit back a smile, remembering how she had protested when Mama made pea soup. "You'll learn to like it," Mama had declared, and Catherine had . . . eventually.

She and the children were in the midst of washing the dishes when a knock at the front door signaled a visitor. It had to be Austin. Catherine's heart began to race as she admitted to herself how much she had been looking forward to his arrival. Ever since she had discovered Hannah with the music box, Catherine had been eager to share what had happened with Austin. The transformation was so dramatic that at times Catherine could hardly believe this was the same girl who'd sat silently in her classroom for more than two months. Was this the way Hannah used to be?

Wanting the changed Hannah to be a surprise, Catherine tried to keep her excitement under control. She greeted Austin with a bright smile, but one that she hoped was no different from the ones she used at the schoolhouse.

"I'm glad you were able to get into town." That was a major understatement. "How are the roads?"

Austin shrugged as he shed his coat, hanging it on one of the hooks Papa had installed near the front door so many years ago. "Not good, but at least passable." He looked around, as if expecting to see Hannah in the parlor. "I'm more grateful than I can tell you that you were willing to give Hannah a room for the night. After the way you took care of Seth when he was ill, I had no doubt that my daughter was safe and warm with you."

She was more than that, but Catherine wouldn't spoil the surprise. "Seth's here too. I left them drying the dishes." She led Austin to the kitchen.

Hannah turned at the sound of her father's footsteps and held out the pot and towel. "Look, Papa," she cried as if she were accomplishing some heretofore impossible task. "I'm drying dishes. Miss Whitfield taught Seth and me how. And, Papa, wait until you see what I found. It's a music box."

Unable to wait, she dropped the towel and ran to the table. Though her impatience was visible, so too was the care with which she wound the box and set it to playing. "Isn't that the most beautiful song you've ever heard? Miss Whitfield says it's Viv . . . Viv . . . Viv what?"

As Hannah turned beseeching eyes on him, Seth grinned and said, "Vivaldi."

"That's it. Vivaldi. Isn't it pretty, Papa?"

Though Austin had been staring at his daughter, clearly speechless at the difference a little more than a day had made, he cleared his throat and nodded. "Yes, it is." Catherine suspected she was the only one who heard the emotion he was trying so hard to disguise.

Austin cleared his throat again. "It looks as if you and Seth still have some dishes to dry. While you're doing that, Miss Whitfield and I need to talk."

They did indeed. Catherine led Austin to the parlor, closing the door behind them for privacy.

"What happened?" Though Catherine gestured toward a chair, Austin remained standing.

"Amazing, isn't it?"

He nodded, his eyes glistening with unshed tears. "This is what Hannah was like before we moved. What did you do to bring her back?"

"I didn't do anything." Catherine would not take undue credit. "She found my mother's music box. The truth is, I believe God led her to it. That's the only explanation I can find for her opening that particular drawer." Catherine smiled at the sound of laughter making its way through the door. "She's been chattering ever since."

Now came the most difficult part of the story, the part Hannah did not want her father to know. "Hannah told me your wife had a music box." When Austin looked surprised, Catherine continued. "Apparently, she found it in a trunk with her mother's dresses. She said she used to play with it. From the way she reacted when she discovered my mother's music box, I'd say it was her favorite toy." Catherine hesitated for a second before adding, "She told me that you didn't bring it when you moved."

Austin was silent for a moment, as if trying to absorb all that Catherine had told him. When he spoke, his voice was hoarse with emotion. "I had no idea she'd found Geraldine's things. If I had, well . . . I'm not sure what I'd have done. Hannah's right, though. I left Geraldine's belongings behind."

Though Catherine wondered whether that was because he was hoping to build a future with fewer memories of his wife and her illness, she wouldn't ask. The question was too personal for even a friend to pose. Instead she focused on Hannah. "You've seen what a difference the music box makes. Perhaps

114

you could send for it. It shouldn't take too long to ship it from Oklahoma."

Austin's expression darkened as he shook his head. "I wish I could, but I can't." And then he muttered something that sounded like, "It's too dangerous."

Austin wished he hadn't said that. Somehow, the words had slipped out. He could tell that Catherine had heard them, though she was too well bred to ask what he meant. He would have liked to have been able to tell her everything, but he couldn't take the risk. Though he'd trusted her with Geraldine's story, no one other than Travis must know what had happened in Philadelphia.

It wasn't difficult to conjure a smile. All Austin had to do was think about the girl drying dishes only a few yards away. "How can I ever thank you for what you've done for my daughter?" Austin had never believed in miracles, but the difference in Hannah seemed nothing less than miraculous.

A strand of silky brown hair came loose from Catherine's chignon as she shook her head. "I told you, I didn't do it. God did." A miracle, or at least an act of God. Austin gave a silent prayer of thanksgiving.

As if she understood what he was feeling, Catherine nodded, then gestured toward the door. "We'd better get back to the kitchen. In my experience, it's never wise to leave two children alone with pots and pans for too long."

She opened the parlor door as she said, "I'm as grateful as you are that Hannah's broken out of her shell. Now my primary worry is Seth. I don't know how his father will react to his being gone. He probably thought Seth should have walked home yesterday to milk the cows."

Austin nodded as he remembered Boone's reaction when his son was ill. "Probably."

Catherine frowned. "It's still hard for me to believe, but it seems Boone Dalton values money more than his son. That's why I'm going to tell him I was afraid Seth would fall and break a leg and that I knew Doc Harrington would charge a lot to set it."

"Good reasoning, but I'll save you the trip out there. I can deliver both Seth and your message." Austin didn't trust Boone Dalton any more than Catherine did. Maybe even less, because he'd heard rumors that Boone was thought to have caused his wife's fatal fall down a flight of stairs. Catherine should never be alone with him.

Austin wouldn't tell her that, because she was just stubborn and independent enough to want to prove that she could handle Boone Dalton. Instead, Austin kept his tone light as he said, "There's only one flaw in your logic: you'd never let the doctor come near Seth." Her vehement opinions of the town's physician were etched in his memory and were another reason why he couldn't tell her about his life in Philadelphia.

She shrugged. "Boone doesn't know that."

Austin couldn't help it. He laughed.

When they entered the kitchen, Hannah and Seth were exchanging guilty glances. The reason wasn't hard to find. In the absence of the adults, the children had engaged in a soapsuds war, leaving wet spots on the floor.

Though Austin was tempted to smile at the evidence that his daughter was once again behaving like a normal six-year-old, Catherine gave the culprits her sternest look, a look that he suspected rarely failed to quell even the most rambunctious child's enthusiasm. "You'll find rags in the pantry, Seth. When you and Hannah have finished drying the floor, Mr. Goddard will take you both home. I'm sure you realize that I'm disappointed in your behavior, but I'm not going to hold that against you. Hannah, you may take the music box with you."

Though her eyes widened and she looked at the instrument with what could only be called a covetous glance, Hannah shook her head. "I can't do that, Miss Whitfield. It belongs here with you."

"Are you certain?" Austin asked. As much as he admired his daughter's lack of selfishness, he could not bear the thought that she might revert to silence. From what Catherine had said, the music box was the key to the new Hannah.

He smiled at his daughter, then glanced at the music box. It was indeed similar to the one Geraldine had loved. "Miss Whitfield said you could have it."

Hannah shook her head again. "She needs it. It was her mama's."

A pang of remorse clenched Austin's heart. If only he'd realized that Hannah had found Geraldine's trunk and that she'd developed such an attachment to the music box. Though they'd left Philadelphia in haste, he could easily have brought what seemed to have been Hannah's favorite possession. What kind of father was he that he didn't know something so important about his own daughter?

Austin looked at the beautiful wooden box, wondering how long it would take to order one for Hannah. Surely he'd be able to get it within a few weeks.

"Perhaps you'd like to borrow it for a week or two," he suggested.

But Hannah was adamant. "I don't want to borrow it. I want to play it every day." Though she shot a glance at Seth, as if expecting him to support her, the boy remained silent as he mopped the largest puddle.

Austin knew the feeling of needing an ally, and he had one. Catherine, He looked from the music box to Catherine and then back to his daughter. "That's why Miss Whitfield offered the music box to you."

"She'd be sad if I took it."

Austin felt as if they were playing ring-around-the-rosy, running in circles, getting nowhere. Unsure what to say to convince Hannah, he looked at Catherine again. Surely she knew how to convince a child. As a parent, Austin had experience with only one, while she dealt with dozens every day.

She met his gaze and gave the smallest of nods, acknowledging his silent plea for help, before turning her attention back to Hannah. "I could bring it to school, and you could play it at recess."

Hannah, practical, stubborn Hannah, shook her head. "Somebody could break it. Seth thinks that's why you won't bring your papa's books to school, 'cuz someone might break them." She gave Seth a glance that made Austin believe there had been more going on in the kitchen than just drying dishes and playing with soap suds. The boy's wink confirmed Austin's belief that the children had been discussing Hannah's fascination with the music box and had concocted a solution. He only hoped it wasn't too outrageous.

Laying a protective hand on the object of the discussion, Hannah turned to Catherine. "Why can't I live here with you? That way I could play it every day, and no one would break it. I'd be very careful."

Austin felt the blood drain from his face. If he'd speculated for the rest of his life, he would not have come up with that suggestion. Was Seth the instigator? Even if he was, why had Hannah agreed? Catherine looked as shocked as Austin felt.

"Your home is with me at the ranch," he said firmly, trying to ignore the pain that the mere thought of Hannah living somewhere else wrought. Didn't she know how much he loved her and that his life revolved around her?

In a surprisingly adult gesture, Hannah shrugged. "You're gone most of the time. You won't miss me."

But he would. Oh yes, he would. He'd missed her last night and this morning, even though he'd known she would be home again this afternoon. "That's not true, Hannah."

When his daughter began to pout, Catherine laid a hand on her shoulder. "Why don't you pack your bag, Hannah? Your father and I need to talk."

"Again!" Seth scoffed at the idea of the adults' need for private conversation.

Austin glared at the boy. "Yes, young man, again. I suggest you leave us alone or you'll be walking back to your farm." When Seth slunk out of the room, Austin turned to Catherine. "I can't believe Hannah doesn't want to live with me."

Her expression was solemn, the furrows between her eyes telling him that this was the first time she'd faced a situation like this. "I won't pretend that I understand what Hannah's thinking," Catherine said softly, "but I suspect this is a passing fancy. Perhaps it's a result of the last time you were riding the range."

Austin was silent for a moment, remembering the misery he'd seen etched on Hannah's face when he'd returned from less than a week away. Though he'd hoped that the change was temporary, it had lasted until yesterday when she'd been here with Catherine and the music box.

"Roundup's coming," he said, dreading the thought of two or more weeks away from home. He fixed his gaze on Catherine. "I don't want to think about how she'll react to that."

Those eyes that reminded him of melted chocolate softened. "This might be the solution. Hannah could be like some of the other children who live on ranches. They board with a family in town during the week, then go home on weekends." Catherine's voice was steady as she said, "I'd be willing to try that, if you are."

Austin took a deep breath, trying to view the proposal impartially. It wasn't easy when his daughter's happiness was at stake. "It's a big step," he admitted, "but the truth is, it would give me more time on the ranch. There never seems to be enough time to get everything done, even with Kevin Moore's help. It would be easier if I didn't have to drive back and forth to town twice a day and if I didn't have to worry about Hannah retreating into her shell." Austin paused, trying to beat back the ache that the thought of leaving Hannah in town wrought.

"Hannah's suggestion makes sense," he admitted. "I wouldn't worry about her if she were with you, but if I don't drive her to school, what happens to Seth?"

"That's a problem." Catherine's lips tightened. "I wish I could keep him here, but Boone would never agree to that. It looks like he'll have to go back to walking."

Remembering the almost emaciated boy he'd seen the first day, Austin shook his head. "I don't like that idea."

"I don't either, but I don't have any alternatives."

Austin walked to the window and stared outside. The ice had begun to melt, leaving the street slushy. While this storm had been an unusual event, the simple truth was that Seth shouldn't have to walk from his farm in any weather.

"There might be a way," Austin told Catherine as the ideas began to swirl through his mind. "You said Boone's motivated by money. What if I hire Seth to work on the ranch and pay his wages directly to Boone? I could claim that I need him first thing in the morning and again after school. Once Seth's at the ranch, Boone wouldn't know if I gave him a horse to ride to school."

A hopeful smile lit Catherine's face. "You'd do that?" When Austin nodded, she continued. "What would you get out of it?"

"Some chores done. I can't have Seth lying when his father asks what he does. Besides, I told you there's more work than Kevin and I can handle. Another pair of hands will be welcome, but more importantly, this arrangement will give my daughter a chance at happiness. There's nothing I want more than that."

He tipped his head to one side, studying the woman who'd made such a difference in Hannah. "So, what do you think? Do we have a deal?"

Catherine extended her hand. "We do."

12

"Oh, Mr. Goddard, you're just the man I wanted to see." Austin tried not to cringe at the sound of Henrietta Brooks's voice. In truth, she had a pleasant voice. It was the subjects she raised that annoyed him. That and the fact that the mere sight of the plump matron made Hannah cling to his hand. They had almost reached the back of the church when Mrs. Brooks marched through an empty pew, her husband and daughter trailing behind as she greeted Austin.

"I heard that dear Hannah has been staying with Miss Whitfield during the week," Henrietta said without bothering to spare a glance for "dear Hannah." "I know how lonely you must be without her, and so I said to Henry, we need to help Mr. Goddard. Didn't I say that, Henry?"

The man whom Austin thought of as the quintessential henpecked husband merely nodded and shot Austin what appeared to be a sympathetic look. Surely it was his imagination that Henry had tipped his head to the left, as if encouraging Austin to keep moving toward the exit.

"I can't tell you how much I hate the thought of you being all alone on that big old ranch of yours." As had been the case each of the previous Sundays when she'd accosted him, Henrietta Brooks did not wait for a response to continue her monologue.

"I told Henry it would only be neighborly to pay you a visit. I know how hard it is for you without a wife to make sure you have good meals. My Anna," she said, pulling the reluctant girl forward a few inches, "is a good cook. I taught her everything I know. It's too early for fresh peaches, but her canned peaches won a prize last year. It's the dash of nutmeg she puts in them, you know."

Austin knew nothing about seasoning peaches. What he knew was that he had to end this conversation before it became any more awkward. Though he'd been taught not to be rude, particularly to ladies, perhaps he needed to make an exception. Henrietta Brooks did not appear to understand polite refusals. Austin took another step forward. Once he and Hannah had spoken to the minister, they could escape.

"We'll bring supper with us—enough to last you a couple days." Without stopping for a breath, Henrietta Brooks added, "I thought we'd come on Tuesday, but if that's not a good day for you, we could come on Wednesday."

As she looked at him, hope shining from her dark eyes, Austin shook his head slightly and took another step toward Pastor Dunn and freedom. "That's very kind of you, Mrs. Brooks, but the reason Hannah stays in town during the week is that I'm rarely at home, and when I am, Mrs. Moore provides meals. I couldn't insult her by asking you to bring food to the ranch, and so I'm afraid I must decline your generous offer. I do thank you for thinking of me." The last was an exaggeration—close to a lie—but Austin would not let his manners desert him.

"Perhaps in a week or two . . ." When Austin did not respond, Henrietta turned to her husband, her voice pitched so that Austin had no difficulty overhearing her. "That man needs a wife. He may not admit it, but he does, and Anna would be perfect."

Anna would not be perfect for many reasons, not the least of which was that her mother frightened Hannah, but there was no reason to say that. It would only hurt Anna and would probably not discourage Mrs. Brooks. Thankfully, Austin and Hannah had reached the back of the church and were next in line to speak with Pastor Dunn.

"An excellent sermon." The minister had preached about loving one's neighbors.

With a twinkle in his eye, Pastor Dunn said, "I fear that some of my parishioners have taken the message too far."

Austin couldn't help but laugh.

He wasn't laughing when he lifted Hannah into the wagon and she turned beseeching eyes on him. "Are you going to marry Miss Brooks?"

"No, Hannah, I am not."

"Good." She gave an exaggerated sigh of relief. "I don't want her to be my mama."

Austin waited until he was seated next to her before he responded. "To be fair, you don't even know Miss Brooks."

Hannah shook her head. "She doesn't smile. Nice ladies smile. Miss Whitfield smiles."

She did indeed. Hannah had stayed with Catherine for two full weeks, and while it was true that Austin missed his daughter, it was also true that she seemed happier than he could recall. At first, he had thought she'd been restored to the Hannah who'd shared his life in Philadelphia, but that wasn't the case. She was visibly happier than she'd been there.

Hannah giggled and laughed like the other girls he'd seen. She even pouted when Mrs. Moore told her she could not bring her doll to the dinner table. Austin had rejoiced over the pout as much as the giggles, because he knew that was normal. His beloved daughter was once again a normal girl, all because of Catherine.

The music box had started the process and had broken through the walls Hannah had erected, but it was Catherine's day-to-day care that kept Hannah from rebuilding barriers. She might not have children of her own, but Catherine knew what little girls needed—smiles and hugs.

Austin flicked the reins as they reached the outskirts of town. He could use smiles and hugs too. Admittedly, Catherine gave him smiles, but there were no hugs. That wouldn't be proper, and Catherine was always proper. While it was true that she had touched his hand when she had told him about her dream and that the warmth of her palm had comforted him as much as her words, that small intimacy had not been repeated.

Rather than risk gossip, with the exception of the day after the storm, she had not invited him into her home. Instead, they remained at the school and conversed when he came for Hannah on Friday afternoons and then again, more briefly, when he brought her back on Monday mornings.

A smile crossed Austin's face, both at the realization that his daughter was staring raptly at the countryside as if she were seeing it for the first time and finding what she saw fascinating and at the memory of his conversations with Catherine. He'd never been able to talk with a woman the way he could with Catherine. She was interested in so many different things, everything from his plans for the ranch and the books she read to the political and economic condition of the world.

Their conversations were invigorating, making Austin wonder what it would be like to come home to her each day. It would be far different from life with Geraldine. That much he knew. Though Catherine was in mourning, grief did not seem to have affected her the way it had Geraldine. He had seen no evidence of moodiness in Catherine. Even when she was worried about a pupil, she maintained a basic level of cheerfulness, and the only time he'd seen her angered had been when the local doctor had treated one of her pupils.

As far as Austin could tell, that anger was well deserved.

The town's physician wasn't simply clinging to old-fashioned remedies; he appeared to be incompetent. If he could have, Austin would have had the man run out of Cimarron Creek and would have taken his place. But that wasn't possible. He couldn't even tell Catherine he shared her opinion of Doc Harrington, for that would open the door to questions he did not want to answer.

"Look, Papa," Hannah cried with delight. "A pretty bird."

It was pretty, perhaps even beautiful. And so was Catherine. Beautiful, intelligent, compassionate—she was the most fascinating woman he'd ever met. If circumstances were different, he would consider courting her, but circumstances were not different.

Mrs. Brooks hadn't been wrong when she'd claimed that Austin was sometimes lonely and that he needed a wife. Both were true, as was the fact that he was unable to change either situation. Not only had Mrs. Moore said that Catherine would observe a full year of mourning before she considered marrying, but he wasn't free to tell her the truth about his past.

Enright was out there, and though Austin wanted to believe the man had given up, he doubted that was true. Sherman Enright was nothing if not tenacious. Travis reported that he was still operating in Philadelphia, and that meant that unless he had found another surgeon to alter his face, which was highly unlikely, he was still searching for Austin.

The man had threatened Hannah. If Austin were courting Catherine, she would be the next in line for Enright's revenge, and that was something Austin could not let happen. Until Enright was gone from Philadelphia and Austin knew that Catherine could put aside her distrust of physicians, they could be no more than friends.

"How do you like instant motherhood?" Lydia wrapped both hands around the cup of peppermint tea Catherine had poured for her.

"Is that what it is?" Catherine sipped her tea, considering both the question and her friend's curious expression. Perhaps Lydia's interest was fueled by her own impending motherhood. It was early evening, a time Catherine had suggested for Lydia's visits because she knew Hannah would be in bed. Now that Hannah lived with her, after-school visits to the candy shop included her, leaving Catherine and Lydia no time for private conversations.

"I'm more tired than I expected," she admitted. "I hadn't realized how much I need quiet time to recover from school. Despite that, I wouldn't change anything. It's wonderful seeing Hannah so happy."

Lydia nodded. "She's blossomed. That's the only way I can describe it, but what about Seth? How is his new arrangement working out?"

"Unbelievably well." That was part of what made Catherine smile each morning. "He's gaining weight from Mrs. Moore's cooking, but more importantly, he's gaining confidence." And that was due to Austin. "I overheard him telling one of the other boys he's going to be a rancher."

"I don't imagine Boone will like that. Most fathers want their sons to follow in their footsteps, and you know farmers and ranchers don't always get along."

But Boone was not most fathers. "I'm not sure he cares what Seth does. Now that he has extra money, I've heard that he's practically a resident of the Silver Spur. Fortunately, Seth has been spending most nights at the ranch, so he doesn't have to deal with a drunken father. Austin told me he found him sleeping in the barn one night and decided to let him stay. When he offered Seth a room in his house, the boy refused, saying that if his father asked where he had been, he could honestly say he'd been sleeping in the barn."

"And Boone would never think to ask whose barn." Lydia chuckled. "Seth's a smart boy."

"He is indeed. Austin said he goes home to milk the cows, but that's about all the time he spends there."

"Just as well, especially if Boone's been drinking heavily. I never did like the man, and the more I hear, the less I like him." In an obvious change of subject, Lydia gestured toward the plate of candy she'd brought with her. "What do you think of the pecan brittle?"

Catherine took a bite, savoring the flavors before she responded. "It's delicious. Almost as good as your coffee fudge." Catherine smiled at the memory of what had become her favorite confection. "I'm always amazed at the new varieties you create. This isn't ordinary pecan brittle, is it?"

Lydia shook her head. "I added a touch of molasses to give it a richer flavor." She paused long enough to eat a piece. "I need to come up with something for Founders' Day. I know it's almost four months away, but it's never too early to start planning."

While Catherine suspected no one would be disappointed if Lydia sold the same special Founders' Day fudge she had last year, she knew her friend wanted to offer something different. "I'll ask my pupils what their favorite flavors are. Maybe that'll give you an idea for a combination of two or more—something like the marble fudge you made last month."

"I draw the line at dill pickle and mint."

Catherine wrinkled her nose. "I doubt even the most adventuresome of them would want to eat that, but one thing's for sure: they're never at a loss for stories, the more outrageous the better. Even Hannah has started. One night last week she said she had a secret to tell me and made me promise not to tell anyone. The problem is, I know it wasn't true."

"Though I'm curious, I won't ask you to divulge it."

"I know, and I appreciate that. I don't want to betray her confidence, but I didn't know what to say. Everyone knows Austin came from a ranch in Oklahoma." While it was true that Austin had admitted they'd lived in Paris, Hannah would have no memories of that. That was why it made no sense that she claimed they'd lived in a big city and that her father made people look pretty.

"I wouldn't worry about it." Lydia nodded when Catherine raised the teapot, offering to refill her cup. "It's not unusual for lonely children to invent imaginary friends and make up stories. Now that she's living with you, Hannah shouldn't need her fantasy world."

"I hope you're right."

The place was a hovel, a far cry from the almost palatial home where he had lived in Philadelphia and the larger, definitely palatial estate he would purchase when he settled near New York.

Small, dirty, and located in the middle of nowhere, this pathetic excuse for a building had no redeeming features other than the fact that no one would expect a man of Sherman Enright's position to be here. And that was precisely the reason he was holed up here, waiting for Austin Goddard to work his magic.

"What excuses do you have for me today?" He leaned back in his chair as he glared at the three men standing before him. He'd deliberately arranged four chairs facing him, though he had no intention of letting any of them sit. They didn't deserve to relax, but they did deserve the reminder that one of their group had breathed his last.

After they'd failed to discover the doctor's whereabouts, Sherman had had no choice but to make an example of Shorty. When he'd put the barrel of his pistol to the man's head, Shorty had pleaded for mercy, sniveling that he had a wife and five children. He should have thought of them and searched harder.

"We haven't been able to find him." Tucker appeared to have been appointed spokesman today.

"Obviously. Why not?"

"He left no trace. The doctor and his daughter didn't take a train or a ship. I checked all the records myself."

"Then they drove his carriage, rented a wagon, or walked. Someone saw them. You simply haven't found that someone." Sherman narrowed his eyes, enjoying the men's discomfort. "Look harder, look further, do whatever you have to. Just find that blasted doctor. I can't go on this way much longer."

The men nodded like the puppets they were. In all likelihood, they were wondering if one of them would meet Shorty's fate today. He ought to kill them all, and he would, once they brought the doctor to him, but right now he needed them. Going into hiding and working only through intermediaries was no way to run a business. He needed to get to New York and build a new empire, but he couldn't do that looking like this.

"Find Goddard, and do it fast."

⁂

"What are you drawing, Seth?"

It was midafternoon on Saturday. For the first time since Seth had begun working for him, Austin had taken him out on the range, ostensibly to check on the calves, but actually to gauge the boy's stamina. As he and Catherine had hoped, Boone had agreed to let Austin hire his son. The man's greed had been apparent when Austin had said he would pay for the boy's services, and he'd haggled over the amount. Though Austin let him think he'd gotten the best of him, the truth was, he would have paid almost anything to keep Seth away from his father.

Initially, Seth tended to the horses, mucking out the stables and grooming them. He milked Austin's two cows and even offered to collect eggs when he discovered that the chickens didn't peck him as much as they did Mrs. Moore. No matter what chores Austin assigned him, Seth did them without complaining, but Austin knew he was hoping to do what he called "real" ranching. That was why they were riding the range today.

So far, Seth was holding up well. It had been a hard day of riding, but he'd shown no signs of fatigue. Instead, he seemed energized by the activity. It was Austin who'd suggested they rest by the creek for half an hour before they continued back to the ranch house.

Though his plan had been to ensure that Seth ate another of the sandwiches Mrs. Moore had packed, as soon as they were both seated, their backs against cottonwood trunks, the boy had pulled a scrap of paper and a stub of pencil from his pocket and began to draw.

According to Catherine, Seth had talent, but his father disapproved of the activity. Perhaps he feared that Austin would be equally critical.

Austin unwrapped one of the sandwiches and handed the other to Seth. Keeping his voice neutral, he said, "I always wished I could draw, but the Good Lord had other ideas."

Seth shrugged as he unwrapped his sandwich and took a bite. "You're a mighty good rancher."

Hardly! Though he'd mastered the basics as a boy, Austin had never enjoyed life on the ranch. That was why he'd left home, determined to find a way to attend medical school.

"Ranching takes common sense, determination, and hard work. It's something almost anyone can master if they want to. Drawing is different. It takes talent, and that's something God doesn't give to everyone." Austin watched Seth carefully, and when he saw the boy's eyes light with what appeared to be pleasure, he continued. "I won't force you, but I would like to see what you've done."

Wordlessly, Seth handed him the drawing, the sandwich forgotten as he waited for Austin's verdict.

Austin stared at the evidence of the boy's talent. Catherine had said she believed Seth had been given the gift of an artist's eye, and she was right. "This is good. It's very good." Seth had captured the scene before them, the creek meandering through the tall grasses, trees forming a canopy over the water, cattle grazing in the background.

"You think so?"

"I know so. I've seen illustrations in magazines that aren't this good. You have real talent, Seth. You shouldn't waste it."

When Seth's gaze met his, Austin saw hope mingled with fear. "But my . . ."

Austin suspected he was going to explain that Boone wouldn't approve, perhaps even that he'd forbidden Seth to sketch. Before he could complete the sentence, Austin interrupted. "I tell you what. I'll order some supplies. As far as anyone will know, they're for Hannah. So long as you finish your chores, you can sketch whenever you're at the ranch. How does that sound?"

"You'd do that for me?" This time hope had chased away the fear.

"Yes."

13

"M iss Whitfield, Miss Whitfield!" Rebecca shrieked as she raced into the schoolroom. "Come quick! Roger's hurt his arm!" Even without the final statement, Catherine would have known something was seriously wrong. Rebecca prided herself on her proper grammar. The fact that she'd said "quick" rather than "quickly" was an indication of extreme stress.

The cause of that stress was apparent the moment Catherine stepped outside. Rebecca's brother lay on the ground under the swing, cradling his right arm. Though Hannah knelt by his side, his older brother stood, an expression of horror on his face. Today was April Fool's Day, and it seemed the boys had been fooling around more than normal.

"What happened?"

"He jumped off the swing." Hannah's disapproving tone left no doubt of her opinion of that particular act. The girl who had once spent most of her free time on it looked at the swing as if it was singlehandedly responsible for Roger's pain.

Catherine knelt next to the boy, trying to assess the extent of his injury.

"It hurts, Miss Whitfield. It hurts real bad." Though Roger

133

tried to maintain a stoic expression, he failed. "Everything went black when I landed."

And that, Catherine knew, was a bad sign. One of the medical books she'd read had said that loss of consciousness often meant a bone was broken rather than simply bruised. She helped the boy to his feet, being careful not to touch his injured arm. "Let's go inside so I can see what needs to be done."

Fortunately, classes were over for the day, and only four pupils had remained in the schoolyard. It was Friday afternoon, which meant that Hannah was waiting for her father to come for her. As had been the case ever since he'd started working for Austin, Seth had left on the horse Austin had told him he could consider his for as long as he worked at the ranch. Normally Hannah would have been the only pupil in the schoolyard, but for some reason Rachel Henderson was late in picking up her trio.

"Should I fetch the doctor?" Sam, the eldest Henderson child, asked. Like all of Rachel's children, he was blond with blue eyes. Today he also wore a decidedly worried expression, making Catherine suspect that the unauthorized exit from the swing had been his idea. It wouldn't be the first time a boy had challenged a younger sibling to do something dangerous.

"There's no need for the doctor," Catherine said firmly. Jumping from the swing, even if it resulted in a fractured arm, was less dangerous than being treated by Doc Harrington. "I'll take care of your brother." She gave Roger a reassuring smile. "It'll be all right, Roger. You can lean on me."

Hannah tugged on Catherine's skirt. "My papa could help you."

Though the thought of seeing Austin again made Catherine's heart skip a beat, she doubted he would be of any assistance in treating a sprained or possibly broken arm. She at least had the benefit of her medical books. Still, it was only natural that

Hannah, who obviously idolized her father, would believe him capable of anything.

"That's nice, Hannah, but your father's not here now, and I am." Keeping her arm around Roger's waist, Catherine moved toward the schoolhouse. "Roger and I are going inside. The rest of you need to stay in the yard." The last thing Roger needed was to have his siblings view his pain. Despite Catherine's declaration that Roger did not need Doc Harrington, if Sam and Rebecca heard him crying, one of them might decide to summon the town's physician. She couldn't let that happen.

"You're a brave young man," she told Roger as they entered the schoolhouse.

The thirteen-year-old nodded, obviously pleased that Catherine had referred to him as a man rather than a boy. Seconds later, she had him seated in the chair next to her desk and had begun her examination. Biting his lip to keep from crying when she rolled up his sleeve, Roger muttered, "That hurts."

It would. Catherine could see the outline of the radius in two distinct sections. Though the bone hadn't punctured the skin, this was obviously a serious fracture.

"Can you move your fingers?" When Roger tried but failed to wiggle them, Catherine nodded. "It appears that you've broken your arm."

"I thought so. I heard a crack just before it all went black."

Catherine took a deep breath, trying to settle her nerves. Though she'd handled a variety of injuries and illnesses, she had never before been called on to set a bone. The medical book she'd bought when Mama had become so ill indicated that the process was straightforward. Fortunately, she had brought it and some basic medical supplies to the schoolhouse when she'd vowed that Doc Harrington would not treat any of her pupils while they were in her care. The question was whether or not

Catherine could steel herself to push the bone back into alignment. She had to. She simply had to.

"Setting the bone will hurt," she told Roger, "so I'm going to give you something to ease the pain." Though she hated what laudanum had done to her mother, there were times when it was needed. She gave Roger a spoonful of the powerful liquid, then bade him lie on the floor. While it would have been easier to set the arm if he'd been awake and could keep it on the desk, Catherine wanted him unconscious when she tugged on the bone.

As the boy drifted into sleep, she pulled out her medical book and turned to the section on fractures. She was studying the diagrams when she heard footsteps.

"I heard you had an injured pupil. Can I help you?"

Catherine tried to ignore the frisson of excitement that rushed down her spine at the sound of Austin's voice. He was her friend—her good friend—and there was no denying the comfort that simply having him at her side provided. Even though he probably knew as little as she did about setting a broken bone, she was no longer alone, and that felt good.

"Roger broke his arm when he jumped off the swing."

As Austin knelt on the floor next to her and looked at the arm, she was grateful that her voice had not betrayed the excitement she felt at having him so close.

"I'm glad to see it's not a compound fracture."

Catherine felt herself stiffen with surprise. While she knew from her reading that a compound fracture was one where the bone protruded through the skin, surely Austin didn't have a medical book at the ranch. "I'm surprised you know the term."

He shrugged, as if the reason should be obvious, the motion wafting the faint scent of leather and soap into the air to tantalize Catherine's senses. It was silly to be acting like a schoolgirl, noticing the masculine scents that clung to Austin when she had an injured boy who needed her help.

"Cattle break bones too. A rancher's got to know what he's dealing with and whether there's a chance of saving an animal." Austin looked at Catherine, his blue eyes serious. "Will you let me help? I know better than to suggest you call Doc Harrington."

"You're right about that. I'd be afraid he would want to bleed Roger as well as set his arm."

"Surely he wouldn't do that. I'll admit I haven't heard many good things about him, but I can't imagine any physician believing that bleeding would help a broken arm."

Catherine wasn't certain of anything concerning the doctor other than that she would do everything she could to keep him away from her pupils. The man who'd killed Mama would not have the opportunity to harm them. "I'm not taking any chances."

Austin nodded. "Then may I assist you? It's often good to have two people dealing with a fracture this serious."

He sounded so confident that Catherine felt herself begin to relax. "All right." It would be a relief to have another adult with her. Maybe Hannah had been right when she'd said Austin could help her.

He glanced at the book that she'd been consulting. "Do you have plaster for the cast?"

Catherine shook her head. "This is the first time I've had to do this."

Though Austin's mouth opened as if he wanted to say something, he closed it. A second later he said, "I'll send Sam to the apothecary. When I was in there, I noticed that Warner had plaster and bandages. I'll be back in a minute."

As Austin rose to his feet and strode toward the door, Catherine moved to the chair behind her desk and gave a silent prayer of gratitude that Austin was here. It felt good to have him with her, and not just to help with Roger's arm. She no longer tried to deny how much she enjoyed his company. Every time she saw him, her heart beat faster, the air seemed fresher, the colors more vibrant. It was as if she'd gone through life half asleep, but when Austin was near, she felt alive.

Catherine couldn't explain it. All she knew was that she'd never before felt this way and that none of the books she'd read had given her any clues. Perhaps she should ask Lydia, but Catherine was reluctant to do that. With her current bent toward matchmaking, Lydia might claim that Catherine was in love.

Though Catherine missed her mother's presence each day, the sense of loss was greater today than it had been in weeks. If Mama were here, she could help her make sense of her feelings, help her understand why she felt so strongly about Austin.

"Sam's going to get the supplies," Austin said as he reentered the schoolhouse, "and he's not going alone. Apparently, Rebecca and Hannah think this is some kind of grand adventure and insisted on accompanying him. He's not happy having two girls tag along."

Catherine smiled, as much at the evidence of the progress Hannah was making as at Sam's discomfort. A month ago, Hannah wouldn't have spoken to him, much less insisted on going to the apothecary. "These are children we're talking about," she told Austin. "It *is* a big adventure. Roger will be the center of attention next week, and Sam will have his part in the story."

"Then let's make sure it has a happy ending. Are you ready?"

"Yes." As ready as she would ever be. Catherine returned to kneel next to the unconscious boy, waiting to see what Austin proposed to do while they waited for the plaster.

He gave her medical book another brief glance. "The first step is to reposition the bone. Can you hold him steady while I move it? I'm afraid that even with the laudanum, he may struggle." When Catherine nodded and positioned herself on Roger's opposite side, gripping his arm and shoulder to prevent movement, Austin moved swiftly and confidently. Within seconds, the bone was back in place. Austin ran his finger along its length, then nodded.

"What does your book say to do next?"

"Wrap the limb in a soft cloth." Catherine pointed to the strips of flannel that she kept in her box of supplies.

"That sounds like a good idea. It'll keep the plaster from irritating the skin." As Austin wound the flannel around Roger's arm, he tipped his head to one side. "I think our adventurers have returned."

Seconds later, Sam entered the schoolroom, followed by his sister and Hannah, all of whom appeared fascinated by the sight of Roger lying on the floor with two adults at his side.

"Is he sleeping, Papa?"

Austin nodded. "Miss Whitfield gave him a medicine that makes him sleep. That way it didn't hurt when we set his arm."

Catherine almost smiled at the plural pronoun. She'd done nothing more than assist, while Austin had performed the actual work.

Austin rose and took the packages from Sam. "Did you tell Mr. Whitfield to put these on my account?"

As the boy nodded, Catherine began to protest. "I can pay for them."

"And so can his parents. Consider this my contribution to the adventure." He turned to the children. "I believe Miss Whitfield instructed you to remain outside."

"But we want to help."

Though Hannah gave Austin her most persuasive look, he shook his head. "You'll help by being outside."

As the children filed out, their slumped shoulders announcing their disapproval of the edict, Austin poured water into the metal bowl Sam had brought and set it to warm on the stove. When it reached a temperature he found acceptable, he poured plaster powder into it and began to stir, nodding when it started to thicken.

"Does your book tell you how many coats of plaster we'll need?" he asked.

Catherine shook her head. "It sounded as if one was all that was required."

"We'll see."

Catherine watched, mesmerized by the assurance with which Austin worked. She had no sense of how much time had passed before he said, "All done. By the time Roger wakens, it will be dry."

She studied the now casted arm. "It looks just like the drawing in my book."

"And you're surprised?"

"A bit. I would have thought that your first attempt would be more . . ." She paused, searching for the correct word, settling on *amateur.*

The grin Austin gave her made her flush with pleasure. "Haven't you ever heard of beginner's luck? C'mon. Let's get off the floor."

As he extended his hand and helped her rise, the door opened with such force that it banged against the wall.

"Will he be all right?" Rachel demanded as she raced toward her son.

Catherine smiled and laid a reassuring hand on the woman's arm. "Yes, thanks to Austin. He's the one who set the bone and applied the cast."

Rachel looked from Catherine to Austin and back again, her eyes narrowing ever so slightly as she studied them. "I don't know how to thank you."

It was Austin who answered. "Just make sure he keeps the cast dry. He'll need to wear it for six weeks."

"I remember. This isn't the first time one of my children

has been injured." Rachel knelt next to her son and inspected his arm. "Doc Harrington couldn't have done a finer job. Sam broke his arm when he was only two, and the cast wasn't this smooth."

Though Catherine said nothing, Rachel's comments confirmed her opinion of the town's doctor. "I'm thankful Austin was here. I doubt I could have done as well."

Looking oddly uncomfortable, Austin touched the cast, pronouncing it dry enough to move, then turned to Rachel. "I'll carry Roger out to your wagon." He scooped the boy into his arms and headed outside.

When the door closed behind him, Rachel raised an eyebrow. "I was wrong."

"What do you mean?"

The pretty blonde leaned against the desk as she faced Catherine. "I thought Nate was the right man for you, but now I see that he wasn't. My brother's a wonderful man, but he's not the one for you. Austin is."

Catherine felt as if the wind had been knocked from her. "You're mistaken, Rachel. Austin and I are friends, that's all."

Rachel's smile was almost a smirk. "So you say. So you say."

Rachel's words lingered in Catherine's mind, popping to the foreground to surprise her at the least opportune times. She had tried to dismiss them, but here she was more than two weeks since the day Roger had broken his arm and his mother had made her outrageous declaration, and the words were just as powerful as they had been then.

Catherine moved slowly toward her destination. It was Easter Sunday, and the day was as beautiful as anyone could wish, with the clear blue skies and soft warmth of spring. The service had stirred Catherine's heart as it did each year, reminding her of the priceless gift God had bestowed on his children, the promise of eternal life. The breakfast that the congregation had shared afterward had been as joyous as ever, the special yeast breads and egg dishes commemorating the risen Lord and the season of rebirth.

Though Easter was normally Catherine's favorite day of the year, she could not ignore the emptiness inside her. The cause was easy to find: she missed her mother.

She had known that this first Easter without Mama would be difficult, but it had been harder than she'd expected, in part because Lydia and Travis had gone to Dallas for a meeting of attorneys. That had left Catherine the sole visitor at Uncle Charles's and Aunt Mary's table. Even though Warner had tried to interrupt, Aunt Mary had been more caustic than usual, and Uncle Charles had patted Catherine's thigh twice. By the time the meal had ended, she had been almost frantic to escape. But now she was alone, walking through the cemetery, planning to plant flowers next to Mama's grave.

Catherine had smiled when she found pansies blooming in a corner of her garden three days earlier. They'd been the last flowers Mama had planted before she'd become so ill, and they'd seeded themselves, their cheerful blooms brightening Catherine's day. She had smiled that day, and she'd smiled again today as she dug up a plant, knowing where it belonged.

When she reached the grave, Catherine knelt beside what the minister had called Mama's final resting place. Mama wasn't here. Catherine knew that, just as she knew her mother couldn't hear her. But that didn't stop her from whispering.

"I'm so confused, Mama. I don't know what to do about Austin and the way he makes me feel. I told Rachel that he's my friend, and he is, but the truth is, I've never had a friend like him. I think about him all the time. That never happened with Nate."

Catherine traced the letters carved into the headstone. "Did you know that Nate wanted to court me? I never talked about it, because I was afraid something would go wrong, and it did. He turned out not to be the man I thought he was. Austin's different. When he smiles at me, my heart races. When I see that distant look in his eyes, all I can think about is helping him overcome whatever it is that's making him so sad. Mama, I care about him in ways I never cared about Nate. Is this love?"

There was no answer, but Catherine hadn't expected one. She might not know whether what she felt was love, but there was one thing she did know: Austin was hiding something from her. There were times when she felt as if he was on the verge of telling her whatever it was, but then he'd draw back. He had secrets, and that worried her almost as much as her feelings for him, for Mama had told her that if a man and a woman truly loved each other, they would harbor no secrets. How could Catherine even consider loving a man who wasn't honest with her?

She closed her eyes, wishing there were someone who could advise her. And then she realized that there was. Mama might not be here, but there was One who was. Slowly, she bowed her head.

"Come see, Miss Whitfield." Hannah's voice carried across the hallway. "There's a strange woman in the cemetery. She looks lonely."

Catherine entered what was now Hannah's room and looked out the window. When she had agreed that Hannah could live with her, Catherine had decided she should stay in the guest room. Not only was it less crowded than Mama's room, but it was also closer to Catherine's. If Hannah had a nightmare or needed her, Catherine would hear her cry out.

One glance was all it took to confirm Hannah's words. A

black-clad woman, her face obscured by a heavy mourning veil, was moving slowly through the cemetery, pausing at each of the gravestones to read the inscriptions. She was a stranger—Catherine was certain of that, for there had been no recent deaths in Cimarron Creek—and yet something about the way the woman moved seemed familiar. Who could she be? There was an easy way to answer that question.

"I want you to stay here," Catherine told Hannah. "I'll see if I can help the lady."

And so, only a day since she had prayed at her mother's grave site, Catherine headed back to the cemetery.

"Good afternoon," she said when she reached the woman. "Can I help you?"

The stranger, who was two or three inches shorter than Catherine, wore traditional mourning clothes, a black gown trimmed in black, a black veil covering her head and face. Though the garments were well tailored, they bore traces of dust, making Catherine suspect the woman had arrived on the stagecoach an hour or so ago. She could distinguish little of the woman's features through the thick veil, but a stray hair on her sleeve told Catherine that the stranger was a blonde.

The woman shook her head. "It's kind of you to offer, but I don't think anyone can help." Her voice was pleasant and well modulated, the voice of an educated woman. Though that combined with the style of her clothing led Catherine to believe she was from a city rather than one of the neighboring towns, it did not answer the question of why she was in Cimarron Creek. The last person who'd come to the town unannounced had been Lydia, and the cemetery had most definitely not been her destination.

"I came to visit . . ." The woman hesitated. "Friends," she said at last. "It seems they've died, so there's no reason to stay."

The despair in the stranger's voice made Catherine's heart

144

clench. This woman sounded the way she had felt when Mama had died, so bereft that she could barely think. Catherine had been fortunate that Lydia and Aunt Bertha had helped her through those terrible first few days, but this woman appeared to be alone.

"You'll need a place to spend the night," Catherine told the stranger. "The next stagecoach doesn't come until tomorrow morning. That's the eastbound one. The westbound arrives in the afternoon." When the woman said nothing, perhaps because she was overwhelmed by the combination of her loss and being stranded here, Catherine continued. "Cimarron Creek has no hotel, but you're welcome to stay with me."

Still, there was no response. "Oh, I've forgotten my manners. I'm Catherine Whitfield. The town's schoolteacher."

The woman nodded and extended her hand, her gesture as graceful as her walk had been. "I'm pleased to meet you, Miss Whitfield. I'm Grace Sims, and I'd be grateful for a room." As she gripped Catherine's hand, pressing it between both of hers as if she were drawing strength from it, she said, "My husband passed away recently. I came to Cimarron Creek, because I'd hoped to find a home here. Now . . ." She let the words trail off.

Catherine took a deep breath, exhaling slowly as thoughts swirled through her mind. When she'd walked through her back-yard and into the cemetery, her only thought had been to help this woman find the grave she sought, but hearing Grace Sims's story had changed everything. Catherine nodded. It might be impulsive, but what she was about to propose felt right.

"You're welcome to stay with me as long as you'd like," she said. "If you decide to remain in Cimarron Creek, you don't need to be in a hurry to find your own home."

"That's more than generous of you." Catherine saw the woman's relief reflected in the angle of her shoulders. They no longer looked as if they were carrying an immense burden. "Thank you, but I'm not sure I should impose."

"It wouldn't be an imposition," Catherine insisted, "though I need to warn you that one of my pupils boards with me during the week. She's a very sweet little girl, but if you're not used to six-year-olds, her exuberance can be overwhelming." There was no need to tell Mrs. Sims that that exuberance was a welcome change from the Hannah who had first entered the schoolhouse.

Mrs. Sims released Catherine's hand and took a step backward. "A child. I see. I'm not sure that would be a good idea."

"Don't you like children, Mrs. Sims?"

"Indeed I do. The problem is, they often don't like me." Slowly, she raised her veil.

14

"You gonna set it the way you did Roger's arm?"

Austin gave his head a little shake as his hands carefully examined the calf's leg. "It's not broken, thankfully. It's a sprain. No need to set that. It will get better on its own."

When Seth had reported that his father had heard coyotes howling, Austin had wasted no time saddling a horse. Even if the coyotes proved to be nothing more than a figment of Boone's imagination, the result of too much time at the Silver Spur, Austin needed to check the cattle. He and Seth were now a half hour's ride from the ranch house, and while they'd seen no evidence of coyotes, they'd found a calf limping. To the boy's immense delight, Austin had allowed him to lasso the animal and had shown him how he'd made sure that the calf had not sustained a fracture.

"That's good. Casts don't work for range animals," he told Seth. "Even if I tried one, this little guy would probably chew it off."

"You're not gonna shoot him, are you?" The faint trembling of Seth's lower lip made Austin suspect that the boy had seen his father kill more than one animal.

"No need," he reassured Seth. "If this guy's smart, he'll take it easy for a few days and be just fine."

Seth nodded, his relief evident.

Austin glanced up at Seth. The boy was watching him wide-eyed, as if Austin were some kind of hero. He wasn't. He was a man who'd deceived a woman he cared about, and that was far from heroic.

Austin hated pretending to Catherine that he had no experience with broken bones. Perhaps he should have remained silent and let Catherine set Roger Henderson's arm, but he couldn't risk the boy's losing use of his arm if the bones were aligned incorrectly.

Book learning was one thing, but nothing beat practical experience. That had been one of the first lessons Austin had learned at medical school. Though Catherine had an excellent book, it was not enough. That was why students worked with experienced doctors to learn the proper techniques. That was why Austin had taken over setting Roger's arm.

He wanted to tell Catherine the truth, but he couldn't until he was certain Enright was no longer a threat and until he had somehow managed to allay her fears of physicians.

"I wish I could do that," Seth said as Austin finished checking the calf's leg. "You make it look easy."

Had he done that in the schoolroom? It was too late to change anything, but Austin hoped he hadn't made Roger's cast look easy. Catherine was an intelligent woman who wouldn't believe the story of beginner's luck if the evidence pointed to a different explanation.

"It's all a matter of practice." And Austin had had plenty of that. He signaled to Seth to release the calf's hind legs, then watched while it struggled to its feet and limped back toward the herd. At least one thing had gone right today: the calf was already limping less than it had been when they arrived.

"So, what did you learn in school today?" he asked, deliberately changing the subject.

"Lots."

Catherine stared at Grace Sims's face, trying not to wince at the badly pitted and scarred skin. No wonder she worried about children's reaction if she removed her veil.

"Smallpox?" That was the only thing Catherine could imagine causing such disfigurement. The woman, whom Catherine guessed to be in her midthirties, had golden blonde hair. Though she would have expected blue eyes with that hair, Mrs. Sims's were an unusual shade of green. Were it not for the scarring, she might have been a beautiful woman, but there was no question that few would look beyond the scars.

Mrs. Sims nodded. "The doctor said I was the worst case he'd seen. He claimed it was more severe because I was an adult." Though Catherine wondered whether her doctor had been as incompetent as Cimarron Creek's, she said nothing, merely listened as the woman continued to speak.

"I was fortunate that Douglas didn't mind the scars. Douglas was my husband," Mrs. Sims explained as tears filled her eyes. "He reminded me that our marriage vows said 'in sickness and in health,' and that he loved me no matter what my face looked like. And he did. I never once saw him wince when he looked at me, but he was also realistic. That's why he encouraged me to wear a veil when I went outside. He said it would make both me and others more comfortable, and he was right. My life was as normal as it could be until he became ill and . . ." She bit her lip in an obvious attempt to control her emotions.

"Died." Catherine completed the sentence.

"Yes. Last month. Afterward, there was no reason for me to stay in San Antonio."

That answered two of Catherine's unspoken questions. She had wondered where the woman had called home and why she had left.

"So you came here only to discover that your friends had died too." And that was strange. If they were friends, why hadn't Mrs. Sims been aware of their deaths? If the deaths had been recent, Catherine could understand the confusion, but there had been no funerals in the last few months.

She looked directly at Grace Sims. Though the scarring was extensive and would appear repulsive to many, the more Catherine talked to her, the easier she found it to ignore the scars and focus on the woman behind them.

"Who were your friends? Perhaps they still have family here." As the town's schoolteacher, not to mention part of the founding families, Catherine knew everyone who lived in the area.

Mrs. Sims drew her veil back over her face as she said, "They don't. They were the last of their line."

Catherine mulled over the recent deaths. Mrs. Sims might be speaking of the Saylors. Both of them had died of yellow fever last summer, along with their only son. Catherine recalled Travis saying it was a shame the foreman couldn't afford to buy the ranch, but the heirs—very distant cousins who lived in Nebraska Territory—had insisted on a high price, and it had remained neglected for a few months until Austin bought it.

"I'm the last of my family. My mother died last year." Catherine wasn't sure why she'd said that. Perhaps she'd wanted Mrs. Sims to know that she understood loss.

"It's never easy to lose a parent." Mrs. Sims cleared her throat. "Are you certain it'll be all right for me to stay with you for a day or two while I figure out what to do next?"

"I'm sure." Catherine glanced at her watch, surprised at how long she had remained in the cemetery talking to Mrs. Sims. Hannah would be wondering what was keeping her. "Let me show you to my house. Then we'll send for your luggage."

"I don't know how to thank you, Miss Whitfield."

Catherine gave her a warm smile, wanting this woman who was all alone to feel welcome here. "You can start by calling me Catherine."

"Only if you'll call me Grace."

When they reached the house, Hannah came barreling out the front door. "You brought the lady home! I'm glad. She looked lonely."

"Where are your manners, Hannah?" Catherine frowned at the girl who was normally better behaved.

"I'm sorry." She hung her head in what Catherine hoped was not feigned regret.

Catherine turned to the visitor. "Grace, this is Hannah Goddard. She spends the week with me. Hannah, Mrs. Sims will be staying with us for a while. Now, let's go inside." She held the door so Grace could enter, then followed, leaving Hannah to trail behind. The veiled woman moved confidently, her gait tickling the edges of Catherine's memory. Something about Grace Sims seemed familiar, and yet she was certain she had never before seen this woman.

Once indoors, Catherine led the way to the only unused bedroom. "This will be your room," she told Grace as she opened the door.

"It's very pretty." The slight hitch in her voice told Catherine she realized this was no ordinary guest room.

"It used to be my mother's."

Grace turned so she was facing Catherine. "Are you sure you want me to stay here?"

"Yes." The reply was immediate. Though she was not normally impulsive, Catherine's instincts told her she had made the right decision and that she could trust Grace. "Supper will be ready in half an hour." She studied her guest for a second, wondering how she could eat while wearing a veil. "You don't need to wear your veil indoors."

"What about Hannah?"

"I'll talk to her."

Catherine crossed the short hallway and entered Hannah's room. "Mrs. Sims left her trunk at the mercantile. I'd like you to ask Mr. Whitfield to have it sent here."

"Yes, ma'am." Hannah reached for her bonnet.

"There's one more thing. Mrs. Sims was very sick, and now her face is not smooth like yours or mine. I don't want you to be surprised when you see her. It's also something I don't want you to mention to anyone. We don't want people gossiping about her, do we?"

"No, ma'am."

Though Catherine had thought Hannah might wrinkle her nose at the idea of a less than perfect complexion, she tipped her head to one side as she asked, "Is the lady scarred?"

"Yes. She had smallpox, and that sometimes happens."

Hannah nodded, as if she had experience with the dread disease. "My papa could make her pretty again."

It was another of her imaginings. Catherine shook her head slowly. "Your father can do many things, but I don't believe that's one of them."

As Hannah opened her mouth to protest, her eyes widened in what appeared to be alarm, and she lifted her hand to her face, pinching her lips together. When she removed her hand, she whispered, "I forgot."

"The least you can do is let me prepare the meals," Grace said as she and Catherine settled into matching chairs in the parlor. The supper dishes were finished, and Hannah had gone to bed, leaving the women alone.

"I don't want to sound as if I'm bragging, but I'm a good cook. That's how I met Douglas. I was working at a hotel in

San Antonio when I saw his advertisement in a newspaper. He needed a cook and a companion for his wife."

Grace looked up from the tatting that had her fingers moving as quickly as her tongue. "You seem surprised. What I didn't mention before was that Douglas was twenty years older than me. His wife's rheumatism became so severe that she could no longer care for the house. That's when he hired me."

A small smile crossed Grace's face. "They were the kindest people I've ever met—almost like parents to me—and when Marjorie died, Douglas said it wouldn't be proper for me to remain unless we were married, so he sent for a minister. Almost before I knew what was happening, I was Mrs. Douglas Sims. We learned later that we were married the same day that General Lee surrendered at Appomattox."

Catherine didn't know which surprised her most, the fact that Grace had married a man so much older or the way words seemed to pour from her. In all her life, Catherine had met only one other person who talked like that: Great-Aunt Bertha, a woman who'd been famous for her monologues.

As the last surviving member of the first generation, Aunt Bertha had been a fixture in Cimarron Creek until her death last fall. Though some had grumbled about Aunt Bertha's tendency to monopolize conversations, Catherine had never minded, for she'd recognized her great-aunt's innate kindness and had always enjoyed her company. The sorrow she had felt about her passing had begun to fade, replaced by regret that Aunt Bertha had died without being reunited with her daughter.

Now was not the time to be thinking of Joan Henderson. Catherine returned her focus to her guest. Grace had raised so many subjects that Catherine wasn't certain where to start her response. When in doubt, Mama had always said, start at the beginning. And so Catherine did.

"I don't expect you to cook. You're a guest here."

Grace's fingers continued to fly as she plied the shuttle and the fine thread. "Then let me rephrase my offer. I enjoy preparing meals and would like a way to repay your kindness. Think of it this way, Catherine: you would be doing me a favor if you'd allow me to cook for you. Please don't say no."

Phrased like that, it became an offer Catherine could not refuse. She smiled, remembering the wonderful meals Mama had made. Even if Grace's were not as good, they would still be an improvement over Catherine's culinary efforts. "Thank you, Grace. I accept your offer with pleasure."

The woman nodded as she released thread from the tatting shuttle. "I'll start with breakfast tomorrow. What time would you like to eat?" When they'd settled that, Grace examined the doily she was making and said, "You've probably noticed that I enjoy tatting. What's your favorite pastime?"

"Reading," Catherine said without hesitation. She had once heard that Thomas Jefferson claimed he could not live without books. She agreed.

Grace smiled as if she'd expected the response. "No wonder you're a teacher. I confess that I don't read many books, but I enjoy magazines. I brought several that might interest you."

Laying her tatting aside, she rose and disappeared into her room for a few seconds, returning with three magazines. "I probably shouldn't admit it, but I yawned when I looked at the bed. If you don't mind, I think I'll retire for the evening. The journey was more tiring than I'd expected."

Catherine bade her guest good night, then picked up one of the magazines. Unlike Grace, she was not ready for bed. She was leafing through the magazine, glancing at an occasional page, when she spotted a small boxed advertisement. It wasn't the type of thing she normally read, and yet it caught her eye. She read the announcement once, then again, her smile turning into a Cheshire Cat grin as the words registered. What an opportunity!

The next day Catherine was as anxious as her pupils for lunchtime to arrive. She'd considered talking to Seth during the morning recess but had decided to wait for lunch and the greater privacy it would afford them. While she thought the boy would be excited by her proposal, there was always the possibility that he would not, and in that case, she wanted no one to overhear them.

The change in Seth since he'd started working for Austin had been dramatic. Not only had he gained self-confidence, but his drawing had also improved. Even without formal training, there was no ignoring his talent. The advertisement Catherine had found could be the opportunity Seth needed to have his talent recognized.

At last! "All right, boys and girls. It's lunchtime." She took a step toward Seth's desk and smiled at him, hoping to dispel any alarm he might feel as she said, "Would you stay for a moment?"

When the rest of the students had left, he approached her desk, his expression clearly alarmed. "Is something wrong, Miss Whitfield?"

"No, not at all." Catherine pulled the magazine that had caught her attention from her bag and opened it to the page she'd marked. "I wanted you to see this."

He read the announcement, then looked up at her, wonder shining from his eyes. "An art contest?"

"Yes. I thought you might want to enter it."

"Do you really think my drawings are good enough?" All traces of self-confidence had vanished, and he was once again the insecure boy who'd first entered her schoolroom.

"I do. You're very talented, Seth."

He looked at her for a second, then dropped his gaze to the floor. "Pa won't like the idea."

Though Catherine knew Boone had discouraged his son's artistic endeavors, she thought he might approve of this. "It doesn't cost anything to enter, and if you win, the prize is five dollars." If Boone was as motivated by money as she believed, surely he would be impressed by the possibility of his son winning such a substantial sum.

"I don't know, Miss Whitfield. Pa thinks drawing is a waste of time."

Catherine hated the way Seth's shoulders slumped. For a moment he had been enthusiastic until the reality of his father's disapproval had intruded.

"I don't want you to get in trouble with your father." She had seen the results of Boone's anger all too often. Perhaps this wasn't such a good idea.

"That wouldn't be anything new." Seth was silent for a moment, clearly weighing his excitement over the possibility of winning the contest against the probability of his father's wrath. He clenched his fists and stared out the window, then looked back at Catherine. "I want to enter. I want to see if anyone other than you and Mr. Goddard likes my drawings."

Seth returned to his desk and pulled half a dozen sheets of paper from his satchel. "Which one should I send?"

Catherine studied each of the drawings, her attention continuing to be caught by one in particular. "This one," she said, pointing to one that showed Austin kneeling beside a calf, examining the calf's leg. "Your pictures of the ranch are excellent, but I think the judges will like the fact that you have a person and an animal in this one as well as background. That gives it more interest."

Seth nodded. "It's my favorite too." The smile that had lit his face as he looked at the drawing faded. "Pa doesn't have to know I'm entering, does he?"

Catherine shook her head. "You don't need his permission to

enter, but you need an address so they can return your drawing when the contest is over and notify you if you win. You can use my address, but you need to use your own name. When you fill out the form, write 'Seth Dalton care of Miss Catherine Whitfield.'"

While she didn't like the deception, she wanted Seth to have a chance. Surely it would be all right.

"Did you have a good week?" If he lived to be a hundred, Austin didn't think he'd ever forget the thrill of having Hannah run from the schoolhouse and fling herself into his arms. It happened every Friday afternoon, and every Friday her spontaneous gesture touched him as much as it had the week before. It was good—so very good—to see his daughter happy again.

"Oh yes, Papa. It was the best."

Austin bit back a smile at the realization that she said the same thing every week.

"Lots of things happened." Hannah began to regale him with stories of the boys catching frogs in the creek and how Roger used one of Rebecca's hairpins to scratch under his cast. "She was so mad. She said he wasn't supposed to do that."

Austin doubted the boy had done any harm. "Arms itch when they're healing."

"That's what Miss Whitfield said. She wasn't mad at Roger." Hannah took a breath, then grinned at her father. "The most exciting thing is that a nice lady came to live with Miss Whitfield and me."

Austin blinked in surprise. Catherine hadn't mentioned expecting a visitor when he'd seen her Monday morning. "Who is she?"

"Her name is Mrs. Sims. She's a very good cook. Even better than Mrs. Moore. But, Papa, it's so sad." Hannah's smile turned upside down. "Miss Whitfield said I wasn't supposed to tell anyone about it, but the lady's face is ugly."

Like many children, his daughter had always been quick to judge others by their appearance. "Not everyone can be beautiful on the outside. It sounds as if Mrs. Sims is beautiful on the inside. That's more important."

Hannah shook her head. "I think she was beautiful once, but now she has scars all over her face. Miss Whitfield said they were from smallpox."

Austin had seen the ravages smallpox could inflict and had no trouble imagining the woman's scars. He also understood why Catherine had cautioned Hannah not to speak of them. Both adults and children could be cruel to a disfigured person. That was the reason he had become a plastic surgeon, to spare people the humiliation of being taunted about something beyond their control.

Scooting across the bench until she was next to him, Hannah turned beseeching eyes on Austin. "Can you help her? She has to wear a veil when she goes outside. It must be hot."

There was only one answer. As much as he hated the idea of anyone being scarred, as much as he wanted to help this woman, he could not.

"No, Hannah, I can't help her. I'm a rancher now, remember?"

Hannah pinched her lips between her thumb and forefinger, then nodded. "I remember," she said as she released them. "I remember."

15

Lydia!" Catherine smiled as her friend entered the kitchen and laid one of her confectionary boxes on the table. "I didn't expect you." Breakfast was over, and Grace had returned to her room to don her mourning veil, leaving Catherine to savor a second cup of coffee before they left for church. Normally Lydia and Travis met Catherine in front of the church, but for some reason Lydia had changed the routine today, perhaps because she shared Catherine's eagerness for them to be together. Though Grace had quickly become more than a boarder, Catherine missed Lydia.

"I couldn't wait another hour," Lydia said as she hugged Catherine. "I haven't seen you in over a week, and from everything I've heard, it's been quite a week. Travis picked the worst time to attend a lawyers' meeting."

"Did you enjoy your time in Dallas?" This trip was Lydia's first visit to the city, and she'd been looking forward to it. She had told Catherine she planned to visit every confectionary in the town, looking for new flavors to offer Cimarron Creek's residents.

"Yes, but . . ."

"Were you ill?" Though Lydia claimed to be as healthy as

a horse, Catherine had worried about her traveling while she was expecting a child.

Lydia shook her head. "Fortunately, no. I seem to be past morning sickness. Now I just feel fat." She laid her hand on her waist.

"You don't look fat."

"That's because I let out the seams in my dresses. Another month and I won't be able to do that." Lydia looked as if the prospect pleased her.

"Then what was wrong with Dallas?"

Wrinkling her nose, Lydia said, "You'll probably think I'm crazy, but I was disappointed in all the shops I visited. Some were larger than Cimarron Sweets with fancier furnishings, but I didn't like any of them as much as mine. I didn't even find any new candy varieties to try."

Catherine smiled. "I'm not surprised. I've always thought Cimarron Sweets was the perfect candy store."

"Not that you're biased, being my friend." Lydia hugged Catherine again. "But I didn't come here to talk about me. Opal said that the town is buzzing with the story that you took in a stranger. She said something exciting happens every time Travis and I go away. Last time it was Austin's arrival, now this woman."

"You probably know that her name is Grace Sims." When Lydia nodded, Catherine continued. "So far folks have been more accepting of Grace than they were of you, because she's not a Yankee. She's a very kind widow from San Antonio."

Lydia's expression said she'd already heard that story. "And she's still in deep mourning, so she wears a veil everywhere. That's part of what's causing the gossip, or so Opal tells me. The other part is that she's staying here. Some folks are even speculating that she's a distant relative."

"If you're speaking of me, that's always possible, isn't it?

We're all daughters of Eve." Grace had entered the room so quietly that neither Catherine nor Lydia had heard her until she spoke.

Her face concealed by the heavy veil, she approached Lydia, extending her hand. "I'm Grace Sims, and you must be Lydia Whitfield. Catherine has told me so much about you."

Instead of shaking her hand, Lydia pulled the box from the table and handed it to her. "I hope you like fudge, because I thought a pound might be a good way to welcome you to Cimarron Creek."

"Thank you. That's very kind of you."

Lydia glanced at her watch. "Travis will be here in a minute or two to escort us to church and then to dinner with Aunt Mary and Uncle Charles."

When Grace made no response, Catherine turned to Lydia. "Grace says she doesn't want to join us for dinner despite my best efforts to convince her otherwise. Maybe you'll have more success." Even though Grace ate the midday meal alone when Catherine was at school, it seemed wrong for her to have a solitary Sunday dinner.

Lydia winked at the woman she'd just met. "You must have heard what a poor cook Aunt Mary is."

"Nonsense. It's simply that it's difficult to eat while wearing a veil." And Grace would not remove it, even for Lydia. While she had accepted the fact that Hannah would see her without the veil, she had been adamant that no one else in Cimarron Creek should see her face.

Grace shrugged. "Besides, if I stay home, I can prepare something special for Catherine's supper. Based on what I've heard, she'll appreciate it."

As everyone chuckled, Catherine felt her heart expand with joy. This was the first time she'd heard Grace refer to this house as her home. Perhaps she should have been affronted that a woman she'd known for less than a week used such a familiar term, but Catherine was not affronted. To the contrary, she was delighted. It felt so right to have Grace living here, filling empty spaces in both the house itself and in Catherine's heart. She would never take Mama's place—no one could—but Grace had found a place of her own.

"There's something odd about that woman you've taken in, Catherine," Aunt Mary announced as she passed the bowl of chicken and dumplings to her. "It seems she ought to have accepted my invitation. That's common courtesy."

As Catherine had expected, Grace had been the center of attention after church, with most of the congregation lingering so they could be introduced to her. Aunt Mary and Uncle Charles had been among the first, and while Uncle Charles had been uncharacteristically silent, Aunt Mary had insisted that Grace join them for the midday meal.

"Her husband died only last month. She's still in deep mourning." Catherine repeated the excuse Grace had given when Aunt Mary had badgered her.

"You're in mourning too, but you don't hide behind a veil. I tell you, Catherine, you need to be careful. What if she turns out to be some kind of criminal?" Aunt Mary, clearly miffed by Grace's refusal, was on one of her tirades.

"Have you seen her face?"

"Of course she has." Lydia answered for Catherine. "Mrs. Sims lives with Catherine. I doubt she wears her veil all the time."

Catherine tried to smile at her aunt. "Grace Sims is no criminal. She's a very nice woman."

But Aunt Mary was not convinced. "Appearances can deceive," she told Catherine before she turned to Travis. "I think you ought to check her story. We can't be too careful. After all, Catherine is a single woman living alone. And then there's the little girl. What's her name?"

"Hannah." Catherine laid down her fork and looked directly at her aunt. "Grace is no threat to either of us."

"That remains to be seen. Right, Travis?"

Travis simply nodded and changed the subject by complimenting Aunt Mary on the dumplings. To Catherine's surprise, Aunt Mary did not pursue the investigation, and the rest of the meal was pleasant, filled with stories of Lydia and Travis's time in Dallas. Still, the idea that anyone distrusted Grace bothered Catherine.

"You're not really going to investigate Grace, are you?" she asked the man who was both her cousin and the town's sheriff an hour later. Today, in addition to Lydia, Travis was accompanying her back home.

Though she'd expected Travis to deny that he'd even considered the possibility, he did not. "It wouldn't hurt," he said firmly. "All it means are a couple telegrams."

Lydia squeezed her husband's arm. "Travis is a firm believer in the truth setting us free. You want to know the truth, don't you, Catherine?"

"Yes, but it feels dishonest—as if I don't trust her. And I do."

"So do I, but I'm the sheriff, and as such I have a responsibility to the town and to you."

Lydia chimed in. "As Travis said, it can't hurt to be sure. You need to be careful, especially now that you have Hannah living with you." She was silent for a moment before she added, "I only talked to her for a few minutes, but I agree with Aunt Mary that there's something odd about Mrs. Sims. She's a stranger in town, and yet she reminds me of someone. If only I knew who, I might feel better. As it is, I'm a little worried about you."

Tucker tipped his head back, emptying the glass, then ordered another shot of whiskey. Another drink, another dead end. If he took a drink for each dead end, he'd be drunk as a skunk in no time, but what was a man to do? He couldn't go back to Philadelphia without the doctor, not if he expected to see the sun rise again once Enright heard that he'd failed.

He'd been so sure about this lead. Everything sounded right. New doctor in town. Came from Philadelphia. No wife in sight, but a little girl living with him. That sure as shootin' sounded like Dr. Austin Goddard. Tucker had hightailed it to the small town in western Pennsylvania that the new doc called home, sure that luck was shining on him. But it wasn't. The doc turned out to have red hair, not yellow. The whelp was too young to be Hannah Goddard, and the wife was still alive. Seems she was staying in Philadelphia with her dying mother.

It was all an honest mistake. Anyone would have thought the same thing Tucker did, that he'd found his man. Anyone would understand. Anyone other than Enright. The man did not tolerate failure. Look what he'd done to Shorty. Tucker shuddered and downed the whiskey. He couldn't tell Enright he'd failed. He couldn't go back without the doc. Somehow he had to find Enright's doc, but where?

"Gimme another." He slid the empty glass across the bar. Pretty soon he'd have drunk half the bottle. So what? If he drank the rest of it, maybe he could forget Enright's face the night he'd told him not to come back alone.

Where was that confounded doctor?

Tucker closed his eyes, wishing he could block the memory of the way Shorty had died. It hadn't been pretty. No, sirree. Not pretty at all. As a man jostled him, his eyes flew open. The bar was getting crowded. Time for him to leave. Time to figure out what to do next. But first he needed another drink. Just one more.

He'd lost count by the time that gal in the red dress started singing. At first the words made no sense, but gradually they made their way through his foggy brain. Something about home. An old Kentucky home. Tucker slapped the side of his head. Home. That was it! Critters went home when they were scared. Folks did too. Tucker would bet his last dollar that's what the doc did. He went home. Now all Tucker had to do was find out where the doc hailed from, and he'd find him.

He'd do that. Right after he celebrated with another shot.

As Catherine awoke to the aromas of coffee and bacon, she smiled. It felt so good not to have to rush to make breakfast. The extra half hour of sleep was wonderful, the food better than any she could have made, but the best part was Grace's company. In the space of a few days she had gone from being a stranger to a friend to something more. The only way Catherine could describe her feelings for Grace was to say that she had become the older sister she'd longed for all her life. She couldn't explain why she felt that way. All she knew was that she was comfortable confiding in Grace, telling her things she hadn't shared with either Mama or Lydia. It was no exaggeration to say that Grace was the answer to her prayers.

"Good morning," Catherine said as she entered the kitchen. "I'm surprised Hannah's not up."

Grace slid the buttered bread into the oven, then turned to smile at her. "She is. She saw a rabbit in the yard and wanted to see if she could catch it. I knew she couldn't, but I didn't see any harm in it."

"It's good for her to burn off a bit of energy. A couple months ago, she wouldn't have done anything other than sit in the corner, but now she's acting like a normal six-year-old. The change in her seems like nothing less than a miracle."

Grace nodded. "If it was a miracle, you had a part in it. Even though I didn't know her before, I can see that you've been good for her. I wasn't surprised when she told me she wished you were her mother."

Though Catherine knew she shouldn't have been surprised, she was, as much at the fact that Hannah confided in the older woman as what she'd said. "I love her dearly, but marriage is not something Austin and I have discussed." It was true that both Lydia and Rachel believed Austin might be the right man for her, but it was too soon for them to be contemplating marriage. Though she'd put off the outward trappings, in her heart Catherine was still mourning her mother. Besides, Austin had secrets, and Catherine had other concerns.

While she had told Grace many things, Catherine wasn't ready to reveal her feelings for Austin. Part of her longed to ask Grace how she'd felt being Douglas's second wife, but part of her held back, wanting to get to know Grace better before she asked such a personal question. Still, Catherine couldn't help admitting that she'd thought of one aspect of marriage to Austin. "I don't know why, but I keep having dreams where Hannah is my daughter. I had one last night."

The smile Grace gave her said she wasn't surprised. "It must have been a night for dreams." She peeked into the oven to check the toast. "I dreamt I was in a city I know I've never visited. I think it must have been somewhere in France, because even though I couldn't understand what anyone was saying, I somehow knew they were speaking French."

Catherine smiled, thinking of the number of times she'd dreamt about traveling to France. With one exception, the dreams had been pleasant.

"I was walking along a river," Grace continued. "I don't

know how long I walked, but suddenly I saw an island in the middle of the river, and on that island was an incredibly beautiful church. There were two square towers in the front and an enormous round stained glass window on the side. I have no idea what they're called, but there were almost lace-like arches on the side, going from the building to the ground."

She looked at Catherine, her eyes bright with unshed tears. "It was all so beautiful that it made me want to cry, and here I'm doing it again, only this time I'm crying because I wanted to be there." Grace brushed the tears from her cheeks. "Have you ever had a dream like that?"

Catherine nodded. "Yes, but I didn't have to be asleep to dream it. There's something I want to show you." Thankful that Hannah hadn't yet returned, Catherine hurried to her room and brought out a book. Opening it to one of the bookmarked pages, she showed it to Grace. "Is this the church you saw?"

"Yes. That's it. Exactly. How did you know?"

"Because as long as I can remember, I've wanted to see that rose window and those flying buttresses. That's what the stained-glass window and the arches on the side are called." She placed her hand on Grace's shoulder, wanting to reassure her. "You were right in thinking your dream was about France. The river you saw was the Seine. It flows through the heart of Paris right next to the cathedral of Notre Dame. That's the beautiful cathedral's name. The island is called Île de la Cité."

Catherine smiled, remembering the hours she'd spent studying the pictures in this book, learning all the details she could of the famous buildings in Paris. "It seems you've borrowed my dream."

16

"H annah's growing up." Catherine said it as calmly as if she'd been telling him that the bluebonnets that carpeted the hillside were particularly beautiful this year. Austin had admired them as he'd driven into town and had even considered asking Catherine if she'd like to take a ride to see them, but the reception he'd received—correction: the lack of reception—from Hannah had chased every other thought from his brain. While Austin didn't doubt that Catherine was correct, the situation wasn't as simple as she made it sound. She wasn't a parent. She couldn't understand the ache that lodged in his heart.

"Hannah's only six," he protested. "I thought it would take longer, but look at her." He pointed toward the trio of girls in front of the school, so intent on their game that they appeared oblivious to the rest of the world. "She's more interested in playing hopscotch with the other girls than going home with me."

And that hurt more than he'd expected. It was Friday afternoon, the time he always came to take Hannah back to the ranch. Every other week, she'd been waiting on the schoolhouse steps and had run toward the wagon when she saw him. Today Hannah had given him a casual wave, then gone back to her hopping.

Catherine's smile said she understood more than he realized. It was warm and comforting, as if she were trying to reassure him that he was not alone. "Hannah's like a baby bird. She's spreading her wings, the way all chicks do as they grow." Catherine's smile broadened. "You haven't lost her, Austin. She'll fly back home once she's tired of playing."

He stared at his daughter and tried to focus on her obvious happiness. That was what he wanted: for Hannah to be happy and safe. Returning his gaze to Catherine, he nodded. "I want to believe you're right."

"I am. Believe me, I've seen this happen so many times I've lost count. Each time the parents wonder if they've done something wrong, and each time the chick comes back to the nest." She glanced at the school's side yard. That, Austin knew, was where the pupils spent their recesses, trying their hands at everything from baseball to jacks.

"You look like you need to play a bit too. When's the last time you swung?"

Swinging? The question was so unexpected it almost made him laugh. Surely Catherine didn't think he was going to engage in such a childish pastime, but she stood next to him, clearly waiting for his response.

He shrugged. "I can't remember. I probably wasn't much older than Hannah."

"Then it's time to try it again. You can't be out of sorts when you're swinging."

A soft spring breeze carrying the scent of freshly cut grass triggered childhood memories of a swing on the neighboring ranch. His family had gone there for Sunday dinner one week, and Austin and the neighbors' son had spent hours trying to outdo each other by swinging ever higher. That was one of his happiest memories of life on his parents' ranch. Odd how he'd forgotten that.

169

He stared at Catherine. "You're serious, aren't you?"

A Cheshire Cat smile was her only answer.

"But I'm a d—" Now, look what he'd done. He'd been so surprised by the mere thought of getting on a swing that he'd almost admitted he was a doctor. Austin swallowed and amended his statement. "I'm a grown man. Grown men don't swing."

"This one should." Catherine started walking toward the swing that hung from one of the live oak trees. "Come on, Austin. Try it."

He couldn't deny the appeal of her smile or the challenge she'd offered. "Only if you show me how. I think I've forgotten." He hadn't, of course, but it would be fun to watch the schoolteacher kicking up her heels on the swing.

"I don't believe that for a moment, but, all right, I'll go first." She looked at the ropes that suspended the board from the tree limb. "We need to tie knots in the ropes or our legs will drag on the ground."

Austin nodded and shortened the ropes until the board hung a couple feet off the ground. "Is this okay?"

"Perfect." Seconds later, Catherine was swinging with as much enthusiasm as Hannah, gripping the ropes as she urged the swing higher and higher, her face wreathed with a smile. When she stopped pumping and the swing slowed, she stepped off and turned toward Austin, a question in her eyes.

"You convinced me." Though memories of enjoying time on a swing had resurfaced, Austin felt a bit foolish as he settled onto the board and gripped the ropes. He was, after all, an adult now, a man with serious responsibilities. But if Catherine could swing, so could he.

Backward, then forward. That's the way to do it. Almost before he'd reminded himself of the basics, he was swinging, going higher and higher with each pump, just as he had that Sunday afternoon more than half a lifetime ago. Catherine was right. This was fun. For the first time since he'd arrived at the school, Austin felt free. Like Hannah, he was testing his wings a bit, enjoying the sensation of doing something different, the novelty enhanced because he knew what was waiting at the end: home. Being on the swing felt good, so very, very good, that he started to laugh from the pure joy of it.

"If that ain't the most doggone thing I ever seen, a grown man acting like a boy. What's the matter with you?"

The man's slurred words brought Austin back to reality. It had been weeks since he'd seen Boone Dalton, and that had been fine with him. Though he'd heard that Boone spent too many afternoons at the Silver Spur, using the money Austin paid for Seth's services to buy whiskey, this was the first time he'd had a firsthand view of the effects of the man's excessive drinking.

Boone was wearing the same ragged shirt and pants he'd had on the other times Austin had seen him. His face sported a few days' growth of whiskers, as it had in the past. His hair was as unkempt as ever. What was different was Catherine's presence and the way Boone was leering at her.

Austin jumped off the swing and moved to Catherine's side. A sober Boone was unpredictable; one who'd imbibed too heavily might be dangerous.

"Is this why you hired the boy?" Boone demanded. "So you could spend your time playing? You dang sure better not be teachin' him to do this. That ain't the way I raised him."

Austin heard Catherine take a deep breath and suspected she was trying to control her tongue. So was he. He knew better than to comment on the way Boone had raised Seth. Nothing would be gained by baiting someone who was oblivious to his shortcomings as a parent. "How I spend my time away from the ranch has nothing to do with you."

"Humph." For a second Boone said nothing, and Austin began to hope that he'd leave. As far as he knew, Boone had no reason to be at this end of Main Street, but perhaps Faith had asked him to leave the Silver Spur when he'd become rowdy and he'd wandered aimlessly. The man had probably been looking for a fight.

Boone blinked his bloodshot eyes, then focused them on Catherine. "I heared you was sparkin' the schoolmarm. This here's a mighty strange way to spark a gal. Unless she's as peculiar as you are." Boone seemed pleased by the fact that he'd managed to pronounce "peculiar."

Though Austin wanted nothing more than to plant his fist on Boone's face and make him retract his insinuation, he took a deep breath, then exhaled slowly, forcing the tension out of his spine. A quick look at Catherine told him she understood why he was refusing to spar with Boone and that she approved. A glance at the front of the school confirmed that Hannah was still engrossed in her game of hopscotch. *Thank you, God.*

Boone planted his fists on his hips and took a step toward Austin and Catherine. "I don't reckon I oughta let the boy work for you no more. There's no tellin' what fool notions you're puttin' in his head."

Keeping his voice as calm as if they were discussing the weather and not Boone's son's welfare, Austin said, "It's your decision, but don't forget that the money I give you for Seth's work pays for your time at the Silver Spur."

A loud hiss was Boone's response, but the look in his eye told Austin he wasn't willing to give up the extra income. He started to stagger away, then turned and glared at Austin. "You think you're so high and mighty. Let me tell you, boy, you'll get your comeuppance."

When he was out of earshot, Catherine spoke. "I've never seen Boone like that. He's worse than I feared." She took a shallow breath, as if trying to control her emotions. "Poor Seth. I keep praying that God will soften Boone's heart, but so far those prayers haven't been answered."

"Boone has to be willing to let God in, and he's not." Austin looked at the man who was making his way back to the saloon. "I've met men like him before. They're bullies who believe force and intimidation are the way to accomplish everything." One of those bullies was the reason Austin was in Cimarron Creek. Sherman Enright was simply a more polished version of Boone Dalton.

"How do you handle people like that?"

"There's no reasoning with them." Austin wished he had more answers. "All you can do is refuse to sink to their level."

"And pray."

"Yes, and pray."

"What's bothering you?"

Catherine tried not to sigh. It had been three days since the encounter with Boone in the schoolyard, and though she'd tried to forget how the man had destroyed Austin's newfound peace, she had failed. She hadn't said anything to Grace, since there was nothing she could do to change Boone, but it appeared that she had not succeeded in hiding her emotions.

"I'm confused," she admitted. "I can't make sense of my feelings."

"About Austin?" The older woman was seated in what had become her favorite chair in the parlor, darning a hole she'd found in one of the bedsheets. Unlike Catherine, Grace enjoyed mending.

"How did you know? Did you hear the same rumors Boone Dalton did about Austin courting me?" Since Austin hadn't mentioned that portion of Boone's diatribe when they'd talked about him, Catherine hoped he believed it to be nothing more than the rantings of a man who'd imbibed too heavily. It would be embarrassing—horribly embarrassing—if he thought she

173

was spreading rumors like Mrs. Brooks, who'd tried to convince Lydia and the other customers at Cimarron Sweets that Austin was on the verge of proposing to Anna.

Grace's needle continued to weave in and out, restoring the muslin. "I don't know that they were the same stories, but there's definitely speculation in town that you two are destined to be more than friends now that his daughter is living here. I get questions every time I go out."

"Oh." Why hadn't she considered that? While no one had confronted Catherine with the rumors, it seemed that Grace had not been as fortunate.

"You needn't worry." Grace reached out and patted Catherine's knee. "I don't encourage the gossip, but I'm also not blind. I see the way your eyes sparkle when you speak of Austin, and you do that more often than you realize. That tells me he's an important part of your thoughts."

"He is. I won't deny that I enjoy being with him. Austin is the most intriguing man I've ever met. When I'm with him, I feel more alive than at other times."

Grace nodded slowly. "That sounds like more than friendship to me."

"I don't know." That was the problem. It had been weeks since Catherine had poured out her feelings at Mama's grave. That day, she had asked God for help, and he'd sent Grace. Perhaps it was time to ask Grace the questions she wished she could ask Mama. "I never thought I'd consider marrying a widower." But Grace had, and from everything she'd said, she had been happy with Douglas.

"Why not? Surely it's not because he has a child. I know you care for Hannah as well as Austin."

"I do, but I always wanted to be a man's first love."

Grace nodded. "I'm not surprised. I think that's part of every girl's dream. We keep ourselves pure, wanting that to be our bridal gift, and we dream that our husband will have the same gift for us." She closed her eyes for a second, her expression telling Catherine her thoughts were not peaceful.

"Life doesn't always happen that way," Grace said as she raised her eyelids. "Sometimes unforeseen things happen, and everything is changed in an instant." She paused again, dropping her gaze to the sheet she had been mending. "I never thought I'd marry a man old enough to be my father, but Douglas was right—God brought us together for a reason. I didn't delude myself by thinking that he loved me the way he did Marjorie, but I knew he loved me. What I learned is that there are many kinds of love. They're all different, but one isn't better than another."

Catherine felt Grace's words flow over her like a benediction. "That's what Lydia said. She told me that being a man's last love was more important than being his first. She claimed that what we call first love is often nothing more than infatuation."

"That could be," Grace agreed, "but it wasn't the case for Douglas. His love for Marjorie was deep and abiding. The love he gave me was different, but I never doubted that it was real." As was typical of her, Grace continued speaking without a pause. "I can't make any decisions for you, Catherine, but I urge you not to dismiss the idea of marrying Austin simply because he's a widower. Second love can be wonderful. Don't fear it."

Catherine closed her eyes for a second, enjoying the way the evening breeze swept over her. The day had been warm enough that Grace had opened all the windows to let the house air out, and though she had closed most of them, she'd left this one half open. As the sweet scents of spring soothed her spirits, Catherine nodded. Grace was right. She had been afraid.

"I'm trying not to be afraid, but there are times when I'm confused by what I feel and what I think I ought to feel. I tell myself I shouldn't, but I can't stop thinking about Austin. Even though I know it's silly, I count the hours until I'll see him again, because the times we're together are the best part of my days."

"That sounds like love to me." Grace's expression was somber, her scars more prominent than usual. "How does Austin feel about you? Has he given you any sign that he considers you more than a friend?"

For a second, Catherine regretted that she had initiated the discussion, but then she realized Grace was asking the same questions she'd asked herself. "Not in words, but when he looks at me, the expression in his eyes makes me believe he feels the way I do." The caring glances Austin gave her never failed to warm Catherine's heart. "I feel as if he's waiting for something—maybe the end of my mourning—before he speaks."

Grace rested the mending on her lap and turned her focus on Catherine. "Then what's the problem?"

Though Grace's tone was even, Catherine felt as if she'd been censured. Somehow, she needed to make her understand. "I'm worried, because I sense that Austin is keeping secrets from me. Important ones." Catherine knew he'd started to say something other than "I'm a grown man" when she'd been trying to persuade him to swing and that he was angry with himself for whatever he'd almost revealed.

"Everyone has secrets." Grace folded her hands together, almost as if she were trying to keep them from trembling, as she added, "Sometimes we need to keep things secret to protect ourselves or someone else."

Though it was an interesting theory, Catherine wasn't sure she agreed. "I don't have any secrets."

"Don't you? What about Seth's entering the contest? You're keeping that secret from his father."

"To protect Seth." Catherine nodded as she recognized the validity of Grace's words. Though she hadn't liked the deception, she believed it was necessary.

"Exactly. We all have secrets."

"Including you?"

"Oh yes, indeed. I've been waiting for the right time to tell you mine, and I think this might be it." Grace laid her mending aside. "It's a long story and not a particularly pleasant one. We need a pot of tea and some of Lydia's chocolate creams to get us through it."

That sounded ominous, leaving Catherine more than a little anxious about whatever Grace was going to reveal. Trying to keep her concerns under control, she arranged an assortment of candies on a plate while Grace put water on to boil. Ten minutes later, she led the way back to the parlor.

Grace settled into the same chair as before, taking a sip of tea before she began to speak. "The first day I met you, I knew you were special. You were being kind to a stranger, but it was more than that. I felt as if you were a kindred spirit, that you would listen and not judge."

Catherine nodded. She felt the same way about Grace. That was why she had finally shared her feelings for Austin with her.

Grace took another sip of tea. Though words normally flowed from her, today the stream seemed to have turned into a trickle. "From the beginning, I didn't want there to be any secrets between us. I knew my secrets were a burden and that they'd be lighter if I could share them. I wanted to confide in you, but I had to be certain I could trust you." She paused for a second, waiting for Catherine's nod before she continued. "No one else can know what I'm about to tell you."

"I won't say anything." Catherine could not imagine what secrets Grace was holding. Travis's investigation had revealed that she was exactly who she claimed to be: a woman named Grace Brown who'd worked for Douglas and Marjorie Sims, then married Douglas when Marjorie died.

Grace pressed her lips together as if unwilling to let the

words escape. Then she gave a brisk nod. "There's no pretty way to say this, so I'll be blunt. The last twenty years of my life have been a lie."

Catherine felt the blood drain from her face. If she'd had a hundred guesses, she would not have guessed that Grace would say such a thing. "I don't understand."

"You will." Grace took another sip of tea, then set the cup aside. Fixing her gaze on Catherine, she said, "My maiden name was not Grace Brown. It was Joan Henderson."

"J-Joan Henderson." Though Catherine never stuttered, the shock of Grace's revelation was so great that she could barely force the words out. "Aunt Bertha's daughter?"

If it was true, it explained so much. No wonder both Catherine and Lydia had thought there was something familiar about her. This woman was part of Cimarron Creek's founding families, just as Catherine was. No wonder she had paused for what seemed like a long time in front of Lydia's house the day Catherine had shown her around town. The home Lydia and Travis now shared had been where Grace had grown up. No wonder her conversations tended to be lengthy. She'd learned that from her mother.

Grace nodded. "I wasn't sure whether you had heard the story or even if you knew my name. My parents tried to hush it up, but the ugly truth is that a man attacked me when I was walking home from my cousins' house." Though she did not elaborate, Catherine knew what that attack had entailed. Lydia had told her of the aftermath.

"When I discovered I was going to have a child, my father accused me of encouraging the man. He wouldn't believe I didn't even know who he was, that he dragged me into the shadows, and that I never saw his face. The man only spoke in whispers, so there was no way of identifying him. All I knew was that he had a scar on the back of his neck. I felt that when I was struggling to get away."

Catherine tried not to shudder at the horror Grace's words evoked. When Lydia had told her that Joan had found herself with child, she had hoped that Joan had not been forced. That had not been the case. *"Sometimes unforeseen things happen, and everything is changed in an instant."* When Grace had spoken those words, she'd been speaking of herself.

"I don't know what to say."

Grace's green eyes were filled with remembered pain. "There's nothing you can say. Nothing anyone can say. Fortunately, Mother believed me when I told her I had done nothing to encourage the attack, but she agreed with Father that the Henderson name could not be besmirched by a child born out of wedlock. They sent me to live with Mother's cousins in Ladreville until the baby was born. The plan was that I would return to Cimarron Creek after the adoption."

"But you didn't."

Grace laid her hand on her cheek. "Even before the smallpox gave me real scars, I felt as if I were scarred inside. I couldn't face my parents again. All the time I was in Ladreville, I kept remembering my father's face. Oh, Catherine, he was so angry that I believed he would never forgive me, and I knew Mother wouldn't stand up to him."

She took a shallow breath. "Looking back, I realize that I was foolish, but I was little more than a child, and I wanted a life where I wouldn't feel ashamed of what had happened to me. That's why I ran away in the middle of the night. I walked for a whole day before I accepted a ride with a farmer and his wife who were headed for San Antonio. Once I arrived, I claimed my name was Grace Brown and that I was an orphan."

She picked up her teacup with hands that had started to tremble. "There were times when I wanted nothing more than to come back here, but then I'd remember Father's anger, and I'd rip up the letter I started to write to my parents." Grace took a sip of her tea before laying the cup back on its saucer. "If I could change one thing in my life, it would be that I didn't contact them, but now it's too late."

Tears filled her eyes as she looked at Catherine. "Though I didn't deserve it, God was good to me and brought Douglas and Marjorie into my life. They loved me. They trusted me. They never knew I was living a lie, but when Douglas died, I knew it was time to make peace with my parents."

"Those were the graves you were looking for in the cemetery." Though her heart ached at the pain Grace had endured, Catherine managed to speak. So much made sense now.

Grace nodded. "When I walked by the house I used to call home and saw a young couple leaving, I realized they lived there. I didn't know who they were, but I did know that if there were strangers in my parents' home, it must mean Mother and Father had died and I was too late. I can't begin to tell you how much it hurt to know that I would never have the chance to tell them I loved them and to learn whether they still loved me."

Reaching forward, Catherine took one of Grace's hands between both of hers, hoping to comfort her with both the gesture and the words she was about to utter. She couldn't undo the pain—no one could—but perhaps she could help Grace find peace.

"Your mother loved you and never gave up hope of being reunited with you. She hired Pinkertons right after you fled Ladreville, but they couldn't find any trace of you. Last fall, she and Lydia and Travis went to Ladreville to see if they could discover any clues to where you'd gone. Lydia can tell you more about the trip."

Grace's eyes glistened with unshed tears as she shook her head. "No. You can't tell her. No one can know. I came back to Cimarron Creek to make things right with my family. I was ready to be Joan Henderson again, but when I realized Mother and Father had died, I knew Joan had too. I'm Grace Sims now, and I'll be Grace until the day I die."

"Are you certain? You have aunts and uncles and cousins galore here." Catherine thought back to the day when Grace had claimed she and Catherine had a right to claim distant kinship. "We're cousins, aren't we?"

"You and Joan would be cousins. I'd rather think of you as my adopted sister."

Though her head was still reeling from Grace's revelations, Catherine managed a smile. "That's how I think of you too."

"I've given it a lot of thought," Grace continued, "and I've decided to put my life as Joan behind me. I'd give almost anything if I could undo the day I agreed to give my baby away, but I know that's not possible. Now I'm praying that God will continue to be good to me and that one day he'll lead me to her so I can tell my daughter I love her. In the meantime, I'm grateful to be here with you. It feels like home."

"It *is* your home. You're the sister I always wanted."

And sisters helped sisters. Catherine wished with all her heart that Aunt Bertha had lived long enough to be reunited with her daughter. That hadn't happened, but surely there was a way to help Grace, the woman who'd become Catherine's sister of the heart, find her daughter. There had to be.

17

I'm so glad you came in," Lydia said as Catherine entered Cimarron Sweets, seeking a few minutes alone with her friend. She was still reeling from the revelation that Grace Sims was actually Joan Henderson, Aunt Bertha's long-lost daughter and the woman Lydia and Travis had tried to find last fall. Though Catherine longed to tell Lydia what she'd learned, she could not, for Grace had been as adamant about keeping her real identity secret as she was about hiding her scars.

The two, Catherine suspected, were related. While she did not doubt that Grace worried that her scars would alarm some people, Catherine now believed that the heavy veil was a way for Grace to keep from being recognized. Though it was possible that the attacker had died or moved away in the last twenty years, it was equally possible that he still lived in Cimarron Creek. Catherine couldn't imagine what Grace would do if she came face-to-face with the man who'd fathered her child.

The attack was not the reason Catherine was here. Grace's daughter was. Ever since she'd heard the story, Catherine had been searching for a way to help Grace. While she could have asked Grace for the information she sought, she didn't want to raise her friend's hopes only to have them dashed. The woman had already endured enough disappointment.

Lydia straightened a nonexistent wrinkle in her apron, smiling as her hand curved over her slightly rounded abdomen. "I hope you can stay more than a minute, because I need you to tell me whether this fudge is good enough for the church social."

And Catherine needed to get some information from Lydia without appearing to pry. When she'd settled onto one of the chairs reserved for guests, Lydia handed her a plate with two pieces of fudge, then returned to the small kitchen.

"I don't need to taste this to tell you it'll be perfect." The store was small enough that Catherine did not have to shout to be heard in the back room. "Everything you make is delicious."

Lydia shook her head as she emerged with two cups and a teapot on a tray. "You're biased. Tell me the truth, Catherine," she said as she took her place at the small table where customers sampled her concoctions. "This is my first social, and I want my contribution to be good." She fixed her gaze on Catherine, relaxing only when Catherine popped the smaller piece of fudge into her mouth.

"Just as I predicted, it's delicious," Catherine announced after she'd savored the bite. "And don't forget that you're not the only one bringing food. There will be a dozen cakes and at least as many pies, not to mention cookies. You don't need to feed all of Cimarron Creek."

When Lydia looked dubious, Catherine continued. "The point of the social is to encourage fellowship. It's not like Founders' Day with all those speeches. This is just an evening for us all to spend together."

"With dancing and singing and food."

"Exactly. What does Travis say about the dancing?" Lydia's apron was no longer able to hide the thickening of her waist, and while the town's midwife had decreed that she was perfectly healthy, Travis had begun to worry about every ache, pain, or even slight twinge that his wife experienced.

"He's grudgingly admitted that if Mrs. Steele says it's all right, we can dance, but he'd prefer that I spent the evening on the sidelines with you." Lydia raised an eyebrow. "Or have you changed your mind about that?"

Catherine shook her head. "As the town's teacher, I need to attend the social, but I don't plan to dance. I want to honor my mother's memory, and going a year without dancing is one way to do that." So too was refusing to think about marriage, but that wasn't something Catherine wanted to discuss today. "Tell me about the baby."

Her eyes sparkling, Lydia patted her stomach. "The little one has been dancing inside me. Oh, Catherine, I can't begin to tell you how wonderful it is. Travis and I are so excited about the thought of having a child. We can't wait to see whether it's a girl or a boy and then watch that tiny infant grow up." Lydia's smile faded. "I can't imagine how any woman could give up her baby."

It was the opening Catherine had sought. "Were you thinking about Aunt Bertha's daughter?"

Lydia took a sip of tea and nodded. "Yes. I can't explain it, but I keep thinking about Joan and wondering what happened to her. Aunt Bertha was certain Ruth and Sterling would have an answer for her, but they didn't."

"Those were Aunt Bertha's cousins in Ladreville, weren't they? The ones you went to visit?" Catherine wanted to be certain.

"Yes. Sterling—I guess I should call him Pastor Russell—was Aunt Bertha's cousin. Ruth's his wife. They're both wonderful people, and they tried their best to help us, even put us in contact with the sheriff and the midwife. It wasn't their fault that Joan left no clues."

Though Lydia's expression reflected the disappointment of that trip, Catherine was not disappointed. Instead, she was exulting over the fact that she had gotten the names she needed so easily.

"Let's talk about happier things," Lydia said as she refilled their cups. "What are you planning to wear to the social?"

They discussed clothing for a few minutes before Catherine announced that she had to return home. There she found Hannah helping Grace cook dinner. For everyone else, it was an ordinary evening, but Catherine found herself counting the minutes until Grace would retire for the night. Once she did, Catherine moved to the desk that occupied a corner of the parlor and pulled out her stationery.

"Dear Pastor and Mrs. Russell . . ."

They might not have learned anything more about Grace's daughter since Aunt Bertha's visit, but if they had, Catherine wanted to find out. She signed the brief missive, sealed it, then redoubled her prayers for Grace.

His singing was bad enough to make the horse's ears twitch, but Austin didn't care. He needed a way to express his newfound joy, and singing was the only way he knew. Besides, there was no one to hear him but his horse, and Dusty would tell no tales.

In just a few minutes he'd be in town, picking up Hannah for the weekend. In the meantime, Austin was rejoicing in the perfect day and all that was right in his life. A large part of that was due to Catherine. The woman was wonderful. She'd changed his life in so many ways, the most obvious of which was Hannah. His daughter was a new girl, a girl who was visibly happy, and that made Austin happy.

Then there was Seth. Though he hadn't expected it, he enjoyed having him around. The boy was a hard worker and definitely gave him a fair day's work, but that wasn't why Austin valued him. It was the boy himself. Seth was intelligent and sensitive. Boone might not recognize it, but his son was a born artist. Though Seth claimed that he wanted to become a rancher, from Austin's view, that would be a waste of a God-given talent, and he planned to do everything he could to steer the boy in a different direction.

The song died on his lips, and Austin blinked at the realization that he had begun to visualize himself and Hannah remaining in Cimarron Creek. He'd started envisioning a future—a long future—right here. What had happened and why? Though Austin could not pinpoint the timing, the reason was easy to find. What had started as a temporary place to hide from Sherman Enright had become a home because of Catherine.

It all came back to her. She was kind and considerate, wise and witty, and she filled his thoughts like no other woman. She'd done so much for him, and what had he given her in return? Not much.

Austin stared into the distance, his mind barely registering the beauty of the rolling hills and the raucous cry of a blue jay. The easy approach would be to buy her a gift. Her cousin Jacob at the mercantile would probably know what she would like. Austin could do that. But a gift wasn't enough. What Catherine had given him was intangible, a gift of her time and caring, and that was invaluable.

Austin wanted to do something similar for her. The problem was, he doubted she'd ask for anything. If Catherine had one flaw, it was that she liked to be self-sufficient. Austin would have to play detective. And if that meant spending more time with her, that was fine. Just fine. More than fine.

He grinned as an idea popped into his mind. He'd start by asking to escort her to the church social tomorrow evening. So what if the town's busybodies would think he was courting her? Let them talk. After all, they just might be right.

Catherine fastened the last button on her cuff, trying to ignore the way her pulse raced at the thought of the evening to come. She'd attended church socials for as long as she could remember, but she'd never taken so much time preparing for one.

Running her fingers down the smooth poplin, she smiled. Though she was glad she'd decided to dispense with mourning clothes, she still wasn't ready to wear her apricot-colored gown. Some members of the congregation, including at least one of her aunts, would find that scandalous. There was no need to invite criticism or gossip, especially since the deep purple dress she'd chosen was equally flattering. Unlike brighter hues, purple was considered an appropriate color for the second stage of mourning.

"He won't be able to keep his eyes off you," Grace said as she entered Catherine's room. "The gown is lovely. Now, let me fix your hair."

When they'd discussed the social, Grace had insisted that Catherine needed a fancier hairstyle than her normal one. "You're a Whitfield," she pointed out, "and you know the Whitfields and Hendersons are supposed to serve as models for everyone else."

It was a refrain both Catherine and Grace had heard so many times when they were growing up that they'd lost count. Their mutual discomfort with the concept of *noblesse oblige* was one of the many things they'd shared with each other in the days since Grace had revealed her kinship. Knowing that they were related had brought Catherine more comfort than she had expected. Though Lydia was still her dearest friend, the fact that she and Grace shared the common bond of having been raised in Cimarron Creek made their relationship special. As Mama had told her often happened, God had answered Catherine's prayers in a way she could not have foreseen. Now she had an almost-sister as well as a dear friend.

She perched on the dressing table stool and watched while Grace wielded the curling iron, creating a series of intricate curls to frame her face. Even Mama, who'd curled Catherine's hair when she was a child, had never made her look like this.

"Oh, Grace, it's beautiful," Catherine said when Grace declared her work done. "I've never had such an elegant hairstyle. It makes me feel different—almost beautiful."

Grace gave her an indulgent smile. "You are beautiful, Catherine. You could dress your hair like this yourself. It's just a matter of practice. You might not want to go to this much trouble on school days, but a girl ought to primp for her beau."

"Austin's not my beau," Catherine protested.

Her friend simply smiled, those green eyes so like Aunt Bertha's filled with amusement. "Let's see if you say that at the end of the evening. My instincts tell me it's going to be a special night for you and the man you claim is not your beau. I can't wait to hear all about it."

Her face flushing at the thoughts Grace's words had triggered, Catherine tried to compose herself. She needed to talk about something—anything—other than what Austin might or might not say or do tonight. "Are you certain you won't come with us?" she asked Grace. "You know you'd be welcome." Though Catherine doubted Grace had changed her mind, she wanted to be certain.

Grace shook her head. "I'm not ready yet. To be honest, I'm not sure I ever will be. Going to church is one thing. I know I'm safe in God's house. Shopping is more difficult, but mostly I encounter other women, so it's not too bad. But being with a group that includes almost every man in Cimarron Creek—especially when it's dark—is more than I can do right now. Just the thought of being out after sunset makes my heart race so much that I'm afraid I'll faint."

"You believe the man who attacked you is still alive and living here." Catherine made it a statement rather than a question.

A nod was Grace's first response. "At the time, something about him seemed old to me, but as I think about it now, I suspect he was only ten or fifteen years my senior, so yes, he could still be here." Grace shook her head again. "Don't think about that tonight. I don't want anything to spoil your evening, but . . ."

She paused, her expression telling Catherine she was weighing her words.

"What is it?"

Grace frowned. "It's just me. I worry about you whenever you go out at night. In my mind, I know you'll be safe tonight because you're with Austin, but my heart doesn't listen, and I still worry." She touched Catherine's shoulder and turned her toward the mirror. "You're especially beautiful this evening. Every man there will see that."

She took a shallow breath, then continued. "Do you know how to protect yourself if someone tries to hurt you?" Without waiting for a response, Grace answered her own question. "Of course you don't, any more than I did. I never told Douglas what had happened to me, but somehow he sensed my fear. He told me there were two things I could do. The first is to raise my knee and hurt a man's privates. If I couldn't do that, he told me to try to gouge out his eyes."

Catherine shuddered at the thought of having to inflict pain, even in self-defense, and yet she recognized the wisdom of the advice. "Thank you."

"God willing, you'll never need to do either of those things, but I'll worry a little less now that I've told you what Douglas said." Though Grace looked as if she wanted to say something more, the knock on the door stopped her. "Are you ready?"

"Yes." Catherine rose and made her way to the front door, opening it to Austin and Hannah.

Hannah's brown eyes, so different from her father's, widened as she stared at Catherine's hair. "You look pretty, Miss Whitfield."

"She's more than pretty, Hannah. She's beautiful."

Wishing she were able to control her blush, Catherine dipped her head slightly, hoping Austin hadn't seen how deeply his words affected her. "You look pretty too, Hannah." She touched the bow that decorated the girl's neatly braided hair. "Is this new?"

Hannah nodded. "Mrs. Sims helped me pick it out. She said it was pretty."

His nose wrinkled with feigned annoyance, Austin turned to his daughter. "What about me? Am I pretty?"

"Silly Papa. Men aren't pretty. They're handsome."

And he was more handsome than ever. Though Catherine had seen Austin's suit each Sunday, tonight she had a heightened awareness of how well it fit him, how the jacket highlighted the breadth of his shoulders, how the impeccably tailored pants emphasized his long, lean legs.

"She's right, Austin. You're not pretty, but you are handsome."

Muffled laughter reminded Catherine that Grace had yet to speak. The veiled woman had been uncharacteristically silent. "Now that that's all settled, I suggest you head for the park. Before you know it, it'll be Hannah's bedtime."

The children's events ended at sunset, and though the children of ranchers and farmers who lived outside town stayed later, sleeping on quilts at one corner of the park while their parents danced and socialized with the rest of the community, Grace had suggested Austin bring Hannah back here and let her remain overnight. She'd return to the ranch with him after church tomorrow.

Hannah's bottom lip protruded as she glared at her father. "You said I could stay up later tonight."

"Later, but not as late as Miss Whitfield and me. Now, no pouting or you won't be allowed to go at all."

Mollified, Hannah grabbed one of his hands and one of Catherine's and began to chatter as they set off for the park. As soon as they arrived, she dropped their hands and scampered off to join her friends.

Austin gave his daughter a fond smile, then turned to Catherine. "I want to thank you again for allowing me to escort you. After what Boone Dalton said, I was afraid it might be awkward for you."

It was the first time Austin had alluded to Boone's diatribe that day on the swing. Though Catherine had hoped that Austin had forgotten, he obviously had not. "I don't like gossip, but I've learned there's nothing I can do to stop it." As a Whitfield, she had lived under public scrutiny her whole life. Gossip, Mama had said, was inevitable. People would undoubtedly notice that she was with Austin and would speculate about what that meant. The truth was, Catherine didn't care, because there was no one she would have preferred as an escort.

Grace might be wrong in calling him her beau, but the way Austin looked at her made Catherine feel beautiful. More than that, it made her feel special. She smiled at Austin, hoping he'd see the thoughts she wasn't ready to put into words, and the smile he gave her in return seemed to say that he did. Tonight was a night to savor, the first time she and Austin had appeared in public together.

They strolled around the park, stopping to chat with Lydia and Travis, who'd been deep in conversation with Opal and her husband. To Catherine's relief, though she saw Rachel and Luke, there was no sign of Nate. While she'd told him numerous times that she was not interested in being courted by him, it was one thing to say that, another to have Nate see her with Austin.

Catherine's relief was short-lived, shattered by her aunt's strident voice. "Ah, there you are, Catherine. Your uncle and I were wondering when you'd arrive." Aunt Mary strode to Catherine's side, the extra fold of flesh at her neck jiggling as she moved. "Warner would have been happy to escort you."

Catherine gave her aunt a perfunctory smile. "Thank you, Aunt Mary, but as you can see, I came with Austin and Hannah. You've met Mr. Goddard, haven't you?"

"I had the honor of being introduced to your aunt and uncle one Sunday." Though Austin's words were polite, the slight twist of his lips made Catherine wonder whether Aunt Mary had shown her acerbic side that day.

With her attention focused on Austin, Catherine did not notice her uncle's approach until he slid his arm around her shoulders and tugged her to him. "You're the prettiest gal here," he announced. "Except for my Mary, of course. I hope you'll save your old uncle a dance."

Feeling as if she had been put on the spot, Catherine shook her head. She didn't want to dance, especially not with the man who was holding her too close. "I hadn't planned to dance. Remember, I'm still in mourning."

"Nonsense, child. No one will look askance if you do." As Aunt Mary spoke, she narrowed her eyes at Uncle Charles, glaring at him until he dropped his arm and took a step away from Catherine. "We all know how you loved Gussie. You don't need to deprive yourself of every pleasure to prove that. Besides, she would have wanted you to enjoy yourself."

Uncle Charles nodded vigorously. "Then it's settled. I claim the first dance."

And so, an hour and a half later, when everyone had feasted on sweets and the children had been put to bed, Catherine found herself being whirled around by her uncle. It wasn't the first time she'd danced with him, so she knew from experience that what he lacked in expertise, he made up for in enthusiasm.

"You need to be careful, Catherine," he said as the dance steps drew them close again. "I don't like the way that Goddard fellow looks at you. There's something about him that rubs me the wrong way."

Before Catherine had a chance to tell him that she liked the way Austin looked at her far better than the way he did, her uncle continued. "I reckon I'd better talk to Travis again about investigating him. I wouldn't want my favorite niece hurt by some shyster."

"He's not a shyster, Uncle Charles. Austin is a good, honest man."

"Then he won't mind Travis looking into his past."

Though they passed the rest of the dance in silence, Catherine's thoughts continued to whirl. Why were Aunt Mary and Uncle Charles so concerned? It wasn't as if their family was without blemish.

When the music died, Catherine returned to the sidelines, grateful to be away from her uncle.

"I thought dancing was supposed to make a girl smile," Austin said as he joined her for his dance.

Catherine tried to smile. She wouldn't tell him what Uncle Charles had said, not wanting the man's plan to put a pall on the evening. Instead, she forced her lips to curve into a rueful smile. "It's hard for a girl to smile when her toes have been trampled more than once."

"Would you rather sit out this dance?"

Catherine nodded. "If you don't mind."

"Not at all." Austin frowned slightly as he looked around the park. "Are your feet up for a short stroll? I wouldn't mind getting away from the crowd for a few minutes."

Though her toes ached, Catherine wouldn't complain, not when Austin was suggesting time alone. They'd need to remain within sight of the crowd, lest tongues begin to wag, but they could go far enough away that their conversation was not overheard.

"That sounds wonderful."

Seconds later, they'd left the park and were walking north on Main Street, Catherine's hand nestled in the crook of Austin's arm. Though they were still close enough to hear the music and the laughter, it was muted, and Catherine felt peace settle over her, a peace that mingled with the excitement of being with Austin.

"Thank you. This is just what I needed," she said as they approached the bridge that marked the north end of the town.

When they reached the center of the span, Austin stopped and gazed down at the water. "I've driven over this bridge dozens of times, but this is the first time I've walked." He gestured toward the slowly moving water. "The creek is beautiful with the stars reflecting in it."

Catherine agreed. It was the perfect evening to be strolling here, and Austin was the perfect companion. Though she wanted to tell him that her heart was beating faster simply from his nearness, that was not something a woman should say, and so she settled on a mundane comment.

"Did you know that it was originally called Muddy Creek? The first Whitfields and Hendersons decided that wasn't an appropriate name, even though it's muddy half the time, so one of them suggested Cimarron. It's been Cimarron Creek ever since."

Though she'd expected Austin to laugh or at least chuckle, he did not. Instead he turned so he was facing her. "You're an incredible woman, Catherine Whitfield." His voice was huskier than she'd ever heard it, the sound sending shivers down her spine.

"Why do you say that?" Somehow, she managed to keep her voice from trembling, when all the while she wondered if he found their closeness as exciting as she did.

"Why? There are a hundred reasons, maybe more. You know so much; you're so good with people; you always put others ahead of yourself."

She wasn't any of those things, and yet the fact that Austin believed them made her want to be that good, that generous, so that she was worthy of his praise.

He paused for a moment, then moved slightly so that only inches separated them. "I've never met anyone like you. I can't explain it. All I know is that I can't stop thinking about you. You're the first thing I think about each morning and the last thing at night."

Catherine knew that feeling—oh, how she knew it—for Austin dominated her thoughts. First thing in the morning, last thing at night, and countless times in between. He was always on her mind. How wonderful it was that he felt the same way about her!

Austin moved again, bringing himself so close that Catherine could feel the warmth of his breath as he spoke. "All I can think about is you and how much I want to do this."

In one fluid motion, he spanned the distance between them, wrapping his arms around her and drawing her to him. Then, slowly, ever so slowly, he lowered his lips to hers.

18

His lips were warm and tender, their gentle touch sending pleasure spiraling through her. Catherine closed her eyes, not wanting anything to distract her from the wonder of her first kiss, for it was indeed wonderful. Mama had told her that the love between a man and woman was one of God's greatest gifts, and with Austin's arms around her, his lips pressed to hers, Catherine knew Mama had not exaggerated.

Afterward she could not have said how long the kiss lasted—seconds, minutes, hours—for time had seemed to stop while she was in Austin's embrace. All Catherine knew was that when he broke away, she felt bereft.

"There's nothing I would like more than to stay here forever," Austin said, his voice husky with emotion, "but I'm afraid people will notice that we're gone. I don't want you subjected to gossip."

And there would be gossip. Catherine knew that. For propriety's sake, they had remained within sight of the park. That meant that anyone who'd been looking this direction would have seen the kiss. Catherine refused to let the thought that there might be new fodder for the grapevine bother her.

"It doesn't matter. I'm glad we came to the bridge. I'm glad . . ." She paused. A lady should not admit how much she enjoyed a man's kiss, at least not until they were married. Catherine knew that, but she also knew that Austin deserved honesty. "I'm glad we kissed," she said firmly.

"So am I."

Though his arms were no longer wrapped around her, Austin extended his hand, enfolding hers in his grip, and they walked slowly back to the park. Catherine's feet may have been planted on the ground, but she felt as if she were soaring. Tonight was a night for firsts: her first kiss, and now her first time walking hand in hand with a man. These were milestones in a woman's life, and she knew she would never forget either, because she'd shared them with Austin.

They spoke little as they returned to the park, and once there they separated, each dancing with other partners until the music ended and the crowd began to dissipate. Somehow Catherine managed to pretend that it was an ordinary church social, but all the while she found herself looking around, hoping to catch a glimpse of Austin. Was this love, this feeling that he was the most important person in the world, that she was complete only when she was with him? Catherine didn't know. All she knew was that her heart beat faster when he approached to walk her home.

They strolled down Main Street, their pace even slower than it had been when they'd had to accommodate Hannah's shorter stride, and once again Austin held her hand in his rather than placing it on the crook of his arm. Catherine welcomed the slower speed. If only this night would never end!

Would he kiss her again? The question reverberated through her brain when they reached her home and walked toward the front door. She hoped he would—oh, how she hoped he would. Their first kiss had been more wonderful than she had dreamed possible. Surely the second would be just as memorable.

As they stood on the front stoop, Austin gave her one of

those smiles that melted her heart, leaving her feeling as if she were the only woman in the world.

"I don't want to say good night," he said softly, "so I won't, although it was a very good night."

He raised his hand and cupped her cheek, his fingers straying to trace the outline of her lips. Catherine closed her eyes for a second, savoring the sensation. When she opened them, she saw Austin smiling.

"Thank you for making my first Cimarron Creek church social special. I'll never forget it." And then her wish came true as Austin punctuated his words with another kiss.

"How was your evening?" Grace asked when Catherine entered the house a minute later.

"Perfect. Simply perfect."

The sermon was longer than usual, causing Hannah and several other parishioners to fidget. Catherine, however, found herself riveted by Pastor Dunn's words. Today he'd chosen the story of the woman who had bled for twelve years but was healed by touching Jesus's robe. Her faith, Jesus had told the unnamed woman, had made her well.

It was a story Catherine had heard dozens of times, but always before the story had ended with the woman's miraculous healing. Today, though the minister spoke of it, he reminded the congregation that before Jesus's ascension, he charged his disciples to continue his work, pointing out that Mark 16:18 specifically mentioned healing the sick as part of that work.

"Each one of us has a God-given talent," Pastor Dunn concluded. "For some, it's raising a family. For others, it's growing crops or ranching. For still others, it's healing. No one talent is better than any other. They're all valuable. That's why God gave them to us. So I charge you to reflect on the talent you've been given and ensure that you're using it to God's glory."

There was a murmur of assent as the congregation absorbed the minister's words. Catherine did not nod. Instead, she bit her lip while questions filled her mind. Was there a reason Pastor Dunn had spoken of Jesus's admonition to heal today? At one point, he had looked directly at her, as if he wanted to be certain she was listening. It almost seemed that he had been prompted to show her that she was wrong to fear doctors.

Catherine continued to gnaw on her lip as she pondered the sermon. Had she been wrong not to trust any doctors? Surely not everyone was like Doc Harrington. The woman in the Bible had been healed by her faith that Jesus could heal her. Faith alone hadn't cured Mama, nor had it restored Grace's skin. Maybe more than faith was needed. Maybe that was why Jesus had commissioned his disciples to go forth and heal the sick. Maybe that was why God had given some of his children the talent of healing.

Catherine felt her shoulders relax as her brain was flooded with new possibilities. It was too late for Mama, but perhaps someone could help Grace. Perhaps there were doctors who specialized in ailments of the skin. Catherine had searched her medical book and found nothing, but she knew the world of medicine was changing. The book had even mentioned how many advances had been made in less than a decade and how many more might happen in only a few years.

She owed it to Grace to continue searching for a way to restore her beauty. When Grace found her daughter—for Catherine refused to stop hoping and praying that that would happen—she needed to be able to embrace her child and talk face-to-face without the worry that her scars would repulse her daughter. There had to be a way to help Grace.

She looked more beautiful than ever this morning, or was it only that he was seeing Catherine with new eyes? Austin settled back in the pew, admitting that he wasn't sure. As he'd returned home last night, he'd wondered if he'd be able to sleep after the kisses they'd shared. His mind kept replaying how wonderful it had felt to hold Catherine close and press his lips to hers and how the scent of her perfume had teased his senses. But the kisses weren't the only things he remembered. He doubted he'd ever forget how good it had felt to walk with her hand clasped in his or how her eyes had sparkled when they'd said good night.

Despite the sweet memories that had whirled through his brain, he'd fallen asleep within minutes of climbing into bed. This morning, he'd wakened smiling and counting the minutes until he'd see her again. He'd planned to take his usual seat in the back of the church, but when he'd arrived, Hannah had insisted they sit with Catherine and Mrs. Sims. So here he was with only Hannah separating him from the woman who filled his thoughts.

When the service began, Austin had pushed thoughts of Catherine aside and gave himself up to worshipping his Lord. The hymns they sang were beautiful; the Scripture readings resonated through him; but it was the sermon that made him grateful he was in this particular church at this particular time, for it touched him more than any message he'd heard Reverend Dunn deliver.

Though Austin had heard numerous sermons about healing, this was the first time a minister had emphasized Jesus's charge to the disciples rather than the miraculous healings he himself had performed. The minister's admonition to use the talents God had given to glorify him resonated deep within Austin. He wasn't a disciple, and he had performed no miracles in Philadelphia, but he knew the surgeries he'd conducted had improved his patients' lives.

When he'd been in Philadelphia, he had believed he was doing God's will, but since he'd moved to Texas, his healing had been limited to cattle. Was God disappointed in him? Was he wrong to have abandoned the calling that had once felt so strong? Austin hated the thought that the answer to both questions was probably yes.

If he'd been asked about the remainder of the service, Austin could not have recounted anything that had occurred, because his mind had continued to whirl with the questions Pastor Dunn's words had triggered. When the congregation began to file out of the church, Austin noticed that Catherine also seemed distracted.

"Is something wrong?" he asked softly. Fortunately, Hannah had pushed past Catherine and was holding Mrs. Sims's hand, leaving Austin standing next to Catherine.

"Why do you ask?" She seemed startled by his question.

"You look like you're worried about something. I hope it's nothing I did." Did she regret the kisses they'd shared? Last night she'd said she had enjoyed them, but perhaps the light of day had made her see them differently.

She shook her head. "It's nothing you've done. I didn't realize it was so obvious, but yes, I am concerned about something."

"Can I help?" Pushing his internal debate aside, Austin wondered if this was the answer to the prayers he'd offered only two days before when he'd sought a way to begin to repay Catherine for all that she'd done for him and Hannah.

Though the church was filled with the sounds of neighbors greeting neighbors, for once no one interrupted Austin's conversation. Perhaps word had spread about that wonderful kiss on the bridge, or perhaps the sight of him sitting with Catherine had discouraged the matchmaking mamas. Regardless of the reason, Austin was grateful he could concentrate on Catherine.

"I don't know." The normally confident Catherine appeared uncertain. "I'm not sure anyone can, but . . ."

When she did not complete the sentence, Austin suspected it was because of her natural reluctance to ask anyone for help. "I'm a good listener," he volunteered. It was a skill he'd learned as he'd trained to be a physician.

He and Catherine had reached the back of the church. When they'd greeted Reverend Dunn and complimented him on his sermon, Austin escorted Catherine to the door. A quick glance outside confirmed that Hannah had remained with Mrs. Sims.

"Why don't we talk under that tree?" He pointed to the largest live oak. "No one will disturb us there, so you can tell me what's bothering you."

When she nodded her assent, he crooked his arm and waited for her to place her hand on it. Though he would have preferred to hold her hand, that seemed inappropriate when they were at church and in full view of the congregation.

"It's Grace," Catherine said when they reached the shelter of the tree. "She didn't want anyone to know, but I suspect Hannah has told you that she wears that heavy veil because her face was scarred by smallpox."

Austin nodded. "Hannah's usually good about keeping secrets, but she told me about Mrs. Sims." He wouldn't tell Catherine that Hannah had divulged the secret because she knew Austin might be able to help the young widow.

"I thought that might be the case. That's one of the reasons I feel comfortable talking to you about her. I also know that I can trust you not to tell anyone else."

"Of course." Confidentiality was another thing Austin had learned at medical school. "What's bothering you about Mrs. Sims?"

"I've gotten used to the scars, but I know that most people would be repulsed by them. That makes life difficult for Grace.

I want to help her, and I wish there were a way to minimize the damage. Today's sermon made me wonder whether there are doctors who specialize in diseases of the skin. If there are, maybe one of them could help her."

As the breeze blew a lock of her hair loose, Catherine tucked it back into her chignon. "My medical books claim that many of the advances originate in Europe. I know it's a long shot, but you're the only person I know who's lived in Europe. I wondered if you'd ever heard of doctors like that."

Though the subject was a serious one, Austin felt a jolt of pleasure. This was the first time Catherine had spoken of physicians as anything other than the devil's spawn.

"I thought you didn't trust doctors." He had to be certain of her feelings before he volunteered anything.

She tipped her head to one side, her eyes filled with something that might have been regret. "It's true that I don't trust Doc Harrington, but what Pastor Dunn said made me realize I shouldn't blame all doctors for one man's failings. Jesus was the Great Physician, and he chose Luke—another doctor—as one of his disciples. It was wrong for me to be biased against all healers just because one did more harm than good."

Thank you, God. Austin took a deep breath, exhaling slowly as he realized that today's sermon was no coincidence. He'd prayed for a way to help Catherine, and he'd been given far more than he'd asked for. Not only had the minister's words opened Catherine's heart, but they'd also reminded Austin of his calling and given him a possible way to use his talent for God's glory.

"There are doctors who can change the shape of a person's face by rebuilding broken noses, jaws, and cheekbones," he told Catherine. When her eyes widened in what appeared to be awe, he continued. "They're called plastic surgeons." And he was one, though it was too soon to tell her.

"A few of them have had good success with severely burned

skin. The technique they used would probably work on smallpox scars." The excitement Austin saw reflecting from Catherine's eyes made him thankful he was able to give her hope.

"That sounds like exactly what Grace needs. Could you help me locate one of those plastic surgeons? I imagine their fees are substantial, but my great-aunt left me a sizeable inheritance. I'm willing to spend it all to help Grace."

That was the Catherine Austin knew—generous beyond all expectations. Though the surgeon he had in mind would not charge a fee, it was too soon to tell her that. He gave another silent prayer of gratitude that she hadn't asked how he knew so much about plastic surgery, because he was not willing to reveal that here.

Austin looked across the yard at Hannah, now happily playing with other girls her age. Though his fears for her safety diminished each day that Sherman Enright or one of his minions did not find them, Austin still worried about the powerful man's reach. Travis had kept his word and had contacted the Philadelphia police each month, but each month the answer had been the same: while no one had seen Enright, his operation continued.

Austin's mind whirled, considering the possibilities. He wouldn't do anything to put Hannah in danger, but there might be a way to help Mrs. Sims without anyone other than Catherine, Hannah, and the patient knowing what had happened.

No one else in Cimarron Creek had seen the scars. Instead, they believed the widow's veil to be a sign of deep mourning. If the surgery was successful, Mrs. Sims would be able to remove the veil, claiming her mourning period had ended. She'd once again have a face she could show to the world, and as a result, she could live the normal life that Catherine wished for her.

Austin said another silent prayer of thanksgiving. Because of the talent he'd been given, he had a chance to help this woman reclaim her life.

"Do you think you can help me?" Catherine repeated her question.

There was only one answer. "I can."

19

Catherine couldn't quite identify Austin's expression. It held hesitation, but something else was mingled with it, something that might be excitement. She was excited—no question about that. The thought that Austin might be able to direct her to a plastic surgeon filled her with eager anticipation.

"You really think you could help me?" If so, it was an answer to many, many prayers.

Austin looked around. Though no one had approached them yet, he was clearly uncomfortable with the number of people who were only a few yards away. "Yes, but there are some things I need to tell you and Mrs. Sims in private."

Catherine understood the need for privacy. Though she'd kept her voice low when speaking of Grace's scars, she had also kept a watchful eye on the other parishioners, prepared to change the subject quickly if anyone approached.

"I wish I could invite you and Hannah to join us for dinner, but you know I always have Sunday dinner with my aunt and uncle. Perhaps supper?"

Austin shook his head. "There's no need for a meal, and this is not something that Hannah should hear. I'll take her back to the ranch. Seth promised to teach her to fish this afternoon."

The corners of Austin's mouth turned up in a wry smile. "I doubt they'll catch anything with the sun so high, but it'll keep her occupied. I'll plan to be back in town by three."

"We'll be waiting." Catherine knew she'd be counting the minutes. She would have done that under any circumstance, but Austin's desire for privacy made her brain whirl with unanswered questions.

Her questions multiplied as Austin took a step closer to her and said, "Please don't tell anyone why I'm coming. You'll understand the reason when you hear what I have to say."

"All right. We'll let the gossips assume you've come courting."

Once again his expression changed, and this time Catherine had no difficulty identifying his emotion. He was apprehensive. Something about courting made Austin wary. There had been a time when she believed he was still grieving for his wife, but Catherine knew that was no longer true. There had been a time when she'd thought he was waiting for her mourning to end, but last night's kisses seemed to disprove that theory. Now, other than the fact that she still believed Austin was harboring secrets, Catherine had no idea why he was wary.

"Three o'clock then," she said as Austin called to Hannah. Within a minute, they had headed home, and Catherine was on her way to Aunt Mary's.

Though she tried to act as if there were nothing unusual about the day, Catherine could hardly concentrate on the dinner conversation. When Uncle Charles repeated his belief that Travis should investigate Austin's background and Aunt Mary seconded him, she wanted to protest, but realized it would have no effect. Fortunately, Travis remained noncommittal, and the subject turned to the upturn in business at Warner's apothecary, leaving Catherine's brain free to worry about what it was Austin was going to tell her this afternoon and what connection that could possibly have to courting her.

Feeling more relieved than normal when the meal ended, Catherine hurried home, making the excuse that she needed to talk to Grace as her reason for not lingering with Lydia.

At last the clock struck three. Seconds later, Catherine heard Austin's knock and ushered him into the house. "You're as punctual as ever."

"I try to be." Though he smiled, the same apprehension she'd seen that morning darkened his eyes. "Did you tell Mrs. Sims why I was coming?"

"Only that you have something to discuss with us." She led Austin to the parlor where Grace was seated, her veil once again covering her face.

When Austin had greeted Grace, he took a seat across from her and leaned forward slightly. "I know you're not comfortable removing your veil, but Catherine told me why you wear it."

Grace shook her head. "Catherine may have told you, but she wasn't the first. Hannah admitted that she'd talked to you. It was almost comical to see how worried she was that I would be angry. Of course, I wasn't, just as I wasn't surprised that she'd told you. It's difficult for a child her age to keep a secret."

"I'm glad you understand." Austin appeared relieved. "Hannah was worried about you. So was Catherine. That's why I'm here. Catherine has been searching for a way to minimize your scarring and asked for my assistance in finding a plastic surgeon with expertise in skin restoration."

Austin tipped his head to the side, reminding Catherine of a bird that was waiting for a response. When Grace said nothing, Austin continued. "I believe I can help you, but I need to see the extent of the damage to be certain."

Catherine felt her eyes widen with surprise. Had she misunderstood? If he was simply going to contact a surgeon, there was no reason for him to examine Grace's face.

"I don't understand."

Austin nodded. "You will." Turning his gaze from Catherine to Grace and then back again to Catherine, he said, "What I'm about to tell you must not be repeated to anyone. I'll explain the reasons, but before I begin, I need your promise of secrecy. Do I have it?"

Catherine felt a frisson of excitement at the realization that her instincts had been accurate. Austin was harboring secrets. Important ones. Though she could not imagine what he'd been hiding that could be connected to helping Grace, she was eager to hear what he had to say.

"Yes, you have my promise," Catherine said without hesitation. "I trust you, Austin." And she did.

He gave her the faintest of smiles before he turned to Grace. "What about you, Mrs. Sims?"

"Of course, I agree. As Catherine knows, I'm no stranger to secrets. I have several of my own. But if we're going to be more than casual acquaintances, I hope you'll call me Grace."

"Certainly, Grace, and I'm Austin. Now, may I see your face?"

There was no hesitation. When Grace raised her veil, Austin rose to stand in front of her, his eyes moving slowly, as if he were cataloging each scar. The intensity of his gaze told Catherine this was a professional examination.

"May I touch you, Grace?" He waited until she nodded, then ran his index finger over her cheeks. When he'd finished, Austin returned to his seat. "The damage is severe, but I've seen worse. I believe it would be possible to significantly improve your skin. There are risks involved, and the recovery will take weeks, but if the surgery is successful—and I believe it would be—you wouldn't have to wear that veil."

Grace fingered the veil but did not lower it. "You speak with authority. How is that possible?" She voiced the question that had been on the tip of Catherine's tongue. Austin spoke as if he had knowledge that only an expert would possess.

Though Grace had asked the question, Austin fixed his gaze on Catherine as he said, "I'm a physician. Before I came to Cimarron Creek, I was one of the few plastic surgeons in Philadelphia."

A doctor. Not just a doctor but a highly trained one. As the image of Doc Harrington and his leeches flitted through Catherine's brain, she dismissed it. Austin was not like Doc Harrington. If he was a doctor, he was a competent, kind one. He would not subject patients to bleeding, purging, and other treatments that did far more harm than good.

She took a deep breath as memories resurfaced. No wonder Austin had been confident he could help Grace. No wonder he'd been able to set Roger's arm with such competence. What he had dismissed as beginner's luck had been nothing of the sort. Speechless at the magnitude of his revelation, Catherine simply nodded, encouraging him to continue.

"I don't want to sound as if I'm boasting, but many in Philadelphia considered me the best. I studied in Paris with two of Europe's most renowned plastic surgeons and developed techniques that were an extension of theirs." Another piece of the puzzle fell into place. That was why he and Geraldine had been in Paris.

"When I returned to America, I became known for my ability to reconstruct faces."

"Then why are you running a ranch in Texas?" Though Catherine had dozens of questions, that was the foremost. It made no sense that a man would abandon a career that brought him satisfaction. Though he hadn't pronounced the words, Austin's expression when he spoke of his work with faces told her he found it gratifying.

He steepled his fingers, the force with which he pressed them together revealing the depth of his emotion.

"I'm here because a powerful man threatened Hannah's

safety if I didn't alter his face. The only thing wrong with the man's face was that it was distinctive. He has a hawk-like nose, high cheekbones, and a very square chin. He wanted me to make him look like one of his underlings, but I refused."

Grace was uncharacteristically silent, perhaps because—like Catherine—she was trying to come to grips with the possibility that the man they knew as a rancher might be able to minimize her scarring.

Catherine fixed her gaze on Austin. "I'm sure you had a good reason for refusing." Didn't professional ethics demand that a physician do no harm? Changing a man's face from memorable to ordinary would be destroying what God had created.

Austin nodded. "I believe I did. The man is a criminal. He extorts small businessmen, threatening them, occasionally torturing them, and arranges for anyone who stands in his way to be killed. The police know what he looks like, so it's only a matter of time before they catch him. That's why he wanted me to make his face unremarkable, so he could move to New York and start up a business there. He insists that it'll take the police longer to find him if he's ordinary looking."

Catherine shuddered at the images Austin's words conjured. "You were right to refuse."

"I want to believe that's true, and I do. My conscience wouldn't let me even consider helping him. The problem is that by refusing, I've hurt innocent people. I used to run a free clinic for Philadelphia's poorest. One of the most rewarding things I did was to repair children's damaged faces. I may not have changed their lives, but I gave them the opportunity to live more normally. I'm sorrier than I can say that I had to abandon them."

"But that awful man threatened Hannah." Grace's voice was filled with compassion. "Your first responsibility was to keep your child safe."

Though Grace was speaking of Austin's daughter, Catherine knew she was also thinking of her own child, wondering as she had so many times whether she had done the right thing by allowing her to be adopted.

Austin's lips tightened. "I don't want to think about what might happen if Enright—that's his name, Sherman Enright—discovers I'm here. The man has no children of his own and, from everything I've heard, takes pleasure in torturing children to make their parents do whatever he wants. I couldn't bear for that to happen to Hannah. That's why I abandoned my life in Philadelphia and became a rancher again."

"Again?"

He nodded. "The story that I came from Oklahoma is true. My parents were ranchers there, but I left that behind when I became a doctor." He looked down at his hands, which now bore the calluses of a true rancher. "I suppose I could have gone back to Europe, but Paris holds too many unhappy memories. Besides, I doubt Enright or any of his men would ever think to look for Dr. Goddard on a ranch."

Dr. Goddard. The man who'd kissed her so tenderly was a doctor. Catherine wasn't certain which surprised her more—the realization that Austin was a physician or the fact that she did not cringe at the idea. The seeds Pastor Dunn had sown in his sermon had done more than take root. They were now full-grown plants, crowding out the weeds of suspicion and distrust.

"I should have realized you were more than a rancher the day you set Roger Henderson's arm. You worked with such assurance."

The corners of Austin's lips curved upward. "I tried not to for two reasons: I didn't want to reveal my past, and you'd made it clear that you distrusted doctors."

Catherine thought back to the times she'd made disparaging remarks about the medical profession and wished she could retract them. It had taken today's sermon to show her the error of her beliefs. "I was wrong about that. I should have known that not everyone was like Doc Harrington."

She let her gaze shift from Austin to Grace. With his infinite wisdom, God had brought them together. "Do you really believe you can help Grace?"

Austin nodded. "I do, but I'll need your help. I can't perform the surgery alone, and we both know that even if I were willing to share my secrets with him, Doc Harrington is not the right person to ask. Are you willing to be my assistant?"

"Of course."

Austin turned to Grace. "Are you willing to let me try? I believe I can make a difference, but I must warn you that there are no guarantees."

Though Catherine had expected immediate agreement, Grace's eyes reflected concern. "I want to say yes. Catherine knows how much I wish I could bare my face, but I don't want to do anything that would put Hannah in jeopardy. I'd never forgive myself if this Enright person learned where you were because of me."

Though he was visibly touched by Grace's concern, Austin shook his head. "I don't see how that can happen. No one needs to know about the surgery. When the healing is complete, you'll stop wearing the veil, saying that your mourning is over." The look he gave Grace was designed to be reassuring. "Neither you nor Catherine will tell anyone I'm a doctor, and no one else has seen your face."

"Except Hannah." Catherine couldn't let anyone forget that. "She's told at least one person."

"That's true," Austin admitted, "but I'm confident that she won't say anything about the surgery. Hannah may be only six, but she's good at keeping secrets. I've taught her never to talk about our life before Cimarron Creek."

Austin sounded so certain that Hannah had not revealed their past that Catherine hesitated for a second, knowing she was going to cause him worry. "She's only a child, Austin. Sometimes children reveal secrets without realizing they're doing it."

"I don't like the way that sounds. What did Hannah say?"

"She mentioned living in a big city and how you made people pretty. At the time, I thought she was inventing a story the way children sometimes do."

Austin's face reflected his concern. "I didn't realize she'd said anything, but I can't undo it. If she told anyone else, I have to hope their reaction was similar to yours."

"It most likely would be," Catherine said, grateful that she could give him some reassurance. "People don't normally take children's stories seriously."

Austin was silent for a moment, absorbing the implications of what Catherine had said. "The truth is, the damage is already done. Even if word somehow gets back to Enright because of what Hannah might have said, performing the surgery won't increase the risk."

He swallowed, then turned to Grace. "Are you willing to take the risk? I am."

She fingered her veil, her expression telling Catherine how much she longed to be able to remove it permanently, but instead of agreeing, she turned the question back to Austin. "Are you certain?"

"I am. From the day I left Philadelphia, I felt as if I were being led. Today's sermon made me realize that God had reasons for bringing me to Cimarron Creek, and one of them is to help you. Let me try."

Grace nodded. "All right."

Tucker took a deep swig of the whiskey. He'd need more than one drink to settle him after what he'd learned.

"Oklahoma. What kind of folks live in Oklahoma?" he asked of no one in particular.

"Okies." The potbellied man seated on the barstool next to him acted as if the answer should have been apparent.

The man on the other side of Potbelly leaned forward, his graying beard dusting the bar as he moved. "I heared they got lotsa cows out there. Big cows with horns longer than any you ever seen."

"Ain't that where them tumbleweeds blow?" Potbelly asked. "I heared they're mighty big too."

Tucker groaned. Great. Just great. Oklahoma sounded like the most godforsaken place on Earth, but that was where he was headed, because that was the place Austin Goddard called home.

He'd poked around, trying to figure out where the man hailed from. No one seemed to know. One man speculated that he'd come from Albany; another said Pittsburgh; still another mentioned Baltimore. Any one of them might have been right, but the cities were all in different directions. Tucker wasn't about to go rushing off on some wild goose chase, especially since that would mean asking Enright for more money. The man didn't need to know that Tucker wasn't already on Goddard's trail. He wouldn't be happy with that news, and an unhappy Sherman Enright wasn't someone Tucker wanted to face.

He needed to be sure before he started chasing the doctor again. That was why he'd broken into the registrar's office at the medical college Goddard had attended. He'd figured they would have records, and they did. There it was, as plain as could be. Austin Goddard's next of kin lived on a ranch outside Tulsa, Oklahoma.

Oklahoma. Land of tumbleweeds and cows. Goddard had better be there. He'd dang well better be there, because if there was one thing on Earth Tucker didn't like, it was cows. And cows with long horns . . . He wouldn't think about them. Not today. Not any day. All he was gonna think about was Enright's face the day he marched Austin Goddard into his office.

"We're finished, Catherine. You can sit down."

She sank onto one of the chairs they'd pushed aside when they'd prepared the dining room for Grace's surgery, her legs suddenly limp, her hands trembling. Somehow she'd kept her hands steady while she'd assisted Austin, but now that the final bandage was wrapped around Grace's head, leaving her looking like one of the mummies whose pictures Catherine had seen in a book, she could not control them.

"Will she be all right?" Her voice was as shaky as her hands.

As if he realized that he might soon have a second patient to treat, Austin strode to the kitchen, returning with a glass of water. "Drink this," he said. "You'll feel better in a few minutes. Your reaction is normal."

Normal was not a word Catherine would have used to describe anything about today.

"Grace's face is in God's hands now," Austin said when Catherine had taken a few sips of water. "You and I've done all we can for right now. Starting tomorrow you need to change the bandages and apply ointment twice a day for a week. After that, you can remove the bandages, but you need to continue the ointment dressings for another week."

"It's a good thing Hannah's not here," Catherine said as she stared at Grace's bandaged face. "She's a sensible child, but this could give her nightmares."

"That's why she's on the ranch." When they'd scheduled the surgery, Austin had declared that Hannah would remain at the ranch for the rest of the school year. Though he'd told Hannah he had a special project for her to work on there, Catherine knew that he didn't want her to see Grace with her face bandaged. It was a wise decision. Grace's scars had been ugly, but the bandages were alarming.

When school had ended this afternoon, Seth had taken Hannah back to the ranch on his horse, and Austin had come to Catherine's house, his medical supplies stashed in a picnic basket. Once inside, he'd begun converting the dining room into an operating room, with Grace lying on the table where Catherine had eaten so many meals.

"I've never read of anything like what you did today," Catherine said, grateful that her hands were no longer shaking.

"The principle has been known for thousands of years." Austin reached for Catherine's hand. Though she'd thought he wanted to hold it, instead he felt for her pulse. It must have satisfied him, because he nodded, then continued his explanation. "The ancient Egyptians used rough stones to remove the top layers of skin. They realized that even though the process was painful, the skin that grew back would be smooth. What I did was something similar."

Catherine closed her eyes for a second, not wanting to relive the memory of the surgery he'd performed. It had seemed almost impossible to believe that something good would come from it, and for an instant she had wondered if this would be as destructive as the purges and bleedings Doc Harrington had inflicted on her mother. But, she'd reminded herself, this was Austin, a man who'd been trained by the best in the field, a man she trusted.

"The important thing now is to prevent infection and keep Grace out of the sun. New skin is very tender, and you know how strong the Texas sun can be."

"Much stronger than me. I feel as limp as an overcooked noodle."

"I'm not surprised. You were tense all the while you were helping me, and now you can relax." He looked at the empty water glass. "Let me make you a cup of tea. I think we both deserve that and some of Lydia's fudge."

"I can make the tea."

Austin shook his head. "Let me wait on you for a change. Your first surgery is a major event. We need to celebrate." When she started to protest again, Austin laid his hand on hers, and this time it was not to check her pulse. "You did a great job, Catherine." The warmth of his hand on hers comforted her as much as his words. "I couldn't have done it without you."

He entwined his fingers with hers as he said, "I've had assistants before, but never one who learned so quickly. Have you considered becoming a doctor?"

"No." While it was true that she gave her pupils as much medical care as she could, that was simply to keep them away from Doc Harrington. If Cimarron Creek had a competent physician, she would gladly relinquish those responsibilities.

"That's not my dream," she told Austin.

"Then what is your dream?"

A husband and a family of her own. That was what she'd wanted for as long as she could remember, but she wouldn't say that to Austin. While it was true that he'd spoken of courtship, until—unless—it became official, she could not be so bold.

"I've already told you my dream. I want to go to Europe."

"Alone?" The look that he gave her made Catherine wonder if he wanted to accompany her. She could think of few things as wonderful as a honeymoon in Paris, but hadn't Austin said that he had no desire to return to Europe?

"No. My mother and I had planned to tour the continent together, but she died before we could do that. Lately Grace has had dreams about being in Paris. When she told me about them, I joked that she had borrowed my dream. Now that she'll have a new face—and, yes, Austin, I'm confident that your skill will help her—maybe she'll be my traveling companion. Instead of a borrowed dream, it could be a shared one."

"Yes, of course." There was no doubt about it. Austin sounded disappointed, and that made Catherine's heart sing.

20

"Are you going to marry Miss Whitfield?"

Austin stared at the boy who was grooming his horse. Though he hadn't actually given Patches to Seth, the boy was meticulous in his care of the aging mare, lavishing love on the animal that carried him to and from school. While he wielded the curry comb carefully, it was obvious that Seth's attention was divided between Patches and his question. Normally Seth's questions centered on the ranch. Why was he asking about Catherine and marriage?

Unsure how much he wanted to share with the boy, Austin countered with a question of his own. "Do you think I should?"

"Yes, sir."

Austin couldn't deny how often he thought of courting and then marrying Catherine. Though life with Geraldine had left him wary, he now knew that Catherine was not like his wife. She was stronger, both physically and emotionally. More than that, she was the woman Austin loved in ways he'd never loved Geraldine.

In the years since her death, he had reflected on his feelings for his wife and had realized that he'd confused the desire to protect Geraldine with love. What he felt for Catherine was not simply compassion. It was love—a deep and abiding love. But he also wanted to protect her, which was why he needed to be certain Enright was no longer a threat before he married her.

"And why do you think I should marry Miss Whitfield?"

Seth smirked. "Because she's pretty."

She was indeed. "That's not a good enough reason to marry someone." Though Boone should have been the one having this discussion with Seth, Austin doubted the man said much to his son other than issuing orders. "Marriage should be based on more than outer appearances."

As he stroked Patches's head, Seth said, "Pa told me a gal needs to be a looker."

That sounded like something Boone would say. "Was your mother pretty?"

Seth shrugged. "I guess. I don't remember much about her. Sometimes I think I just dreamed her. Pa said we were better off without her, but I don't believe that. Everybody needs a ma. That's why I think you should marry Miss Whitfield—so Hannah can have a ma."

It was the longest speech Austin had heard Seth make, and it gave him pause. "Did Hannah say she wanted Miss Whitfield to be her mother?"

Seth nodded. "She misses living with her."

And she hadn't said a word to Austin. He had believed she was content being back on the ranch and working with Mrs. Moore to decorate a picnic basket as a gift for Catherine, but he'd been mistaken. Was he as poor a father as Boone? The thought was appalling.

⁂

Another day without mail. Catherine told herself not to be concerned. There were many reasons why she might not have heard from Sterling and Ruth Russell. Her letter could have been lost. Their reply could have been lost. Or—more likely—they'd been too busy to answer. She needed to be patient, but right now she needed the company of a friend.

"Did you come for a piece of fudge or a chocolate cream?" Lydia asked as Catherine entered the confectionary.

"I was thinking about one of each."

Lydia gave her a sympathetic look, then wrapped her arm around Catherine's waist in a quick hug before she headed for the back room. "Sounds like you've been having a bad day. I thought that might be the case with Hannah gone and Mrs. Sims ill."

Since Grace would not be able to attend church for at least two weeks, she and Catherine had decided to spread the story that she was recuperating as a reason for her absence. It was not a lie.

"Grace is doing better, but you're right—I do miss Hannah." Even though she saw her at school, it wasn't the same as having her living with her. Last night, Catherine had gone into what she now thought of as Hannah's room and had played the music box. The lilting melody that had once evoked bittersweet memories of her mother now reminded her of Hannah's almost miraculous change from a silent child to one with a zest for life.

She had been right to share the music box with Hannah. That thought was followed by the memory of Seth's request for her to bring her father's books to school. At the time, she'd done nothing, but now Catherine wondered if he was right. Perhaps something good would come of sharing them with her pupils. She pursed her lips, then nodded. She'd take them one day next week. Feeling a sense of peace over her decision, Catherine smiled as her friend emerged from the back of the shop.

When Lydia had placed a tray laden with a teapot and two cups as well as a selection of candies on the table, she motioned to Catherine to take a seat. "Hannah's going to be one very happy little girl when you and Austin marry."

"Lydia!" Catherine practically shouted her friend's name. "We haven't even talked about marriage."

"You will." Lydia's smile was almost a smirk. "And Hannah won't be the only one who's happy. Rachel Henderson keeps talking about that cousin of hers who wants to teach here."

Catherine pretended to be annoyed. "So Austin and I should marry to make Hannah and Rachel happy. Is that what you're saying? What about us?"

Lydia's eyes sparkled with mirth. "You'll be the happiest ones of all."

Catherine couldn't disagree.

Austin watched his daughter. There was no doubt about it. The closer they came to the church, the more animated she became, and when she spotted Catherine walking toward the front door, she leaned over the wagon's side and called to her.

"Miss Whitfield! Miss Whitfield! Can I sit with you?"

Catherine turned, her smile almost as jubilant as Hannah's, making Austin hope she was as happy to see him as she was his daughter. Though the ever-proper Catherine did not shout a reply, she nodded and waited at the entrance until he and Hannah joined her.

"Oh, Miss Whitfield, I'm so glad to see you!" Hannah grasped Catherine's hand between both of hers and grinned when Catherine bent down to give her a quick hug. For a moment Austin wished he were Hannah's age. Of course, Catherine couldn't hug a grown man in such a public place. It wouldn't be proper.

"How is Mrs. Sims?" he asked when he'd greeted Catherine. Though he now thought of his patient as Grace, he would not refer to her so casually when he might be overheard.

"I can see improvement each day," Catherine told him. "The change is quite remarkable." As they'd agreed, their comments were circumspect. They could be discussing nothing more than a recovery from the grippe, but Austin knew the truth: his surgery had been successful. His heart overflowing with gratitude, he said a silent prayer of thanksgiving to the One who'd given him the ability to heal.

"Can I come visit her?" Hannah asked as they walked down the aisle toward Catherine's pew. "I miss her."

Catherine shook her head. "Not yet. She can't have any visitors until the healing is complete."

"Oh." Hannah tipped her head to one side as if considering a new approach. "Then can you come visit us? We have baby chicks, and Papa let me hold one 'cuz I was very careful. They're soft."

"I'm sure Mrs. Moore has more than enough food if you'd like to join us for dinner." And Austin would be more than happy for the opportunity to spend the afternoon with Catherine. "You could ride back with us. I know you normally have Sunday dinner with your aunt and uncle, but perhaps they'd excuse you today."

Catherine slid into the pew, waiting until Hannah and Austin were seated before she said, "I told them I need to eat with Grace today, but perhaps I could come out later."

Austin was certain Hannah's squeal of delight could be heard at the back of the church. "Perfect," he said. "I'll have my two favorite girls together." And if the day ended the way he intended, both of them would get good night kisses.

"You brought them!"

Catherine couldn't help smiling at Seth's enthusiasm when he saw the books in her arms. Once she'd made the decision, she had sought the perfect day to implement it. Today was that day. When the class had seemed more distracted than normal, she'd promised them that if they finished all their assignments before noon, she would read them a new story after the lunch-time recess. The ploy had been successful, and they'd worked more diligently than ever to win their reward.

"I promised you we'd see," she said, remembering Seth's skepticism the day she'd told him that.

"I know you did. It's just . . ." When he didn't complete the sentence, Catherine suspected it was because he'd been about to say that he wasn't used to adults keeping their promises.

Though she'd seen no signs of Boone using his fists on Seth recently, there was no doubt that he was not a good father, and that made Catherine's heart ache. As much as she'd hated having no father, she had had a devoted mother, and she was confident that had Papa survived the war, he would have been a tender parent. Poor Seth had no mother and a far from loving father. The least she could do was make his time at school as pleasant as possible.

"This was Seth's idea," Catherine told the class five minutes later, "so he's going to have the privilege of choosing the first story." She held up the books. "Which one would you like?"

To her surprise, Seth did not select one. Instead, he gave the class a brief description of the three books and let them vote. Wouldn't Austin be proud when he heard how mature the boy had become?

"Are you certain you're ready?" Two weeks had passed since Grace's surgery, and throughout that time, Catherine had in-sisted that Grace not look in a mirror. She had covered the one that hung over the dressing table in what had been Mama's room and had even removed Grace's small handheld mirror from the bureau. But today Grace was adamant.

"I can feel the difference," she insisted. "I want to see it."

And so Catherine removed the sheet that had shrouded the mirror. Austin had advised her to keep Grace from seeing her reflection for at least ten days, lest the scabs alarm her, but that time had passed.

Grace stared into the mirror, her eyes widening in astonishment. "I didn't think it was possible." Her fingers stroked the skin covering her cheek bones. "I look almost like I used to."

Tears filled Grace's eyes. "The day I arrived back here and discovered that both of my parents had died, I was angry with myself for not having come sooner. I was even angry with God." Grace brushed the tears aside. "I know it's wrong, but I blamed him for not urging me to come home sooner. Now I know that the time I came was right. I won't say it was perfect. I still don't know why God didn't let me see my mother again, and I probably won't understand that this side of heaven, but I do know that if I'd come for a visit a year ago, Austin would not have been here, and I would have had to wear a veil for the rest of my life."

"The change is remarkable, isn't it?" Each day as she had cleansed and dressed Grace's face, Catherine had marveled at the way the previously pocked skin had responded to Austin's treatment. For the first time in her life, she had witnessed a doctor healing rather than hurting his patient.

Grace continued to stare at the mirror, almost as if she could not believe what she saw. "God has been good to me. He's answered what I thought was a selfish prayer. Now I pray that he'll answer two more."

"Finding your daughter is one of them." That had to be the thing Grace wanted most.

"Yes. The other is keeping that horrible Sherman Enright from finding Austin and Hannah."

Those were Catherine's prayers too.

"Oh, Catherine, I don't know what I'm going to do . . ." Lydia stopped abruptly. She'd entered the kitchen without knocking, giving neither Catherine nor Grace any time to prepare for a visitor. Her eyes widened, and she gripped the doorframe as she stared at the woman seated at the table, whatever she was about to say clearly forgotten.

"Come in, Lydia." Catherine pulled out a chair. She wasn't surprised by Lydia's shock. This was the first time her friend had seen Grace's face. It had been three and a half weeks since the surgery, and while her skin was still red, the scars were barely visible, revealing Grace's beauty and something else, something that was undoubtedly the cause of Lydia's wide eyes.

"I'm sorry for staring, Mrs. Sims," Lydia said. Despite the offer of the chair, she remained standing in the doorway, almost as if her limbs were frozen. "I know it's rude to stare, but you look like someone I used to know. The resemblance is uncanny. If I didn't know better, I'd say you were a young Bertha Henderson."

Catherine exchanged a look with Grace. They'd both commented on the now-evident resemblance between them, a resemblance that was strong enough that most people would believe them related, though their coloring was different. Still, Grace had hoped everyone would accept her claim that she was a distant relative, not the daughter of one of the town's first generation. Though some might believe that, it wouldn't be as easy to convince Lydia. She might have been in Cimarron Creek only a year, but she had lived with Aunt Bertha and knew her better than most of the townspeople.

Grace nodded briskly. "Sit down, Lydia. A woman in your condition shouldn't be on her feet when she's upset. I wouldn't want you to collapse." She turned to Catherine. "You might want to get Lydia a glass of water." It was only when Lydia sank onto the chair that Grace continued. "I hadn't planned for anyone other than Catherine to know, but it seems you've guessed my secret. There's a good reason you think I look like Bertha: I'm her daughter."

Blood drained from Lydia's face, then rushed back. "You're Joan?" She shook her head as if to clear it. "Of course! It's no wonder I kept telling Travis and Catherine that you seemed familiar. You look just like the portrait your mother showed me."

Tears misted Grace's eyes. "She kept that? I wasn't sure she would. She and Father were so upset when they learned I was going to have a child that I didn't know what they'd do. Father threatened to disown me if I didn't do exactly what he wanted."

Catherine reached over to lay her hand on Grace's. "I think they may have been trying to protect you as much as themselves when they refused to let anyone talk about you."

Lydia nodded, confirming Catherine's supposition. "But your mother never stopped loving you. She kept your clothes for years, hoping you'd return to wear them, and that portrait was one of her most treasured possessions."

Her voice husky with emotion, Grace said, "I wish I'd had a photo of her and Father. As the years passed, my memories faded."

"You only need to gaze at a mirror to see what your mother looked like." Catherine was still in awe of the difference Austin's surgery had made.

"There's a daguerreotype of your parents in the house," Lydia told Grace. "I'll bring it to you today along with your portrait. They're both on the bureau of what used to be your mother's room."

A shadow crossed Lydia's face as she considered the implications of Grace's revelation, and she took a sip of water. As Catherine watched, color fled from her friend's face again. "The house should be yours. The only reason Aunt Bertha left it to me was because she feared you would never return. Now that you're here, Travis and I will move out." She took another sip before continuing. "Travis has been worrying about leaving his cousin's house vacant. We can go there."

Grace shook her head. "I don't want the house. It's right that you and Travis live in it, especially since you're going to have a baby. It's a wonderful house for a child to grow up in."

"But it's your house."

Grace shook her head. "No, it's yours. All I want is to learn more about my mother. Catherine says you were closer to her than anyone in Cimarron Creek."

Lydia kept her eyes fixed on Grace as she appeared to catalog each of her features. "You look so much like her." She smiled before she said, "I don't know where to start. I only knew Aunt Bertha for a few months, but she became one of the most important people in my life. She was kind, loving, and generous. It's thanks to her that I have my store, a beautiful home, and the love of the most wonderful man in the world. I can never repay her for all that she did for me."

As tears filled Grace's eyes, Catherine wondered whether that was the way she remembered her mother or whether the unpleasantness of Grace's final days in Cimarron Creek had colored her memories.

Her smile tinged with sadness, Lydia continued. "The most important thing you need to know is that your mother loved you dearly. It almost broke her heart when she couldn't find a trace of you in Ladreville. To be honest, it almost broke my heart to watch her. She told me that if she could redo any part of her life, it would have been the day she agreed to send you away. She knew she couldn't undo that, but she wanted to see you and beg your forgiveness."

The tears that had been gathering in Grace's eyes began to fall in earnest. She brushed them aside as she said, "I forgave her and Father years ago after my husband's first wife helped me realize that my anger was only hurting me. Marjorie was right. I needed to forgive, and once I did, I felt better. I wish I could have told my parents that." Grace took a shallow breath, then continued. "I wanted to send them a letter. The truth is, I wrote dozens but never mailed them. I was afraid they'd be returned unopened." She shook her head. "I'm such a coward."

Catherine couldn't let her believe that. "You're the least cowardly person I know. You made difficult choices in your life, but they were all because you wanted life to be better for someone else." Though Catherine didn't pronounce the words, she hoped Grace realized she was referring to her decision to give her daughter up for adoption. "That's not cowardly. That's brave."

"I agree." Lydia gave Grace a warm smile. "What I don't understand is why you told us your name was Grace Sims."

"It's a long story." Grace closed her eyes for a second, perhaps remembering all that had happened since the day she left Cimarron Creek. "I've been Grace for so long that being called Joan feels wrong. The girl who was Joan is gone. I'm Grace now."

"I understand, Grace. Believe me, I do, but once you stop wearing the veil outdoors, people will notice the resemblance." It wasn't the first time Catherine had made the argument.

Lydia nodded her agreement. "It is a remarkable resemblance."

But Grace would not be swayed. "Folks already believe I'm a distant relative. I'd like to keep it that way. The only reason I told you the truth, Lydia, is that I want to learn more about my mother."

"I'll tell you everything I know, and I won't tell anyone you're Joan, but . . ."

As if she'd read Lydia's mind, Grace said, "It's all right to tell your husband. Catherine assures me that he's trustworthy."

"He is," Lydia concurred. "And if he knows the truth, he can tell you about your father. Travis was Uncle Jonas's protégé."

"I'd like to hear what he has to say." Grace looked at Catherine, a question in her eyes. "I know this is Catherine's home, but she's told me to do whatever makes me happy. What would make me happy is to spend more time with you and your husband. Will you come for supper tomorrow?"

Lydia nodded and started to rise, but Catherine stopped her. "When you first came inside, you seemed upset. What's wrong?"

Her eyes darkening, Lydia laid a protective hand on her abdomen. "It's Mrs. Steele. She had an apoplectic attack last night, and now she can't move her left arm or leg. What am I going to do, Catherine? I don't want Doc Harrington delivering my baby."

Catherine tried to find something positive to say. "You've got more than three months before the baby is due. Mrs. Steele may recover." Even as she pronounced the words, Catherine knew how unlikely the possibility was. "Maybe it's time for Cimarron Creek to hire a new midwife."

Lydia's smile returned. "I'll talk to Travis about that. He'll have an answer."

And if he didn't, Austin might.

⁂

But Austin did not.

"I wish I could promise that I'd be able to deliver Lydia's baby," he said when Catherine told him what had happened to the midwife. "It's possible that everything with Enright will be settled by then, but I wouldn't want to bank on that. Lydia may have to rely on Dr. Harrington."

Catherine looked at Austin, horrified. "How can you even suggest that? I told you what he did to my mother."

To Catherine's surprise, Austin did not agree with her. "I'm not condoning his techniques, but I also don't think he intended to harm her. I've spoken to him several times, and—"

"You did? You've talked to that man?" Catherine felt outrage rise within her. Though she forced herself to nod civilly when he greeted her, she had never initiated a conversation with the town's physician. "Why did you do that?"

"Because I wanted to learn just how much of a threat he was." Austin's reply was as calm as Catherine's had been angry. "I didn't tell him my background, but I wanted to get to know him. He's not a monster, Catherine. I don't believe he's evil or cruel like Boone Dalton. Doc simply hasn't kept up with the changes in medicine. He's probably perfectly capable of delivering a healthy baby."

Catherine wasn't convinced. "I wouldn't trust him with Lydia."

"Then the town needs to find a new midwife."

That was the only answer that made sense.

21

"The healing is complete," Austin said as he finished his examination of Grace's face. When he'd told Catherine he wanted to check the results of the surgery, she had suggested they meet at her house during the lunch break. The schoolchildren were accustomed to being on their own then, and there'd be enough time for Austin and Catherine to combine a quick meal with the examination.

Austin's smile confirmed his satisfaction with the healing. "In another week or two, you can go outside without your veil."

Grace rose and began to dish out bowls of stew. "It's a big step. I'm not sure I'm ready." Though both Travis and Lydia had added their arguments to Catherine's, Grace was still reluctant.

"Why not? You're beautiful." Austin glanced at the portrait of Grace that had been taken more than twenty years ago. Though she hadn't divulged Grace's secret, Catherine had wanted him to see the daguerreotype so that he could see how successful the surgery had been.

"You look almost as young as you did then," he told his patient.

Though Grace flushed at the compliment, she continued cutting squares of cornbread to accompany the stew. "That's thanks to you and Catherine."

"We're not the ones to thank. It was God who gave you your beauty. All Catherine and I did was help restore it."

"And I'm grateful—more grateful than I can say." She laid the plates on the table, then took her seat. "Let's give thanks for this food and for the many blessings we've received."

When the prayer ended and Austin and Catherine had taken their first bites of the stew, Grace looked up from the cornbread she was buttering. "I was worried, but now I know that coming back to Cimarron Creek was the right decision."

"Back?" Though Austin had a spoonful of stew in his hand, he paused with it halfway to his mouth. "That sounds as if you lived here before." His eyes narrowed slightly as he kept his gaze fixed on Grace. "I'm guessing it's no coincidence you look so much like the Hendersons and Whitfields."

He turned his attention to Catherine, cataloging the resemblance between her and Grace. Though Catherine had hated keeping Grace's true identity secret from him, it was not her secret to reveal. She said a silent prayer of thanksgiving that Grace had chosen to confide in Austin.

"You're right. I'm a Henderson," Grace admitted, "but I left more than twenty years ago. Like the prodigal son, I wasn't sure I'd be welcomed back. Fortunately, being here has been better than I dared hope."

And while her newly restored face was part of that, Catherine knew it wasn't the only factor. She'd seen how Grace blossomed when Lydia and Travis shared stories of her parents. Her spirit was healing as well as her face.

Catherine glanced at the clock as she finished her last bite of cornbread. "I need to get back to school."

"And I promised Mrs. Moore I'd pick up some supplies for her," Austin added.

Grace nodded. "Of course." She started to rise, then frowned. "Oh, Catherine. I'm so sorry. I forgot to stop at the post office this morning."

"That's all right." Catherine knew Grace didn't like to leave the house in the afternoon when more people were out and about. "If I hurry, I can stop there on my way back to school."

"Grace seems happy," Austin said two minutes later as they made their way toward Main Street.

"She is, and so am I. What you were able to do is almost miraculous."

"I told you. I'm only the tool."

Though Catherine appreciated Austin's modesty, she said, "You've been given a marvelous talent. I wish you didn't have to hide it." Just as she wished Grace didn't feel the need to hide her past.

"This is a temporary hiatus. That's what I tell myself."

He held the post office door open so that Catherine could enter. She blinked, trying to accustom her eyes to the relative darkness. "Good afternoon, Cousin Matthew," she said, greeting the man who stood behind the counter. "Do you have any mail for us?"

"Nothing for Austin, but there's something for you. Actually, it's for Seth Dalton." Matthew raised an eyebrow. "I didn't know you were getting his mail."

Mama had once told Catherine that as postmaster, Matthew Henderson was privy to many of the town's secrets, and that what he couldn't surmise from the return addresses on letters and packages, he often embellished with speculation. Though that would probably happen today, Catherine had no intention of satisfying his curiosity. If she had mail for Seth, it must be the results of the contest he had entered. She said a quick prayer that the news was good.

"Here you go." Cousin Matthew handed her a large envelope bearing the name of the magazine. "Looks like he ordered some magazines. Reckon he didn't want Boone to know he was spending money."

Catherine kept her expression noncommittal, though her

heart was singing with happiness. The entry form had said that finalists would receive several copies of the magazine. "Whatever it is, I'll take it to Seth now. Thank you, Cousin. I know we can rely on your discretion."

Matthew nodded. Though he might like to speculate about his customers' business, he would not gossip if someone specifically asked him not to.

"What was that all about?" Austin asked when they were once again outside.

"I encouraged Seth to enter one of his drawings in a contest. This is the answer. Oh, Austin, I hope he won. The boy has so much talent."

"And you don't want him to hide it under a bushel basket."

"Exactly." She clutched the envelope to her chest. "I'm fairly certain he's a finalist, but wouldn't it be wonderful if he won first prize?"

Austin's lips curved into a smile. "There's only one way to know."

Though she normally would have preferred to linger with Austin, Catherine increased her pace. When they reached the schoolyard, the children were still playing outside.

"I'll say good-bye to Hannah, then leave."

Catherine nodded her approval of Austin's plan. She approached one of the groups of boys and laid her hand on Seth's shoulder. "I need to see you. Please come inside."

He followed her into the schoolhouse, his hunched shoulders bearing witness to his apprehension. "What is it, Miss Whitfield?" he asked as soon as they were inside. "Did I do something wrong?"

Though her heart ached at the further evidence that Seth's life was one of criticism rather than praise, Catherine gave him a reassuring smile. "Not at all. I have some mail for you."

As she handed the envelope that she'd been holding at her

side, as hidden by her skirts as possible, to Seth, he stared at it, comprehension sending color to his cheeks. "It's from the magazine. What do you think it says?"

"Open it and find out." Catherine reached into her desk and withdrew a pair of scissors, knowing that while other children would rip the envelope, Seth would not.

He slit one end, his hands trembling the way hers had the day of Grace's surgery, then paused before he withdrew the contents. As Catherine had surmised, the envelope contained half a dozen copies of the magazine as well as a letter.

Seth stared at the letter, not noticing the piece of paper that fluttered to the floor. His eyes scanned the carefully penned words once, then again, as if he couldn't believe what he was reading. Then a grin as wide as the state of Texas creased his face.

"I won! Miss Whitfield, I won!" He held out the letter for her perusal. "That's what this says. Do you believe it? I won!"

He laid all but one of the magazines on the desk before opening the remaining one. "Page eleven. They said to look at page eleven." When he reached the page, his grin broadened. "There it is! It's my drawing!" He held the magazine so Catherine could see the picture.

The picture was beautifully rendered, but what was even more beautiful and what filled her heart with joy was the sight of Seth's happiness. She'd never seen him with such unfettered emotions.

"That's wonderful news," she said, giving his shoulder a brief squeeze. "But don't forget this." Catherine bent down and retrieved the paper that had fallen to the floor. "This is your prize money."

He stared at the bank draft as if he'd never seen one before. In all likelihood, he had not. As Catherine watched, he swallowed deeply, then smiled again. "This is the best thing that's ever happened to me, and it's because of you."

A dead end. Tucker kicked the gravestone, wincing as his foot connected with the large marble slab topped with an equally large angel. Another dead end. He stared into the distance for a moment before giving the stone another kick. The problem was, if his luck didn't change, something else would be dead—him. He'd be as dead as Austin Goddard's family.

Wiping the sweat from his face, he looked around the cemetery and wished he was somewhere—anywhere—else. He'd come all the way to Oklahoma, sure he'd find the doctor or at least someone who knew where he was holed up. Instead, he'd discovered that the Goddard ranch had burned two years after Austin left. His parents were burned to a crisp, or so the owner of the mercantile said.

The man had been eager to share the details. According to him, when the doctor had learned what happened, he hadn't bothered to come back for the funeral. Instead, he'd sent word they were to sell what was left of the ranch and use the money for a gravestone.

The man was a fool, but Tucker already knew that. He should have kept the money instead of wasting it on a monument. His family wouldn't have cared, and he'd have had an extra couple hundred dollars. Most men would have realized that marble monuments were a waste of good money. But Austin Goddard wasn't most men. He'd vanished, and no one knew where he'd gone.

It was another dead end, and this time Tucker had run out of ideas. All he knew was that he couldn't go back to Enright without the doctor.

Tucker gave the cemetery one final look, then strode toward the entrance. Maybe he should follow the doctor's example and disappear. He hadn't told Enright he was coming here. All he'd said was that he had a good lead and was following it.

For the first time since he'd heard about the fire that had ended Austin Goddard's family's life, Tucker felt a surge of hope. No one would look for him out here. Disappearing wasn't a bad idea, not a bad idea at all.

***

Austin pulled out his watch and looked at it for what felt like the hundredth time. Half past eight. Where was the boy? Seth was an early bird, arriving no later than six each morning, but today there'd been no sign of him. Worry sent prickles down Austin's spine. Shaking his head at the futility of worry, he straightened his shoulders. There was only one way to find out why Seth hadn't come to the ranch.

"Kevin, I'm heading over to the Dalton farm to find Seth," Austin told his helper. "I wanted us to check the area by the creek today, but you don't need me for that."

"No, sir." Though Kevin was Austin's senior, he insisted on addressing him formally. "I'll make sure the calves are all right." Last week one had caught its leg in a gopher hole and broken it so badly that Austin had known there was no point in trying to set it. They'd dined on veal for days afterward.

Compelled by an urgency that startled him, Austin saddled Dusty and raced to the farm, covering the distance in half the normal time. As he barreled down the poorly maintained lane, he saw nothing amiss, and for a second he wondered if he'd been mistaken in his worry. There was no one out and about, but that wasn't unusual. Seth had told him his father slept late most mornings when he'd visited the Silver Spur the previous night. Boone was probably trying to sleep off too much whiskey, but that didn't explain Seth's absence.

Austin dismounted and looked around. A cow's plaintive mooing made the hair on the back of his neck stand up. This was no ordinary morning sound. He sprinted toward the small pen outside the barn. Sure enough, there was the Daltons' sole cow, a heifer in obvious need of milking. No wonder the poor critter was bawling.

Austin clenched his teeth at this further evidence that something was wrong. Milking the cow was Seth's job. He would never neglect that.

"Seth!" There was no answer. "Seth!" he called again. This time he heard what sounded like a moan coming from inside the barn. It was so faint that Austin wasn't certain he'd heard it, but he pushed the door open and entered the ramshackle structure, trying not to gasp at the sight of a form lying on the ground. His years of training and his work in Philadelphia's most dangerous neighborhoods had shown Austin the effect of men's brutality, but nothing he had seen had prepared him for this.

"Seth." He recognized the shirt, though the boy's face was so battered as to be virtually unrecognizable. He lay curled in a ball, a mangled mass of flesh where his right hand had once been. The rest of his body appeared to be in little better shape. Rage, deeper and more intense than he had ever experienced, filled Austin with the desire to inflict the same pain on the man who'd done this.

"Seth, can you hear me?" Austin knelt next to the boy who'd been so brutally beaten that he was barely breathing. He was a doctor, a healer. What mattered now was helping his patient, not seeking vengeance.

Seth moaned.

"Who did this?" Though Austin was certain he knew the answer, he needed the confirmation.

"Pa." The word escaped through lips that were twice their normal size.

"He won't ever do that again." Austin wasn't certain how he'd prevent it, but he would find a way.

Austin's hands moved quickly, cataloging the damage the man had done. A few more blows, and he might have killed his son. But, Austin suspected, Boone hadn't wanted Seth to die. His goal had been causing the maximum amount of pain a body could sustain without shutting down. And, it appeared, he'd accomplished that. Though the pain must be excruciating, Seth was still alive. *Thank you, God.*

"I'm going to take you home with me," Austin told Seth. The sooner they were out of here, the better. Though the boy was still alive, his shallow breathing told Austin that Seth's grip on life was tenuous.

Austin rose and glanced at the Daltons' wagon. As dilapidated as the barn itself, the wagon was unlikely to withstand the trip to the ranch. The best answer would be to bring his own wagon and transport Seth in that, but Austin had no intention of leaving the boy unprotected. As painful as it would be, he'd tie Seth onto Dusty and take him home that way.

"I don't want to hurt you," he said as he lifted Seth from the ground and carried him to his horse. Fortunately, before he began to strap him onto Dusty's back, the boy lost consciousness. *Thank you, God.* For the second time in less than a minute, God had answered his prayer.

Austin mounted Dusty and was heading away from the barn when Boone staggered out of the farmhouse. "What's goin' on?" The way the man slurred his words confirmed Austin's assumption that he'd drunk too much whiskey yesterday. "What you doin' with the boy?"

"I'm taking him somewhere where he has a chance of living." It took every ounce of self-control Austin possessed not to leap down from Dusty and pummel Seth's miserable excuse for a father.

Boone shook his head, then frowned, obviously regretting the pain the simple act had caused. "You ain't got no right."

"And you've no right to kill." Austin kept his hands on the reins. Though they were moving slowly to avoid injuring Seth further, each step Dusty took brought the boy closer to safety. "You're lucky I got here when I did. Another hour and the sheriff would have been stringing you up for killing your son."

Boone's shrug said he would have had few regrets. "He had it comin'. A man's gotta teach the whelp a lesson."

Though Austin wished he could teach Boone a lesson, now was not the time. Instead, he asked as casually as he could, "Just what did Seth do that you thought deserved a beating?"

"He made the fellas laugh at me. One of 'em pulled out some magazine. Showed me a drawin'. It had the boy's name on it, plain as could be. Seth Dalton of Cimarron Creek." Boone's eyes narrowed, and he clenched his fists in remembered anger. "I tole the boy he weren't supposed to waste his time drawin'. I tole him what would happen if he did. He ain't gonna be doin' that no more."

Boone took a step toward Austin. "And don't you try blamin' me. You wanna blame someone, look in the mirror. It was your picture the boy drew." He shook his fist at Seth's battered body. "This is your fault."

22

The rich aroma of rising yeast filled the kitchen as Grace began to give the bread its second kneading. Catherine smiled. It was a beautiful Saturday in her favorite month of the year, June. That alone would fill her with happiness, but the icing on the cake, as it were, was the memory of Seth's face when he'd seen his drawing in the magazine. He'd radiated so much happiness that even now, twenty-four hours later, she grinned at the thought of what the boy had accomplished.

She was still smiling when she heard the knock on the front door. Puzzled over who might be calling during what was normally the time when the women of the community either visited the shops or began their supper preparations, she hurried to open the door, then stopped, shocked by what she saw.

"What's wrong, Austin?" She'd never seen such pain and anger on his face. Fear clutched her heart. "Is it Hannah? Did Enright find her?"

Austin shook his head. "She's safe, but . . ."

"Come inside." Though hardly anyone walked this direction, Catherine did not want a casual passerby to witness Austin's distress. Even though he'd said Hannah was safe, something was worrying him.

"I need to see Travis," he said when she closed the door

behind him, "but I want your advice before I approach him." Austin's voice was low and ragged, filled with the pain and anger Catherine had seen in his eyes.

"Austin, you're scaring me. What's wrong?"

"You might want to sit down while I tell you what happened."

"Now you're really scaring me." He sounded as if he expected her to faint over whatever it was he was going to say.

Her heart pounding with anxiety, Catherine led the way into the parlor and took one of the chairs, motioning him to the other so she could watch his face as he spoke.

"It's Seth." Furrows formed between Austin's eyes. "There's no easy way to say this, so I'll be blunt. Boone just about killed him."

Catherine gasped. "What did he do?" She had seen bruises in the past and knew Boone was a violent and vicious man, but never had he come close to killing his son.

"He beat him more severely than I've ever seen a boy beaten and survive. When I found him, he could hardly breathe thanks to three broken ribs." Austin clenched his fists, then took a shallow breath, as if remembering Seth's tortured breathing. "God was definitely looking after Seth, because one of those ribs could have easily punctured a lung. His whole body is a mass of welts and bruises."

Catherine closed her eyes, trying but failing to control her shudders. How could anyone be so brutal? She had thought that Boone was more content now that Austin was paying him for Seth's services. Obviously, she had been wrong. Catherine forced her eyes open.

"And then there's his hand." Austin's frown deepened. "I did what I could, but the bones were so badly crushed that it will take a miracle for them to heal properly. Seth will be lucky if he regains any use of it."

Catherine shuddered. Hands were so sensitive. Even a paper cut hurt more on a finger than it would on any other part of the body. But Seth had suffered far more than a paper cut. He must be in agony. And knowing that he might never again be able to draw . . . Catherine let out another shudder.

"Poor, poor Seth. What I don't understand is why Boone would do something so horrible." Unless he'd been drunk, in which case anything could have triggered his anger. "Had he been drinking?"

"Yes, but that wasn't what caused the anger. It seems he learned about the contest and wasn't happy that his son had defied him and was still drawing. That's why he stomped on Seth's hand, so he wouldn't be able to hold a pencil again."

The impact of Austin's words made Catherine's head reel. The contest. "It's my fault." The pain that swept through her was unlike anything she had ever experienced as guilt mingled with anguish over what Seth had suffered. "It's all my fault." Her voice was as ragged as Austin's as her heart thudded more loudly than a drum. "I wanted Seth to have something good in his life. That's why I encouraged him to draw and why I told him about the contest."

Catherine shuddered again as the images Austin's words had conjured whirled through her mind. "Oh, Austin, I was wrong, so very wrong. My pride made me think I knew what was best for Seth, and now he's paying the price."

Leaning forward, Austin placed his hand on hers in a gesture designed for comfort. Didn't he realize that nothing could comfort her, not when she knew she was the reason for Seth's being battered?

"You're not alone in feeling guilty," Austin said softly. "When I confronted him, Boone told me I was to blame because I encouraged Seth." Austin's eyes darkened. "I believed him at first, and it hurt. But when I was treating Seth's wounds, I realized that only Boone is to blame. He's the one who chose to injure his son."

While that was true, it was little comfort.

"You know this isn't the first time he's hit Seth," Austin continued.

"But it's the worst. Based on what you said, he'll never be able to draw again."

Catherine looked around the parlor, remembering the day of the ice storm and how Seth had retreated to one corner to sketch when he'd grown tired of Hannah's playing the music box. The room had been colder than the kitchen, but he'd insisted he didn't mind. There would be no more days like that, no more sketching for Seth.

"I'm afraid that's true." Austin lifted her hand, perhaps comparing it to Seth's mangled one. "As I said before, it'll take a miracle for him to regain full dexterity in his right hand."

"His right hand?" For the first time since Austin had told her what had transpired at the Dalton farm, Catherine felt a ray of hope.

"Yes."

She closed her eyes and bowed her head. "Thank you, God."

"You're thanking God that Seth's hand was destroyed?" Austin's voice was filled with incredulity.

"No," Catherine said, opening her eyes and fixing her gaze on Austin. "I'm thanking him that Seth's left hand was spared." She looked down at her hands. While the right one was in Austin's clasp, the left rested on her lap. She raised it and turned it palm upward. Five fingers, all intact. Thanks to God, that's what Seth still had.

"Haven't you noticed that he's ambidextrous?" she asked. "I believe he's naturally left-handed, but he told me that Boone would hit him if he ate with his left hand, so he learned to use his right. Seth can do most things with either one, but he writes and draws with his left hand."

"And Boone didn't pay enough attention to his son to know that."

"Apparently not." This was the first positive thing Catherine had seen in Boone's neglectful parenting. "Where is Seth now?"

"At the ranch. That's why I wanted your advice. I don't want Seth to return to the farm, because there's no telling what Boone might do. The next time he might actually kill him." Austin closed his eyes for a second, his pained expression telling Catherine he was reliving the scene he'd found at the farm. "I was hoping Travis could help me and thought you might have an idea of how to approach him, since he's your cousin as well as the town's sheriff."

It was Catherine's turn to give comfort. She entwined her fingers with Austin's as she said, "Don't forget that he's also an attorney. A good one." Catherine tried not to sigh as she recalled the conversation she had had with Travis about Seth and Boone. "I'm not sure there's anything Travis can do, but if there is, I know he'll try. Let me tell Grace what's happened. Then I'll get my hat and gloves and go with you."

"It's no secret that I don't particularly like Boone Dalton and that I trust him even less than I like him," Travis said ten minutes later when he'd heard Austin's story. "The problem is, Boone is Seth's father. Legally, he can discipline his son any way he sees fit."

"Even killing him?" Travis hadn't seen what Austin had, and even if he had, he might not have recognized the severity of Seth's injuries. A layman would have seen the welts and bruises, the bleeding flesh, but as a physician, Austin had been able to identify the even more dangerous internal injuries.

"No, Boone can't kill him, but the fact is, he didn't."

And so Boone was free to continue his brutality. For the first time in his life, Austin understood why some men resorted to vigilante justice.

Before he could respond, Catherine leaned forward, placing her hands on the sheriff's desk. "Isn't there any way to keep Seth away from Boone?"

"Legally, no." Once again, Travis confirmed what Austin had feared. Travis wanted to help, but his hands were tied. That meant it was up to Austin to protect Seth.

"What if I worked out a deal with Boone? From everything I've seen, he only cares about the work Seth does at the farm. What if I sent Kevin Moore to do Seth's chores? Kevin's big enough and old enough that Boone won't be able to intimidate him."

The more Austin considered it, the better he liked the plan. "I could argue that Boone wouldn't have to spend any of that money he prizes so highly to feed or clothe Kevin. He'd be getting totally free labor in exchange for agreeing that Seth can remain on the ranch. If I have to, I'll agree to keep paying him for the work Seth used to do for me, despite the fact that it'll be weeks before he can handle even light chores."

Travis nodded slowly. "That might work. You might be able to convince Boone to relinquish custody. If that happens, I'd be happy to draft the papers."

"Do you think he'll agree?" Catherine posed the question to her cousin.

"Probably not, but it's worth a try."

Catherine steeled herself not to cry. When she and Austin had arranged for her to join him and Hannah for Sunday supper, it was supposed to have been a happy occasion. They had both agreed that it was time to tell Hannah about Grace's surgery so that she would not be surprised when Grace removed her veil. Though Grace had not set a date for that, Catherine suspected it would happen within the next few weeks, and she wanted

Hannah to be prepared. Today was supposed to be a day for rejoicing, not witnessing the result of Boone's brutality.

"Oh, Miss Whitfield, I'm so glad you could come." Hannah's face was wreathed in a smile, and she grasped Catherine's hand as soon as she climbed out of the rented buggy. "You need to see what Seth made. It's a drawing of Papa, and it looks just like him."

The drawing. Catherine's heart clenched at the thought of the pain Seth had endured because of that drawing.

"He won, you know." Hannah sounded as pleased as if she'd been the one whose picture had been awarded first prize. "Come. You need to grad him."

"Grad?" Catherine looked at Austin, who'd been watching his daughter with a bemused expression.

"I think she means congratulate."

Hannah nodded and gave Catherine's hand another tug. "C'mon. Seth's waiting."

He looked as bad as Catherine had feared, his face so bruised and swollen that it was almost unrecognizable, his right hand encased in a cast that extended almost to his elbow. But, despite the pain he must be in, he managed a smile.

"This is the first thing I ever won," he said. And in that instant, Catherine knew she had witnessed another miracle. Somehow, despite everything he had endured, Seth did not regret having entered the contest. The judges had given him something Boone could not destroy.

"I have a secret, Papa. Do you want me to tell it to you?"

Austin smiled at his daughter. With all the secrets she'd had to keep, it was not surprising that she'd invented one of her own. "Are you sure you want to tell me?"

Both he and Catherine had impressed the need for secrecy

on both Hannah and Seth when they had told them about the surgery Austin had performed on Grace. Initially, he hadn't planned to include Seth in the discussion, but Catherine had pointed out that the boy was smart. It was likely he'd realize that Austin had greater knowledge of bodily injuries and how to repair them than an ordinary rancher would, and so Austin had agreed.

To his surprise, neither Hannah nor Seth appeared startled by the fact that Austin had been able to restore Grace's face. Hannah had simply nodded and said, "I knew you could," while Seth had declared that Austin could do anything. He couldn't, of course, and the hero worship in Seth's eyes had made him uncomfortable, but he'd been grateful that the children had accepted the announcement so calmly.

Hannah nodded so briskly that her braids bounced against her shoulders. "It's all right, Papa. I want you to know my secret."

"Then I'd be glad to hear it."

Her face glowing, she climbed onto his lap and whispered into his ear. "I like Seth. I want him to be my brother."

"I'd like that too." Austin hugged his daughter as he thought about all that had happened in the two weeks since Seth's beating. The boy had made a remarkable recovery. His bruises were almost gone, and though he still had trouble taking deep breaths because of the broken ribs and could do little with his right hand in a cast, he'd settled into life on the ranch.

When he'd first regained consciousness and learned that he was going to stay with Austin and Hannah for a while, Seth had volunteered to sleep in the barn, a suggestion that Austin had quickly vetoed. Seth would sleep in the bedroom across from his own. Like Travis, Austin did not trust Boone.

The man had refused to consider relinquishing his rights to Seth, although he made no protest when Austin offered to have

Kevin take over Seth's chores. When he'd left the farm, Austin had felt as if he were part of an uneasy truce. Boone had agreed that Seth could remain on the ranch until he was completely healed, declaring that the boy was of no use without two good hands, but he would make no promises beyond that. Unsure of what Boone would do the next time he drank too much whiskey, Austin was determined to keep Seth as safe as he could, and that meant ensuring that the boy was never alone.

Because he could do none of his normal chores, Seth had volunteered to keep Hannah amused. From Austin's perspective, it was an ideal solution. Not only did he not have to worry about his daughter when he was riding the range, but she'd blossomed under the attention Seth had showered on her. In less than two weeks, Seth had become part of the family.

If only that could be permanent.

"Are you ready?"

Grace nodded as she pinned her veil in place. "I think so. And yet . . ."

Catherine understood her hesitation. Today would be the first time the majority of Cimarron Creek's residents saw Grace's face. After some deliberation, Grace had decided that church was the right place for the unveiling. The plan was for her to wear the heavy veil into the sanctuary as she did each week, but remove it once she and Catherine were in their customary seats in the front of the church.

Though Hannah knew that Grace's scars were gone, Austin had said they would sit in the back of the church, since neither of them could predict Hannah's reaction when she first saw Grace.

If everything went as planned, few would see her face until the service was over, delaying the inevitable questions and speculation and giving Grace a chance to bask in the peace that worship always brought her. All that would change once the benediction was pronounced and the congregation began to file out of the church.

Both Grace and Catherine knew the grapevine would buzz at the sight of the widow without her veil. As Lydia and Travis had pointed out, the familial resemblance was remarkable. Catherine prayed there would be no unpleasantness, but there was no way to know how some of the town's busybodies would react.

That concern was trivial compared to the fear that Grace's rapist would recognize her. If he did, what would he do? Would he flee, or would he feign innocence? Though part of Catherine hoped the man who had attacked Grace was long gone from Cimarron Creek, another part knew that Grace needed to know who had fathered her child.

Grace held out her hands. "Look at me. My hands are trembling like leaves in the wind. I keep telling myself he won't be there, that a man who did what he did wouldn't be enough of a hypocrite to attend church, but I haven't managed to convince myself."

Grasping Grace's hands to still the trembling, Catherine said, "It's possible that he repented and that if he is there and recognizes you, he'll ask for your forgiveness."

"Do you believe that?" The catch in Grace's voice said she did not.

"I'd like to. But even if that doesn't happen, you won't be alone." Besides Catherine, Lydia and Travis would be in the pew with Grace.

Grace managed a weak smile and lowered her veil. "I know. Thank you."

Ten minutes later, they walked down the central aisle of the sanctuary and took seats in their usual pew. Grace gripped Catherine's hand for an instant before releasing it to lift her veil.

The unusual act did not go unnoticed. Catherine heard mur-

murs from several women in the pews behind them and a gasp coming from the pew opposite them. Aunt Mary's eyes were wide with surprise. As Catherine watched, she nudged Uncle Charles. He turned, obviously annoyed, but the annoyance vanished the instant he saw Grace. Blood drained from his face, and though he did not speak the name, Catherine saw his lips form the word *Joan*.

Afterward she could not have said which hymns they sang and what subject Reverend Dunn had chosen for his sermon. Though she tried to focus on the service, Catherine's mind was whirling with the memory of the fear she'd seen in Uncle Charles's eyes. It was so strange. She couldn't imagine why he would look afraid when he saw Joan. Unless . . .

Was it possible that her uncle was Grace's assailant? As memories of the way he'd treated her—the touches, the leers, the overly long hugs—flooded through her, Catherine knew it was not only possible, it was likely.

"There's something we need to do," she told Grace as they filed out of the church. Fortunately, Grace had kept her eyes fixed on the altar when she'd lifted her veil and was unaware of Aunt Mary's and Uncle Charles's reactions. "I hope I'm wrong, but I'm afraid I'm not."

Grace closed her eyes for a second. "You think he's here?" There was no question of who she meant.

"Yes, but we need to be sure." Dodging parishioners who wanted to talk to Grace, Catherine led her toward her aunt and uncle, who were standing with Warner. It wasn't her imagination, Catherine was certain, that Uncle Charles was nervous when he saw them approaching.

"Good morning, ladies." His greeting sounded forced.

Aunt Mary studied Grace's face. Though Catherine knew she had observed the resemblance to other Whitfields, she said only, "I'm glad to see that your mourning is ending, Mrs. Sims.

Will you both be joining us for dinner today? I'm serving roast chicken."

Catherine cared nothing about the menu or her aunt's attempt at friendliness. She needed an answer to her question. Grace had said that the man who attacked her had a scar on the back of his neck. Was that the reason Uncle Charles wore his hair longer than fashionable? There was only one way to find out.

Catherine walked boldly to her uncle's side and raised her hand to brush aside the hair that covered his neck.

Tucker settled back in one of the rocking chairs on the front porch of the boardinghouse that he now called home and looked around. Oklahoma wasn't as bad as he'd feared. Thanks to men with more money than sense when it came to poker, he had no trouble paying for his room. Six days a week he played cards in the saloon. Six days a week his pockets were full. The problem was the seventh day.

There was nothing to do on Sunday. Everything was shut tighter than a miser's purse. No stores, no saloons, nothing to do but go to church, and that was one thing Tucker had no intention of doing. He'd heard enough about fire and brimstone when he was growing up. He didn't need another preacher telling him what would happen if he didn't repent and walk the straight and narrow. He knew what fate awaited him, and it was too late to change. That was why he was stuck here leafing through one of the magazines someone had left in the parlor.

He frowned as he turned a page. There was nothing to interest a man, just a bunch of words and too many advertisements for those patent medicines the ladies seemed to like.

Tucker flipped another page. Figures. The only real picture was a drawing of some rancher tending to a cow. Tucker had no interest in cows, and his only interest in ranchers was in parting them from their earnings. He turned to the next page, then stopped. There was something familiar about that picture, something that tickled his brain. He turned back to it and stared, his heartbeat accelerating at what he saw.

Yes, sirree! He'd found the mother lode right here in the land of cows with long horns. Tucker grinned as he studied the picture again. No doubt about it. That was no ordinary rancher looking at a cow's leg. That was Austin Goddard, the man he had traveled halfway across the country to find. And thanks to some artist named Seth Dalton, Tucker knew exactly where the good doctor was hiding out. Yes, sirree. Lady Luck was with him today.

Gripping the magazine in one hand, he strode down the street, practically running until he reached the telegraph office. "Send this to Philadelphia, Pennsylvania," he directed the man when he'd written out the message. One of Enright's cardinal rules was that someone checked for messages every day. Before he ate breakfast tomorrow morning, Enright would know of Tucker's success. Now all he had to do was find his way to Cimarron Creek, Texas.

23

W hat is going on?" Aunt Mary slapped Catherine's hand as she brushed the hair from Uncle Charles's neck, revealing a curved scar. Knowing how vain he was, Catherine suspected hiding it was the reason he'd always worn his hair longer than fashionable. He hadn't wanted anyone to see that his skin wasn't perfect.

"How dare you be so familiar with my husband?"

Ignoring her aunt, Catherine turned to Grace, who'd shifted her position so that she had a clear view of the older man's neck. "Is this what you remember?"

Her face as pale as Uncle Charles's had been, Grace nodded but said nothing. For once in her life, the woman who delivered almost as many monologues as her mother had was speechless. Catherine's fears had been confirmed. She looked at her aunt, wondering if she had any idea what had just transpired and how many lives would be impacted if the truth were revealed.

"This is not the place to have this discussion," Catherine said firmly. While no one was close enough to overhear them now, that could change, particularly if the conversation became heated. And then there was Grace. As Catherine watched, she fingered her veil, as if she wanted to pull it over her face. Though she left it swept back, the pallor in her cheeks told Catherine she was shocked by the revelation. While Grace had known it was possible—perhaps even probable—that her attacker still lived in Cimarron Creek, Catherine doubted she had expected him to be a part of the family.

"Grace and I are unable to accept your invitation to dinner," Catherine told her aunt. She could not imagine sitting at the same table as Uncle Charles, knowing what she now did. "She and I need some time alone, but we will call on you this afternoon. You may expect us at two."

Aunt Mary bristled. Her lips thinned and her eyes radiated anger as she glared at her niece. "I resent your tone, Catherine. I am not one of your pupils. If you intend to continue like this, you will not be welcome in my home, neither you nor Mrs. Sims."

"Joan." Uncle Charles spoke for the first time, his voice little more than a croak. "She's Joan Henderson, Bertha's daughter."

Grace nodded. "Yes, I am. Or rather, I was. But as Catherine said, she and I need to reflect on what we've learned this morning." Her voice had returned, and so had her determination. She laid her hand on Catherine's arm. "It's time for us to return home."

Though it was not the shortest route, Grace turned onto Oak, clearly wanting to avoid the curious parishioners clustered around the front of the church. Grace's obvious resemblance to the founding families coupled with the heated discussion with Aunt Mary and Uncle Charles was certain to set tongues wagging. Fortunately, no one had any reason to link Austin to Grace's smooth skin. As he had promised, Austin had kept Hannah in the back of the church and had ushered her out as soon as the service was over, lest she inadvertently say something that might trigger speculation. As far as the congregation knew, Grace's face had always been beautiful. That was good. The scene with Aunt Mary and Uncle Charles was not.

Once they were inside the house and had put away their hats

and gloves, Catherine turned to Grace. Though it was time for the midday meal, she suspected Grace had as little appetite as she did. "What do you want to do about Charles?" Catherine couldn't bear to refer to him as "uncle" and admit that they were related, if only by marriage.

Grace sank onto one of the chairs, waiting until Catherine was seated across from her before she spoke. "There's only one thing to do. I need to forgive him."

Though it was the right thing to do, it wasn't Grace's only choice. "Even if you do that, you could still press charges against him. What he did was wrong."

Tears filled Grace's eyes, but her voice was firm as she said, "Nothing good would come from that. If Charles's conscience hasn't punished him, sitting in jail won't make him repent. It would only cause his family pain. Mary and Warner don't deserve that."

Once again Catherine was struck by Grace's kindness. This was the woman who had hesitated over having life-changing surgery because she did not want to endanger Hannah. Now she was worried about her attacker's family. But they weren't the only ones to consider.

"What if he hurts another woman? How would you feel if you let him go unpunished and that happened?"

Though she hadn't intended it, something in Catherine's voice must have betrayed her personal concerns, for Grace laid her hand on Catherine's. "Did he hurt you?"

"Not the way he did you, but there were touches and looks that made me uncomfortable. The only reason I went to Sunday dinner at their house was to support Warner."

Grace was silent for a moment, considering. "You're right. We'll talk to Charles. After I've forgiven him, we'll tell Travis what Charles did. It'll be up to him to decide on the punishment." Once again, Grace was magnanimous.

"I doubt I could be as generous as you and offer forgiveness for something so horrible." Though she knew it was wrong, Catherine still had not forgiven Doc Harrington for his role in her mother's death.

"You might be surprised at how strong you are. Douglas used to tell me that adversity forces us to search deep inside us and that it reveals who we truly are. I've made my decision. Now I hope that I can follow through with it." Grace stared at her hands for a few seconds. "I'm not looking forward to this afternoon, but I am looking forward to it being over."

⁂

"Come in." Aunt Mary's voice was curt, and her customary smile was missing. "Charles is in the parlor. He said this had nothing to do with our son, so Warner is visiting Travis." She led the way to the sitting room and gestured toward the chairs facing the settee where Charles was seated. Catherine noticed that he did not pay them the courtesy of rising when she and Grace entered the room.

"What is this all about, Joan?" Aunt Mary's voice held more than a hint of rancor. "I thought you'd died years ago." Her belligerent tone was only making a difficult situation worse.

Apparently refusing to sink to Aunt Mary's level, Grace kept her voice neutral. "As you can see, I did not die. I left Cimarron Creek because my parents did not want the shame of having an unwed mother for a daughter. They did not want anyone to think that a Henderson was less than perfect."

Charles frowned but remained silent while his wife smirked. "So, you got yourself in trouble," she said, a note of gloating in her voice. Catherine could almost hear her thinking, *How the mighty are fallen.* If this was how family reacted, it was no wonder Aunt Bertha and Uncle Jonas had not wanted their daughter to remain in Cimarron Creek and be subjected to the town's censure.

"What does this have to do with us?" Aunt Mary demanded.

"Grace didn't get herself in trouble, as you put it." Catherine leapt to her friend's defense, not wanting Grace to have to deal with what Catherine suspected would soon become verbal abuse. She had seen the way Aunt Mary had attacked Lydia after Aunt Bertha's death and wanted to spare Grace that pain.

"Grace was raped." Though she had planned to say "attacked," the defiance on her aunt's face made Catherine use the harsher word. She wanted there to be no doubt of exactly what Charles had done. "It was dark and she didn't see the man, but when she was struggling to get away, she felt a curved scar on the back of his neck—a scar like the one your husband has."

Blood rushed to Aunt Mary's face, and she clenched her fists in anger. "You can't be suggesting that Charles would have done such a vile thing. It's preposterous."

"Ask him." While her aunt had raised her voice to little less than a shout, Catherine kept hers low.

"Preposterous!" Aunt Mary repeated the word. "I trust Charles. He would never hurt a young girl. He loves me." She turned to her husband. "Isn't that right, Charles?"

"Of course it is. She's lying." His words were brave, but they held no conviction, and judging from the way Aunt Mary moved closer to the edge of the settee, putting a distance between herself and her husband, she knew it.

"Are you planning to tell Travis of your suspicions?" Aunt Mary glared at Grace, as if daring her to involve the sheriff. Aunt Bertha and Uncle Jonas hadn't been the only ones in the Henderson-Whitfield clan who worried about having the family name besmirched.

"No. There's been enough suffering. I don't want to cause you any pain." Grace kept her gaze fixed on Aunt Mary as she said, "I've forgiven Charles for what he did. The only thing I want is for him to admit to those of us in this room that he was the father of my child."

As Grace turned to look at him, Charles sneered. "You can't be sure. Anyone could have seen you leaving your cousins' house."

He'd convicted himself and he hadn't even realized it. Catherine shook her head. "Grace didn't say where or when the attack took place. Only one other person would have known that."

The blood drained from Aunt Mary's face, leaving her as pale as a ghost. She stared at the man she'd married, horror on her face. "You did it, didn't you? What kind of man are you?"

He lowered his head under the force of her fury. "She was so pretty. All the fellas said that."

Aunt Mary rose and pointed a finger at Grace. "There's your answer, Joan. He admitted it. Are you happy?"

Though she'd flinched at being called Joan, Grace shook her head. "No, I'm not happy, but at least I know the truth."

"And so do I." Aunt Mary took a step away from the settee, as if distancing herself from the man who'd betrayed his marriage vows and dishonored Grace. "The man I loved, the man I thought loved me, was no better than a rutting stallion." She glared down at her husband. "How will I ever be able to hold my head up in this town? First my son, now my husband."

She strode to the small desk in the corner of the room and tugged the drawer open. Before Catherine realized what she intended, her aunt pulled a revolver from the desk. "I hate you, Charles," Aunt Mary said as she aimed the weapon at him. "I hate you."

Catherine jumped to her feet. "Stop it, Aunt Mary. You don't want to do that."

Aunt Mary shook her head. "I do." A single shot punctuated her words.

Catherine stared in horror as her uncle slumped forward, his head landing on the small table between the settee and the chairs.

"Oh, dear God, what have I done?" The older woman slid onto the settee and cradled her husband's head to her bosom. She stared at the lifeless eyes, then began to cry. "He's gone. I loved him, but I killed him." A low keening turned into a wail. "How can I live without him?" She shook her head wildly, her cries intensifying.

As Catherine moved toward her aunt, praying for a way to comfort her, Aunt Mary pressed the gun to her head.

"No!"

It was too late.

"Mrs. Sims is beautiful."

Austin had been expecting comments ever since they'd left the church. He'd seen Hannah's expression when she'd spotted Grace without her veil and had known that the magnitude of the change was more than she had expected. Though Hannah knew about the work he'd done in Philadelphia, this was the first time she had seen the results. Somehow she'd managed to contain her excitement until dinner was over and Seth had gone outside to sketch one of the barn cats.

"You made her beautiful, Papa."

"Yes, I did, but remember that you mustn't tell anyone. Papa is a rancher now, not a doctor. No one must know I used to make people look better." No one except Catherine, Grace, and Seth. Even Travis didn't know that Austin had been a plastic surgeon.

"Not even Mrs. Moore? I like her."

"I know that, Hannah, but it's important—it's very important—that you don't tell anyone."

Though Hannah looked disappointed, her eyes were luminous as she remembered the woman she'd seen in church. "Mrs. Sims is almost as beautiful as Miss Whitfield."

"I agree." No one could be as beautiful as Catherine, but if there were a beauty contest in Cimarron Creek, Grace Sims would win second place.

"Can we visit them today?" Hannah tugged on Austin's shirt. "I miss seeing them."

So did Austin. Admittedly, what he missed most was seeing Catherine. Now that school was out, he had fewer opportunities to spend time with her. They usually talked for a few minutes after church, but today she and Grace had been engrossed in what appeared to be a serious discussion with her aunt and uncle. He hadn't wanted to interrupt, and so he hadn't heard her lilting voice or seen her sweet smile directed at him.

"I miss them too," he told his daughter. "Why don't I ask Mrs. Moore to pack us a picnic supper? You and Seth and I can go into town and invite Miss Whitfield and Mrs. Sims to join us."

"Yay!" Unable to contain her enthusiasm, Hannah jumped up and down. "I love you, Papa."

"And I love you." Though Austin hated to dampen his daughter's high spirits, he needed to add a note of caution. "Don't forget that you can't tell anyone that I operated on Mrs. Sims's face."

"Not even Mrs. Moore?" His daughter was nothing if not persistent.

"Not even Mrs. Moore."

Austin grinned as he crested the hill leading into Cimarron Creek. Like the two children seated in the back of the wagon, he was excited, but his excitement was due to more than the novelty of a picnic. Its cause was twofold: the opportunity to spend time with Catherine and the satisfaction that he'd been able to restore Grace's beauty. Seeing her in church this morning reminded him of how much he missed helping his patients and how, if his prayers were answered, he would be able to spend the rest of his life as a doctor.

As he'd ridden the range, as he'd branded cattle, even as he'd done things as mundane as shaving, he'd thought and prayed about his future. There had been no great revelations, but he'd realized that he didn't have to practice medicine in Philadelphia. He didn't even have to be a plastic surgeon. What mattered was healing others. Humans, not simply cattle. He wanted to be a doctor again, a doctor with Catherine as his wife.

The problem was, it was too soon for both. Until Travis's reports confirmed that Enright no longer had a reason to search for him, Austin could not take the risk of letting the town know that he was a physician. And, no matter how much he loved Catherine and wanted to marry her, he would respect her wishes and wouldn't begin to court her until her year of mourning ended. That wasn't until September, more than two months from now. He might not be courting her, but nothing would stop him from spending time with her. And if they shared another kiss or two, well . . .

Austin's grin widened at the prospect. He'd invite both Catherine and Grace to come to the ranch for supper at least once a week. While being a rancher might not have been his dream, he was proud of what he'd accomplished here. And if it was God's will that he continue to be a rancher, he needed to know whether Catherine would be happy as a rancher's wife.

Slowing the wagon as they entered the town, Austin looked around. It appeared to be a normal Sunday afternoon in Cimarron Creek. Though a few people strolled Main Street, it was mostly deserted. Folks usually spent Sunday afternoons at home or visiting friends, grateful for the day of rest.

As they reached Mesquite Street, Austin prepared to turn right toward Catherine's home, but Hannah's cry stopped him.

"Look, Papa," she said, pointing in the opposite direction. "There's Miss Whitfield and Mrs. Sims. They're with the sheriff and Mrs. Whitfield."

Though he was too far away to hear what was being said, the rigidity of Catherine's posture and Grace's bowed head told Austin something was wrong. And, judging from the fact that they were all standing in front of Mary and Charles Gray's home, that something had to do with Catherine's aunt and uncle.

Austin directed the wagon toward them, addressing Hannah and Seth when he stopped a few yards short of the Grays' home. "You two need to stay in the wagon while I find out what's going on." If the situation was as serious as he feared, he did not want the children exposed to it. He would shelter them by censoring what he told them.

"Catherine," Austin said as he climbed down and approached her. No matter what had happened, his heart still leapt at the sight of the woman he loved.

She broke away from the others and rushed to his side, the lines of strain that etched her face confirming the gravity of the situation. "What are you doing in town?"

"I came to invite you and Grace for a picnic supper. Hannah and Seth wanted to see you again, and so did I, but I'm guessing this isn't a good time."

Catherine closed her eyes for a second, as if trying to blot out painful memories. "No, it's not." She gestured toward her relatives' house. "There's been a tragedy. Mary killed her husband and then herself." Her voice caught as she added, "Grace and I were there."

"Oh, Catherine." Austin had dealt with the aftermath of violent death, but he'd never actually witnessed it. He knew that people sometimes did and said unexpected things while they were recovering from shock. That could be the reason Catherine hadn't referred to Mary Gray as Aunt Mary, but Austin doubted it. He suspected the reason was connected to the discussion she and Grace had been having with her aunt and uncle after church and that that discussion had somehow led to the killings.

It could be coincidence that the deaths occurred the same day that Grace had revealed her face, but Austin did not believe it. Though he wanted to know what had triggered something as seemingly senseless as a murder-suicide, that was of less importance than supporting the woman standing so close to him.

"How can I help?"

She shrugged. "I don't know. I don't think there's anything anyone can do right now." She turned toward the wagon. "I'd better talk to Hannah and Seth."

That was the Catherine he knew and loved, thinking of others before herself. He extended his arm and escorted her to her wagon.

"Thank you both for inviting me and Mrs. Sims for a picnic," she said when they were standing by it. "I wish we could accept, but I need to help Mr. Gray. His parents died this afternoon, and he's all alone."

As if he'd heard her words, Warner Gray emerged from the home he'd shared with his parents. Though his head was held high and his shoulders were straight, even from this distance Austin could see the pallor of his face.

"Did my pa kill them?"

Austin's heart clenched at the worry he heard in Seth's voice, but it was Catherine who responded. "Of course not," she said in her best schoolmarm tone. "Why would you think that?"

"'Cuz he didn't like Mr. Gray. He said he cheated at poker and that's why my pa didn't have any money."

Knowing Boone, Austin suspected that if there was any cheating, it was on Boone's part. Still, he had no trouble picturing the scene when Boone discovered he'd lost yet another game.

"I haven't seen your father in town all day." Catherine reached into the wagon and laid a reassuring hand on Seth's arm.

"That's good," he said.

"It's sad that people died." Hannah spoke for the first time, her little face solemn. "Mamas and papas shouldn't die." She scooted to the edge of the wagon and threw her arms around Catherine. "I miss you, Miss Whitfield."

"I miss you too, Hannah. Maybe we can have our picnic next week."

Her face scrunched into a frown. "The food will spoil."

If the situation hadn't been so serious, Austin might have laughed at Hannah's pragmatism. "Mrs. Moore will make more. You and Seth and I will have our picnic today." He turned to Catherine. "I'll come back this evening, if that's all right with you."

"Yes." Relief washed over her face. "Thank you."

24

It felt like the longest afternoon of her life. Once Catherine had realized there was nothing she could do for her aunt and uncle, she and Grace had hurried to Travis and Lydia's home. As sheriff, Travis needed to know what had happened. Even more importantly, Warner needed to be told what his mother had done.

Poor Warner! Tears filled Catherine's eyes as she thought about her cousin. It had been less than a year since his brother's death, and now this . . . He'd lost his entire family. Like her, he was now an orphan.

"Why?" Warner demanded when she told him, Travis, and Lydia what had happened. "Why would Ma do that?"

Catherine looked at Grace. Though Grace had said she wanted to spare Warner, Catherine had warned her that he wouldn't be put off with platitudes. He wanted the truth. And so when Grace nodded, Catherine told the trio what Charles had done more than twenty years ago, omitting only the fact that Grace had borne a child. Both Lydia and Travis already knew that, but Catherine and Grace had agreed that Warner didn't need to know that he might have a half-sister somewhere.

Though Travis and Lydia had been shocked by the identity of

Grace's rapist, it was Warner's expression that haunted Catherine. She'd seen sorrow, shame, and disillusionment on his face. Unlike Catherine, he no longer had untarnished memories of his parents. He'd weathered the scandal that had followed his brother's death, but this would be more difficult.

"No one else needs to know," Lydia said. "Isn't that right, Travis?"

Before he could respond, Warner shook his head. "They'll speculate."

He was right. "Of course they will," Catherine agreed, "but if we ignore the gossip, it'll die down. It's hard to keep a fire burning without fuel."

Travis was silent for a moment, obviously trying to balance his duty as sheriff with his desire to protect the man who was as close as a brother. "I agree with Catherine that we should do nothing to fan the flames. I suggest our story be that they argued and that the argument got out of control. That's true, and it's no one's business why they argued."

Warner had appeared relieved, although nothing could erase the grief that colored his expression. Realizing there was nothing more they could do here and sensing that Grace was on the verge of collapse, Catherine had urged her to return home. They'd no sooner closed the door behind them than Grace burst into tears.

"None of this would have happened if I hadn't come back," she sobbed. "I thought I was doing the right thing, but look what happened. Because I returned to Cimarron Creek, two people are dead."

Catherine wrapped her arm around Grace's shoulders and led her to a chair in the parlor. Catherine's legs were wobbly from shock, and she suspected Grace's were no stronger. "You didn't kill Mary and Charles," she said, wondering if she should insist Grace drink a glass of water. Austin had claimed that was important for people dealing with shock. "You can't blame yourself, Grace. You were the victim."

"But poor Warner. What will he do now? Even with the story Travis suggested, he'll be subject to gossip." Grace shuddered and gripped the chair arms, as if seeking strength from the inanimate object. "I know how this town is. That's the reason my parents insisted I leave. They didn't want everyone talking about me. That may have been twenty years ago, but I know nothing has changed. You saw how Mary reacted when she learned the reason I left Cimarron Creek. Until she realized Charles was involved, she was ready to visit everyone she knew to spread the news. Warner will be subjected to the gossip for a long, long time."

Catherine did not doubt that Grace was right. She'd seen how stories circulated, and even though no one knew the details, that wouldn't stop them from speculating. Warner would indeed suffer, unless . . .

She took a deep breath, hoping Grace would not be offended by what she was about to suggest. "If you want to help Warner, you could give Cimarron Creek something else to talk about."

Grace brushed the tears from her cheeks. "You mean admitting that I'm Joan?"

"Yes." There was nothing like solving a mystery, particularly one that was more than two decades old. "You don't have to tell them about the baby. You could simply say that you ran away from the cousins in Ladreville and started a new life in San Antonio."

The pain that had clouded Grace's green eyes began to lift. "That would be almost as sensational as the Grays' deaths."

"And it would deflect attention from Warner, especially if you spent some time in Lydia's shop each afternoon. She'll never admit it, but I think she could use more time sitting." Catherine remembered the tall stool Lydia had brought to Cimarron

Sweets last week, claiming it gave her a place to rest when the store was empty.

"You could help by serving customers, leaving her to work behind the counter." Once word spread, the store would be busier than ever. "The women will claim they're there to buy candy, but the real reason is they'll want to learn what they can about you."

Grace was silent for a moment, perhaps considering the magnitude of what Catherine had suggested. Instead of being a veiled woman who spent the minimum amount of time in public, she would be opening herself up for inspection. The women who visited Cimarron Sweets would stare at her face, but—more importantly—they would attempt to discover what she had done during all the years she'd been away.

She took a deep breath, exhaling slowly before she said, "All right. I'll do it for a few days, but then it will be time for me to leave Cimarron Creek."

Her words hit Catherine with the force of a blow. Surely Grace wouldn't leave! "You can't leave."

Grace shook her head. "I can, and I must. I've loved being here with you, but now it's time for me to find my daughter. She may not want me in her life after what I did, but I need to see her once more. I need to know that I made the right decision when I gave her up for adoption."

But what if she hadn't? What if the parents were neglectful or even abusive? How would Grace handle that? Oh, how Catherine wished she had heard back from Aunt Bertha's cousins in Ladreville. They were the only possible link to Grace's daughter.

"Where will you go?"

"I keep dreaming about Paris. Maybe God is sending me a message. Maybe he wants me to go there."

"Do you really believe your daughter is in Paris?" That seemed highly unlikely to Catherine.

"I don't know," Grace admitted. "All I know is that I can't stop thinking about France. I picture myself walking along the Seine and going into Notre Dame."

That had been Catherine's dream for years, but for her it would have been a holiday, not a quest for a loved one.

"Please don't make any hasty decisions." Neither of them was thinking clearly, and the fact that Grace blamed herself intensified the effect of the tragedy.

Grace nodded. "I'll stay until after the Fourth of July. Then we'll see. In the meantime, I want to get out of these clothes. I don't think I can bear looking at them a minute longer."

They'd eaten a light supper, neither of them tasting much. When Grace went to her room, Catherine moved to the porch, waiting for Austin. She wasn't sure what they'd say, what they'd do. All she knew was that she could barely wait to be with him again. Today more than ever before, he represented stability. And in a world that had tipped on its axis, that was more valuable than gold.

When she saw his wagon, Catherine rose and met him halfway down the front walk.

"Would you like to go for a drive?" he asked.

She had suspected he would offer that. Though the thought of even a brief escape from the town was appealing, Catherine felt a need to remain closer to Grace. "I'd rather walk," she said, gesturing toward the west end of Mesquite. "There's a path that leads to the creek. When I was a child, I used to go there to think."

Austin gave her a smile that made her heart beat faster. "It sounds like a good place to talk as well as think."

As he had once before, he took her hand in his. It felt good—so very good—to feel the warmth of his palm on hers. Though the town gossips might have been scandalized by the fact that she had not worn gloves this evening, Catherine was glad she'd forgone them and that Austin had tossed his driving gloves back into the wagon when she'd said she didn't want to go for a ride. The touch of skin on skin reassured her as nothing had done since the moment she'd exposed Charles Gray's scar. For a moment, the ugliness of the day faded, replaced by the pleasure of being with Austin, the man who figured in so many dreams, the man she loved.

They walked in silence until they reached what Catherine had always thought of as her spot. There the meandering creek that had given the town its name took another bend, this time toward the west. Ancient cottonwoods lined the banks, their roots drawing sustenance from the water. A few birds flitted from branch to branch, searching for a roosting spot. For them it was just another day, and the ordinariness of the scene helped calm Catherine.

"Is it time to talk?" Austin asked when she stopped in the shade of one of the cottonwoods. When she nodded, he reached for her other hand, as if he realized she needed the comfort of his grasp. "How are you feeling?"

"I don't know," she admitted. That was part of the reason Catherine was so grateful for Austin's company. Perhaps talking to him would help her make sense of her emotions. "Part of me is numb. The rest feels as if I've been sliced open. Oh, Austin, it was horrible."

She had told herself she wouldn't cry, for tears solved nothing. She'd learned that when Mama had been so ill and again when she'd died. But the caring she'd seen on Austin's face released the floodgates, and Catherine found herself sobbing.

He dropped her hands, and for a second, she felt bereft. But then he drew her into his arms, pressing her head against his chest as he stroked her back. "I won't tell you it will be all right. Seeing something like that changes a person." His hand moved in gentle circles, comforting her as if she were Hannah, and her sobs subsided. "Death is always difficult to accept, and violent death . . ." He paused for a second. "It's not easy to recover from that."

Catherine wondered if he was thinking of his wife and the despair that had led her to plunge into the Seine. It had been years since that day, but some pain never ended.

"I feel as if everything in my life has shifted. I believed I knew my aunt and uncle, but today proved that I didn't—not really." She'd realized that Charles had a roving eye, and she'd known that Mary was a proud woman who feared scandal, but she'd been unprepared for the reality of Charles's past or Mary's reaction to it.

"Do you know why Mrs. Gray did what she did?" Austin asked as Catherine dried her tears. She'd moved back slightly, but remained in the shelter of his arms.

"Yes. Grace said I could tell you, because she knew she could trust you to keep it secret." Catherine took a breath and wiped a stray tear from her cheek. "Twenty-two years ago, a man attacked Grace, leaving her with child." Catherine related what had happened to Grace and why she had not returned to Cimarron Creek until recently, concluding, "It was only today that she learned Charles was the father of her child."

"She looks so much like the portrait you showed me that Charles must have known immediately who she was. I imagine he was shocked to see her face."

"He was. He looked horrified and incredulous at the same time. Seeing that reaction was how I knew he was the one. All I had to do was prove it." Catherine closed her eyes for a second, reliving the moment when she'd revealed Charles's scar. "What bothers me is that I never guessed there was such evil inside him."

"You shouldn't blame yourself." Austin's eyes were warm and caring. "Some people are very good at hiding their true selves."

"This was someone I've known my whole life." Catherine frowned as memories resurfaced. "Ever since Mama died, he's been overly friendly to me, but until today I didn't think he was capable of attacking a woman."

A bird squawked a protest as another settled on the same branch; the light breeze ruffled the cottonwoods' leaves; the creek burbled as it made its way around the bend. Catherine took a deep breath, trying to let the pastoral beauty chase away her regrets.

As if he understood her conflict, Austin gave her a reassuring smile. "There was no reason you should have realized what your uncle was hiding. Based on what happened, I'd say his wife had no idea what he'd done."

"She didn't."

"Then why do you think you should have? She lived with him. She knew him better than anyone else." That was Austin—logical, pragmatic, and comforting all at once.

"You're right, but I still wish there were a way to undo today."

Austin nodded, his expression empathetic. "I felt that way the day Geraldine died. I wondered what I could have done differently." His words confirmed Catherine's belief that he was still suffering from his wife's death, that while there must have been some healing, it was incomplete.

"Did you find an answer?"

"No. I knew I couldn't change what she'd done, but it was more painful than I'd thought possible to remain there surrounded by memories. Everywhere I turned, there was a reminder of Geraldine. Our home even had a view of the Seine, but after that day, I couldn't bear to look at it. That's why I went back to Philadelphia."

"Did that help?" Catherine hoped Austin didn't think she was prying into his past, but she wanted to learn everything she could about what had made him the man he was.

"It did."

Perhaps that was the answer she sought. It wouldn't be a permanent move like Austin's, but perhaps a temporary change of scenery would help her regain her equilibrium and relegate today's horrors to the back of her mind.

"Grace wants to go to Paris," Catherine told Austin. "I tried to dissuade her, but maybe I shouldn't have. Maybe I should go with her."

As she pronounced the words, Catherine felt a sense of peace settle over her. It was true that Grace had not mentioned having a companion when she searched for her daughter, but Catherine could not ignore how right the idea felt.

Though Austin looked stunned, all he said was, "What about your pupils? They need you."

Another piece of the puzzle fell into place. "What they need is a teacher, not necessarily me. Rachel Henderson has a cousin who'd like to move here if she could figure out a way to earn a living. She could teach school this fall."

Austin stared at the creek for a long moment, his expression solemn. "I know going to Europe has been your dream, but it wouldn't be easy for two women to travel alone, especially since neither of you speaks French."

"We can hire a guide. That's what Mama and I had planned to do."

He nodded but appeared unconvinced. "There's another alternative." He swallowed deeply, seemingly uncomfortable with whatever it was he was going to propose. When he spoke, his voice was low and fervent. "Would you let me be your guide?"

For a second Catherine wondered if he was speaking a foreign language. Was Austin, the man who'd told her he had no desire to return to Europe, the man who'd confirmed how painful it had been to remain in Paris after his wife's death, now proposing to accompany her and Grace?

"You?" The word came out as little more than a croak.

He nodded, his expression more serious than she'd ever seen it. "I had planned to wait until you were out of mourning. I know how important it is for you to honor your mother with a full year of mourning, and I'd hoped that by then the threat from Sherman Enright would be over. Today changed everything. I don't want you to leave."

And, if she were being honest with herself, she did not want to leave him.

As Catherine opened her mouth to tell him that, Austin pulled her closer. "I love you, Catherine. I think I have since the first day I met you."

His eyes shone with the love he was professing, sending shivers of delight along Catherine's spine. This was not the way she'd pictured a declaration of love. Today was hardly the day she would have expected it, and yet she could not deny the joy that rushed through her as Austin pronounced the words she'd longed to hear.

He cupped her chin in one hand as he said, "Dare I hope that you love me too?"

"I do." She wanted to shout it so the world would hear, but she couldn't. Not yet.

His lips curved into the sweetest of smiles. "Then marry me. I'll take you and Grace to Paris."

It was tempting, oh so tempting, but Catherine knew it would be wrong. "I want to say yes, but you're right: it's too soon. Mama was both mother and father to me. It seems only right that I give her a full mourning period. And, as I told Grace when she said she wanted to leave Cimarron Creek, neither of us should make any decisions right away. I'm not sure we're thinking clearly, especially not today."

Though Austin made no attempt to disguise his disappointment, he said only, "But you love me?"

Catherine would not deny him the answer he sought, not when it was what her heart had been telling her for so long. "Yes, Austin, I love you. I love you so very much. I love Hannah too." She smiled, thinking of the girl who'd captured her heart her first day of school. "I doubt I could love a child of my own any more than I love her, but I need to finish mourning before I begin a new phase of my life. Will you wait?"

Austin nodded. "I'm not a patient man, but I'll learn. I'll wait as long as it takes for you to be ready." The corners of his mouth turned up in a wry smile. "There is one thing I hope you won't make me wait for."

When he looked the way he did now, Catherine knew there was nothing she'd deny him. "What is that?"

"Another kiss."

He tightened his grip on her chin, tipping it up. When she nodded, he lowered his lips to hers. His mouth was firm, his touch so tender that Catherine felt herself melting. For the first time since Charles had stared at Grace in church, Catherine was fully at peace. This was where she was meant to be—in Austin's arms.

25

T his is the nicest Fourth of July I can remember."

Austin stared at the beautiful woman seated next to him. If he was going to stay in Cimarron Creek, he needed to buy a carriage. Catherine deserved to ride in something nicer than an ordinary wagon.

"I agree," he said. Philadelphia had had more elaborate parades, and the fireworks were more spectacular, but there'd been nothing to compare to the pleasure of spending the day with Catherine. They'd watched the parade together, listened to the seemingly interminable speeches, and laughed at Hannah and Seth's attempt to run a three-legged race.

Though the boy's hand was still in a cast and his ribs were still taped, making breathing difficult, he'd done his best when Hannah had declared that the thing she wanted most was to enter the race. She had claimed she didn't care about winning, which was fortunate, since a six-year-old girl and a gangly thirteen-year-old boy were hardly ideal partners. But Seth had done his best, enduring what had to have been a painful fall, all to make Hannah's wish come true. The boy would do anything for Austin's daughter, just as Austin would do anything for Catherine—including returning to Paris.

He tipped his hat at Kevin as the man drove past them. When they'd planned the day, Mrs. Moore had suggested everyone return to the ranch for supper and had decreed that Kevin would drive a second wagon so that no one would be crowded. With Kevin, his mother, and Grace on the seat and Hannah and Seth in the back, that wagon was far more crowded than Austin's, but he wasn't complaining. Being alone with Catherine was a reason to rejoice, not complain.

It had been a wonderful day, because he'd had Catherine at his side. But the pleasure Austin had experienced wasn't due solely to Catherine. As the day had progressed, he'd realized that he felt as if they all belonged together—Hannah, Seth, Catherine, and himself. Even Grace. She'd spent much of the day discussing recipes with Mrs. Moore, the two women acting as if they were lifelong friends rather than new acquaintances.

Austin took a deep breath, inhaling the sweet smell of the wildflowers that dotted the countryside. For the first time since Geraldine's death, he felt as if he were once again whole and part of a family. As dearly as he loved Hannah, he needed more. He needed a wife and perhaps another child.

"I can't believe the change in Seth."

Catherine's words brought Austin back to the present, and he smiled as he glanced at the wagon ahead of them. Both Seth and Hannah were laughing, looking like the carefree children they deserved to be.

"Seth's broken bones are healing well. He has the resilience of youth on his side. I haven't told him, because I don't want to raise his hopes and then have them dashed, but I think there's a possibility that eventually he'll be able to do a few things with his right hand."

Though Catherine appeared pleased by the prognosis, she shook her head. "That wasn't what I meant. Of course, I'm glad that he's healing and that he may regain some use of his hand, but it's more than that. Seth's more relaxed and happier than I've ever seen him. He's talking more too. He even told me that his bed is soft."

What a strange thing to confide in his teacher. "It's an ordinary mattress, but compared to sleeping in a barn, it probably feels like down." Austin closed the small distance between him and Catherine and laid his hand on hers, wanting the reassurance that touching her always brought. "I keep praying that Boone will relinquish his rights." Though Austin was grateful he was able to keep Seth safe while his wounds healed, he hated the knowledge that the situation was temporary.

Catherine turned her hand so that they were palm to palm. Even with gloves between them, he could feel the warmth of her skin, and it filled him with happiness.

"So do I," she said. "It would be wonderful if he could live with you permanently."

Though Austin wanted to amend her wish, changing "with you" to "with us," he did not. It was too soon. He'd promised he wouldn't rush her, and he would keep his promise.

It had been a wonderful week, knowing Catherine loved him, knowing there was a good chance she would marry him before summer's end. That had buoyed his spirits more than he'd thought possible. Even the solemnity of the double funeral had not destroyed Austin's happiness. If only Enright would give up his search, his life would be complete.

"I keep telling myself to be patient, that God's timing is perfect."

Catherine's eyes filled with understanding. "But it's hard to wait, isn't it?"

"Yes."

"Your daughter shares your impatience. She said you promised her a new dress for school, but she doesn't want to wait. I think she's afraid you'll forget."

"I won't." Austin had made himself a note to visit the mercantile the week before school opened and select a dress for Hannah.

Giving his hand a little squeeze, Catherine said, "I know, but two months feels like forever to a six-year-old. I thought I might be able to help. If you wouldn't mind, she could spend next Monday with me. We'll buy material for her dress and start making it. That way she'll be part of the process. If she enjoys it, we can sew together every Monday until it's finished."

It was a generous offer and one Austin knew Hannah would appreciate. Just this morning she'd told him for what felt like the thousandth time that she wished Miss Whitfield were her mother.

"Are you sure you don't mind?"

Catherine gave him one of those smiles that made him feel as if he were the most interesting man on Earth. "It would be my pleasure. I may not be a great cook, but I can sew. It's time Hannah learns how."

"Perfect." The plan was perfect, and so was Catherine.

As towns went, he'd seen worse. Tucker rode slowly down the main street of Cimarron Creek, looking at his surroundings. The trees were a nice touch, and that candy store sure smelled good. The proprietor had left the door open, letting the smell of fudge fill the air all the way to the street. Tucker dismounted and tied his horse to a hitching post. It was time to do a little exploring on foot.

He looked in the window of the candy store. A man could use a piece or two of fudge, but he wouldn't find his answers there. He needed a saloon. Most likely it was at the other end of the street. Folks in towns like this usually put their saloons on the edge of town where the old biddies who didn't appreciate a fine glass of whiskey didn't have to look at them when they came into town to do their shopping.

He might mosey back to the candy shop when he'd found what he needed, but first things first. He needed to see whether Enright had sent him a telegram. That was why he'd left his horse here, close to the post office. Chances were the man who ran the post office also handled the town's telegrams.

"Welcome to Cimarron Creek," a friendly voice said as Tucker entered the building. He'd heard Texans were neighborly, and though this man's eyes narrowed as if he realized Tucker was no ordinary visitor, he kept smiling. "What can I do for you?"

"Name's Tucker. I'm checkin' to see if you got a telegram for me."

"Yes, sir." The smile didn't falter. "It came in a few days ago." He riffled through a small stack of papers, pulling one out. "Here you go. Will there be a reply?"

Tucker scanned the few words and shook his head, though the content surprised him. *Don't lose package.* He'd expected that. *Am on way.* Hadn't expected that. He'd figured he'd be taking the doc back to Philadelphia so he could fix Enright's face there. Something must be going on back East if Enright was coming all this way.

"Thanks." He spun on his heel and headed toward the door. He needed to find out where Austin Goddard was holed up, but he couldn't ask this man. No, sirree. The man knew his name. That was all he was gonna learn. Enright had taught him good. Tell folks only what they needed to know, not a bit more.

Tucker swung his leg over the saddle and headed north on Main Street. Just like he'd figured, the saloon was on that end of town.

"Welcome to the Silver Spur. What can I get you?" The woman was a looker with all that red hair and the streaks of silver near her ears. On another day, Tucker would've wanted to get to know her better, but there was only one thing he was gonna do today.

He gestured toward the shelves behind the bar. "Your best whiskey. A whole bottle." Another thing Enright had taught him was that the surest way to learn something was to wet someone's whistle.

While the woman retrieved the bottle, Tucker looked around, grinning when he saw a man seated by himself, his expression as forlorn as an abandoned pup's. Unless Tucker missed his mark, Mr. Lonely would have loose lips.

"Mind if I join you?" Without waiting for a response, Tucker grabbed the chair on the opposite side of the table and plunked the bottle on the table. "I'm new to town. Lookin' for a friend to share a drink or two." He turned the bottle so the man could read the label. When Mr. Lonely's eyes widened with respect for the fine liquor, Tucker spoke again. "Folks call me Hunter." It wasn't the name his pappy had given him, but it was a good name. After all, he was a mighty fine hunter.

The man's greedy eyes moved from his empty glass to the bottle. "Name's Dalton, but you can call me Boone." Boone held out his glass. "Fill 'er up." He downed the liquid in one slug, then slid it back for a refill. "What brings you to town?"

"Thinkin' about staying here. Need a place to stay for a few days. Nothin' fancy, mind you. Just someplace quiet. I like privacy, if you know what I mean." Tucker gave the man a wink. "You know any place like that?"

Boone nodded. "I reckon I got a place for you. Ain't fancy, but it sure has got all the privacy a man could want. Wouldn't nobody know what was goin' on there, if you know what I mean." He returned the wink Tucker had given him as he repeated Tucker's phrase.

"Where is this place?"

AMANDA CABOT

Boone drained his glass and reached for the bottle, frowning when Tucker kept it in his grip. "Corner of my farm. A couple miles out of town."

"No one's livin' there now?"

"Nope. Cabin's been empty for a year or two."

The way Boone looked at the floor when he said that told Tucker it had been more than two years since anyone had called the cabin home. Except maybe varmints. Still, beggars couldn't be choosers, and at this point, Tucker was a beggar. The less time he spent in town, the less chance the doc would find out he was here. The timing had to be perfect.

"How much you chargin'?"

The man who was eyeing the bottle of whiskey like a drowning man would eye a boat quoted a price that almost made Tucker laugh. Did he think he was dealing with a fool?

"Tell you what," he said. "I'll give you half today, the rest in a week." That was safe enough. Within a week, he and Enright would be long gone.

"You give me half and another bottle of whiskey and we got ourselves a deal."

Tucker pretended to consider the offer. "Another bottle of whiskey and you'll need a doctor." If he said so himself, that was a mighty clever way of getting the man to talk about doctors.

Boone shrugged. "Doc Harrington wouldn't do nothin' but laugh."

"Harrington?" That wasn't what Tucker had expected. "I thought somebody said your doc was named Goddard."

The man who was swigging whiskey like it was water looked up, his gaze steely. "You got it wrong. The only doc is Harrington. Goddard . . ." He spat on the floor, his disgust apparent. "He ain't no doctor. He's the lily-livered coward what stole my boy."

A memory teased Tucker's brain. Dalton. Boone had said

285

that was his name. And Dalton was the name of the boy who'd done that drawing. Tucker practically shouted with glee. Lady Luck sure was on his side today. Boone Dalton was just the man he needed, a man with a grudge against the doctor who'd refused to help Sherman Enright.

Tucker pretended to study his glass. "Sounds like somebody oughta run this Goddard fella out of town."

"You're dang right about that. Problem is, he's got himself some allies, includin' the sheriff. Ever since he started sparkin' the schoolmarm, everybody thinks he's some kind of hero. He ain't. I can tell you that."

Tucker lifted the glass to his mouth to hide his smile. This just kept getting better and better. If Austin Goddard had a sweetheart, Enright had two pieces of . . . Tucker scratched his head. What was the word? Leverage. That's what Enright had said. A man needed leverage, and Boone Dalton had just given Tucker some of it.

"Guess I better make sure I don't cross tracks with him. Where does this Goddard fella live?"

Boone took another swig of his drink, his lips curving into a sneer as he said, "Right next to me. He stole the ranch just like he stole the boy. I sure wanna see him get his comeuppance."

If Lady Luck continued to shine on him—and Tucker was sure she would—Boone just might get his wish.

"Here, have another drink." The man deserved that. "Now, tell me more about this schoolmarm."

26

So, you're going to teach Hannah to sew." Grace cut a slice of bacon into small bites, then mixed them with her scrambled eggs. Catherine tried not to smile at the routine. Each day of the week, Grace ate a variation of bacon and eggs. Today was Friday, the day for the meat to be stirred into the eggs. The one other day when she scrambled eggs—Wednesday—she cut the bacon into thick slabs and sandwiched one between two slices of toast, keeping the eggs separate.

"When I lived in San Antonio and saw mothers and daughters in the dry goods store picking out fabric and lace, I would wonder if someone was doing that with my daughter." A frown crossed Grace's face. "You'd think that by now I'd be used to the idea that I might never know where she is or what her life is like, but not a day goes by that I don't think of her."

Catherine wasn't surprised. Not a day went by without her thinking of her mother.

"It's the oddest thing, Catherine. I keep dreaming about Paris. Even though I never see my daughter in the dream, I always waken with the belief that she's there." Grace took a breath and fixed her gaze on Catherine. "It's time for me to plan my trip."

That meant it was time for Catherine to present her proposal. She had thought about it numerous times since the idea had floated into her head, and the more she thought about it, the

287

better she liked it. Both she and Grace would see their dreams become reality.

"Can you wait until fall? We might have a guide who speaks French then."

Grace looked up from the toast she was buttering, her eyes wide with surprise. "We? What do you mean?"

"You know I'd planned to tour Europe with my mother and that visiting Europe, especially Paris, has been my dream for years. I'd almost given up on it, but if you're going, I thought maybe we could go together." Catherine hesitated as a thought assailed her. "Unless you'd rather go alone."

Grace laid her knife on the plate and shook her head. "What a ridiculous idea! I'd love to have you as my traveling companion. But you can't just leave the school, can you?"

When Catherine explained about Rachel Henderson's cousin, a smile lit Grace's face. "God has worked everything out, hasn't he? He means for us to go to Paris. But you said something about a guide. Who would that be?"

"Austin."

A frown was not the reaction Catherine had expected. Grace had been so excited about the thought of their traveling together, and now she looked like a deflated balloon. "I suppose that would be all right," she said slowly. "He'd be our guide, and I'd be your chaperone."

Though she hadn't planned to say anything yet, Catherine didn't want Grace to worry. "I might not need a chaperone. Austin has asked me to marry him."

There was a moment of silence as Grace digested the news. Then her frown turned upside down. "That's wonderful! I knew you two were meant for each other, and I was right." Her smile widened. "Now sweet little Hannah will have a mother. Oh, Catherine, it's perfect! When is the wedding?"

This was the Grace Catherine knew and loved—exuberant

and easily excited. "There's no date, because we're not officially courting yet. We both agreed that we need to wait until my year of mourning ends and he's convinced that Sherman Enright is no longer a threat."

"That makes sense, but when he does propose, your answer will be yes." Grace was like a terrier digging for a bone. Nothing would deter her from her goal.

"It will." Catherine had thought of little else since Austin had asked her to marry him, and each time she thought of it, her decision became more clear. Austin was the man she loved, the man God intended for her.

"Oh, Grace, I love him so much. I can't wait to be his wife."

Grace's smile was as bright as the summer sun. "I couldn't be happier if it were my own wedding I was planning. This is just what Cimarron Creek needs—some good news. The fact that I'm Joan Henderson didn't excite people for very long."

"But it did take attention away from Warner." Though Catherine knew he would never fully recover from the loss of his family, he had looked less haunted when she'd seen him at the Independence Day Celebration.

Grace glanced at the wall clock. "It's time for me to do some shopping. I wish I could share your news with everyone, but I won't."

"You'd better not, since it's not official."

"But it will be soon, and then the town will have something new to talk about. They'll be as happy for you two as I am."

Catherine stared out the window after Grace left, wondering why she felt so unsettled. She ought to be happy—and she was—that many of her dreams were coming true. In a few months, she would be Austin's wife and Hannah's mother. In a few months, she would experience the beauty of Paris. She ought to be satisfied, and yet she felt as if something was missing from her life, as if there were something important she needed to do.

She turned, intending to retrieve her Bible from her room, then stopped. She knew what it would say. Every time she had opened it lately, her eyes had lit on a passage exhorting forgiveness. Seventy times seven, Jesus had said when his disciples had asked how often they needed to forgive, yet she had not forgiven a single time. She still harbored anger and resentment in her heart, as corrosive as the purges Doc Harrington had administered.

"Forgiveness helps you," Mama had said.

"He acted out of ignorance, not malice," Austin had told Catherine.

They were both right. She knew that. But, oh how difficult it was to lay aside the anger she had felt for so long. It had been easier to blame the doctor for her mother's death than to remember that Mama had willingly submitted to his treatments, even though Catherine had begged her not to. She had wanted someone to blame, because anger kept her from dwelling on the loneliness that had engulfed her after Mama died. It was time to move forward.

Catherine looked around the kitchen, nodding when she spotted the pudding Grace had made for today's dinner. Mama had often commented on the fact that Doc Harrington lived alone and probably did not eat well. Perhaps he would appreciate a bowl of tapioca pudding.

Before she had a chance to reconsider, Catherine dished out a serving of pudding, adding two of the cinnamon rolls she had made yesterday. Three minutes later, she was knocking on the doctor's door.

When the heavyset man with gunmetal gray hair opened the door, his eyes widened in surprise. "What do you want?"

Catherine couldn't blame him for his hostility, not when every encounter they'd had for the past few years had been fraught with hostility on her part.

"I thought you might enjoy some pudding and rolls," she said, wondering if this had been a mistake. When he said nothing but looked at the food as if it might be poisoned, she continued. "I paid your bills, but I never thanked you for trying to cure my mother. I know you did your best." His treatments may have seemed barbaric, but they were the only ones he had been taught.

The doctor's eyes narrowed, and Catherine knew he was gauging her sincerity. At length, he nodded. "Are those cinnamon rolls I smell? They're my favorite."

As the man she had distrusted for so long accepted her peace offering, Catherine felt her anger disappear. She could not change the past; she could not predict the future; what she could do was control the present, and right now the present felt good.

When Grace returned from running her errands, Catherine was leafing through *Godey's Lady's Book*, searching for a pattern for Hannah's dress. It was a mundane activity, yet she found herself humming as she turned the pages. Her time with Doc Harrington, brief though it had been, had left her filled with peace.

She smiled and looked up when she heard the door open and her friend approaching the parlor. To Catherine's surprise, Grace did not remove her hat or gloves, but marched toward her, her face redder than usual, as if she'd been running. Catherine's smile faded when she realized that something was amiss.

"What is it, Grace? You look upset."

"There's a letter for you," she said, holding out an envelope. "It's from Ladreville. I didn't know you were in touch with anyone there." Curiosity and something else, perhaps fear, tinged Grace's voice.

Catherine accepted the envelope, her happiness over receiving the answer to prayer mingled with concern for Grace. Though it had taken far longer than she had expected, the wait was over. Within minutes, she would know whether the Russells remembered anything about Grace's daughter. But first she needed to soothe Grace and pray that the results of her impulse to send a letter were not as harmful as her urging Seth to enter the contest had been.

"I'm sorry, Grace. I probably should have asked you before I did it, but I didn't want to raise any false hopes. Now I'm afraid you'll feel I was meddling when I wrote to Pastor and Mrs. Russell. I wanted to know if they had any idea where your daughter might be living. You see, when Lydia and Aunt Bertha visited them, they only asked about you."

Grace sank onto a chair, the color that had flushed her face beginning to fade. "You *were* meddling, but how can I be angry? I should have done that myself. I don't know why I didn't think of it, other than that I was convinced I'd find my parents here and that they would have the answers." She gestured toward the envelope. "Go ahead. Open it."

Unwilling to tear the letter open, Catherine retrieved the letter opener from the desk and slit the envelope. Withdrawing the one sheet, she scanned the contents, then began to read.

Dear Catherine,

You must think I'm either rude or uncaring not to have responded to your letter sooner. I assure you neither is the case. The truth is, your letter arrived only a week ago. The envelope was filthy and water-stained, as if it had been dragged through mud or left out in a storm, leaving the address barely legible. Perhaps that is the reason it took so long to be delivered. I am thankful that it did reach us, albeit much later than it should have.

Unfortunately, neither Sterling nor I recalled the name of the couple who adopted Joan's daughter. She was not baptized in either Ladreville church, so there are no records. I thought we had reached a dead end until our midwife Priscilla remembered that Isabelle Lehman had acted as an interpreter, since the couple spoke little English.

Though Grace nodded as if the names were familiar to her, Catherine was puzzled by the fact that the adoptive parents were obviously immigrants. She had thought that immigration had slowed by the time Grace had gone to Ladreville and that those who came to Texas were primarily from the eastern states. It appeared she was wrong.

"Let me finish," she said.

Unbeknownst to us, Isabelle remained in contact with the couple for the first year after they adopted Joan's daughter. It seems their plans to emigrate to San Francisco failed, and they returned to their home in France.

Catherine paused for a second as her brain registered the final word, then she continued quickly.

Isabelle has not heard from them since, but she told me their names were Jean-Joseph and Denise Jarre, and they lived in a town called Maillochauds. Sadly, she cannot recall what they named the girl.

There was no need to read the remainder of the letter, for it was only the usual pleasantries. When Catherine looked up at Grace, she saw that the woman was beaming.

"I was right. Those dreams were a message from God. My daughter is in France!"

27

"Y ou have perfect timing," Lydia said as Catherine entered the candy store. "I have news for you."

"And I have some for you, but you should start." Though Catherine was bubbling over with the thought that Grace was closer to being reunited with her daughter, she could see by the gleam in Lydia's eyes that her announcement was equally important. The fact that Lydia kept rubbing her abdomen made Catherine suspect the news was about her baby.

"Are you having twins?" she asked mischievously. Lydia had claimed there was so much activity in her womb that she must be carrying more than one child.

"I don't know about that, but I know that we need some mint tea and a piece or two of fudge." Lydia turned toward the small kitchen at the rear of the store. "Would you brew some mint tea for us, Opal?"

The woman who was now Lydia's partner appeared in the doorway. "It's all ready, but you might want to drink it back here. That way you won't be interrupted by customers. I can help them while you rest."

A minute later, Catherine and Lydia were perched on stools next to the counter. They weren't as comfortable as the padded window seat and chairs in the showroom, but the kitchen had the benefit of privacy.

"So, what's happening?" Catherine asked as she sipped the tea that never failed to soothe her. "I'm guessing it has something to do with the baby."

"It does," Lydia confirmed. "Travis and Matthew have hired a new midwife." She smiled as she rubbed her stomach again. "Matthew's taking credit for it, of course, saying that as mayor it's his job, but Travis was the one who sent telegrams to all the nearby towns, asking the other sheriffs to put the notice in their papers." Lydia broke off a piece of fudge and held it between her thumb and index finger as she said, "They received three responses. One of them sounds perfect." The candy disappeared into her mouth.

Catherine nodded, encouraging Lydia to continue once she'd swallowed. She wasn't surprised that Travis had done most of the work in finding a midwife. Cousin Matthew was a good postmaster, but he viewed his role as mayor as mostly ceremonial. Fortunately for the town, Travis's training as an attorney and his contacts now that he was sheriff made him eminently qualified to hire people to serve Cimarron Creek. And of course he had a vested interest in choosing the best midwife.

"Her name is Mrs. Thea Michener," Lydia said. "She comes with the highest of recommendations, but her story is so sad that I cried when Travis told me what she'd gone through."

Catherine closed her eyes in a silent prayer for the unknown midwife. "What happened to her?" She hoped Mrs. Michener hadn't been the victim of rape or abuse.

"Her husband was killed, and her baby was stillborn." Lydia's voice wavered as she pronounced the words. "Oh, Catherine, I can't imagine what I would do if something like that happened to me." She cupped her arms around her abdomen, cradling her unborn child. "The only reason she's willing to come here is that she wants to move to a new town. She said there are too many unhappy memories in Ladreville."

"Ladreville?" Catherine laid her cup on the counter and stared at Lydia. "Mrs. Michener is from the same town where Grace once lived?"

Lydia nodded. "That's one of the reasons Travis was eager to hire her. Her recommendation came from Priscilla, the midwife who attended Grace. We both met her when we went to Ladreville with Aunt Bertha, and we trust her. If Priscilla says Thea Michener is a good midwife, I know she is."

Catherine nodded slowly, marveling at the links between Cimarron Creek and what Grace claimed was one of the prettiest towns in the Hill Country. "My news came from Ladreville too."

"It sounds as if you had an eventful Friday." Austin smiled at the woman he loved so dearly. When he and Hannah had slid into the pew beside her and Grace, he'd noticed that Catherine looked different, but he had been unable to identify the difference. Now that the service had ended and they were outside waiting for Hannah to finish regaling Rebecca with the story of her plans for tomorrow, he was still mystified.

"Lydia's excited about the new midwife," Catherine said, "but that's understandable. I'm happy for her."

Austin nodded, although the thought of midwives did not excite him.

Ignoring his lack of enthusiasm, Catherine continued. "I'm looking forward to meeting Mrs. Michener, but I have to admit that I was more excited by the news about Grace's daughter."

That had been the first thing Catherine had told him, and the way she'd grinned while she'd recounted the contents of the letter had told him that Grace wasn't the only one looking forward to a trip to Europe.

"Will she wait until September to go to France?"

Catherine nodded. "Of course, she's anxious, but she said that after waiting more than twenty years, a few more months won't matter." Catherine hesitated for a moment. "Are you certain you want to go? I know your memories of Paris aren't happy ones."

While that was true, Austin had been surprised at how much the pain had faded over the past few months. Being here—being with Catherine—had helped him put the sorrow of Geraldine's death behind him. Instead, he found himself remembering the happy times they'd shared.

"You and I will make new memories," he said firmly. "I want to be with you when you see Notre Dame for the first time." He lowered his voice, not wanting to be overheard, even though no parishioners were near. "I'm beginning to feel confident that Enright has given up his search, even though it doesn't appear that he's left Philadelphia. It's been more than six months. By now he's likely to have realized that he won't ever find me and has made other arrangements."

"What would those be?"

"Consulting another doctor." Changing his appearance and moving to a different city was the only way Sherman Enright thought he could continue doing business without fear of being arrested.

"But you were the best."

"That doesn't mean that someone else couldn't have tried to alter his appearance. The results may not have been the same, but they could have been enough to achieve his goal. Chances are, any physician he'd consulted would have tried to help if Enright spun a good enough story and if he hadn't recognized the man as a criminal. We all try to do our best."

"Even Doc Harrington."

Austin blinked in surprise. This was the first time Catherine had spoken the man's name without rancor. What had happened?

"I surprised you, didn't I?" Without waiting for his response, Catherine continued. "I surprised myself too. I kept remembering what you and my mother had said, and I realized it was time to let go of my anger. I don't agree with the techniques he used, but I now know that he didn't deliberately harm my mother. He acted out of ignorance, not malice."

Catherine's smile turned mischievous. "You should have seen his face when I knocked on his door and gave him a peace offering of tapioca pudding and cinnamon rolls."

As Austin chuckled, imagining the crusty physician's shock, his heart filled with warmth. This was the reason Catherine looked so different today. She had found peace.

"What a happy day! What a happy day!" Hannah's clear soprano rang out in a tune Catherine did not recognize. While she was certain those were not the original words, she couldn't quarrel with the sentiment. It had been a happy day, despite the summer cold that had left Catherine with red eyes and a stuffed nose.

Though Austin had said he'd bring Hannah into town, Catherine had decided to rent a buggy and pick up Hannah, believing that would make the day more special. And it had. The girl had reveled in the novelty of riding in something other than her father's wagon and had chattered constantly about both the buggy and the upcoming thrill of her new dress.

To Catherine's delight, Hannah had insisted on bringing the doll Rebecca Henderson had given her. Though she had said nothing to Hannah, the doll figured into Catherine's plans.

When they'd arrived at Catherine's home, they'd spent an hour looking through *Godey's Lady's Book* to choose a pattern before going to Cousin Jacob's mercantile to select fabric.

Catherine doubted it was the first time Hannah had been inside the mercantile, but she wandered the aisles, exclaiming over the variety of merchandise, before she joined Catherine at the fabric table. Once there, she insisted on examining half a dozen bolts before she spotted a navy poplin with small white flowers and declared that nothing else would do.

The girl had practically bubbled over with excitement when Catherine suggested a white cotton lace as trimming. Sturdy but pretty, the lace would set the dress apart from the plainer ones Hannah normally wore and would make her feel special. Everyone—young or old—deserved to feel special.

After Catherine had cut out the pattern, allowing Hannah to make a few of the cuts, they'd begun the sewing lessons, with Hannah making a dress for her doll from the remnants. As Catherine had expected, she'd been delighted by the idea of her doll wearing a dress that matched hers. Hannah's sewing wouldn't win a prize at the county fair yet, but it was good for a first attempt. Now they were headed back to the ranch.

As the song ended, Hannah turned toward Catherine. "Sewing was fun. Can we do it again?"

"Of course. We need to finish your dress. Your father and I agreed you could spend every Monday with me until school begins."

"Yippee! Yippee! Yippee!"

Hannah was yelling so loudly that Catherine did not hear the approaching horse until the rider was next to them. Though the man's appearance was so ordinary that he would blend into any crowd, the way he looked at them made the hair on the back of Catherine's neck rise.

"Look what I found here. Two purty gals out for a ride."

His voice sent shivers down her spine, increasing the alarm she'd felt at the sight of him. His accent told Catherine he was an Easterner, while his grammar betrayed his poor education.

Under ordinary circumstances, neither of those would have bothered her, but Catherine's instincts warned her that this was no casual visitor and that she needed to get away from him. Instead of giving him a friendly greeting, she remained silent, planning her escape. It would be difficult for the buggy to outrun a man on horseback, but she would try.

"I reckon you're the schoolmarm and that there's Doc Goddard's daughter."

Catherine's instincts were shrieking now, telling her that something was very wrong. No one was supposed to know that Austin was a doctor, but somehow this man—this man with the evil glint in his eye—did.

She laid her hand on Hannah's and spoke so softly that she hoped the man could not hear her. "Don't say anything. Just hang on tight." She reached for the whip, intent on escaping from the stranger.

"That ain't a good idea, schoolmarm." The man pulled out a revolver and pointed it at Hannah. "You do one thing wrong, and that girl's gonna get hurt. Bad. Now just drop them reins. The three of us are gonna take a little ride. There's a man waitin' to meet you both. He's mighty curious about anyone connected to the doctor."

Catherine's feeling of dread increased as the man climbed into the buggy and grabbed the reins, then wrapped his arm around her, tugging her close to him. "Don't get no notions about tryin' to escape. I'll shoot both you and the little one. I won't kill you. Not yet. But it sure will hurt."

"I'm scared, Miss Whitfield," Hannah whispered. "He's not a nice man."

Catherine clasped Hannah's hand, searching for a way to comfort her. "We need to be brave." There had to be a way out of this situation. She closed her eyes and prayed to the One who could help them.

"Where are we going, Mr. . . ." She let her voice trail off, hoping he'd tell her his name.

He did not. Instead, he smirked. "Don't you worry none, missy. You'll find out soon enough where I'm takin' you. As long as you and the little one do your part, won't be no need to kill you."

Hannah shuddered and buried her face in Catherine's lap.

"He's only interested in the doc," the man who refused to give his name said.

Catherine sent another silent prayer heavenward. Unless she was mistaken, Austin's worst fear had come true. "Who is he?" she asked as calmly as she could.

The man let out an evil laugh, as if he knew the answer would hurt her. "He's a man no one crosses." Another laugh made Hannah tremble again. "Leastwise no one crosses him and lives to talk about it. You're gonna meet Mr. Sherman Enright."

28

I didn't expect you back so early." Mrs. Moore wiped her hands on the towel she'd tucked into her apron pocket, raising her eyebrows as she looked at Austin.

"I didn't want to overdo on Seth's first day in the saddle." It had been four weeks since the boy had sustained the injuries, and though his hand was still in a cast, Austin knew it had healed enough that he wouldn't reinjure it, even if he took a tumble. What had worried Austin was possible fatigue. As it had turned out, that should have been the least of his worries. Seth's energy outstripped his own.

Mrs. Moore nodded, though her expression said she wasn't buying the story. "That's mighty thoughtful of you. The fact that now you can get all cleaned up before Catherine arrives never crossed your mind, did it?"

Austin couldn't help laughing at how well she'd read his intentions. "I can't put anything over on you, can I?"

"Not where that gal's concerned. You perk up every time someone mentions her name, and when she's in the same room, you don't seem to notice anyone else. Face it, Austin. You're a lovesick boy."

He shook his head in pretended annoyance. "The least you can do is call me a man."

"I notice you aren't saying anything about the lovesick part."
There was no point in denying the truth.

Catherine tried to hide her surprise as the man turned the
buggy into the road leading to Boone Dalton's farm, but her
mind continued to whirl with the terrifying realization that
somehow Sherman Enright had tracked Austin to Cimarron
Creek. As Austin's stories of the man's cruelty crept into her
brain, she tried desperately to brush aside the thoughts of what
might lie in store for Hannah, instead focusing on this unexpected turn. She had thought the man intended to take her and
Hannah to the ranch, but he clearly had other plans.

Why here? Was Seth's father somehow involved with Sherman Enright? Though she wouldn't put anything past him, she
had no idea how Boone could have learned about Enright and
his search for Austin.

"This goes to Seth's house," Hannah whispered.

"That's right, little one." The man had obviously heard Hannah. "The boy's drawing tole me where I could find your pa. His
pa was mor'n happy to rent his cabin to a fine fella like me."

Shock bludgeoned Catherine like a club, and for a second
the world went black. She forced herself to take a deep breath.
She could not faint, not when Hannah's safety depended on
her, not when she knew this was all her fault.

Drawing. The word echoed through her brain, taunting her
with the knowledge of what she had done. Mama had told her
that deeds could be like pebbles tossed into a pond, sending
ripples farther than the person intended. Unintended consequences, Mama had called them. Sherman Enright's arrival in
Cimarron Creek was yet another unintended consequence of
Catherine's pride.

Why, oh why had she told Seth about the contest? Doing

that may have given him confidence and a sense of self-worth, but that had come at a high price—first his beating, now this. Thanks to her, Sherman Enright had found Austin, and, just as the pebble could not stop the ripples, there was nothing Catherine could do to stop the evil from spreading.

When they reached a fork in the road, the man who would not reveal his name turned onto a little-used track that Catherine assumed led to the cabin he had mentioned. Seth had never spoken of it, but why would he? He probably wanted to forget everything associated with this place. Catherine knew she would, if she'd been in his position.

"I'm scared." Hannah clutched Catherine's arm and began to whimper.

Catherine wouldn't tell her that she was more than scared, she was terrified. She couldn't let fear cloud her brain. Somehow, she had to find a way to save Hannah. Austin had lost his wife. She couldn't let him lose his only child.

"It's your pa what oughta be scared." The man punctuated his words with a nasty laugh.

Stroking Hannah's hair, Catherine tried to ignore the man who'd pulled her closer. Even though her nose was stuffy from the cold, she was close enough that the man's rank odor made her want to gag. "Pray, Hannah," she said softly. "Pray as hard as you can."

"You think prayer will save him? Not a chance." The man spat over the side of the buggy.

While Hannah continued to whimper, Catherine saw the cabin come into view. Though the location at the edge of the woods was appealing, the building was even more dilapidated than the farmhouse. If it had ever been painted, the color was long since gone, and the roof appeared in need of replacement. Judging from the size, she guessed there was only a single room serving as kitchen, parlor, and bedroom. That wasn't a surprise.

What was a surprise was the smoke coming from the chimney. Since no one needed heat on a July day in Texas, someone must be cooking.

The driver reined in the horse. "Get out nice and easy, both of you," he ordered. "We're goin' inside."

Catherine scrambled out of the buggy, grateful to be away from the man, if only momentarily, then raised her arms to help Hannah dismount. "Stay close to me," she whispered into the girl's ear as she held her. "You need to do exactly what I say. Do you understand?"

"Yes, ma'am."

The man strode before them and pushed the door open. "After you, ladies." He chuckled at his patently false gallantry. When Catherine and Hannah were inside, he followed. "I got 'em."

Catherine blinked, trying to let her eyes adjust to the relative darkness. As she'd expected, there was only one room. A surprisingly sturdy table, empty save for a lighted kerosene lamp, stood in the middle, flanked by two chairs. The only other furniture was a cot placed under the room's sole window. If the window had been opened, it might have vented some of the heat from the stove. As it was, the room was oppressively hot, a fact that did not seem to bother Sherman Enright.

He rose from the chair and stood next to the table. "Good work, Tucker." So the man had a name. "You know what's next," Enright continued. "I want the doctor here within the hour."

As Tucker left, Enright turned his attention on Catherine. She met his gaze without flinching, determined to show no fear. The man was as different from his minion as possible. While Tucker could blend into almost any crowd, Enright had a face few would forget. No wonder he wanted Austin to alter it. Even though Catherine had never met him, she would have known him simply from Austin's description. There could not be two people on Earth who looked like Sherman Enright.

If she had seen him on a city street, she would have thought him a successful businessman with his finely tailored suit, his carefully cut hair. If she'd spoken to him, she would have marked his cultured voice and excellent grammar, so different from Tucker's. It was only when she gazed into his eyes that she saw the similarity between the two men: their cruelty.

"So you're the one who caught the doctor's eye." Enright's smile held no mirth. "Turn around, Miss Whitfield, so I can see the whole package."

He was treating her as if she were an object. Catherine bristled. "That hardly seems appropriate."

Enright raised his right hand, displaying the gun that had been hidden by the table. "I make the rules here. If I tell you to dance on the table, you'll do it, or the girl will pay the price. Do you understand?"

"Yes." Catherine turned slowly, trying to ignore the cool appraisal Enright was giving her. This was worse than the way Uncle Charles had leered at her. She could almost understand lust, but Enright's scrutiny was devoid of passion. He was assessing her as he would have a piece of furniture, searching for flaws. His gaze made Catherine uncomfortable, a fact she was certain brought him satisfaction.

"You can sit down now. You and the girl. I just wanted to ensure you knew who was in charge."

When her eyes met his, Catherine tried to keep her face impassive, even as ripples of horror made their way down her spine. Enright's eyes told her he had no intention of releasing her or Hannah. Once Austin had performed the surgery, Enright or Tucker would kill them. They'd need to keep Austin alive until Enright's face had healed, because someone would need to change the bandages and apply the salve, but Catherine and Hannah were disposable. That meant she had to take action before Austin arrived.

Catherine glanced around the room. There had to be a way to get Hannah to safety. Without her, Enright had limited leverage over Austin. She would worry about how to alert Austin once Hannah was out of the cabin.

She kept her voice as calm as if she were discussing the weather. "No one's challenging you, Mr. Enright, but Hannah is tired. Would you mind if she lies on the bed?" Catherine wouldn't think about the critters that might have nested on the cot. All that mattered was saving Austin's daughter.

"Suit yourself."

She turned her attention to Hannah. "It's time for your nap."

When Hannah started to protest, Catherine gave her head an infinitesimal shake, and the girl nodded, remembering Catherine's admonition to obey her. "All right, Miss Whitfield."

"Do you want me to tell you a story?" Catherine accompanied her word with the tiniest of nods.

"Yes, please, Miss Whitfield." Hannah was playing her part well.

"Is that necessary?" Enright's voice held more than a note of annoyance.

Catherine turned and gave him her most guileless expression, grateful that the man had no children and didn't realize that most six-year olds did not take naps. "I'm afraid it is. I'll speak softly, though. She'll fall asleep faster that way and won't cause you any trouble."

When he was once more seated, she began. "Once upon a time there was a princess, a very pretty princess." With each phrase, she lowered her voice. Keeping the gentle cadence of the fairy tale, she said, "I need you to be very brave, Hannah. I'm going to try to get the window open. If I do, I'll help you climb out. You'll fall, but you won't be hurt. It's only a short distance. When you land, stand up and run as fast as you can to the woods out back. I want you to hide there until your father or I call you." She cupped Hannah's cheek, then bent over and gave her a soft kiss. "Now it's time to pretend you're asleep."

Catherine turned and walked slowly toward the table. Brushing her hand across her forehead, she said, "It's awfully warm in here. May I open the window?"

Enright shrugged. "You might as well. The doctor will need hot water for the surgery. That's why I had Tucker fire up the stove." He glanced at the stove and the two big pots of water that simmered on top of it. Several split logs were stacked on one side, while a rusted bucket held kindling. "There's no reason why you can't be comfortable. Now that the whelp's asleep, you and I can get to know each other better."

Though his words were ordinary, the leer that accompanied them sent shivers down Catherine's spine. Gone was the cool appraisal he'd given her before. Now his eyes were glazed with lust. She wouldn't think about what he intended to do. What mattered now was Hannah.

Catherine returned to the cot and bent down, pretending to check on Hannah as she whispered, "It's time. Get ready." She straightened up and fumbled with the window sash, waiting until Hannah was crouched in front of her before she flung it open. With one quick movement, she pushed Hannah through the opening. Perfect! The girl had rolled a few feet from the cabin, but was now upright and running toward the trees.

Slowly, as if nothing had happened, Catherine turned toward her captor. She saw the instant his brain registered the empty cot. Rage colored his face, destroying the image of a cultured businessman. At this moment, he was nothing more than an angry man.

"No!" he bellowed, the word echoing through the cabin as he raised his revolver and pointed it at Catherine. "You'll pay for this."

29

Tucker whistled a happy tune. It was a mighty fine day. Enright was pleased with him. Why wouldn't he be? Tucker had succeeded where the others had failed. He'd discovered where Austin Goddard was hiding, and he'd brought the brat and the schoolmarm to his boss. Now all he had to do was get the doctor. That would be as easy as fleecing a minister. Once the doc heard where his daughter was, he'd do whatever Tucker said.

He grinned and started whistling a new song. It sure was nice to have the upper hand. That high and mighty doctor would bow down to Tucker if he told him to. Just the thought made him grin again. Before they left the doc's ranch, he'd do that. He'd make the man bow. Better yet, he'd make him kneel in the dirt. Yes, sirree. Today was a mighty fine day.

Tucker was still grinning as he approached the point where the road to the cabin joined the one that led to Boone's farmhouse, but his grin faded when he spotted the man on horseback. He didn't have time to talk to that sniveling farmer.

"Howdy, Boone," he called out. He'd keep riding. Whatever the man had to say, it couldn't be important. What was important was fetching the doctor and keeping Enright happy.

"Not so fast." Boone reined his horse in front of Tucker's.

"You got somethin' of mine, and I want it." The farmer's words were slurred, telling Tucker he'd spent too much time at the saloon. What a fool! Tucker had known from the beginning that Boone wasn't able to handle his liquor like a man. The way he was swaying made it look like he was about to fall off his nag.

"What do you want?" Tucker tried to edge by Boone, but his horse wouldn't budge.

"The money you done promised me."

Money. Of course. That fool farmer had probably spent everything he had on whiskey—cheap whiskey—and now he wanted more. "The week's not over," Tucker said firmly. Time was a-wasting. He needed to get this settled and get to the ranch.

"No, it ain't," Boone agreed, "but the price went up. Seein' as how you got somebody else livin' there, I figger it's only fair you pay me more." He wobbled in the saddle, obviously having trouble maintaining his balance.

Tucker glared at the farmer. He'd needed him once, but he didn't need him now. "You're right. I do owe you something.'"

Before Boone had a chance to recognize the danger, Tucker pulled out his revolver and shot him in the gut. Good riddance. As the farmer toppled off the horse, Tucker laughed. "You ain't dead yet, but purty soon you'll wish you was."

"You let her go!" Enright glared at Catherine, his eyes narrowing as he considered his options. "I ought to kill you right now."

His words confirmed what she had suspected, namely that he planned to kill both her and Hannah as soon as the surgery was complete. "If you do that," she said as calmly as she could when a gun was pointed directly at her heart, "you'll have no hold over Austin. The fact that you had Hannah and me kidnapped tells me you realized the only way Austin would help you is if you coerced him."

The look Enright gave her was designed to strike fear into the recipient's heart. It was cold, steely, and promised no mercy. No wonder the man was as successful as he was. He'd mastered the art of intimidation. Though she was trembling internally, Catherine refused to cower. She kept her gaze focused on him while she said a silent prayer for deliverance.

"You're two of a kind, aren't you?" Enright demanded. "You and the doctor think you're smarter than me. Let me tell you something, schoolmarm. No one's smarter than Sherman Enright."

Underneath all his fancy clothes, Sherman Enright was nothing but a bully. She'd dealt with them before, both as a teacher and earlier when she had been a pupil. There was no point in trying to fight with a bully. Since she wasn't big enough to intimidate him, Catherine had to outsmart Enright. If she could distract him, she might be able to reach the door.

"The evidence would seem to refute that allegation," she said, infusing her words with sarcasm. If she could make him so angry at what she was saying that he didn't notice that she was moving, she might have a chance. It was a small chance, but even a small chance was better than none at all.

"Big words don't scare me."

She took another step forward. The table that separated them was only a foot away now. "Nothing scares you, does it, except for the thought of spending the rest of your life behind bars?"

Another step. She'd need to do more than run. Positioned as he was between her and the door, he'd stop her before she reached safety. She needed to slow his progress. There was only one way.

Catherine placed her hands on the edge of the table and sneered at Enright. "That's where you'll be. Behind bars. I doubt you'll be so brave then."

"Why, you little . . ."

He cocked the gun. It was time. With all her might, Catherine shoved the table.

⁂

She'd be here soon. Austin smiled as he sat on the front porch waiting for the woman he loved. Mrs. Moore was right. He was lovesick. Even when he'd been courting Geraldine, he hadn't felt this way. He'd loved his wife, but it had been a different kind of love. What he felt for Catherine was stronger, more intense than anything he'd ever experienced. It was wonderful and frightening at the same time. In just a few months she had become the most important part of his life. Soon . . .

The sound of hoofbeats brought Austin back to the present, and his heart leapt at the thought that Catherine was here. But instead of a buggy, he saw a solitary rider racing down the lane. Austin narrowed his eyes, wondering who was in such a hurry to pay a visit. When he'd practiced medicine, he'd grown accustomed to people knocking on his door at all hours of the day and night, desperate to have him rush to an ailing person's bedside, but there was no reason for such haste here. Other than Catherine and Grace, no one knew he was a doctor.

The feeling of uneasiness that had swept over Austin intensified. He didn't recognize the horse, and the rider was too far away for him to identify him. Probably a stranger, but that made no sense. Why would a stranger be coming here and at such a pace?

Austin rose and entered the house to retrieve his rifle. Though Texans were noted for their friendliness, it never hurt to be prepared, especially when his instincts told him this was not an innocent visit. He'd never killed a man, and he hoped he wouldn't have to break that record, but he needed the reassurance of a weapon in his hand.

Feeling more confident, Austin returned to the porch and

waited. It took only seconds before his stomach roiled. He never forgot a face, not even one as ordinary as this man's. Austin's worst fears had come true.

"What are you doing here, Tucker?" It was a rhetorical question. There was only one reason one of Sherman Enright's minions would be in Cimarron Creek.

The man reined in the horse and grinned at Austin. "That ain't no way to greet a friend." He pointed his own weapon at the rifle. "You might as well set that down. You ain't gonna need it where you're goin'. Mr. Enright don't take too kindly to weapons in the operating room."

It was worse than Austin had thought. Not only had Tucker found him, but it sounded as if Enright himself was in Texas. Not once had Austin considered the possibility that Sherman Enright would leave his comfortable home to search for him. The fact that he had must mean that the situation in Philadelphia had become too dangerous for Enright to remain there. That would make him a desperate man, and Austin knew that the only thing predictable about desperate men was their unpredictability.

Forcing back thoughts of what a desperate Sherman Enright might do, Austin kept his voice level. "I'm afraid you've both wasted your time coming to Texas. I already told Enright I wouldn't do what he asked."

Tucker's grin broadened, his smirk announcing that he was enjoying the situation. "I reckon you're wrong. If you want to see that girl of yours and the schoolmarm again, you'd better collect those doctorin' things of yours and come with me."

Austin had always believed "blood running cold" was nothing more than a colorful phrase some people used to describe deep emotions. As Tucker's words registered, he knew it was more than a phrase. His blood did chill at the thought that the two people he loved most were in the hands of a ruthless man like Sherman Enright.

Dear Lord, don't let it be true. But Austin knew that it was true, just as he knew that he would do everything in his power, including performing the surgery he'd once refused to consider, to keep Catherine and Hannah safe.

"You'd better hurry up, doc." The self-satisfied note in Tucker's voice infuriated Austin almost as much as the knowledge of what this man had done. "Mr. Enright ain't one to wait long. If we ain't at the cabin soon, he just might take it into his mind to get to know the schoolmarm better . . . if you know what I mean."

Austin knew exactly what Tucker meant. As his mind blurred with images of Sherman Enright's hands on Catherine, he took a deep breath and forced the images away. Anger solved nothing. What he needed was a plan, for one thing was certain: he couldn't—and he wouldn't—let anything happen to either Catherine or Hannah. With God's help, he would rescue them, but to do that, he needed to know where they were.

"You win," he said, feigning surrender. Tucker wasn't very bright, but he obviously liked the idea that he had the upper hand. That was probably part of the reason he'd remained on his horse, so that he could look down on Austin. Austin would play to that. As casually as he could, he asked, "Where are we going?"

"Just a piece up the road. Boone Dalton's got a mighty fine cabin waitin' for us."

Austin doubted that anything belonging to Boone Dalton was fine, but he gave thanks that Enright hadn't taken Catherine and Hannah too far from town. That could be a crucial point in the plan that had begun to take shape in his brain.

He turned toward the front door. "It'll take me a couple minutes to get everything together."

Tucker seemed uncomfortable with the idea of Austin entering the house alone. "I reckon I oughta come with you."

Austin couldn't let that happen. "Suit yourself," he said as if it made no difference to him, "but if I'm talking to you, I might forget to pack something important. You don't want that, do you?"

The man shook his head. "Make it quick. Mr. Enright ain't too patient."

Nor was Austin, not when his loved ones were in danger. Though his medical bag was hidden in his room, his first stop was the kitchen.

Mrs. Moore looked up from the carrots she was peeling. "I saw you had a visitor. Is he staying for supper?"

"No." Austin laid his index finger across his lips. If Mrs. Moore cried out at his news, Tucker might hear her. "I don't have time to explain now, but that man is a criminal from Philadelphia. His boss, who's even more dangerous, is holding Hannah and Catherine hostage in a cabin on the Dalton farm."

Though his housekeeper's eyes widened with shock and she gripped the counter to keep from falling, she said only, "What do you want me to do?"

"Do you know where the cabin is?"

Mrs. Moore nodded. "Kevin told me about it. It's on the far corner of the property."

"I'm going to try to rescue them, but I may need help. As soon as I leave, I want you to go into town. Tell Travis and his deputy about the cabin and that it's a matter of life and death."

When Mrs. Moore nodded her understanding, Austin sprinted to his room and grabbed his medical bag. Carrying it and the rifle, he rejoined Tucker.

"I tole you, you ain't got no need for that rifle."

Austin had no intention of relinquishing it. Only a fool would face Sherman Enright without some form of protection, and Austin was not a fool. "This is Texas, not Philadelphia," he informed the ruffian. "There are poisonous snakes

315

and wild boars called javelinas. A man does not ride without a weapon."

Though Tucker appeared dubious, the threat of wild animals seemed to convince him. "Don't try nothin' funny. I'll be right next to you with my gun pointed at you."

Austin nodded and mounted his horse. Fortunately, he'd kept Dusty saddled when he'd returned from the range. At the time, he had intended to accompany Catherine back to town so they could spend some time together. Now Dusty would be part of what he hoped would be a rescue mission.

Austin looked at the man riding by his side. The gun in Tucker's hand didn't worry him. Though Tucker might threaten him, he knew the man wouldn't shoot him until he'd performed the surgery. That was the reason Tucker and Enright were in Texas. They needed Austin, at least for the next few days, but they did not need Hannah and Catherine. From everything Austin had heard about Sherman Enright, he might kill them out of sheer orneriness even before the operation was complete. Austin could not allow that to happen.

Travis and his deputy would come. Austin knew that. What he didn't know was when. It was possible both men were out of town dealing with other crimes. Austin needed to do whatever he could as quickly as possible, but he knew the odds of overpowering two armed men were slim. Somehow, he needed to disarm Tucker. But how?

"That schoolmarm is a mighty purty gal," Tucker said as they rode toward the Dalton farm.

Though the words were meant to goad him, Austin refused to respond. He needed to focus all his attention on finding a way to disable Tucker. *Show me the way, Lord.* He prayed more fervently than he had in years, knowing that he could not accomplish anything alone. *Show me how to save Catherine and Hannah.*

Tucker kept up a stream of inane comments as they left the ranch and headed toward the Dalton farm, while Austin's mind whirled, trying to find a way to overpower the ruffian. When they turned onto the ill-kempt lane leading to Boone Dalton's home, Austin studied his surroundings. Everything looked the same as it had the last time he had been here—rundown and sad. He'd heard that the farm had once been prosperous, but under Boone's stewardship, it provided less than a subsistence living.

Austin kept his eyes on the lane. There was no point in thinking about Boone Dalton and the mistakes he'd made in his life. What mattered now was disarming Tucker before they reached the cabin. There had to be a way. Austin blinked, thinking he was mistaken. Another blink and he knew his eyes had not deceived him. The lump he'd seen in the road was a body.

"What's that?" he demanded, speaking for the first time since he'd mounted Dusty. Instinct told him to reach for his rifle.

Tucker turned toward the body and spat. "That's your neighbor. He won't be needing none of yer doctorin'. I saw to that."

It was the break Austin needed, the one he'd prayed for. While Tucker stared at Boone Dalton's lifeless body, Austin slid the rifle out of the holster. Knowing he'd only have one chance, he aimed carefully, bludgeoning Tucker's head with the butt of the rifle. The man slumped.

Mindful that every moment was precious, Austin leapt from Dusty and dragged Tucker off his mount. Grabbing the rope he always carried on his saddle, he secured Tucker's arms, then his legs behind his back. One more step was needed. Using the same technique he did with calves, Austin ran the rope between Tucker's bound arms and legs, effectively hobbling the man. Even when Tucker recovered consciousness, he wouldn't be going anywhere.

Thank you, Lord. Now if only he was in time to save Hannah and Catherine.

30

The table barely budged. Catherine heard the tinkle of glass as the lamp slid off the edge and landed on the floor, but that was overshadowed by the sound of Sherman Enright's laughter as he kept the table from moving.

"You're not as smart as you think, schoolmarm," he said, the cultured tone of his voice slipping, making him sound more like Tucker. Was that part of his plan, changing his voice as well as his face?

He glared at Catherine, his lips curving into a sneer. "Those eyes of yours are a dead giveaway. I knew what you were going to do almost before you did. Like I said, a dead giveaway. Dead. That's a good word, because you're going to be the one who's dead." Enright's laughter sent shivers down Catherine's spine.

"We've had ourselves a little change of plan here. Since you started the fire, I'm going to let you burn to death while I find that little girl the doc prizes so much. Once I've got her, the doc will have no choice. He'll fix my face and let me recuperate in his house, but you'll be gone. How do you like the idea of being Joan of Arc?" He jerked his head to the right.

Catherine's eyes widened in shock. If her nose hadn't been stuffy from the cold, she would have smelled the smoke from the overturned lamp. Now flames licked at the edge of the wall.

Though the fire was still small, the cabin was as dry as tinder. Enright was right. The fire would escalate. It had been only a few seconds since the lamp had overturned, but the fire was already growing more quickly than she'd thought possible, so much so that even the water on the stove might not be enough to quench it. She had to reach the door. She had to get outside and protect Hannah, but Enright stood between her and the door.

Mindful of his assertion that he could read her thoughts, Catherine looked at the stove, as if planning to grab one of the water buckets, but instead darted toward the door.

"Not so fast, missy." Enright sounded amused as he extended his leg in front of her, knocking her off balance and sending her sprawling to the ground. "You can't fool me. I know all the tricks."

Catherine refused to give him the satisfaction of groaning, though splinters from the floor dug into her hands. There had to be a way to escape. She couldn't let him find Hannah.

"Fire's too slow," he said, his voice as cold as steel in winter. "I want to watch you die."

For a second, there was no sound other than the crackle of the flames and the pounding of Catherine's heart. *Help me,* she prayed. *Keep Hannah safe.* Sherman Enright was as evil as Austin had said, a man who took pleasure in others' pain, and Hannah would be his next victim unless Catherine could stop him.

"C'mon, schoolmarm. It's time for you to meet your maker."

Enright reached down to grab Catherine's hair, tugging until she winced. Slowly, clearly enjoying the pain he was inflicting, he dragged her into the center of the cabin, then yanked her to her feet.

"I like watching people die," he said as he wrapped his hands around her neck and began to squeeze. "Slow and painful. That's the best way."

She tried to pull away, but it was to no avail. She pushed, but he was too strong. She kicked, but he didn't seem to notice. With each second that passed, Catherine could feel her lungs constrict. She needed air. She needed it now.

Dear Lord, show me the way. As she lifted the silent prayer heavenward, Douglas Sims's advice to his wife rushed into Catherine's brain. She wasn't helpless. Not totally. She had one more chance to save herself. Catherine raised her hands and, mustering every ounce of strength she possessed, jabbed her fingers into Sherman Enright's eyes.

He screamed, and as his face contorted with pain, he released his hold on her throat, leaving Catherine gasping for fresh air. The door. She had to find the door. Instinctively, she moved in that direction.

"No!" Enright's voice held both anger and pain. "You're not getting away." He reached for Catherine, but as he did, he lost his balance and tumbled, landing face forward against the stove.

Smoke! The moment of relief Austin had felt when he'd overpowered Tucker vanished at the sight of smoke rising from the cabin. There was far too much for this to be an ordinary stove fire. The way it seeped around the door and through the cracks in the walls told Austin the cabin itself was on fire. Boone Dalton would no longer care about that, but Austin did, for Catherine and Hannah were inside.

He spurred Dusty to cover the final yards in half the normal time, then flung himself to the ground and raced toward the door, flinging it open at the same time that he heard a blood-curdling scream.

"Catherine, are you and Hannah all right?" Austin blinked at the smoke that had begun to fill the room and tried to make sense of the scene before him. The woman he loved was reaching for the door with one hand while the other rubbed her throat. Her hair hung loose around her face, and lines of strain added years to her age, but she was alive. Austin said a silent prayer of thanks as he looked around, searching for his daughter. The body on the floor next to the stove had Sherman Enright's blond hair, but there was no sign of Hannah. His daughter, his precious daughter, was missing.

"Where's Hannah?" Tucker had said Enright had both her and Catherine, but Austin knew Catherine would not leave his daughter in peril.

"She's safe." Though Catherine's voice was hoarse, her words reassured him. "I got her out of the cabin before the fire started." She staggered toward the door and took in deep gulps of fresh air.

Though Austin's heart leapt at the confirmation that his daughter was safe, he feared that Catherine had not been as fortunate. Smoke inhalation could be dangerous, and there was no telling what Enright had done before he'd arrived.

As if she'd read his thoughts, Catherine said, "I'll be all right." She moved to the doorway and inhaled deeply, her color improving with each breath. "I'm not sure about him." She tipped her head in Sherman Enright's direction. The stench of burned flesh mingled with the growing smoke, while blood continued to pool beneath the man's body. No doubt about it, the man was seriously injured.

Austin's gaze returned to Catherine. When she'd tipped her head, she had revealed red marks on her throat. Those were the reason she'd been rubbing it when he'd flung the door open. Anger welled up inside him at the realization that there was only one logical explanation for her injured throat. Enright hadn't been able to hurt Hannah, and so he'd taken out his anger on Catherine.

Austin stared at the man who'd threatened everyone he loved.

It would be easy to leave him to die. With the amount of blood he'd lost, death would not be long in coming unless he received medical care. Austin knew that if the tables were turned, Enright would leave without a second thought. But Austin was not Sherman Enright. No matter how evil the man was, Austin had to help him. It was his duty as a doctor, a duty he took seriously. More importantly, it was his duty as a Christian. *Thou shalt not kill.* It would be killing if he, a man trained to save lives, let this man die.

Austin turned back to Catherine. "We've got to get him out of here. Can you help me?"

When she nodded and reentered the burning building, Austin knelt beside the injured man and turned him over, trying not to grimace at the sight of a piece of kindling embedded in Enright's abdomen. While the hot stove's effect on his face was obvious, there was no telling how much harm the wood had done.

"We'd better drag him." That would do less damage than lifting the man and would keep him from inhaling the worst of the smoke. The one good thing Austin could say about being close to the floor was that the smoke was less dense here. His eyes stung and his throat hurt, but that was nothing compared to what both Catherine and Enright had endured.

While the injured man continued to moan, Austin and Catherine pulled him from the burning cabin. "Would you get my bag?" Austin asked her when they were a safe distance from the fire. "It's on Dusty."

While she was gone, he began to assess Enright's injuries, almost smiling at the irony of the fact that the stove had accomplished what he'd refused to do: it had changed the criminal's face. No one would recognize this badly burned man as the one who'd terrorized so many Philadelphia shop owners. Enright wouldn't be pleased, though, because although he was currently unrecognizable, his face was still distinctive. The scars would be as extensive as Grace's had been, but this time Austin would do nothing to remove them.

Enright opened his eyes and stared at Austin. "I bet you never thought you'd see me like this. You might as well let me die."

"I ought to, especially after what you did to Catherine, but I won't. I'm going to do my best to ensure you can stand trial."

When Catherine returned with his medical bag, there were furrows between her eyes. The sight of a man as badly injured as Enright would do that to even a hardened professional. What must it be like for a woman like Catherine to see so much blood and suffering, especially so soon after witnessing her aunt and uncle's deaths?

To Austin's surprise, her voice was calm as she asked if he wanted her to assist him. That was more than he'd ask of her, so he shook his head.

"If you're sure." He was. Catherine looked toward the building that was now engulfed in flames. "I want to find Hannah. She must be terrified that one or both of us is in there." Catherine grimaced as she glanced at Enright. "I don't want her to see him. Even though I know she'll want to be with you, I think I should take her back to the ranch."

Austin agreed. "You don't need to worry about me. Enright's not going anywhere, and Travis or his deputy will be here soon. I sent Mrs. Moore into town to get them."

Though she still looked reluctant to leave him, Catherine nodded and headed toward the stand of trees behind the burning cabin.

By the time Travis arrived, Austin had staunched the bleeding. Enright had been fortunate. He would live, although Austin suspected he might have preferred death to life in prison. When he'd sutured the wound and covered Enright's face with a soothing salve, he watched as Travis handcuffed the man and bound his ankles together.

"That'll keep him until I return," Travis said, explaining that he would bring a wagon from town to transport Enright and Tucker to the jail. He and his deputy had found Tucker still trussed but once again conscious and surprisingly talkative, more than happy to tell the authorities what he knew about his boss's activities in hopes that his own sentence would be lighter.

Travis almost smiled as he told Austin that Cimarron Creek's sole jail cell would be crowded with two men, particularly men who were now at odds with each other.

"After all the telegrams I've exchanged with Philadelphia about this man, I feel like I've been part of the case, but I never thought I'd be the one arresting Sherman Enright."

Travis gave a final tug on Enright's bindings, then shot Austin an appraising look. "How does it feel knowing you won't have to pretend to be a rancher any longer?"

The answer was more complex than Austin had expected. "I am a rancher." The time in Cimarron Creek had shown him that there was much satisfaction to be gained from raising cattle.

"But you're also a doctor and a man who's in love with my cousin."

Austin wouldn't deny that, nor would he deny that it felt good to talk about something other than the tragedy that had almost occurred in the now destroyed cabin. "I never tried to hide my feelings for Catherine. Speaking of . . ."

"She should be at the ranch by now. I saw her and Hannah on the road when I was coming in."

Austin expelled a sigh of sheer relief. It had been a horrible day, a day in which he'd feared that he would lose everyone he loved, but God had been merciful. Both Hannah and Catherine were safe, and the threat from Enright was over. Austin's prayers had been answered.

31

Catherine kept her arms wrapped around Hannah as she gave the porch swing another gentle push. "Your father will be here soon," she promised.

Though only an hour had passed, it had been an eventful one. When she'd left Austin, Catherine had found Hannah cowering behind the largest live oak, her hands pressed against her eyes as if eyelids were not enough to blot out the sight of the fire. At the sound of Catherine's voice, she'd lowered her hands and shrieked, "You're safe!"

Seconds later, she was in Catherine's arms, sobbing with relief. "I thought you'd burned up with that mean man. I didn't care if he died, but I was so scared for you."

"No one died in the cabin." Since Catherine wasn't sure whether Enright was still alive, she had phrased her words carefully. "Your father is here. He's helping the man."

Hannah simply nodded, not finding anything odd in the fact that her father was attempting to heal the man who had threatened her.

Not wanting Hannah to see the extent of Enright's injuries, Catherine had left the girl in the woods while she brought the buggy back to her, then skirted the cabin as she headed toward the ranch. She'd gone close enough that Hannah would see that her father was alive and well but not close enough that she could view his patient's face. The girl was likely to have nightmares as it was. Catherine would not add that sight to them.

They'd both washed their hands and faces, and Catherine had pulled the splinter from her right hand and twisted her hair back into a semblance of a chignon when they'd reached the ranch. She knew she still looked disheveled, but at least both she and Hannah were alive. Now they were sitting on the front porch, waiting for Austin to arrive.

"I was scared, Miss Whitfield," Hannah said. "He was a mean man."

"Yes, he was, but you were very brave. You did what I asked you to do, and that was brave."

Hannah looked up at Catherine, tears threatening to leak from her eyes. "I don't want you to leave me—not ever. I was so scared when I was in the woods. All I wanted was for you to be with me. Please say you won't leave me."

Though there was nothing Catherine wanted more than to tell Hannah her wish might come true, she couldn't. Not until she and Austin had talked. And then there was the news they'd have to give Seth. As if summoned by her thoughts, Seth rode in on Patches.

The boy dismounted and looped the reins over the porch railing. It was only when he'd climbed the steps and stood in front of the swing that his eyes widened. "You've got blood on your dress, Miss Whitfield."

She looked down. "So I do. It's not mine, though." She hadn't bothered trying to rinse out the stains, because this was one dress she would never wear again. As soon as she returned home, it was destined for the rag bag.

Hannah slid out of Catherine's embrace and stood next to Seth. "It belonged to a very bad man. He wanted to kill me, but Miss Whitfield wouldn't let him."

While Catherine tried not to gasp at the fact that Hannah had recognized Enright's intent, Seth had less self-control. He let out a short cry, and the blood drained from his face so quickly Catherine feared he might faint. "Was it my pa?" Seth's voice squeaked as he forced the words out.

Catherine's heart ached at the realization that this boy equated every cruel man with his father. "No, it wasn't your father." Boone Dalton would never again hurt Seth or anyone else.

When Catherine had seen the body and realized what had happened, she had distracted Hannah. That was another sight she hadn't wanted the girl to witness. Eventually, Hannah would need to know what had happened, but now wasn't the right time, nor was it the time to tell Seth. That was something she and Austin needed to do together.

"This man was someone Mr. Goddard knew before he moved here."

"Oh." Seth's relief was palpable. He turned to Hannah. "Do you want to play checkers with me?"

To Catherine's surprise, Hannah agreed and followed Seth into the house. Ah, the resiliency of the young. A traumatic event could be dismissed, if only temporarily, by the prospect of a game. Catherine wasn't complaining. Not at all. The children's absence meant she and Austin could have a few minutes alone when he arrived.

She settled back in the swing, watching for the dust that signaled an approaching rider. Soon, she told herself. He'd be here soon. And he was. When she recognized the rider as Austin, Catherine stepped off the porch and walked toward him, her walk turning to a run when he dismounted and opened his arms. Seconds later she was enfolded in his embrace.

This was where she wanted to be—close to the man she loved. Like hers, his clothing was bloodstained. Like hers, his face was lined with fatigue from the day's ordeal. Like hers, his heart beat faster now that they were together, and that was how it should be.

"Oh, my love," Austin murmured against her hair, "I was so afraid I'd lost you."

Catherine tipped her head back so she could smile up at him. It was the first time he'd called her his love, and oh, how wonderful the words sounded.

"I'm safe and so is Hannah. She and Seth are playing checkers, if you can believe it." The words were prosaic, but Catherine heard the tremor in her voice as she looked at the man she loved so dearly, the man Sherman Enright had planned to take from her. Austin wasn't the only one who had feared the loss of his love.

His eyes were solemn as he looked at her. "I never thought I'd be grateful for a checkers game, but I am. I wanted to talk to you before I saw Hannah and Seth. There are some things we need to discuss." Though Austin's words sounded ominous, the corners of his mouth lifted in a small smile of reassurance.

Slowly, he lowered his arms, as if he were reluctant to release her, but then he reached for her hand. "Will you come with me where we can have a little privacy?" he asked, gesturing toward the shade of an oak tree.

Catherine nodded. Didn't he realize she'd go anywhere with him?

When they stood beneath the canopy of the oak's branches, once again Austin's expression turned somber. "I know I promised to wait until your mourning was complete, but what happened today changed everything. It reminded me that life can end without warning. Catherine, my love, I don't want to wait any longer."

He'd said it again. It hadn't been a slip of the tongue or an aberration. The day they'd walked by the creek Austin had told her he loved her, but calling her his love was different. It felt more intimate. "My love" was the kind of endearment a husband would use with his wife. If she was right—and how Catherine hoped she was—Austin was about to ask the question that could have only one answer. As her heart began to pound, she realized he wasn't the only one who didn't want to wait.

"I love you, Catherine. I love you more than I knew it was possible to love a woman." His eyes gleamed with love and tenderness, the expression so sweet Catherine's breath caught in wonder. Her prayers were being answered; her dreams were coming true.

Austin tightened his grip on her hand as he spoke. "Will you make me the happiest man on Earth? Will you marry me and be a mother to Hannah and any children God gives us?"

A bird chirped as it landed on a branch above her; a rabbit scurried through the grass; Dusty neighed at the horse still hitched to the buggy. They were ordinary sounds, proof that there was a world beyond Catherine and Austin, but for the moment all that mattered was being here with him.

"Yes, Austin, yes." Her heart overflowing with happiness, Catherine smiled at the man who'd offered her the future she'd dreamt of, a life of love and laughter, a life where family and faith combined to bring true happiness.

His smile matched hers, and then he found a better use for his lips, touching them to hers in a kiss that sent tingles down her spine. When at length he ended the kiss, the smile that curved Austin's lips was mischievous.

"Hannah will be almost as happy as I am. She keeps telling me she wants you to be her mother."

Catherine snuggled closer to Austin, resting her head on his chest for a moment before she looked up at him again. This might not be the time for her next question, but Catherine had to ask it. As Austin had said, today had changed everything. "Being your wife and Hannah's mother will be wonderful, but

I can't help worrying about Seth. I saw Boone's body. I don't know what happened, but I know he was dead."

Austin nodded. "That's the next thing I wanted to discuss. You're right. Boone is dead. Tucker shot him. While I don't condone murder, Boone's death makes one thing easier. If you agree, I'd like us to adopt Seth. I know it's asking a lot of you to take on two children as well as a husband, but Seth deserves a better life than he had with Boone."

And she and Austin could give him that. Though she hadn't thought her happiness could increase, it did. "I think it's the perfect solution. I've done what I could for Seth, but you've done more. You've been a better father to him than Boone ever was."

"You're selling yourself short, Catherine. You're the one who saw Seth's talent and encouraged it."

Catherine closed her eyes, remembering the consequences of her decisions. "I shouldn't have done that. Look at all the pain that caused. It's because of my encouragement that Seth was so badly beaten and that Sherman Enright found you."

When she saw the confusion on Austin's face, she realized he didn't know. "Tucker saw Seth's drawing in the magazine. That's how he knew you lived here."

Austin raised his hand and cupped Catherine's chin, tipping it so she was looking at him. "Don't blame yourself for any of this. It wasn't your fault. Boone was always looking for an excuse to vent his anger. If it hadn't been the drawing, it would have been something else."

Though Catherine did not feel exonerated, she knew there was some truth to Austin's words. Boone Dalton had been an angry, cruel man, but Tucker's bullet ensured that he would never again hurt his son. Catherine nodded at Austin, accepting what he had said.

"It seems I was deluding myself when I thought Enright would abandon his search for me and seek out another physician. He isn't used to anyone refusing him and had no intention of letting me be the first. One way or another, he would have found me. What angers me is that he hurt you." Austin touched her neck. Though the pain had subsided, there were still tender spots where Enright's fingers had dug into it.

"It will heal. It already feels better," Catherine told him. "At least now you don't have to worry about Enright any longer. You don't have to hide the fact that you're a doctor. You could even return to Philadelphia." And though she knew she would miss her family and friends in Cimarron Creek, Catherine would go with him. Her future was with Austin, wherever he chose to live.

He shook his head. "I've given it a lot of thought, and I realized I don't want to go back East. It's true that I miss my patients, but we both know Cimarron Creek could use a new doctor. What do you think about being a doctor's wife?"

Catherine pretended to consider the question. "It might be all right, if . . ." She paused, hoping he knew she was teasing.

"If what?" he asked.

"If *you're* the doctor. It doesn't matter to me whether you're a rancher or a doctor. You're the man I love, no matter how you earn a living."

She lifted her hand and traced the outline of his lips with her index finger. "I love you, Austin Goddard. I always will." And then she placed her lips on his, returning the kiss he'd given her.

"I like the way you show your love," he said when they broke apart, both a little breathless, "but it makes waiting difficult. Do you still want a September wedding?"

Catherine shook her head. As Austin had said, what had happened today changed many things, including her perspective. "Not anymore. I think we should marry as soon as possible." It would take a few days to arrange the ceremony, but if Austin agreed—and she was certain he would—they could be married within the week.

"Mama would have been the first to tell me not to waste a day. She always wanted me to find a love like she and my father shared, and now that I have, she wouldn't have wanted us to wait."

His eyes filled with happiness, Austin stroked Catherine's cheek as he said, "All that leaves to settle is our wedding trip. We've talked about my accompanying you and Grace to Paris, and I still like that idea. Although . . ." His lips curved into a grin. "Grace would actually be accompanying us. The problem is, I don't feel comfortable leaving Hannah and Seth behind for as long as it will take to go to Europe. It won't be conventional, but what do you think about taking them with us?"

"Oh, my love," Catherine said, repeating his endearment, "who cares about being conventional? That sounds like the trip of a lifetime. We can show Hannah the city where she was born, and think of all the sketches Seth will be able to make. Even better, we can help Grace find her daughter."

"And she can watch over the children when we want to be alone." The way Austin was staring at her lips told Catherine he was looking forward to their time alone as much as she was.

"It will be perfect." Catherine smiled again. "Thank you, Austin. You're making all my dreams come true."

As Austin lowered his head for another kiss, a familiar voice called out from the porch. "Papa, are you kissing Miss Whitfield? Does this mean she's going to be my mama?"

His eyes reflected his amusement as Austin turned Catherine so they both faced Hannah and Seth. "Come over here, Hannah. You too, Seth. Catherine and I have something we want to tell you."

Author's Letter

Dear Reader,

If you're like me, you enjoy learning why an author chose a particular setting for her book or a specific profession for her characters. You probably already know that the Hill Country is one of my favorite parts of the country, so my using it as a setting for another book shouldn't have surprised you. Austin's profession might have. Did you wonder why I decided to make him a plastic surgeon?

When I started plotting the series, I knew that Catherine's experiences with the local doctor made her fear the entire medical profession. From her point of view, Austin was absolutely the wrong person for her, but as the author, I knew he was exactly the man she needed. Austin had to be a doctor to help Catherine overcome her fears. Why a plastic surgeon? That sounds too modern, doesn't it?

Writers' inspiration can come from almost anywhere. When a close friend told me she was considering cosmetic surgery, I was curious and started researching the subject. Since I'd always thought of plastic surgery as a twentieth-

century branch of medicine, I was surprised to learn that it had its origins far earlier than that and that the ancient Egyptians—a culture that valued beauty as much as modern society does—had developed rudimentary techniques. Just as importantly, they performed what we would call dermabrasion to reduce scarring.

That was one of those "aha!" moments for me, because it meant that Austin could have been a plastic surgeon in the nineteenth century and that he could have known how to repair the damage smallpox had wrought on Grace's face. Once I knew that, the rest of the book fell into place.

If you're wondering, as some of my early readers did, whether a doctor in the nineteenth century would have used the term "plastic surgeon," the answer is yes. While we think of plastic substances as being modern inventions—and they are—there's no plastic involved in plastic surgery. The adjective "plastic" was used for almost three hundred years before plastic (a noun) was invented in the early twentieth century.

If you enjoy learning the origin of words as much as I do, you probably already know that the English word "plastic" comes from the Greek "plastikos," meaning to mold or shape, which is, of course, what reconstructive plastic surgery does.

As for "plastic surgery," although the procedures have been practiced for thousands of years, it wasn't until the early nineteenth century that the word "plastic" was used to describe them. A German surgeon, Karl Ferdinand von Gräfe, is credited with the first published use of "plastic" in this context when he released his 1818 book Rhinoplastik, *in which he described his work reconstructing noses. Once he used the term, others followed his lead, so by the time Austin became a physician, the term "plastic surgery" was one a trained surgeon would have known.*

I know that's a long answer to the question, but since I'm always annoyed by anachronisms in historical fiction, I wanted to assure you that "plastic surgery" was indeed a nineteenth-century term.

I hope you enjoyed Catherine and Austin's story and that you're looking forward to returning to Cimarron Creek next year when A Tender Hope *is released. The town's in for a lot of changes. Between the arrival of a new midwife, a new teacher, a lovely Frenchwoman, and a Texas Ranger with a mission, not to mention an abandoned infant, it's definitely not business-as-usual in that part of the Hill Country.*

A year is a long time to wait, so I've included a sneak peek at the story. Just turn the page, and you'll find the first chapter.

While you're waiting for A Tender Hope *to be released, I invite you to read my earlier books. If this is your first Cimarron Creek book, you might enjoy* A Stolen Heart, *Lydia and Travis's story. And, if you'd like to learn a bit more about Thea, the heroine of* A Tender Hope, *pick up a copy of* Paper Roses.

I also encourage you to visit my website, www.amanda cabot.com. You'll find information about all of my books there as well as a sign-up form for my newsletter. I promise not to fill your inbox with newsletters, because I only issue one when I have important news to share, but it's a way for us to keep in touch. I've also included links to my Facebook and Twitter accounts as well as my email address. It's one of my greatest pleasures as an author to receive notes from my readers, so don't be shy.

Blessings,
Amanda

Stay tuned for
Amanda Cabot's next story from
CIMARRON CREEK!

Revell
a division of Baker Publishing Group
www.RevellBooks.com

1

August 8, 1881

She was free.

Thea Michener smiled as she checked the harness, then climbed into the buggy. Within minutes, she would be leaving the only home she could remember. As much as she loved Ladreville, whose half-timbered buildings and Old World charm made visitors declare it to be one of the prettiest towns in the Hill Country, it was time for a change. While others might have trembled with fear over the thought of leaving family, friends, and all things familiar, the prospect filled Thea with relief. A new town, new possibilities, a new life beckoned her. Although a year ago she would not have dreamt of it, that was a year ago. So much had changed in the past year, most of all Thea.

"But you haven't changed, have you, Maggie?" Her smile widened into a grin as she looked at the bay mare that had carried her on countless journeys. The horse was the one part of her old life that she was taking with her, that and the tools of her trade. What she was leaving behind were the need for secrecy and the fear that someone would discover the truth she had tried so hard to hide.

Waving good-bye to the liveryman who'd cared for Maggie whenever Thea's business brought her into town, she set off down the street. It was time to be gone. The sun was already high in the sky, although a layer of clouds promised some relief from the heat of a Texas summer. Not for the first time, Thea was grateful for her buggy. The padded seat that some in Ladreville had considered an extravagance would make the long journey more comfortable, while the top—another extravagance according to the town's more frugal residents—would block most of the sun's rays.

"You sure you won't change your mind?" the mayor's wife asked as Thea passed her home. Though she had hoped to escape last-minute farewells, that hope was stillborn. A number of the town's matrons were outside their homes or strolling along the main street, apparently waiting to say good-bye to Thea or perhaps, like the mayor's wife, hoping to persuade her to remain.

Thea shook her head. Though she would miss the friends she had made, not to mention her sister, brother-in-law, and their children, she wanted—no, she needed—a complete change. Cimarron Creek would provide that.

Thea smiled as she waved at another woman, then smoothed a wrinkle from her skirt. Another change was coming. Tonight, when she was miles away from those who would look askance at her action, she would remove her black garments for the last time. Just the thought brought Thea a sense of peace, as if she'd shed a heavy burden. She knew she would never stop mourning her husband and son and the dreams that had died with them, but the outward trappings weighed her down, both literally and figuratively.

Not only did she hate black clothes, but the sight of them wasn't good for her patients. Women who were *enceinte*, to use the French word that sounded so much more genteel than the English "pregnant" with its harsh consonants, needed no reminder that not all babies were born healthy and that not all fathers lived to hold their sons in their arms. They didn't need the reminder, and neither did she.

Thea took a deep breath, trying to block the painful memories. She wouldn't dwell on what had happened. Not today. Today was a day to celebrate the beginning of a new life, a day to put the past behind her.

Less than a minute later, she reined in Maggie in front of the parsonage.

"Bonjour, Aimee," she said as a blonde woman, only a couple inches taller than Thea's own five foot two, hurried from the building and stowed the modestly sized valise that contained all her earthly belongings in the back of the buggy. Thea was surprised that Aimee, the woman who'd explained that her name was pronounced eh-MAY, not Amy, was alone. She had expected the couple who had been her hosts during her time in Ladreville to accompany her to the buggy. Evidently, they'd said their farewells in private.

Aimee returned the greeting in the same language, then shook her head and said, "Good morning. We should speak English, though. I need to get in the habit." Her hazel eyes held a note of apprehension, perhaps at the prospect of going to a town where English was the only language. Cimarron Creek did not share Ladreville's history.

Though almost everyone in Ladreville spoke English now, the town had been founded by immigrants from Alsace, and when Thea and her sister had arrived almost a quarter of a century ago, most of the residents had spoken either French or German. As a result, Thea had grown up trilingual. It was a skill she rarely needed now that her generation had adopted English as their primary language, but it had proven helpful the day Aimee Jarre arrived. The woman had been so exhausted

340

from her journey that she had struggled to find more than a few English words.

"Are you certain you want me to accompany you?" Aimee asked as she settled onto the seat next to Thea. While her English was practically faultless, when she was distressed or fatigued, she struggled for words, and whenever she spoke, her accent belied the fact that she was a native Texan, born right here in Ladreville.

"Yes, of course, I am." Thea's heart ached for the painfully thin woman who'd traveled all the way from France to the heart of the Texas Hill Country in search of the mother who'd given her up for adoption. As heartbreaking as the past few months had been and as heavily as her fears had weighed on her, Thea's life had been easier than Aimee's.

The day Aimee had arrived in Ladreville, it had been obvious to Thea that she had not eaten in days, for she'd practically fainted when she'd climbed down from the stagecoach. Fortunately, Thea had been passing by and had taken her to the parsonage, knowing Pastor and Mrs. Russell would care for her, not knowing that Aimee had been born in their house.

As the light breeze teased her bonnet strings, Thea smiled. If it continued, the midday heat might feel less oppressive. Even if it did not, she was on her way, and that felt oh, so good.

"I'm glad you're coming with me," she told the young Frenchwoman. Though Aimee had been born in Ladreville, she had spent the rest of her life in a small French town and was, for all intents and purposes, French. It was virtually impossible to think of her as a Texan.

As they reached the town's limits, Thea continued. "My sister was having a conniption at the thought that I might drive to Cimarron Creek alone. Sarah forgets that I'm twenty-seven and not a child any longer."

"*Ancienne.*"

Thea laughed, both at the thought and the fact that Aimee had already forgotten her resolution to speak only English. "There are days when I do feel ancient," she admitted, "but today's not one of them." There had been times when her fears had made her feel far older than Sarah, who was twenty years her elder. The need to escape those fears, to put the past behind her, was one of the reasons the position in Cimarron Creek had sounded so attractive.

"You seem happier this morning than I've ever seen you," Aimee said.

"I am." The thought of a new life filled Thea with an almost unbelievable sense of freedom. "The announcement that Cimarron Creek needed a midwife came at exactly the right time."

"For me too." Aimee turned to glance back at the town where she'd been born. From this distance, it appeared peaceful, a place where nothing could go wrong. Thea knew otherwise.

"God's timing is perfect," Aimee continued. "He was looking out for me when he brought me to Ladreville and you."

And for Thea. "I hope you find your answers in Cimarron Creek," she said, changing the subject, "but even if you don't, it will be wonderful having you with me. Travis Whitfield—he's the man who hired me—said the town would welcome me, but I'll still be a stranger for a while. I'm glad I'll have a friend with me."

Aimee had become a friend more quickly than Thea had thought possible. The young Frenchwoman had arrived in Ladreville less than two weeks ago, but from the first hour she had spent with her, Thea had felt a connection to her. Though she couldn't identify the reason, she felt as if Aimee was the younger sister she'd always wanted, and when it had turned out that Aimee's mother had come from the same town that had hired Thea as its midwife, she had known that was no coincidence. They were meant to go together.

If all went as planned, Aimee would find her mother, and

Thea would begin a new life, a life free from secrecy, fear, and worry. No matter what anyone said, no matter what anyone thought, she was not running away.

⸎

She was trying to run away from him. Jackson Guthrie scowled as Ladreville's sheriff told him the woman he'd tracked this far had left town only hours before he arrived. Somehow—and he didn't know how, since there'd been no sign of the rest of the Gang—she must have realized that he was searching for her. Admittedly, the story that she'd accepted a position as a midwife in a new town sounded plausible, but the timing was suspect. It was more likely that with her husband dead, she'd decided to operate from a different location.

The Gang had done that before. That was part of what made finding them so difficult. They kept moving, and when they weren't robbing stagecoaches or trains, from everything he'd learned, they appeared to be ordinary, law-abiding citizens. Three men and a woman. The Gang of Four. And unless his information was totally wrong, she was one of them.

She was running. Jackson didn't doubt that for a minute. What she didn't know was that she couldn't outrun him. Texas Rangers always got their man, or in this case, their woman.

"C'mon, Blaze," he said as he swung into the saddle. "We've got a ways to go."

As the sun rose the next morning, Jackson yawned. The journey was taking longer than he'd expected. When Blaze had stumbled and injured his fetlock, he had had no choice but to slow their pace. He wouldn't risk further injury by pushing the gelding, nor would he do what some men might have and return to Ladreville to find another horse. He and Blaze had been together for five years now. They were partners, and one partner didn't abandon the other.

And so, although he'd thought he would overtake his quarry before nightfall, he had not. When he'd realized how slowly he'd have to travel, Jackson had abandoned the idea of apprehending her along the way and had decided to head straight for Cimarron Creek. Rather than stop, he'd ridden all night. If there were no other delays, he should reach the town before Thea Michener and the Frenchwoman who was accompanying her did, for the sheriff had said they'd planned to stop at an inn along the way.

Arriving before her would give Jackson an element of surprise, a weapon of a sort. If he combined that with a plausible reason for being there—something other than his official reason—he might lull her into making a mistake and revealing her guilt.

He yawned again, then smiled at the realization that he was within hours of achieving his goal. The day was beautiful. Hot, of course, but at least it was cooler here in the Hill Country than it was on the plains. Blaze's leg seemed better than yesterday, which was little short of a miracle, and Jackson himself was filled with anticipation. By nightfall he would have met the woman who held the key to his brother's killers, and if she slipped up and admitted what he suspected, he'd have her in custody faster than a rattler could strike.

His smile widened into a grin at the thought that he would be in Cimarron Creek in little more than an hour. From everything he'd heard, it was a friendly town. Why, it might even have a hotel. A night or two in a bed sounded good right now. Jackson didn't consider himself old—after all, thirty wasn't decrepit—but he had to admit that sleeping on the ground had lost its appeal. So had . . . His thoughts were interrupted by the unmistakable sound of a baby crying.

Jackson reined in Blaze as he surveyed the area. There was no one in sight, and he hadn't passed any houses in the last hour. What was a baby doing out here in the middle of ranch territory? He tipped his head to one side, listening intently. There was no question about it. A baby, an unhappy baby, was nearby.

"C'mon, Blaze. Let's see what we can find."

It didn't take long to discover an infant lying beside the tallest prickly pear cactus in the field, its face red from crying and sunburn. The poor thing must be hungry. Jackson took a deep breath, then frowned. Judging from the smell, it was also in dire need of clean clothes.

Though Jackson's saddlebags held the essentials of life for himself, he'd never had a reason to carry a diaper. He rummaged through the contents, pulling out a spare bandanna, and made short work of changing and cleaning the little boy. It had been years since he'd done that for his youngest brother, but he hadn't forgotten how.

As he hefted the baby into his arms, the crying that had subsided momentarily resumed. Hunger, no doubt, and that was a problem. The boy was clearly too young for jerky or hardtack, but Jackson had no milk. He'd have to settle for drizzling some water into the child's mouth. That wouldn't fill an empty stomach, but it might help prevent dehydration.

Sure enough, as soon as he'd swallowed a little of the warm water, the boy's cries stopped, and he looked up at Jackson with eyes as blue as the summer sky. It might be fanciful, but Jackson thought the baby was grateful for his rescue. The question was, why had he needed to be rescued?

As far as Jackson could see, there was nothing wrong with the child. He'd heard of parents abandoning babies with deformed limbs or faces marred by birthmarks, but this one had no defects. Why was he here? Even when parents abandoned children, they usually left them at a church or on the porch of a home where they knew someone would find the infant. Why would anyone leave a baby here where his chances of survival were slim? As soon as he'd taken care of Mrs. Michener, Jackson resolved to track down whoever was responsible for this baby's plight. It might not be official Ranger business, but what had happened to this boy was criminal.

"All right, son," he said as he mounted Blaze. "You're coming with me to Cimarron Creek." The boy wasn't his son, of course. Still, the name sounded right. He couldn't simply call the baby "you," could he?

"We'll figure out what to do with you there," he promised the infant in his arms. A smile curved his lips at the thought that had popped into his mind. "You may be just what I need—an innocent-sounding reason for meeting Thea Michener."

Dreams have always been an important part of **Amanda Cabot's** life. For almost as long as she can remember, she dreamt of being an author. Fortunately for the world, her grade-school attempts as a playwright were not successful, and she turned her attention to novels. Her dream of selling a book before her thirtieth birthday came true, and she's been spinning tales ever since. She now has more than thirty novels to her credit under a variety of pen names.

Her books have been finalists for the ACFW Carol Award as well as the Booksellers' Best and have appeared on the CBA and ECPA bestseller lists.

A popular speaker, Amanda is a member of ACFW and a charter member of Romance Writers of America. She married her high school sweetheart, who shares her love of travel and who's driven thousands of miles to help her research her books. After years as Easterners, they fulfilled a longtime dream and now live in the American West.

The future she dreamed of is gone.
But perhaps a better one awaits...

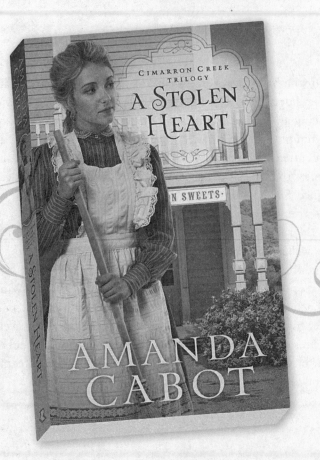

When Lydia arrives in the Texas Hill Country
in 1880 to find that her fiancé has married another,
what kind of future awaits her?

"Crafting characters rich with emotion, Amanda Cabot pens a compelling story of devastation and loss, of healing and second chances. But most of all, of transcending faith."
—Tamera Alexander, bestselling author

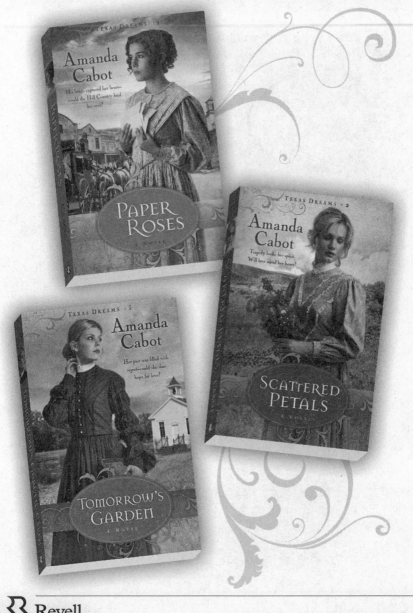

"One thing I know to expect when I open an Amanda Cabot novel is heart. She creates characters that tug at my heartstrings, storylines that make my heart smile, and a spiritual lesson that does my heart good."
—Kim Vogel Sawyer, bestselling author

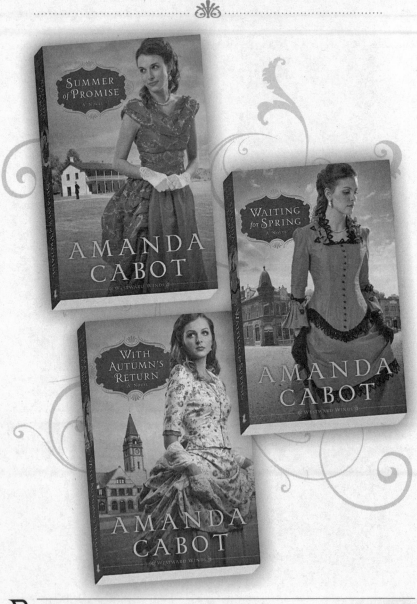